MATAGORDA
&
THE FIRST
FAST DRAW

Bantam Books by Louis L'Amour
ASK YOUR BOOKSELLER FOR THE BOOKS YOU HAVE MISSED.

NOVELS

Bendigo Shafter
Borden Chantry
Brionne
The Broken Gun
The Burning Hills
The Californios
Callaghen
Catlow
Chancy
The Cherokee Trail
Comstock Lode
Conagher
Crossfire Trail
Dark Canyon
Down the Long Hills
The Empty Land
Fair Blows the Wind
Fallon
The Ferguson Rifle
The First Fast Draw
Flint
Guns of the Timberlands
Hanging Woman Creek
The Haunted Mesa
Heller with a Gun
The High Graders
High Lonesome
Hondo
How the West Was Won
The Iron Marshal
The Key-Lock Man
Kid Rodelo
Kilkenny
Killoe
Kilrone
Kiowa Trail
Last of the Breed
Last Stand at Papago Wells
The Lonesome Gods
The Man Called Noon
The Man from the Broken
  Hills
The Man from Skibbereen
Matagorda
Milo Talon
The Mountain Valley War
North to the Rails
Over on the Dry Side
Passin' Through

The Proving Trail
The Quick and the Dead
Radigan
Reilly's Luck
The Rider of Lost Creek
Rivers West
The Shadow Riders
Shalako
Showdown at Yellow
  Butte
Silver Canyon
Son of a Wanted Man
Taggart
The Tall Stranger
To Tame a Land
Tucker
Under the Sweetwater Rim
Utah Blaine
The Walking Drum
Westward the Tide
Where the Long Grass
  Blows

**SHORT STORY
  COLLECTIONS**

Beyond the Great Snow
  Mountains
Bowdrie
Bowdrie's Law
Buckskin Run
The Collected Short Stories
  of Louis L'Amour
  (vols. 1–5)
Dutchman's Flat
End of the Drive
From the Listening Hills
The Hills of Homicide
Law of the Desert Born
Long Ride Home
Lonigan
May There Be a Road
Monument Rock
Night over the Solomons
Off the Mangrove Coast
The Outlaws of Mesquite
The Rider of the Ruby
  Hills
Riding for the Brand
The Strong Shall Live
The Trail to Crazy Man

Valley of the Sun
War Party
West from Singapore
West of Dodge
With These Hands
Yondering

SACKETT TITLES

Sackett's Land
To the Far Blue
  Mountains
The Warrior's Path
Jubal Sackett
Ride the River
The Daybreakers
Sackett
Lando
Mojave Crossing
Mustang Man
The Lonely Men
Galloway
Treasure Mountain
Lonely on the Mountain
Ride the Dark Trail
The Sackett Brand
The Sky-Liners

**THE HOPALONG CASSIDY
  NOVELS**

The Riders of the High
  Rock
The Rustlers of West Fork
The Trail to Seven Pines
Trouble Shooter

NONFICTION

Education of a
  Wandering Man
Frontier
THE SACKETT COMPANION:
  A Personal Guide to the
  Sackett Novels
A TRAIL OF MEMORIES:
  The Quotations of
  Louis L'Amour,
  compiled by
  Angelique L'Amour

POETRY

Smoke from This Altar

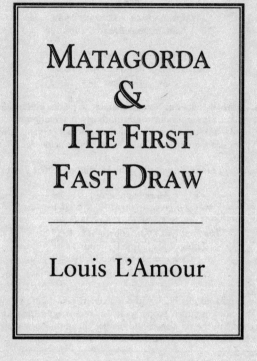

Matagorda
&
The First
Fast Draw

Louis L'Amour

BANTAM BOOKS

MATAGORDA / THE FIRST FAST DRAW
A Bantam Book / March 2008

Published by Bantam Dell
A Division of Random House, Inc.
New York, New York

This is a work of fiction. Names, characters, places, and incidents
either are the product of the author's imagination or
are used fictitiously. Any resemblance to actual persons, living
or dead, events, or locales is entirely coincidental.

Photograph of Louis L'Amour by John Hamilton—Globe Photos, Inc.

Bantam Books and the rooster colophon are registered trademarks
of Random House, Inc.

ISBN 978-0-553-59180-4

Printed in the United States of America
Published simultaneously in Canada

www.bantamdell.com

OPM   10 9 8 7 6 5 4 3 2

MATAGORDA

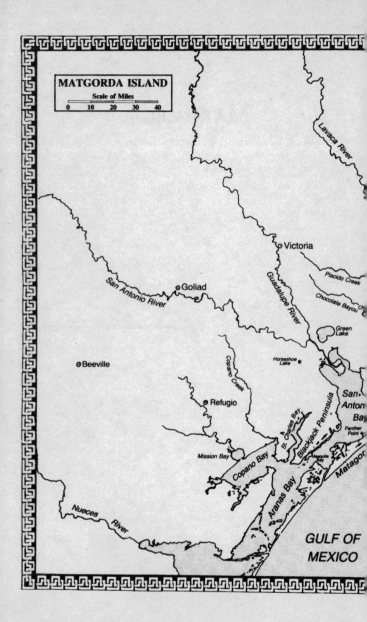

MATGORDA ISLAND

Scale of Miles
0   10   20   30   40

Lavaca River

Victoria

Placido Creek

San Antonio River

Goliad

Guadalupe River

Chocolate Bayou

Green Lake

Horseshoe Lake

Beeville

Copano Creek

San Antonio Bay

Refugio

St. Charles Bay

Blackjack Peninsula

Panther Point

Mission Bay

Copano Bay

Aransas Bay

Matagor

Nueces River

GULF OF MEXICO

Map by Alan McKnight

CHAPTER 1

MAJOR TAPPAN DUVARNEY rested his hands on the rail and stared toward the low sandy shore. It was not what he had expected of Texas, but whatever lay ahead represented his last chance. He had to make it here or nowhere.

He listened to the rhythmic pound and splash of the paddle wheels and looked bleakly into the future. Behind him lay the War Between the States and several years of Indian fighting with the frontier army; before him only the lonely years at some sunbaked, windswept frontier post, with nothing to look forward to but retirement.

When the war had broken out he was a young man with an assured future. Aside from the family plantation in Virginia, his father owned a shipping line trading to the West Indies and Gulf ports—four schooners and a barkentine, and good vessels all.

Tap Duvarney had made two trips before the mast on the barkentine, had taken examinations for his ticket, and had made two trips as third mate, one aboard a schooner, the other on the barkentine. His father wanted him to know the sea and its business from every aspect, and Tap liked the sea. He had taken to the rough and rowdy life in Caribbean ports as if born to it.

The war changed all that. His sympathies and

those of his family were with the Union. He had gone north and joined up. Renegades had burned the plantation buildings and run off the stock; one schooner had been lost in a hurricane off this very coast, two others had been confiscated by the Confederacy and sunk by Union gunboats. The barkentine had disappeared into that mysterious triangle south of Bermuda and left nothing behind but the memory. The last schooner, beat and bedraggled, had burned alongside the dock when the war came to Charleston. Tap Duvarney returned from the war saddled with debts, his father dead, his home destroyed.

There seemed only one thing to do, and he did it. He went back to the army and a series of frontier posts. During the nine years following the war he fought Indians from the Dakotas to Arizona. He managed to keep his hair, but picked up three scars, one from a knife, two from bullet wounds.

Finally, his father's estate had been settled and he emerged from the shambles with a bit more than seven thousand dollars.

It was then he heard from Tom Kittery.

———

CAPTAIN WILKES STOPPED beside him now on his way to the pilot house. Duvarney knew that Wilkes was worried about him, and genuinely wished to help. The captain was a good man who had served on one of his father's ships.

"You'll find Texas a fast country, Major. Do you have friends here?"

"One . . . so far as I know. I met him during the war."

"You haven't seen him since? That's quite a while,

Major. Is that the man you've gone into partnership with?"

Duvarney thought he detected a doubtful note in Wilkes's voice, and he was not surprised. He was a bit doubtful himself from time to time.

"I know the man, Captain. Whatever else he may be, he's honest . . . and he's got guts. I go along with that."

"The cattle business is good," Wilkes said. "Indianola has been the biggest cattle-shipping port in Texas for a good long time, so I've had a good deal to do with it. I may know your partner."

"Kittery . . . Tom Kittery. Old Texas family."

"Kittery, is it? Yes, he has guts, all right. There isn't a man in Texas would deny that. And he's honest. But speaking as a friend, I'd never leave the ship, if I were you. Come on back to New Orleans. You're a good man, and you know the sea. We'll find something for you there."

"What's wrong with Kittery?"

"With *him*? Nothing . . . nothing at all." Wilkes glanced at Duvarney. "I take it you haven't heard about the feud?"

Wilkes paused, then went on. "You're walking right into the middle of a shooting war . . . the Munson-Kittery feud. It has been going on since 1840 or thereabouts, and from the moment it is discovered that you are associated with Kittery you'll be a prime target."

"I know nothing about any feud."

"You say you knew Kittery during the war? He may have thought the feud was a thing of the past because it seemed to be over. Until the Kittery boys left for the war there hadn't been any shooting for several years.

"In the years before the war the Kittery faction numbered some of the toughest, ablest fighting men in Texas; so the Munsons laid low and played their music soft. And when the Kittery boys went off to war, the Munsons stayed home.

"Even so, they kept quiet until Ben was killed at Shiloh. That started them stirring around a bit, but it wasn't until Tom was captured—reported dead, in fact—that they began to cut loose.

"They ran off a bunch of Kittery cattle, then burned a barn. Old Alec, Tom's uncle, rode out after the Munsons and they ambushed him and killed him. After that they really cut loose. They killed two Negro hands who had worked for the Kitterys for years, and burned the old home—one of the oldest houses on the coast.

"Cattle were beginning to be worth money, and the Munsons thought they were rich on Kittery beef. Only somebody stampeded the biggest herd one night and ran them into the Big Thicket. Well, you don't know the Thicket, but finding cattle in there is like hunting ghosts. The Munsons never were much on hard work, and rousting those steers from the Thicket would be the hardest kind of work. So the steers, and a lot of other cattle, are still in there."

"Maybe those are the cattle I bought," Duvarney commented ironically. "It's my luck."

"Are you wearing a gun?" Wilkes asked.

"I have one." As a matter of fact, he had two guns. "From what you've said, I should be wearing one."

"You should." Wilkes straightened up. "I'm going

up to take her in, but my advice to you is: stay on the ship. . . . If you do leave her, be ready for trouble. They laid for Johnny Lubec, and they laid for Tom. They were waiting for him when the boat docked . . . my boat."

"Tom?"

Wilkes smiled grimly. "Tom was no fool. I told him what had happened to Johnny, so he left the ship as we were going past the island, entering the bay.

"The fog was thick that morning, and he lowered himself over the side on a raft we'd built for him, and paddled ashore. He slipped ashore on Matagorda Island, and nobody knows the island better than Tom. It's long, but so narrow you wouldn't think a man could hide there, but he managed it. Anyway, he was still alive the last time we were here, and I hope he still is."

"You mentioned Johnny Something-or-other?"

"Lubec. Johnny wasn't a Kittery, just an orphan kid they took in and treated like one of the family. Folks said that Johnny's pa was one of the Jean Lafitte pirates . . . they had a hideout on Matagorda themselves and used to careen their ships on the landward beaches.

"Anyway, Johnny grew up with the Kitterys, so when he came home the Munsons were laying for him. They shot him down and left him for dead, then went off to have a drink, and Johnny crawled away. He got to the house of an old Indian who lives on Black Jack Point, and the Indian cared for him.

"The Munsons were fit to be tied when Tom gave them the slip. If they'd known Tom was alive they would never have reopened the fight, not even with

Jackson Huddy or the Harts around to help. At that, they almost got Tom."

"What happened?"

"Tom rode over to his old home. Nobody had told him the place was burned out, and I guess he figured some of his people might be there. He rode home and the Munsons were laying for him. They heard him coming and shot him out of the saddle, put two bullets into him.

"Jim Hart and two renegade riders of the Munson crowd were there, and when Tom fell they just knew they had him. They ran in on him and he killed one of them and burned Hart a couple of times. Then he crawled to his horse, pulled himself into the saddle, and rode off.

"Tom must have figured he was dying, or he wouldn't have done what he did. He rode to the Munson place and hollered up the folks. Well, they'd no idea Tom was even alive. Word hadn't got back from Indianola yet, so old Taylor Munson, the bull of the woods, came to the door. Tom told him who he was, and shot him down. And then Tom dropped from sight."

Tap Duvarney stared gloomily toward the nearing shore. He had bought a partnership in a herd of cattle to be driven to Kansas ... not a feud. He wanted no part of it.

"Months went by," Wilkes went on, "and nobody saw hide nor hair of Tom. The Munsons hunted him high and low, and finally they were ready to believe he was dead. Cattle had become big business, so the Munsons rounded up a herd and started for Kansas. When they were close to Doan's Store, Dale Munson rode over to pick up the mail and some tobacco, and ran right into Tom Kittery.

"First any of the Munson crowd knew of it was when Dale's horse came into camp with Dale tied over the saddle. There were two bullet holes in Dale's chest you could cover with a silver dollar."

"You mentioned a Jackson Huddy," Duvarney said.

"He's a killer. Some say he's kin to the Munsons. Anyway, he runs with them, and after old Taylor Munson was killed Huddy sort of moved into command. And I mean it is a command.

"When it looked like the fight was going their way, Munsons began showing up from all over. I'd say there were forty or more gun-packing men in the clan. And they've played it smart. Two of their kin are elected to office, a sheriff and a judge. Another one is a deputy over to Victoria."

When Wilkes had finished speaking he went to the pilot house, and Tappan Duvarney lingered by the rail.

He had no choice, he was thinking. Every cent he owned beyond what he carried in his money belt—and that was little enough—was invested with Tom Kittery, who was supposed to be buying cattle and hiring an outfit.

It was an odd friendship that had developed between the two men. Tap Duvarney, then a lowly lieutenant in the Union forces, had been sent south on a secret mission. His southern accent was perfect for it, as was his knowledge of the country. Trouble developed when he ran into Captain Tom Kittery. He captured Tom, but he was more than a hundred miles from the nearest Union outpost.

He had a choice of turning Tom loose, which would mean his own pursuit and capture, shooting him in cold blood, or trying to take him back. Tap Duvarney decided on the last.

On the way, although Tom was continually trying to outwit Tap and escape, the two developed a respect and a liking for each other. During the long hours en route, Tom talked a good deal of Texas and the cattle business, suggesting that if they came out of the war alive they should become partners. And that had been the beginning of it.

Walking back to his cabin now, Tap Duvarney dug down into his sea chest and got out a Russian .44 Smith & Wesson. The holster was worn from use, but he belted it on. He hesitated a bit over the second pistol, then thrust it into his waistband.

Pausing before the mirror, he straightened his cravat, and studied the hang on his coat to see if the pistol showed a bulge. It did not.

For a moment then, he looked at himself.

What he saw was a lean, spare-built man with a brown, quiet face and hazel eyes. His shoulders were broad, and the coat fitted admirably. He was, he thought wryly, what he had heard people say of him: "a handsome man," or "a fine figure of a man." He was also a man of thirty-three with a wealth of experience, and nothing to show for it but the scars. When most men of his age were well established in their life work, he had nothing, was nothing.

He had found it all too easy to slip into the routine of army life, but the peacetime army offered little chance for advancement, and he had been lucky to make major. He knew of many older men who had done just as much who were captains, and a few who were still lieutenants. But his early life had been geared to ambition, and he felt he must accomplish something, do something, make himself a better man, and his country a better place. This he had been taught as a child, this he still believed.

He turned from the mirror, gathered up his gear, and swung his sea chest to his shoulder with practiced ease. Then he picked up the carpetbag and walked out on deck, placing his things near the gangway.

Several passengers had come out on deck to watch the steamboat's approach to Indianola. Most of them he knew by sight, and had measured and catalogued them. All except two fell into familiar categories. One of these was a tall, wiry man in a tailored black broadcloth suit, a hawk-faced man with a saturnine expression, as if he viewed the world with wry amusement. The other was a girl.

She was young, and beautiful in the way a ranch girl is beautiful who does not know the skills or artifices of the city. She was blond, with blue eyes and a clear, fresh complexion, but she looked somewhat sullen now, and seemed to be approaching the Texas coast with no anticipation of pleasure.

Several times Duvarney had caught her eyes upon him, showing curiosity but nothing more. He lifted his hat. "Ma'am, I presume you are acquainted in Indianola?"

"Yes, I am," she answered. "My home is in Texas."

"A fine state, I've heard. I was wondering if you could tell me where I could locate Tom Kittery."

Her eyes were suddenly unfriendly. She looked at him, a hard, measuring glance. "If you are looking for Tom Kittery you will have to find him yourself. If there is anyone who knows where he is, I don't know about it."

"I see. Well, no harm done. I expect he will find me soon enough, when he knows I am here. He has enemies, I believe?"

"He has . . . too many of them."

Then they stood silently together, watching the approaching shore, and Tap found himself wondering about her. She was dressed neatly but not expensively, in the style of a ranch girl going to the city, or coming back from a visit. From her attitude, she was not happy about coming home.

"You enjoyed New Orleans, ma'am?"

She turned quickly. "Oh, I did! It's a wonderful place, so many people, beautiful clothes . . . so many nice places to go—if there was somebody to take you."

"You have friends there?"

"I have an uncle and aunt there. I'm afraid they did not approve of a lot of the most exciting places."

"Quite properly," Duvarney commented dryly. "The most interesting places in New Orleans are no place for a young girl.

"As for me," he added, "I look forward to Indianola, and to Texas."

"You're going to *stay* there?"

"I hope to. As a matter of fact, I have some investments there. An investment, I should say. In cattle."

She looked at him. "You did not mention your name. Or where you were from."

"Sorry, ma'am. The name is Tappan Duvarney, and I am from Virginia."

"*You're* Tap Duvarney?"

He was surprised. "You've heard of me, then?"

"I'm Mady Coppinger." She glanced quickly around to be sure no one else was listening. "Tom Kittery is my...he is a friend of mine. He told me about you. As a matter of fact," she added, somewhat irritably, "he has been talking of very little else since you decided to come down."

She looked hard at him again. "Tom said you'd lived in Richmond and Charleston."

"A long time ago. For years I've only visited there. I've been in the army...out west."

"I envy you. Any place is better than Texas." The sullen look was on her face once more. "I wish I had never come back. I hate it."

"Do you go to New Orleans often?"

"I've never been there before, and it isn't likely I'll get to go again." She looked suddenly defiant. "Unless somebody takes me."

He avoided the opening, if that was what it was, and watched the shore. He could see the buildings now. The coast was low and flat, but there seemed to be hills beyond the town which were vague at that distance. The two long dark fingers of pier thrust into the bay waters.

"I've never been anywhere before," the girl said. "Only to Indianola or Victoria...and once over to Beeville. My pa owns a ranch."

"Does he live near Tom?"

She shook her head. "Mr. Duvarney, you must understand something. Tom Kittery is a hunted man.

The Munsons are looking for him and when they find him they'll kill him. If you want to stay alive, don't you dare mention his name, or they'll be gunning for you."

"I will have to find Tom."

"Don't you go asking for him. I'd say you'd best hire yourself a rig...or a horse." She looked up at him. "Do you ride?"

"I was in the cavalry."

"Then get a horse and ride south. Take your time. Ride south toward Mission River. If nobody stops you keep on riding, but don't be in a hurry. Tom will find you."

"It doesn't seem a very good time to gather a herd for a cattle drive," Duvarney commented.

"Tom usually does what he starts out to do," Mady said. "I'll have to say that. Like the business with the hides."

At his questioning look, she went on. "The Munsons have been branding Rafter K stock. The Rafter K is the Kittery brand, but the law is a Munson and there wasn't much Tom could do, or so folks thought. Then one morning they woke up and found fresh hides tacked up where everybody could see them. They were nailed up with the hair side against the wall so any western man could see the Rafter K had been changed into a Munson Circle M."

She smiled, and suddenly her face was changed. "Everybody in the country was laughing about that, and telling the story, until Jim Hart killed a man over to Beeville. Since then nobody feels much like talking, but the hides are still going up. Tom has nailed up hides in Beeville, Indianola, and Victoria, and even clean down to Brownsville. The Munsons are mad enough to eat nails."

Tap chuckled. "No wonder they're mad." He straightened up. "How about you? Do they know you're a friend of his?"

"They know it. But mister, nobody bothers a woman in Texas. They may not like me, but they won't do anything or say anything. Even if they weren't afraid of Texas people, they wouldn't say anything because of Jackson Huddy."

"But I thought he was one of them?"

"He is. Jackson Huddy is probably the quickest man alive with a gun...quicker than Tom, some think. But whatever else he is—and he has the name of being the coldest killer this country ever saw—he respects a woman. He respects women and the church, and very little else. You look out for him."

Duvarney tipped his hat and moved away from her. It would never do to invite trouble for her by staying near her. The possibility that they knew about him was slight, yet somehow they had known that Johnny Lubec and Tom were coming home, and they had been waiting for them. Somehow they might also know about him.

He stood by the gangway and watched the lines go out, and then the gangway. Captain Wilkes came down from the pilot house to bid his passengers good-bye. One by one he saw them down the gangway and onto the pier.

Several rigs were waiting there, and in turn they drove away with passengers and their luggage. Only one remained behind.

Warily, Tap Duvarney studied the men on the

dock. There was the usual collection of loafers who gathered to see any boat or train arrive. But there were three who drew more than his casual attention. He had lived too long on the frontier not to know trouble-hunters when he saw them, and two of these seemed to be in that category. The third man was a tall, high-shouldered man with a clean-shaven, hard-boned face and small eyes. Once, briefly, his eyes met Duvarney's.

The others on the dock were familiar types. In most towns there are men or boys who want to try their strength, usually against somebody they feel confident they can whip. Often the man they choose is a stranger—if a well-dressed stranger, so much the better. Such men he did not mind, for they started their fights and they took their medicine, learning their lesson as all must do.

But there was another kind, the real bullies, those with a drive to meanness and sadism. These three, he felt sure, were of that sort. He had been the butt of the joke before, knew the dialogue, and was ready.

Only he had not wanted it to happen here, when he had just arrived in the town where Tom Kittery had enemies. A fight he would not mind, and might even welcome as a way to initiate himself into the local scene, but he did not want a bullet in the back because of it.

When the last of the passengers had gone, he lifted his sea chest to his left shoulder, then picked up his carpetbag with his right hand, following the last man by a few steps.

The buckboard with the two paint mustangs was

still standing at the end of the pier. If the driver was around, he was not in sight.

Duvarney walked along to the end of the pier and put down his sea chest and carpetbag near the buckboard. He glanced around, hearing the boots of the two young men as they came up behind him. He turned slowly when they were still several feet off.

They had moved apart a little, so he waited, somewhat bored by the familiarity of the pattern. "You fixin' to ask that man for a ride, mister?" one of them asked.

"I might at that. Is he around?"

"Name of Foster. Got a way of comin' an' goin', Foster has. He might be around, and he might not. Thing is, have you got any right to be here? Seems to me a man comin' to a strange town should have some money, and if he has money he should stand up for the drinks."

"That's fair enough. You boys carry my trunk up to the hotel and I'll buy you each a drink."

"Carry your—What do you think we are, mister? Beggars?"

"No," he said, "only I figured you could earn money enough for a bath and a shave. Might seem nice to be clean again . . . after so long a time."

They stared at him, then the taller one took a step nearer. "You tryin' to be smart, mister? You sayin' we're dirty?"

Duvarney widened his eyes. "I wouldn't think of such a thing. I'm not a man who stresses the obvious. I just offered you a chance to earn the drink you asked for."

"We never asked for no drink," the tall one argued.

"We figured a gent like you, so dressed up an' all, we just figured you might have money enough to treat the boys up yonder. Suppose you let us see how much you got."

"Sorry. If you intend to rob me, you'll have to try it the hard way."

Duvarney stepped back, as the tall one started for him, but as he stepped back he kicked the carpetbag into the other's path, tripping the young man so that he fell to hands and knees. As Duvarney kicked the carpetbag, he shifted his feet and met the lunge of the second man.

He was coming in low, and Tap jerked his knee up hard into the man's face, smashing nose and lips. Catching him by the hair, he jerked him upright and swung a right into his belly. The man went down hard as Tap wheeled and caught a wild right on the shoulder from the first man, now on his feet. Tap looked at him and laughed, then he feinted and the man's hands flailed wildly. Tap stabbed a left to the mouth, then three more as fast as he could jab. He feinted again, hitting him in the wind, and when he bent over gasping, a hammer blow on the kidney stretched him out.

Calmly, Duvarney straightened his coat. Captain Wilkes was standing by the rail of the steamboat, watching. The tall, lean man who had apparently been with the two he had just beaten, looked on without emotion, or evidence of more than casual interest.

"That there was mighty neat," he said. "Looks to me like you've fought some with your fists."

"A little."

The man gestured toward the two on the dock, who were groaning now, and beginning to stir. "Don't let that set you up none. They never was much account." He started to turn away toward town, then paused. "If you're huntin' the man who owns that rig, you'll find him yonder. You can tell any who ask that he just kept the wrong company."

"How does a man choose his company around here?"

The tall man looked at Duvarney with cool, almost uninterested eyes. "He chooses any company he likes, just so it ain't Kitterys. We don't cotton to Kitterys."

"Afraid of them?"

The man looked at him. "I am Jackson Huddy," he said, and walked away up the street.

CHAPTER 2

DUVARNEY WATCHED JACKSON Huddy walk slowly away and his eyes went beyond him to the weather-beaten frame buildings, the signs hanging out over the streets, the hitching rails. It looked not at all like a port on the Gulf of Mexico, but rather like a cow town in the Plains country or the Rockies.

The two roughnecks were getting up. One, whose face had had a hard encounter with Tap's knee, had a badly broken nose, by the look of it; the swelling had already almost closed his eyes, and his lips were a pulp.

Neither of them had known anything about fist-fighting. As for Duvarney, he had served a harsh apprenticeship when he made those two trips to the West Indies as a deck hand, to say nothing of two trips as a mate. In those days no man could hold down a job aft unless he could fight. He was expected to be ready and able to whip any man in the crew, and any three if necessary.

Duvarney stood watching the two, but as they got up they backed off. He was wary of a shot in the back, but neither man seemed to remember that he carried a gun.

When they had gone he glanced reluctantly at the

stack of cotton bales toward which Jackson Huddy had gestured.

With another glance up the street, Duvarney walked over to the bales. A man lay behind the pile, sprawled on his face, and there was blood in the dust where he rested.

Duvarney turned him over. The man had been stabbed twice in the belly, the long blade striking upward. He was dead, the body not yet cold. On his holster was burned a Rafter K, the brand of the Kitterys.

Returning to the buckboard, Duvarney made a space in the back for the body, then brought it over and laid it out in the back, covering it with an old tarp that lay there.

In the buckboard was a nose bag for the horses and a sack of oats, as well as two sacks of groceries. He saw that the mustangs also carried the Rafter K brand.

He stepped up to the seat and turned the buckboard around. He drove up the street, aware of the eyes that followed him. He drove to a sign that said Hardware, got down, and went inside. A small group congregated around the buckboard, and more than one of them lifted the tarp to look at the dead man.

"Is there an undertaker in town?" Duvarney asked.

The gray-haired man behind the counter shook his head. "Nobody will lay out a Kittery man," he said "and Foster was a Kittery man. And there ain't nobody will dig a grave for him, either. Nor pray for him."

"It's that kind of town?"

The man shrugged. "We live here, mister. We live

here all the time, and that Munson crowd are here. I'm sorry, right sorry."

"Is there a Kittery lot in the cemetery?"

"Two . . . maybe three of them."

"I'll need a pick and a shovel."

"You'll need more than that, mister. You'll need a rifle."

"All right, hand me down one of those Winchesters, and I'll want about five hundred rounds of ammunition."

"*Five hundred* rounds? That would fight a small war."

"You can pass the word for me that I have no part in this feud, and I want no part in it; but if they ask for any kind of trouble they can have it.

"You can also pass the word around that I am going to bury this man, and that I am asking for no help. I will read over him myself."

The storekeeper was silent, putting the order together swiftly. When Duvarney paid him, he said, "Don't think we're unfeeling. This fight has been going on for nearly forty years now, and a lot of good men have been killed. Nobody wants to get involved anymore. It's their fight, so let them have it."

"All I want to do is bury a man."

"You won't do it. They won't let you."

The crowd moved back for him when he put the pick and shovel into the wagon beside the body. They stood back even farther when he loaded the ammunition and a few items in the way of food. Then he got up on the buckboard and spoke to the team. They started with a rush.

At the cemetery he drove the buckboard through

the gate and closed it after him. He scouted among the graves until he found the Kittery lot; then he peeled off his coat, which he put over a tombstone beside him, one of his guns hidden beneath it. The other he left in its holster. The Winchester he leaned out of sight near the buckboard. Then he went to work.

He worked swiftly down through the top soil for a good two feet. Then it became slower work, but he kept on. He was a strong man, in good condition, and used to hard work, but he realized that he would be lucky to finish before dark. He had the grave less than half dug when the riders began to come. He slipped the thong from his six-shooter and continued to dig.

There were three of them. All the horses wore the Circle M brand of the Munsons. Within a few minutes there were four more, then others, some of these hanging back, obviously come to see the fun.

"You diggin' that grave for one or two?"

Duvarney ignored it, managed three more spadefuls of dirt before the question came again. He straightened up, leaned on his shovel, and looked at them. He was waist-deep in the hole with a parapet of dirt thrown up in front of him. Three large tombstones formed almost a wall along his route to the buckboard.

"I asked was you diggin' that for one, or two?"

The speaker was a wide-hipped, narrow-shouldered man with a narrow-brimmed hat.

"For one," Duvarney replied. "You'll have to dig your own, if you want one."

Somebody among the spectators snickered, and the man turned sharply around. The snickering stopped.

"When you get that grave deep enough, you'll find out who it's for. We aim to bury you right there."

Jackson Huddy had ridden up, and he was watching and listening. Duvarney leaned on the shovel. "You boys aren't very smart," he said. "I've got a lot more cover than you. I figure to get three or four before you get me . . . if you ever do."

For a moment that stopped them. He had only to drop to his knees to leave only head and shoulders in view. There was no cover for them outside the fence, and a man at that range should do pretty well. Nobody spoke, and Duvarney resumed his digging.

Suddenly the man with the narrow-brimmed hat started to crawl through the fence.

"Shab," Huddy was saying, "you come back here. That man is buryin' the dead. There'll be no botherin' him. Anyway, he ain't a Kittery."

"That's a Kittery man he's buryin'!"

"Leave him be. I like a man with nerve."

There was no more talk, but nobody walked away. Slowly, Duvarney completed his digging; then he wrapped the body in the tarpaulin and placed it in the bottom of the grave. He filled in the grave, while the men stood quietly. After that he went to the buckboard for his carpetbag and took out a Bible. He removed his hat, and began to read, and when he had finished the funeral text he had chosen, he sang *Rock of Ages*.

His voice was fairly good, and he managed to sing it well. Here and there a voice joined in. When he had finished the hymn he picked up his tools and went back to the buckboard, then returned for his coat. As he lifted it his right hand gripped the six-shooter. He brought it up, and walked back to the buckboard and placed the coat and the pistol on the seat. As he started to get up he lifted the rifle from where it had been hidden and with an easy motion swung to the seat.

He gathered the reins with his left hand, his right holding the Winchester. He drove to the gate, and when he reached it he pointed the Winchester at the nearest man, smiling as he did so. "Friend, I'd be pleased if you'd open the gate for me."

The man hesitated for a moment, then he walked over and opened the gate, standing back with it until Tap Duvarney had driven through.

"Thank you," Duvarney said. "Thank you very much." He glanced at Huddy, still sitting his horse, and regarding Duvarney with an enigmatic expression. "And thank you, Mr. Huddy. It hurts no man to respect the dead."

He spoke to the team and they moved forward down the road, but at the point where the road to the cemetery reached the main trail he turned sharply and took the trail south from town.

There was no sound behind him, but he did not turn his head to look back. He had a straight quarter of a mile before there was any cover, and despite the bouncing the buckboard was giving him, he could be hit by a good shot. He held the good pace at which they had started, wanting as much distance as he could get. He had no doubt he would be followed, and a buckboard leaves a definite trail.

When he had two miles behind him he drew up, and with a wry grin he loaded the rifle. "You damn fool," he muttered. "Forgetting a thing like that can get you killed."

The sun was down, the breeze cool off the Gulf, which lay some distance off on his left, beyond Powderhorn Lake, close by. He had a good memory for maps and charts, as a result of both his early training at sea and his years in the army. To go south he must first go inland, find the Green Lake road, and let it take him past the head of San Antonio Bay. Beyond that there stretched a wide piece of country, but between here and there he knew of no place to hide.

The twin tracks of the trail were plain enough, even at night, so he pushed on. The paint mustangs seemed to be glad to be moving and he held them to a good trot, which seemed to be the pace they liked. From time to time he drew up to listen for sounds of pursuit.

He was under no delusions about Jackson Huddy. Whatever else he might be, the man had a code of ethics of his own, and only that had prevented a bloody gun battle in the cemetery. He was sure that under other circumstances Huddy would never hesitate to kill him . . . if he could.

He had studied the charts in Wilkes's wheelhouse and had a fair understanding of the country, so after a while he took a chance and left the trail, cutting across toward Green Lake. By day they would find his tracks, of course, but by then he hoped to be far away.

Several times he drew up to give the mustangs a brief rest, but they seemed tireless and impatient to keep going. Give them their heads, he thought, and likely they'll take me right where I want to go.

It was well past midnight when he saw the shine of water on his right. That would be Green Lake. The mustangs were tired now, trotting only when they started down a slight grade...which was rare enough. But they had held the pace well.

The last miles before daylight were weary ones, but he kept the team moving until they reached the breaks of the Guadalupe.

The sky was gray with morning when he turned off into the trees and found a hollow screened from the trail. Here he unhitched the team and led them to water, and after that he picketed them on a patch of good grass not far from the buckboard. Then, a gun at hand, he drew a blanket over him and went to sleep.

It was high noon when the sun woke him, shining through the leaves of a cottonwood tree. For a minute or two he lay perfectly still, listening. Then he sat up.

The horses were not twenty yards off, heads up, ears pricked.

Duvarney came up off the ground like a cat, thrust his six-shooter into his belt, and reached for his gun belt and his other pistol. As he belted it on, he listened. The horses were looking back the way he had come.

He got the team and brought them back. Not wanting the jingle of trace chains to warn anyone of his presence, he tied them to the buckboard. Taking his rifle, he worked his way through the trees and brush to a place where he could watch the tracks he must have left.

He recognized the girl before he could make out any of her features. It was Mady Coppinger.

She was riding in a buckboard driven by a stalwart Negro. Two riders followed close behind. As they drew nearer he could see that the Negro's features looked more like those of an Indian. He was a lean, intelligent-looking man with watchful eyes.

He drew up as he neared the place where Duvarney had turned off. "I'm thinkin', ma'am, that he wouldn't have gone no farther than this. That team will be plumb wore out by now. You want I should find him?"

"No..." She hesitated, then turned to one of the riders following. "Harry, do you think Huddy will follow him?"

"Huddy? No. He won't foller, but Shabbit will. Shabbit and those boys Duvarney whupped down to the dock. They'll be after his scalp, an' you can bet on it. Huddy won't do anything until Duvarney declares himself."

"We should find him and warn him."

Tap Duvarney made no move to leave the shelter of the brush. He did not know these men, and although they seemed to be riders from the Coppinger outfit, he did not want to chance it. His attention was on the girl. Mady was lovely, no question about it, and the figure that filled out the dress she wore was something to think about...or for Tom Kittery to think about. She was his girl.

Besides, Tap had a girl. Or he had one when he left Virginia.

The Negro spoke. "Ma'am, I think it best we leave him alone. I've been watching his trail, and he's a cautious man. The way I see it, going into the brush to hunt for him might prove a chancey thing."

"Caddo's right," Harry agreed.

Caddo spoke to the horses and they moved out. Harry turned slightly in his saddle and glanced back at the pecan tree under which Duvarney was crouched. Had something given him away? Some bird, or perhaps a squirrel? Some movement he had not seen or felt?

When their dust had settled he harnessed the horses and emerged from the copse where he had been hiding. At the point where he went back on the trail he got down and wiped out the tracks as best he could, then drove on. An Apache would have read the sign without slowing his pace, but these men might not be as good at reading sign.

The air was fresh and clean, and the mustangs, rested after their morning grazing and rest, were prepared to go. They were tough, wild stock, bred to the plains, and only half-broken. Duvarney drove on with only an occasional backward glance, holding to the trail followed by Mady Coppinger.

Somewhere to the south he would find Tom Kittery and whatever was left of his seven thousand dollars. He had already made up his mind about that. He would take whatever money was left and ride out, writing off the rest of it as a bad investment.

He had no part in the Kittery-Munson feud, and he wanted none. No mention had been made of it when they had discussed the buying of cattle for a drive north.

Having no knowledge of exactly where Tom Kittery might be, Duvarney decided just to drift south, scouting the country as he went. He had supplies and ammunition enough, and the terrain was easy for buckboard travel, being generally level or somewhat rolling, with good grass and clumps of trees. Along the rivers there were oaks and pecans, as well as dogwood, willow, and redbud.

Taking a dim trail, Tap drove down toward Blackjack Point, following the shore of the peninsula whenever possible. On the third day after seeing Mady Coppinger, he was camped near some low brush within sight of the sea. He had made a small fire of driftwood and was brewing coffee when he heard a rustle behind him.

He reached for the coffeepot with his left hand, drew his six-shooter with his right. Moving the coffee a little nearer the coals, he straightened up, then took a quick step back to his left, which put him into the deep shadow of a pecan tree, gun ready.

There was a chuckle from the brush, and Tom Kittery stepped out, followed by two other men. "See? I told you," Kittery said. "Ain't no catchin' him off-guard. I never knew such a skittish hombre."

Tom Kittery looked good, but he was thin. He was honed down by hiding out, worn by constant watching, but humor glinted from his eyes as he stepped forward, hand thrust out in greeting.

CHAPTER 3

MAN, YOU ARE a sight to behold! Look at him, boys. This here's the on'y man ever took me. Captured me alive an' on the hoof, and I'd never believed it could be done! And then he smuggled me right by some renegades that would have strung me up like a horse thief for bein' a Johnny Reb. And him a Yank!"

"Hello, Tom," Tap said. "It's been a while."

Kittery grinned at him. There was genuine welcome in his eyes, and his handclasp was firm and strong. "I've thought of you a good bit, Tap. I surely have."

"Have we got a herd?"

Some of the smile left Kittery's face. "Sort of. I've got to talk to you about that." He turned. "Tap Duvarney, this here's Johnny Lubec. And that's the Cajun...a good man, right out of the Louisiana swamps."

Lubec was a small, wiry man, scarcely more than a boy, but a boy with old eyes, a boy who had seen trouble. The Cajun was tall, thin, angular, sallow of face, with dark, lank hair and a gold earring in each ear.

"What about the cattle?" Tap asked. "That was every cent I had in the world, Tom. I gambled on you."

"And you won't regret it, Tap. I've had troubles—I suppose you've heard about that?"

"I heard about it."

"When we talked I thought the feud was a thing of the past. It was just a matter of rounding up some of Dad's cattle. I didn't have any money, so with your money, our cattle and know-how, we could drive to Kansas and make some money. That's what I planned. The trouble was, the cattle had been stolen. Most of them, at least."

"So the drive is off?"

"Not on your tintype! We're rounding up cattle now. Fact is, we've got a good part of a herd stashed away. But that's a small part of it. Somehow we've got to slip three thousand head of cattle out of the country without the Munsons gettin' wind of it."

They walked back and sat down around the fire, and the Cajun disappeared into the darkness. "He'll keep watch, so don't you worry none. He's one of the very best."

"I met Mady Coppinger on the boat."

Tom Kittery shot him a quick glance. "Came back did she? I wouldn't have bet on it."

"I thought you two had an understanding."

Tom shrugged. "We have, sort of. Mady's fed up with Texas, fed up with dust, cows, bronc riders, and cookin' for ranch hands. She fell heir to a stack of Godey's Lady's Books, and since then all she does is pine. I keep tellin' her I ain't no city man, but she won't listen."

With another glance at Duvarney, he said, "How'd she look?"

"Great. She's a very pretty young woman."

Tom filled two cups with the hot coffee. "Did you see any Munsons? I mean, around Indianola."

Tap ignored the question. "How did you know I'd arrived? Or did you know?"

"Cap'n Wilkes. He dipped the flag when he passed the point. We'd agreed on the signal." He paused a moment. "You're drivin' the rig...where's Foster?"

"They killed him. He was killed just about the time we were coming up to the wharf. I buried him in your family lot."

"You *what*?"

"You didn't want him buried there? Didn't seem that I had much choice."

"They let you bury him? Of course, we'd want him in our lot, or anywhere we could manage, and the best. But Indianola is mostly a Munson town. There's two or three of the clan live there, and always some of them are circulatin' about."

Over coffee, Tap Duvarney told about the burial and the brief encounter with Shab, or Shabbit. Of the brief fight on the wharf he said nothing at all.

"Tom," he said abruptly, "let's get the herd together and get out. The feud is none of my business, and I don't intend to make it mine. Every dime I've got in the world is tied up in that venture."

Tom Kittery looked at him, his eyes suddenly hard. "That's right. It isn't none of your affair, and I'm not expecting you to take a hand in it. Nonetheless, you may have to before we get those cattle out of the state."

Johnny Lubec got up angrily. "I thought you said he was a friend of yours? He sure don't sound like it to me!"

Kittery said nothing, but stared into the fire. Tap Duvarney looked at Lubec. "I consider myself Tom's friend, but that does not involve me in a shooting war that began God only knows how—and years ago, from all I've heard. If I were a member of his family, I might feel otherwise, but I am not. Furthermore, Tom and I made an agreement, and I expect him to live up to it."

"Don't count yourself any friend of mine!" Lubec responded, his tone harsh. "Far as I'm concerned, them as ain't for us is against us."

Tap turned to Kittery, "Tom, if you don't like the sound of this, just give me back my money and we'll forget it."

Kittery looked up. "You know damn well I can't give that money back. I spent it. I bought cattle."

"Then we've got a deal." Tap reached across the fire for the coffeepot. "I'll be ready to go after those cattle in the morning."

"You got to wait." Lubec spoke with cool triumph. "We're goin' after them as killed Foster."

Tap Duvarney sipped his coffee, and when Kittery did not speak he said quietly, "I'll be ready at daybreak, Tom. If necessary, I'll get the cattle out and make this drive on my own; but if I do, I'll sell the cattle and keep every dollar of the money."

"Like hell you will!" Kittery was suddenly angry. "Half those cattle are mine!"

Tap grinned at him. "Don't be a damn fool, Tom. Our deal was my money and your savvy. If you aren't in there working and telling us how, what part can you have? I'm here. My money is in the pot. I made an agreement, and so did you. I understood that in Texas men lived up to their agreements."

"Are you sayin' I don't?"

"I'm saying nothing of the kind. I am only saying that the Munson feud is your personal affair, but I can't let it interfere with my business."

"You're right," Tom said glumly. "Damn it, I am sorry. I got no right to expect you to horn in on my fight."

Johnny Lubec leaped to his feet. "Tom? You backin' down for this—this—"

Tap Duvarney looked up. "Johnny, if you finish that sentence it better be polite or you'd better be reaching for a gun when you say it."

Lubec backed off. "On your feet, damn you! I'll—"

"*Johnny!*" Kittery's voice rang with authority. "Stop it! Tap would kill you before you got a gun out. I've seen him work."

Lubec hesitated, still angry but suddenly wary. Tom Kittery was as near to a God as he could recognize, and if Tom said this stranger was good, he must be good. Abruptly, he turned his back and walked away into the brush.

Tap finished his coffee and got to his feet. "I'm tired. I'm going to turn in."

"Sorry, Tap. Losin' Foster like that—. We're on edge, all of us."

"Forget it."

Tap walked back into the brush and unrolled his bed. He folded his coat neatly, then pulled off his boots and placed them for a pillow. He put his Winchester beside him, and also his gun belt. His spare gun he placed under the blanket and near his hand.

The Cajun came in from watch, drank coffee and ate without talking, and disappeared again. Tom

Kittery sat alone by the fire. After a while Lubec returned and crawled into his blankets.

The fire sank low, and Tap slept.

What made him awaken he did not know, but a dark figure loomed above him. The fire was only a few red coals, the columns of the trees against the stars were dark and mysterious. A faint light gleamed on the gun held in the man's hand. The gun was not aimed, it was simply hanging at arm's length against the man's leg. The man was Tom.

Tap's own hand held his gun, pointed up at Kittery through the blanket. "Go to sleep, Tom. You'll feel different in the morning. Besides, this Colt I'm holding on you would rest mighty heavy on your stomach."

Tom Kittery chuckled. "Damn it, Tap, I never knew anybody like you! Nowhere! All right, to hell with the feud! We work cattle."

TAP DUVARNEY'S EYES opened on daylight. For a moment he lay still. The fire had been built up, and he could smell coffee. Lifting his head, he saw the Cajun was slicing bacon into a frying pan. Tap slid out of the blankets and into his boots. Standing up, he slung his gun belt around his lean hips and settled the holster into place against his leg.

He felt good. The air was fresh and cool off the Gulf, not many miles away to the east, and he was a man who had lived most of his life in the open.

The War Between the States had been a blood bath, a desperate, bitterly contested war in which he had been constantly in action, often on secret missions behind the enemy lines. He had been born in

Virginia, and his southern accent was a distinct advantage on such jobs. But it was the frontier that honed him down, made keen the edges of his senses, his will to survive. For he had faced the American Indian—a wily, dangerous adversary, a fighting man of the first rank, and one familiar with every aspect of wilderness warfare and survival.

The Cajun glanced up as Duvarney approached the fire. Tap gathered a few sticks for additional fuel and placed them close at hand. It was evidence that he was expecting nobody to serve him. He was here to pull his own weight, no matter what the circumstances.

The future looked bleak enough to him. Every cent he'd owned was tied up in the cattle; a feud and the violent hatreds it generated hung over them. When such a fire burned no man within range was free from it, and the very fact that he was riding with the Kitterys would make him a target. The Kittery faction, too, was filled with hatred. The cattle drive, Tap was quite sure, had been put aside because of the feud; and had he not come along might never have been carried out. They could think of nothing now but striking back, striking hard.

When the coffee was ready, he filled his cup and squatted on his haunches by the fire. Tom Kittery was tugging on his boots. Lubec was nowhere to be seen.

"We got our work cut out for us," Kittery said. "If we round up cattle now we'll be likely to lose 'em. The Munsons will stampede them some night, scatter 'em from hell to breakfast."

"Then we'll find a place where they can be guarded,

and hold them there until we've completed the gather."

"You got any idea what you're gettin' into?" Kittery asked. "Most of those cattle are back in the brush. It won't be easy to get them."

"And you're holding some on Matagorda Island? All right, we'll just round the others up and push them out to the island. Or hold them on Black Jack Peninsula."

Tom Kittery looked over his cup at him. "You said you'd never been in this country before."

"I can read a map," Duvarney answered dryly.

By the time the sun was over the horizon they had pulled out, Duvarney riding the buckboard with Tom Kittery, whose horse was tied behind. The others rode on ahead, or scouted off to one side or the other.

"They're hunting us," Tom said matter-of-factly, "and one day they'll find us. All we've been hoping to do was thin them down a mite before the show-down."

"How many can you muster?"

"Mighty few. Eight or ten at most. We're outnumbered, four or five to one."

"Tough."

They rode on, and from time to time they saw cattle grazing, and several times saw the tracks of horses.

"Comanches raided clear to the Gulf coast some years back," Tom commented, noticing some tracks. "We don't see them anymore. At least, I haven't. Back around 1840 they burned Linnville and attacked Victoria. My folks were at Linnville, and nobody expected any Indians. When they came, everybody who could climbed on a barge and pushed out on the water. Saved their lives, but lost everything they had but the land."

"Was Indianola a port then?"

"No...not until sometime around 1844, I think. It was started by a German prince, and he called it Carlshafen, after himself, I guess. His name was Prince Carl ZuSolms-Braunfels. He brought a colony of immigrants into Texas.

"Back in those days they came from everywhere—Germans, French, Swiss...we still have a lot of them. Castroville, D-Hanis, Fredericksburg, all those places were settled by foreigners. Over by Fredericksburg half the talk a body hears is in German.

"Indianola picked up for a while, then about 1846 the cholera hit the town—nearly wiped it out. I've heard tell of it. I was too young to remember it."

"Where's Shanghai Pierce's outfit?"

"You've heard of him? I guess ever'body has. He's north of here, up on Tres Palacios Creek. He's got the biggest outfit around here, unless it's Cap'n King." Tom Kittery glanced at Tap. "You two should get along, you going to sea, and all. He was a steamboat captain before he settled in this country. A mighty good man, too. I met him a couple of times."

After this neither man spoke for several miles, and there was no sound but the clop-clop of the horses' hoofs and the jangle of the harness. Johnny Lubec had pulled off and ridden away into the brush. When he returned an hour or so later, he was leading a sad-dled horse, a tough-looking buckskin with a black mane and tail.

"We'll leave the rig," Tom said to Duvarney. "You'll ride the buckskin."

Tap Duvarney looked doubtfully at the horse, which rolled an inquisitive eye at him as if it had already been informed who its rider was to be, but Tap pulled up and swung down.

"What about the team?"

"We'll take off the harness and turn 'em loose. The buckboard can stay right here in the brush until we have reason to pick it up."

Taking the reins, he drove the buckboard into the brush. Tap took his gear from the wagon, then gestured at the supplies. "I'll need those," he said.

Kittery noticed the ammunition boxes for the first time. "You figure on usin' all that? What you goin' to do? Fight all the Indians in the Nation?"

Tap shrugged. "They told me you were in a feud. It isn't my fight, but if somebody starts shooting at me I want to be able to shoot back as long as I'm in the mood."

Lubec merely looked at him, while the Cajun took the boxes from the wagon-bed and placed them on the ground. He went to the seat, and from under it he took the sack of oats and dumped what remained on the ground. Then he filled the canvas sack with the contents of the boxes.

With all the packages and sacks loaded behind their saddles and the mustangs turned loose to go home, they took off through the scattered brush and trees. Several times they passed through extensive stretches of prickly pear, and twice they followed stream courses, keeping under the cottonwoods and pecans for concealment.

It was sundown when they rode into a small clearing. For several miles they had been moving through thick brush and timber, and the clearing came as a surprise. There was a small fire going, and three men were standing nearby, all with rifles.

"Howdy, Tom!" A stocky, barrel-chested man with a black beard walked toward them. "Johnny? Howdy, Cajun."

He smiled as he saw Duvarney. "How are you, Major? I never had the luck to run into you during the war, but we came nigh it a time or two. I am Joe Breck."

"You're Captain Joseph Breck? I remember your outfit, sir. I am just as glad we missed our meetings. You had some good men."

Breck smiled. "I've still got a couple of them, and one of yours."

"Mine? Who?"

"Me, Major." A tall, ungainly man with a large Adam's apple stepped from behind a horse he was grooming. "Corporal Welt Spicer."

Duvarney grinned. "How are you, Spicer? I'm not likely to forget you." He looked around at Kittery. "Did he tell you? He was in my outfit. We covered a lot of country together."

Kittery threw a sharp look at Spicer, but made no comment.

The hideout was a good, if temporary, one. It was on a small knoll in a dense growth of brush; tunnels through the brush showed their dark openings here and there. Obviously the thicket was a network of underbrush passageways and trails. A small spring was nearby, and although the water was brackish, it was potable.

"What's on the program, Tom?" Breck asked.

"We hunt cattle," Kittery replied shortly. "We start at daybreak. We'll make up a herd and strike out for Kansas."

They looked at him, but nobody offered a comment. A few minutes later, Duvarney caught Breck studying Kittery with care. Obviously, Tap thought grimly, he had altered their plans, and they didn't like it.

Tired from the long riding, he rolled up in his blankets. The last he remembered was seeing the others huddled around the fire, drinking coffee and talking in low tones.

Well, he reflected, let them talk. Tomorrow they work cattle.

CHAPTER 4

FOR THREE DAYS they kept at it, daylight to dark, working the cattle out of the brush, branding them and bunching them at a clearing in the woods that consisted of several hundred acres of good grass, with a trickle of water running across one corner. A few of the cattle still wore the Kittery brand, but most were mavericks.

The work was hard, punishing, and hot, yet they made time. Tap Duvarney had never worked cattle before except on the few occasions when he had hazed a small herd into an Indian camp that was being fed by the government, or when it was cattle to be beefed for the army itself. However, he had watched a lot of cowhands work on the range, and had listened to them yarning over campfires. As he could match none of these men with a rope, he devoted his time to finding the cattle and driving them from the brush or the grassy hollows. By the end of the fourth day they were holding four hundred head of mixed stuff, and their horses were played out.

Most of the cattle had been found within a few miles, but they were wild, some of them being old mossy-horns that had lived back in the brush for years. These made most of the trouble. At first it was not much more than a matter of riding around the cattle and slowly bunching them; but the older stock would have none of that. Time and again some of the mossy-horns would break for the brush, and it was hard work, and hot work, rousting them out again.

There was no chuck wagon. Every rider carried a small bait of grub in a sack behind his saddle, and ate his noonday meal out on the range . . . if he had time.

On the evening of the fourth day, Kittery said, "We've got to ride for horses. We'll need about forty head, and the nighest place is over to Coppinger's."

"Give you a chance to see Mady," Johnny Lubec said, grinning. "Want I should go along to kind of cool you off after you leave there?"

"I wouldn't trust you. Ever' time we get near the C-Bar, you head for those Mex jackals down in the wash. I think you've got eyes for that little Cortinas girl."

Lubec made no comment, and Kittery said, "All right. We'll ride out at daybreak. Johnny, you can come, and I'll take Pete and Roy." Then he glanced over at Duvarney. "You want to come, Tap?"

"I'll stay here."

After they had gone, Duvarney worked over his guns and equipment, then saddled up to ride out. "I'm going to scout around," he said to the others. "I may drive a few cattle if I see them, but I'm going for a reconaissance."

Welt Spicer got to his feet. "Mind if I trail along?"

"All right with me."

The Cajun watched them with eyes that told nothing, but Joe Breck looked at Duvarney and said, "You be careful. There's Munsons around, and if they see you they'll shoot first an' ask questions afterward."

When they'd been a few minutes on the trail, Welt

Spicer commented, "We're nigh Copano Creek. Empties into the bay yonder."

"Mission Bay?"

"Copano. Mission's smaller, and opens into Copano Bay.... You ever been in this country?"

"No, this is my first time east of the Brazos in Texas. But I've seen the maps."

The trail was narrow. Only one rider could follow it at a time, the other trailing behind. Branches brushed them on either side. It was hot and still. The only sound except the muffled fall of their horses' hoofs was the hum of insects or the occasional cry of a bird. Sweat trickled down Duvarney's face and down his body under his shirt. Sometimes they saw the tracks of cattle. Cow trails branched off from time to time, but the riders held to the main trail.

They came on Copano Creek unexpectedly. It was a fair-sized stream, with many twists and turns. Both men dismounted and drank upstream from their horses. The water was clear, and not unpleasant.

"Low tide," Spicer said. "At high tide you can't drink it." He squatted on his heels and took a small Spanish cigar from his pocket. "You got your work cut out for you, Major."

"Call me Tap."

"That Tom, now. He's a mighty good man, but he's mad. He's Munson-killing mad, and so are the others. All of 'em want to fight, not run cattle."

"How about you?"

"I'll string along with you. I figure we're a sight better off drivin' cows to Kansas." Spicer pushed his hat back so he could see Tap's face without tilting his head. "You're goin' to need men—men you can depend on."

It had been that way in the army. There had always been men he could depend on, the right sort of men in the right places when they were needed, and they made easier whatever needed to be done. His had been the responsibility of command, of decision. There had always been the sergeants, many of them veterans of the War Between the States as well as of Indian fighting. They were tough, dependable men. Now he was alone.

Somehow he had to hold the reluctant men to putting the herd together, somehow he had to get them started on the trail to Kansas. He had to ride roughshod over their resentment of him, over their hatreds, their reluctance to leave a fight unfinished. It had been easy enough when he had tough non-coms to whom he could relay his orders, and enlisted men whose duty it was to obey. This was different.

He was going to have to get the herd together faster than they had planned, get it ready to move before they expected it. If he started the herd they must come along, like it or not.

"Spicer, you're right. I will need some men. You've been around here a while ... where can I find them?"

"Fort Brown ... Brownsville. I happen to know they're breakin' up a cavalry outfit down there, and there'll be some good men on the loose. As far as that goes, there are always a few hands around Brownsville or Matamoras, anyway."

"All right, Spicer. You ride down there. Pick maybe ten good men, thirty a month and sound. Tell 'em they may have to fight. But they are hiring out to me—and to me only. You know the kind of men I want. Men like we had in the old outfit."

"It'll take me a week at least. Ten days, more likely."

"Take two weeks if need be, but get the men and get them back up here."

After Welt Spicer had gone, Duvarney rode on along the trail, emerging finally on the lower Copano, and following it along to the bay. He saw cattle from time to time; most of them were unbranded, a few were wearing the Kittery brand, and there was a scattering of other brands unfamiliar to him.

The creek ended in a small inlet, and he cut across to the bay itself. Copano Bay was almost landlocked. From his saddlebag Duvarney took the chart Wilkes had given him and studied the bay, its opening into Aransas Bay, and the island beyond. All this country was low, probably less than twenty feet above sea level, and much of it was certainly less than half of that.

He made a camp on the shore of the bay, made coffee, and chewed on some jerked beef. He went to sleep listening to the sound of the salt water rippling on the sand, and smelling it. At daybreak he was up, drank coffee, and rode off toward the northeast along the coast.

Several times he saw cattle, and as on the previous day he started them drifting ahead of him, pointing them toward the roundup area. They might not go far, but he might be able to drift some into the country to be covered for the drive. He swam his horse across the inlet at the mouth of the creek and made a swing south to check for cattle tracks on the peninsula that separated Copano from St. Charles Bay. He found a good many, and worked his way back to camp.

Joe Breck was on his feet, rifle in hand, when Tap rode in. "I wondered what happened to you. Where's Spicer?"

"Sent him down to Brownsville."

"You sent him *where?*" Without waiting for an answer, Breck went on, "Tom won't like that."

"He'll like it." Duvarney spoke shortly. "There are a lot of cattle on the peninsula east of us. We'll drift some of this lot in there."

"Wait and see what Tom says," Breck objected. "He's got his own ideas."

"And I have mine. We'll start drifting them in the morning."

Breck stared at him, his eyes level, but Tap ignored the stare and went about getting his bed ready for the night.

"I'll wait and see what Kittery says," Breck said. "He hired me."

"You wait, and then tell him to pay you what you have coming. You won't be working with us anymore."

"For a new hand," Breck said, "you swing a wide loop."

"Breck," Duvarney replied, "you're a good man, too good a man to get your back up over nothing. You want to fight the Munsons; but if you do, do it on your own time. They're no damned business of mine, and I'm going to drive cattle. I've got money tied up in this drive, and I can't work up any interest in somebody else's fight."

"It may get to be your fight, too."

"Not if it interferes with this cattle drive. Get one thing through your head. These cattle go to Kansas. If anybody gets in the way, and that means you or the Munsons, I'll drive right over them."

Breck gave him a hard look, but Duvarney paid no attention to it. He rolled up in his bed, and slept.

At daybreak the Cajun had a fire going and coffee on. Duvarney joined him. "Don't you ever sleep?" he asked.

The Cajun grinned; it was the first time Tap had seen any expression on his face. "Time to time," he said. He reached for the pot and filled Tap's cup. "Where do you think we should start?"

Duvarney drew a rough line in the sand. "Ride southeast, start sweeping the cattle north, then turn them into the peninsula."

Joe Breck came up to the fire wearing his chaps and spurs. Thirty minutes later they all rode south to begin working the brush.

It was a wide stretch of country. They rode back and forth, making enough noise to start the cattle moving out of the brush to get away from them, then pushing them toward the cattle trails that led to the peninsula. Some of them would move along those familiar trails easily enough, but a few would be balky. It was little enough the three men could do; but working in that way, there was the chance they could move quite a few head.

It was hot and sticky in the brush. Not a breath of air stirred. From time to time Duvarney found himself pulling up to give his horse a breather, and each time he did so he turned in the saddle to study the sky. It was clear and blue, with only a few scattered clouds.

They came together on the banks of a small creek flowing into St. Charles Bay, where they made coffee, ate, and napped a little. Through the afternoon they worked steadily, and drifted back into camp at sundown, dead tired.

"We covered some country," Breck commented, "and we moved a lot of beef—more'n I expected."

Tap nodded. He was no longer thinking of cattle. His thoughts had turned back to Virginia, and to the quiet night when he had said good-bye to Jessica Trescott.

Old Judge Trescott, who had known his father—had in fact been his father's attorney—had offered him a job. There were half a dozen others, too, who came up with offers, partly because of his father, and partly because he was to marry Judge Trescott's daughter. He would have none of it. He would take what cash he had, make it his own way.

Was it a desire for independence that brought him west? Or a love of the country itself? Everything he had grown up with was back there in the coast country of Virginia and the Carolinas. His father and his grandfather had operated ships there since before Revolutionary times. There had been Duvarneys trading to the Indies when George III denied them the right. In those days they had smuggled their goods. Duvarneys had been privateers during the Revolution and the War of 1812.

His was an old family on that coast. His service in the War Between the States had been distinguished; on the Indian frontier it had been exceptional in many respects. His position in Virginia was a respected one, and many doors were open to him. Yet he had left. He pulled his stakes and headed west again, to the country he had come to know.

Now here he was, struggling to get a herd together, and so deeply involved that he could not get out of it.

Jessica had rested her hands on his arms that night. "Tappan, if you don't come back soon I'll come after you. No Trescott ever lost a man to a sandy country, and I'm not going to be the first."

"It's no country for a woman," he had objected. "You wait. After I've made the drive and have some cash money, we'll talk."

"You mind what I say, Tappan Duvarney. If you don't come back, I'll come after you!"

He had laughed, kissed her lightly, and left. Perhaps he had been a fool. A man would never find a girl like that in this country. Not even Mady Coppinger.

Tom Kittery would be seeing Mady about now. He was a lucky man, Tap was thinking, a very lucky man.

"Somebody coming," the Cajun said, and vanished into the brush with no more sound than a trail of smoke from the campfire.

Tap listened, and after a moment he heard the faint sounds. One horse, with a rider—a horse that came on steadily at a fair pace and was surely ridden.

He got up and moved back from the flames, and the others did the same.

The rider came on, then drew up while still out in the darkness. "Halloo, the fire! I'm riding friendly, and I'm coming in with my hands empty."

Nobody spoke, and the stranger's horse started to walk: After a moment they could see the rider. He was a stocky, thick-shouldered man with a wide face. Both hands were in the air.

He rode into the firelight and stopped, his hands still

held shoulder-high. "I'm hunting Major Duvarney," he said. "Is he here?"

Tap stepped out. "I am Tappan Duvarney."

"And I am Darkly Foster, brother to Lightly Foster, the man you buried at Indianola."

"I know him," Breck said to Duvarney. "He's all right."

" 'Light, and move up to the fire," Tap said. "There's coffee on."

He watched the man lower his hands, and then step down from the horse. It was a fine animal, and Darkly Foster himself moved with a quick ease that told of strong muscles beneath the homespun clothes. "I am sorry about your brother," Tap said.

Darkly turned to him. "No need to be sorry. Lightly lived a full life, and a good one. Feel sorry for those who did him in."

He took a tin cup from his saddle pack and moved to the fire. When he had filled his cup and squatted on his heels he said, "I have come to meet the man who buried my brother. It was a fine thing you did."

Tap filled his own cup. "I never knew him," he said, "but he had the look of a good man."

"He was that. A solid man, a trusted man, and a man of courage. Not many would have dared to do what you did, burying him, with Shabbit and the Munsons looking on. Especially after what happened on the wharf."

"What happened?" Joe Breck asked.

Foster gestured toward Duvarney. "He treated Wheeler and Eggen Munson to a whipping. They started it—picked him for a tenderfoot, and he whipped the two of them so fast he never even mussed his hair. The town's talkin' about it."

"You never mentioned that," Breck commented.

"No need. They were feeling their oats and decided to try me on. Neither one of them could fight."

Joe Breck was silent, and in the silence the fire crackled, and off in the brush one of the horses stamped and blew. A nighthawk wheeled and turned in the sky above.

"Whatever you're planning," Darkly Foster said, "I'll offer a hand. I can use a gun as good as average, and I can handle horses or cattle."

"We're driving to Kansas . . . nothing more."

"You got yourself a hand," Foster said. "I like the way you travel."

It was long after midnight when Duvarney awakened suddenly. The fire had died to coals, with one thin tendril of flame winding itself around a dry branch. The only other man awake was Darkly Foster, who sat across the clearing, back from the fire.

Tap listened for a moment, then sat up and reached for his boots. Riders were coming.

Foster had disappeared from his seat, but could be vaguely seen, well back in the darkness. Duvarney stamped into his boots and skirted the clearing toward Foster.

"It could be Tom Kittery," he said. "He's due back."

They waited. Several horses were coming, moving slowly. When they rounded into the clearing, Tap Duvarney swore bitterly.

Roy Kittery was swaying in his saddle, his face drawn and pale. Pete Remley lay across his saddle, tied on to keep him from slipping off. Tom Kittery had a bloody shirt; only Johnny Lubec seemed to have come off without a wound.

"They were laying for us," Tom Kittery said as he slid from the saddle. "They'd been watching the Coppinger place, and when we left they let us have it. They killed Pete."

Duvarney helped Roy from the saddle. "Get over by the fire, Tom," he said, over his shoulder. "Let's have a look at those wounds."

He turned to suggest the Cajun keep a lookout, but he was gone.

"Did you get any of them?" Breck asked.

"I doubt it. We never even saw them. They were down in the brush off the road, waiting until they had us full in the moonlight. We're lucky to have any of us alive."

Neither Tom nor Roy was hit hard, but Roy had lost a lot of blood. Tap bathed and bandaged the wounds, treating them as well as he could under the circumstances. He'd had a good deal of rough experience in the handling of gunshot or knife wounds, picked up while in the Indian-fighting army.

He was beginning to have his doubts. Nothing was said about the horses they had supposedly gone to get. It began to look as though the group had actually ridden off hunting a fight, or at least hoping to run into some of the Munson party.

Tom Kittery got up and walked to the fire. "It was Huddy," he said bitterly. "Nobody else could have figured it out. Of course, I figured they'd be watching Mady's place, so we didn't go there. We went to a spring up back of the place—at least I did. I left the others a quarter of a mile down the road by a deserted corral. From the spring a man can see Mady's windows on the second floor, and she can see a fire at the spring . . . and there's just no place else a fire like that can be seen. I lit the fire, and Mady came up the slope through the trees about half an hour later and told me it was safe to come on down to the ranch.

"The Coppingers have taken no part in the feud. Fact is, they won't allow me to marry Mady until it is settled, somehow. The Munsons want no truck with them, because the old man has about thirty tough cowhands, and the Munsons don't want to tangle with them.

"I spent the evening there, mostly talking to Mady, then I went back up the hill to the spring, and then back to the corral. The boys had seen nothing and heard nothing. We mounted up and started down the hill toward the Victoria trail. They were waiting for us."

Duvarney stared at him in astonishment. "You blame it on Huddy? How could he know you were there?" He was thinking that Tom Kittery must be naive not to realize that somebody had sold him out; that he had been set up for a killing.

"He's uncanny," Kittery said. "Yes, there's something uncanny about that man," he insisted. "He ain't natural."

Nobody else was saying anything, but from their expressions Duvarney decided they must agree.

"Of course," he said, "I don't know the people on the Coppinger place, but can you trust them?"

Tom Kittery looked at Duvarney in surprise. "Them? Of course . . . Hell, I'm goin' to marry Mady.

That's been understood. It's been an agreed-on thing since before the war."

Duvarney said nothing more. He was an outsider here, knowing nothing of what had gone before, but to him it seemed likely that someone on the Coppinger ranch was accountable for this. He had no faith in the uncanny cunning of Jackson Huddy.

Duvarney was feeling that the sooner he could start the herd out of this country the better. There was too much going on here that was no concern of his, too much that might wreck all his plans. And although he kept trying to force the thought from his mind, he was thinking more and more of Jessica.

Tom looked up at him. "Sorry, Tap. This will hold things up a mite. I mean our getting shot up like this. If you'll just stand by—"

"Stand by, hell! We're going right on with it," Tap said. "When you boys can ride you can join us. I'm still working cattle."

Tom looked sour. "Well, Breck can help, and Spicer." He looked around, suddenly realizing that Spicer was not there. "Where is Spicer?" he asked.

Joe Breck answered. "Duvarney sent him to Brownsville."

"He *what?*" Kittery was angry. "Damn it, Tap, what d'you mean, sending one of my men off?" He paused. "What did you send him for?"

"Men. I'm hiring more men."

Kittery was silent, his face set in hard lines. "You figure to pay them yourself? I hope you've got the money."

"You have, Tom. You've got the money I loaned you, or whatever of it was saved to finance the drive. You certainly didn't spend it all for cattle."

Joe Breck was staring at the ground, jabbing at it angrily with a stick. Johnny Lubec, hands on his hips, looked equally angry. Duvarney glanced around at the others. He was alone here, that was obvious.

"I figured that money was mine. You bought yourself a partnership," Tom Kittery said.

"I bought half of a cattle drive, not a gun battle. And we'll need some of that money to lay in supplies and pay our way north."

"There's money," Tom protested. "I never used it all. I figured—"

"Whatever you planned, Tom, that money is partnership money, not a war chest."

"All right, all right! Forget it! You want to drive cattle, we drive cattle." Tom looked at Tap. "Damn it, man, I don't want to fight you. If ever a man had a friend, you've been a friend to me. You saved my bacon a couple of times back yonder, and I ain't likely to forget it."

———

EACH MORNING AT daybreak, Tap Duvarney was in the saddle. He drifted cattle toward the peninsula, and several times at low tide he swam his horse across to the island to check the cattle there. Breck or the Cajun worked with him, and when Roy Kittery had regained some strength he worked as well. Lubec was usually off scouting for enemies, and working out a trail by which they might move the cattle without being seen.

It was ten days to the day when Welt Spicer rode into camp. With him were eight rough-looking ex-soldiers, three of them still wearing partial uniform.

All of them were armed; all looked fit and ready for whatever came.

Gallagher, Shannon, and Lahey were New York–born Irishmen, Lawton Bean was a long-geared Kentuckian, Jule Simms was from Oregon, and wanted to go back. Doc Belden was a lean, sardonic Texan; and Judson Walker and Lon Porter were Kansans. All had served in the cavalry against Indians and Mexican bandits, and were veterans of the rough and ready life of the frontier.

Tom Kittery stood beside Tap Duvarney as the men rode in and unsaddled. "With an outfit like that," he said, "we could run those Munsons clear out of the country."

"Forget it. I hired them to run cattle."

"You've made that plain enough," Tom said dryly. "Come on, let's have a cup of coffee and hear what Johnny has to say."

Lubec squatted on his heels and, taking a twig from the fire's edge, traced the route as he talked. "The way I see it, our best chance is to head northwest of Goliad, cross the San Antonio east of there, and strike due north. We're going to have to camp away from streams and hold to sheltered country, but there's a couple of places where we can bed down without being seen unless somebody rides across country."

Lubec paused, and glanced from one to the other. "Unless"—he hesitated—"unless you decide to drive to Indianola and ship from there."

"Indianola?" Tom Kittery shook his head. "It wouldn't work. We'd never make it."

"Look," Lubec suggested. "Before we get that

herd together the Munsons will know about it. In fact, they already know we're planning a drive. So they'll be expecting us to try for Kansas. They'd never dream we'd have the nerve to try for Indianola."

"It's a thought," Breck said. "And it just might work."

"Supposing," Lubec went on, "we started our drive like I said, across country to the San Antonio. Then we drive northeast from there, as if we planned to pass Victoria on the south. There's a chance we could pull every Munson out of Indianola and have the cattle in the loading pens there before they knew what had happened."

No one spoke. Tap Duvarney stared into the fire, thinking about the suggestion. It might mean trouble, big trouble; on the other hand, it might mean a quick and adequate return on his money. The profit would not be as great, but neither would the risks be as great as those of the long drive to Kansas and the trail towns.

Indianola was only a few miles away. If the cattle could be driven there, sold there...

Then Tom said, "I like it. I think we can do it." He turned to Duvarney. "What about it, partner?"

"Let's wait. We can decide when the cattle start, but once we start nobody leaves the herd, not for any reason at all."

"What's the matter?" Lubec demanded. "Don't you trust us?"

"Do you trust me?" he countered. "If nobody leaves the herd, nobody can talk. It is simple as that."

CHAPTER 5

MATAGORDA WAS ALL of seventy miles long, and anywhere from one mile to five miles wide, depending on the state of the tide and the wind. On the Gulf side there were dunes, and a fairly even beach. The west, or landward side, was cut by many little coves or inlets, most of them shallow. There was also a good bit of swampland, with occasional patches of higher, wooded ground. Down the middle of the island was some good grassland, enough to feed a lot of cattle.

It was also a land of catclaw, mesquite, and prickly pear, with the usual allowance of rattlesnakes, jack rabbits, and deer.

Tap Duvarney rode out to the island with Welt Spicer, Jud Walker, and Doc Belden. There were a lot of cattle, most of them wearing the Rafter K, the Kittery brand. Among the others, they found a dozen old cows with calves, carrying no brand at all.

"Doc," Tap suggested, "you're carrying a running iron. You start a fire and heat it up."

By noon they had roped and branded fifteen head—branded them with a Rocking TD.

"Your brand?" Belden asked. "If it ain't registered, you'd best ride to the county seat and do it. Else somebody will beat you to it. Whoever registers that brand owns the cattle."

"I'll do just that, Doc, and thanks. We'll ride in tomorrow."

Spicer watched the last of the cows walk away, then looked around at Duvarney. "What's that for? I thought the Kittery brand was Rafter K?"

"It is ... until we've road-branded; and until we've a road brand for both of us, I've nothing to show for my investment, so I'm starting my own brand. I'll have something to build on, something to use as a bargaining point."

Spicer nodded doubtfully. "You got to be careful," he warned. "Tom may not like it."

"He'll like it. Half the cattle in Texas wearing brands got them just that way. And remember? I bought a piece of this outfit."

They rode on, and finally branded two more cows; then they crossed back to the mainland. Now there were not only a lot of cattle on the island, but also a lot of cattle on the peninsulas, and there was no reason why they should not start the drive.

Tom Kittery had thrown up a brush corral, and there were twenty new horses in it when they returned. They all wore the Coppinger brand. Tap Duvarney studied them thoughtfully, then looked at the tracks on the ground, the tracks of three horses that had carried riders. The men were at the fire when he came up.

Tap's own men had drifted in and were gathered around a smaller fire.

Two of the Coppinger riders were Mexicans—tough, salty-looking vaqueros. The third was a lean, stoop-shouldered man with a perpetual smile that did not quite reach to his eyes. He wore a tied-down gun and bowie knife.

"Lin Stocker . . . Tap Duvarney, my partner."

"Howdy," Stocker said, sizing him up coolly as Duvarney acknowledged the greeting. He started to speak, but Duvarney squatted on his heels near the Mexicans.

"That *grulla* looks like a tough little horse," he commented: then addressing the shorter Mexican, he asked, "How do you like him?"

"Bueno. That one is my own horse."

"I figured so. I like him." He turned to the other Mexican. "How do you like the paint?"

The Mexican shrugged. "He runs fast." He grinned. "He pitches a leetle, too."

Duvarney had already decided that Stocker was a trouble-maker, and he wanted to have as little to do with him as possible. The three had brought the horses over from the Coppinger outfit, which meant they knew where to find Tom Kittery, and also that a drive was in prospect. Tom Kittery did not seem to be as wary as Duvarney remembered him. Either he had changed or he was inviting attack . . . perhaps inviting attack because the Munsons could not know of the new men Duvarney had brought in.

Tap found himself growing more and more irritated and more anxious. He had bargained for no feud. What he had made was a simple business deal, and that was exactly what he wanted.

"How'd you know Pedro rode the grulla?" Stocker demanded. "Did you see us ride in?"

"He wears Mexican spurs, with big rowels. He left

some sign where he tied his horse and where he dumped his saddle."

Duvarney felt sure that Stocker was not to be trusted. The tall, stoop-shouldered cowboy did a lot of looking around. Duvarney drifted over to where Tom Kittery sat, and dropped to the ground beside him.

"I'm taking some of my boys and riding into Refugio," he said, "and then we'll swing around by Victoria. Any business I can do for you?"

Tom Kittery took the makings from his pocket and began to build a smoke. "If you aren't in this fight," he commented, "you'd better ride careful. There's those who wouldn't believe it."

"Tom," Duvarney said quietly, "I know you'd like to have me take up this fight of yours, but I say again that I joined up only for the cattle business. I think this feud is a foolish thing. You and the Munsons are fighting a fight that should have died out years ago. I know they burned you out, I know they killed some of your kin, but you killed some of theirs, too. All I want is to make my drive, and I'd like you to make it with me.

"If we get these cattle to Kansas or sell them in Indianola, whichever proves out, we'll have some cash money, enough to start ranching up north...in Wyoming or Montana."

"I'm a Texas man," Kittery protested.

"Hell," Duvarney said, "I've been up there. Half the cattlemen in Wyoming and Montana are from Texas...or England. There's good grass up there, and I know the country. We could sell our steers, then drive the young stuff and the breeding stock to northern grass. You could leave this feud behind, own your own outfit, marry Mady Coppinger, and live happily ever after."

"You make it sound good, Tap. You surely do."

"Which sounds better? That, or to roust around the country hunting for Munsons all your life? Until they're all dead, or somebody dry-gulches you?"

"When do you want to pull out?"

"A week from today, with whatever we have. We can try for Indianola if things work out: if they don't, we can strike north for the Red River, fatten our stock on Indian grass, and push into Kansas when the market is right."

REFUGIO WAS A sleepy-looking cowtown that belied its appearance. The four riders rode into the dusty street and tied to the hitching rail in front of the courthouse.

Boardwalks ran along both sides of the street, and back of the walks were adobe or frame buildings with a few galleries hanging over the walks. The courthouse was open, and Tap strolled across the street and went up the steps. Doc Belden stayed near the horses; Jud Walker and Welt Spicer had gone into the nearest saloon.

"Rocking TD?" The clerk opened the brand book. "I don't recall that one, so you're probably all right on it." He registered the brand, studying the name he had written . . . *Tappan Duvarney*.

"I've heard of you," the clerk commented. "Friend of Tom Kittery's, aren't you?"

"Met him during the war," Duvarney replied.

"He come in with you? If he did, you might tell him Mady Coppinger's in town."

Despite himself, Tap felt excitement. Was it because he hadn't seen any woman in so long? Or—

He shook himself to escape the thought, settled his hat in place, and went out. For a moment he paused in the doorway, his eyes studying the street. One of the ways to avoid trouble was to see it before it got to you.

Doc Belden was still standing near the horses, smoking a small cigar. He was looking down the street toward the saloon, which Tap could not see. Almost without thinking, Tap reached up and unbuttoned his coat. He carried two guns, one in its holster, the other in his waistband.

He walked directly to the horses and stood near Doc. "Everything all right?"

Doc gave him a quizzical glance. "Half a dozen riders just pulled in...lathered horses...like maybe they'd hurried to get here."

"Mount up," Tap said; "we'll ride down and join the boys."

They tied the horses at the rail in front of the saloon, listening for voices. There were six horses tied nearby; all had been ridden hard, all bore the Circle M brand.

"Sit loose in the saddle, Belden. This may be it, but let me open the ball."

They pushed through the swinging doors into the shadowed coolness of the saloon. Spicer was at the end of the bar, facing the room, and Jud Walker stood close by.

Two of the Circle M riders stood well down the

bar from Walker. Two others were seated at a table behind him but about fifteen feet away. The other two were down the room, but facing Walker and Spicer, boxing them neatly.

Tap stepped to one side of the door, his eyes taking in the scene at a glance. Doc Belden had moved easily to the other side of the door.

One of the men at the tables turned his head, squinting his eyes against the outside glare, to see who had come in. It was Shabbit.

"How are you, boys?" Tap said quietly. "Let's all have a drink, shall we?"

The situation had suddenly reversed itself, and it was now the Munson party who were boxed. If they faced the two men at the bar they could not face the two at the door. And shooting against the sunlight was not too easy a thing.

Shabbit hesitated, and the moment passed him by. "To the bar, gentlemen," Tap insisted. "I'm buying the drinks. Bartender, set them up ... *right there.*"

He was pointing at the center of the bar, and he was pointing with a gun.

Nobody had seen him draw it ... it was simply there.

One of the Munson men, whom Tap remembered from the graveyard, pushed back his chair and got up. "Don't mind if I do," he said coolly. "You ridin' with the Kitterys now?"

"I'm in the cattle business with Tom Kittery," Tap replied calmly. "I'm not mixed up in any feud, and don't intend to be."

As the first man started to the bar a second man got up. Shabbit was the last to move, muttering under his breath. When all had lined up along the bar and their drinks were poured, Duvarney motioned Walker and Spicer back to the door. Then he went to the bar and paid for the drinks.

"Oblige me, gentlemen," he said, "and stay with your drinks. My finger is very touchy on the trigger, and I'll need at least ten minutes to complete my business here. I would regret killing a man for merely putting his head out of the door."

Retreating to their horses, they mounted and walked them slowly down the street. They left town on the road to Victoria, but soon turned off it and went toward the San Antonio River. It was after dark when they made camp in the breaks along the San Antonio, and before daylight they were moving again. By late morning they were riding into Victoria.

Spicer and Walker stayed with the horses, while Duvarney and Doc Belden walked down the street. Mady Coppinger was on the boardwalk on the other side. Tap crossed over, removed his hat, and bowed.

"Miss Coppinger?" he said. "It is good to see you again."

His eyes went up and down the street, scanning the buildings, even the second-story windows.

"I don't understand you, Major Duvarney. Why would a man like you want to come to Texas? Tom says you have connections in Virginia, that you've lived all over, know all sorts of people."

"I like Texas."

"You *like* it? I find that hard to believe."

"It's a man's country, I will admit, but you would find the cities less attractive after you had been there a while."

"Anything is better than this," she replied. "I wish ... I wish I could just move away and never see it again. You men may like the dust, the cattle, the sweating horses ... I don't. I want to be where there's life ... excitement."

"You would find it just as dull there after a while," Tap commented. His eyes swept the street again. "Have you time to eat with me? I see there's a restaurant up the street, and I'd be pleased if you'd be my guest."

"I'd like that very much," she agreed, "after I get some things I need." While she went on down the street to do her shopping, Tap Duvarney walked back to the horses.

"We'll be in town for a bit," he said. "I'm going to have dinner with Miss Coppinger."

"You sure do pick 'em, Major," Walker said, grinning. "That's a mighty handsome figure of a woman."

"She's spoken for," Duvarney replied shortly. "That is the girl Tom Kittery is going to marry."

"You'd never know it, the way she was lookin' at you," Jud commented. "But that's none of my affair." He looked around uneasily. "You want us to stay close? I smell trouble."

"There's a grove of pecans on the edge of town. After you boys do whatever buying there's to do, meet me there ... in an hour."

Welt Spicer hesitated. "You sure you don't want us to stay by you? I've heard tell this here is a Munson town."

"No ... just be there when I come. I'll be all right."

The restaurant was a small place, with white curtains at the windows and white tablecloths and napkins. Mady came in a moment after he arrived, moving gracefully. Her eyes lighted up when she saw him. "You may not believe this," she said, "but I've lived near Victoria all my life and this is only the second time I have eaten here."

He glanced at her thoughtfully. She was uncommonly pretty, and especially so today. She was, he thought, one of those girls who love company, who like to be going and doing. There was little chance of that on a cattle range.

"But you're in town often," he protested. "Where do you eat?"

"We bring our lunch. But sometimes we eat at the home of friends." She looked up, her blue eyes resentful. "You haven't been here long enough to know, Major Duvarney, but cash money is hard to come by in Texas these days. My father has more cattle than most folks around Victoria, but he sees very little cash money. I had to skimp and save to make that trip to New Orleans. Not that Pa isn't well off," she added. "It's just the way things are in Texas."

She looked unhappy, and it caused him to wonder about her relationship to Tom Kittery. Tom was the sort of man who would appeal to women. He was tall and well set-up, he carried himself with a manner, and had an easy, devil-may-care way about him. His family had standing in East Texas, and but for the feud might have been living in prosperity ... on a par with her own family.

Obviously, that was not enough for Mady Coppinger. She wanted the life of the city and its real or fancied excitements. Her one brief visit had only served to whet her appetite for more, and had been brief enough to bring no disillusionment. Such a girl was the last person in the world for Tom Kittery, a man committed by birth and inclination to the wilder West.

"Cities aren't the way you seem to think them," he said, "and most of the people living there have no part of what is supposed to be the glamour and the excitement. You probably have a better life and a more interesting life right here."

They talked on, and in spite of himself he was led to talk of New York and Washington, of Richmond and Charleston. The time went by too quickly, and more than an hour had passed before he broke away and joined his men, who were growing restive.

He had learned a little. Mady was in love with Tom, but was torn between her love for him and her desire to be rid of Texas and all it stood for. She loved him in her way, but she wanted him away from Texas, and she doubted his ability to win the feud. The fighting itself disturbed her less than he expected, yet somewhere, somehow, she had been offered some powerful and fairly consistent arguments to indicate that Tom had no chance of winning.

He had a feeling that when she talked of this she was not using her own words, but words she had heard. From her father, perhaps? Or from somebody else? Had Tom any inkling of her doubts? Or that there might be some who lacked faith, someone close to Mady or himself?

He had no doubt that somebody had informed the Munsons that he and his men had ridden to Refugio the day before. Those hard-ridden horses were hard to explain in any other way.

Somebody had informed the Munsons in time for them to get some fighting men to Refugio. That they had failed in their mission was largely due to the fact that they had failed to catch Duvarney and his men together in a single group.

Tap Duvarney had lived too long to trust anyone too much. It was his nature to like people, but also to understand that many men are weak, and some are strong. In the rough life of the frontier, strengths and weaknesses crop out in most unexpected places, and there is less chance to conceal defects of character that in a less demanding world might never become known . . . even to their possessor.

Someone close to Tom Kittery, someone whom he trusted, was betraying him. It would pay to ride carefully and to study the trail sign before revealing too much to anyone.

Riding back to the hideout in the brush, Tap Duvarney considered his moves with care, trying to foresee the moves the enemy would make, and to plan his own accordingly.

They must do the unexpected, always the unexpected.

Tom Kittery got up from the fire and approached as Tap swung down. "We'll drive for Kansas," Tap said, "and we'll start day after tomorrow."

CHAPTER 6

OVER THE SULLEN coals of a mesquite-root fire, Tap Duvarney told his men: "Roll out at first light, bunch on Matagorda, and sweep south. Start about here." He drew a rough map of the island. "Push down and swim them over to here."

He turned to Kittery. "Tom, how about you taking your boys and sweeping kind of east by north from Copano Creek? Scatter out and gather what you can, but waste no time chasing the tough old ones.

"Darkly Foster can take Shannon, Lahey, and Gallagher over to the tip of Black Jack Peninsula and drive north. We'll work fast and we'll miss a lot of stuff, but we should rendezvous on Horseshoe Lake with a good-sized herd."

Kittery nodded. "Seems likely. How about you?"

"I'll take Doc, Lawton Bean, Spicer, and Jule Simms over to the island. Walker and Porter can work with you."

"You'll never make it. Not in the time you're givin' us. That's a whole lot of country."

"I know it is, and we can't make a clean sweep. Just start driving and keep moving. What we get we'll take, and what's left we can get the next time."

"All right, Major," Kittery said ironically, "you're givin' the orders."

Breck and Dubec stared stubbornly at the ground,

ignoring Tap. The Cajun showed no feeling one way or the other. Tap said mildly, "If we all do our part, this should be quite a drive. We'll slip out of here without a fight."

Lubec laughed contemptuously. "You don't know them Munsons, Major." Lubec emphasized the title. "They'll wait until you bunch your stock and they'll move. You'll see."

"I hope you'll be there shooting when they do, Johnny," Tap replied pleasantly. "Now I'm going to hit the hay. I'm tired."

Slowly, they drifted away to their beds, all but Breck, Lubec, and Kittery.

"They don't like it much, Major," Spicer whispered, "you takin' command like this."

The night was still. The crickets' chirping was the only sound. Tap clasped his hands behind his head and stared up at the stars, which winked occasionally through the black mantilla formed by the branches and leaves overhead. He liked the smell of the earth, the trees, the coolness of a soft wind from off the Gulf.

Despite his outward assurance, he was far from confident. There were too many things that could happen, too many things to go wrong, and there was too much that was doubtful about his own relationship with Tom Kittery.

The man was moody and solitary, and when not alone he kept close to those who had been with him from the beginning. The bitterness of the feud was upon him, the memory of good men dead, of his burned-out home, of the graves of his family. Nor could Tap blame him. In Tom's place, he too would have fought. But he was not in Tom's place.

His future lay in that herd of cattle they were to gather, his future and perhaps that of Jessica. He wanted to return to her without empty hands, and if he could not return that way, he made up his mind suddenly, he would not go back at all.

He was too proud to accept a position from her family, or from friends of either his family or hers. His father and grandfather had walked proudly, had made their own way, and so would he make his. He could return to the service, but he knew what it meant—fighting Indians or living out a dull existence on some small post on the frontier.

With the few men they had, they could not hope to make anything like a clean sweep. They could only do their best, then move the herd; with luck they would get out without a fight. He was not at all as hopeful of that as he had sounded at the campfire.

Finally he slept. In the night he stirred restlessly, the sea in his bones responding to something on the wind, some faint whisper from out over the wastes of the ocean. Something was happening out there, something he knew by his instincts. Several times he muttered in his sleep, and when he awakened he was not refreshed.

The Cajun was at the fire. Did the man never sleep at all? He looked up at Duvarney and, taking his cup from his hand, filled it from the coffeepot.

Brooding, the Cajun sipped at his coffee. Presently he glanced around at Duvarney. He nodded to indicate a huge log that lay over against the edge of the clearing. It was an old log measuring at least four feet through, and was perhaps sixty feet in length.

"He big tree . . . grow far off."

Tap Duvarney looked at the log. It certainly was larger than anything he had seen along the Gulf Coast, although there might be something as big in the piney woods to the north.

"How did it get here?"

The Cajun jerked his head toward the Gulf. "Storm. Big storm bring him on the sea."

Tap looked at the log again. They were at least five miles from the Gulf Coast. To come here by sea, that log would have to cross Matagorda Island and then be carried this far inland.

"Have you seen the sea come this far in?"

"One time I see. My papa see, also. One time there was a ship back there." He turned and pointed still farther inland. "Very old ship. It was there before my grandpa."

The Cajun relapsed into silence over his coffee. There was no light in the sky, but a glance at his watch showed Duvarney that the hour was four in the morning. When he had finished his coffee he went out and caught up his horse, then bridled and saddled him.

Standing beside the horse, he thought over the plans he had made. There was much about them he did not like, but he could see no alternative that would improve the situation.

The night coolness had gone. The air was still, and it was growing warmer. He led his horse back and tied him to a tree not far from the fire.

He accepted a plate of beef and beans from the

Cajun, and ate while the others crawled sleepily from their beds. It was going to be a long, hard day.

There is no creature on the face of the earth more contrary than the common cow. Not so difficult as a mule, not so mean or vicious as a camel, the cow beast can nevertheless exhaust the patience of a Job.

Duvarney and his men started on the island, and contrary to his announced intention, they did not drive south, but north.

It was not until they reached the island that Tap pulled up and hooked a leg around the saddle horn. He pushed his hat back and got a small cigar from his pocket. "We're going to do a little different from what I said." He paused to strike a match. "We're going to drive the cattle north, cross from the tip of the island over to the mainland, at low tide or close to it, and take our part of the herd right into Indianola."

"Suits me," Spicer commented.

"Me too," Doc said. "We'll get to town that much sooner."

"Somebody," Duvarney went on, "has talked too much, or else somebody has too much confidence in their friends. So if you should meet anybody, don't let them get the idea we're driving north."

"That's marshy country," Jule Simms said doubtfully. "We're liable to bog down the herd."

Tap reached into his saddlebag and brought out a folded chart, now much crumpled. "Look here," he pointed. "This is an old smugglers' trail. It was an Indian trail before that. We'll have to watch the herd, but if we keep them on that trail we can go right through."

They scattered out and began to work back and

forth across the island, pointing the cattle north. Here and there other brands were found, and those they cut out and turned back. It was slow, painstaking work. The cattle were loath to be driven, stubbornly resisting, and a few were allowed to go.

The weather was hot and sultry. Not a breath of air circulated among the low-growing brush, or moved in from the sullen sea. Tap mopped his face again and again, fighting the flies, but he kept driving the cattle out. By noon they had a good-sized herd moving up the island ahead of them.

Jule Simms had gone back for fresh horses, and they took a long nooning by a brackish waterhole near Panther Point. Kittery was to have started horses to them, and with luck Simms would meet them halfway.

Lawton Bean held his cup in his gnarled, work-hardened fingers "You figure this'll turn into a scrap?" he asked.

"Not if I can help it," Duvarney said. And then he added, "But I'd say the odds were against us making it all the way without a fight."

"You figure to drive the other herd thisaway?"

Duvarney shook his head. "No . . . and this isn't to be talked about. We'll drive this bunch in and sell them right in Indianola. If things work the way I figure, they already know we've a drive under way over on the Copano; and unless I'm mistaken, that will pull all the Munson crowd out of Indianola."

The grass was good, and the cattle, fortunately, showed no inclination to go back. When Duvarney had put out the fire and they had saddled up again, they merely nudged the cattle along. On the landward side of the island there were inlets and coves, and small scattered lakes, and the cattle took shelter from the flies in some of the thick brush there. But Duvarney led the way, working the reluctant cattle out of the brush and starting them north.

Welt Spicer met him at the end of one of the narrow necks of land that lay between the ponds and lakes. He mopped his face and swore. "Hotter'n hell," he said. "Cyclone weather, if I ever did see it."

"Jule should be along," Duvarney said. He stood in his stirrups, but it offered him no advantage. He could see nothing but the tops of willows. "My horse is played out," he added.

"So's mine. How far to the end of the island?" Spicer asked.

"Twenty miles."

"We ain't goin' to make it today. Maybe not tomorrow."

"Tomorrow. We should cross over to the mainland before noon. The brush thins out farther along, and the island narrows down. I'm going to send you and one of the other boys ahead to keep the cattle to the Gulf side of the island."

Their horses started reluctantly. A big red steer lifted his head and stared at them defiantly. His horns would spread an easy seven feet; he would weigh fifteen hundred pounds if an ounce, and all of it ready for trouble. Both men started for him and he lowered his head a little, then thought better of it and turned away.

Spicer started a cow and a calf from the brush, the cow wearing the Rafter K brand, as the steer had.

"We'll get that brindle calf in the roundup," Spicer said.

They had moved no more than two miles from their nooning when Simms caught up with them, bringing ten head of horses.

Tap Duvarney stripped his saddle from his own weary horse and saddled one of the new ones—a strawberry roan with three white stockings. It was a mustang, but there had been some good blood in it somewhere, for the horse had fine lines. It looked strong and tough.

Jule Simms sat his horse, studying Duvarney. "I heard some talk," he said at last.

"I'll listen."

"They're goin' to kill you—Breck an' them."

Tap rested his hands on the saddle and looked across the horse at Simms. "Do they know you heard this?"

"I was saddling a horse—they didn't even know I was around. They want you out of the picture. With you gone, they figure to fight the Munsons."

"Does Tom know this?"

"Not from the way they talked. Of course, I couldn't say for sure. Breck hates you for bein' a Yankee-lover, and Lubec thinks you rate yourself too high. Mostly they think you're ridin' roughshod over Tom and keepin' them from killin' Munsons."

"Do you know just what they're planning?"

"I didn't hear that part, only it's supposed to come soon. Maybe at Horseshoe Lake, maybe somewhere else."

"Thanks, Jule," Duvarney said. "Thanks."

"The boys and me, we figure you're our boss. We're

riding for you. If you want us to, you say the word and we'll ride down there and talk it over some."

"I appreciate that. I surely do." Tap stepped into the saddle. "Let's get on with the drive."

Several times he came within sight of the Gulf. The sea looked sullen and heavy. The water scarcely rustled on the sandy beach. He drew up, smelling the air and looking seaward. There was a sort of swell to the sea, scarcely discernible.

The island had narrowed, and the cattle could be moved faster. He threw himself into the work.

Lawton Bean rode in, hazing a mixed lot of stuff, mostly young, with a couple of old mossy-horns. He had been working among the tidewater ponds and stringers of land that ran out among the maze of inlets and channels along the inland shore of Matagorda. His faded blue shirt was dark with sweat, and the dust on his face was streaked with it.

"I swear that Tom Kittery must've branded everything that wore hair!" he said. "A couple of times back in the brush I'm sure I seen a cougar wearin' his brand."

"There was a cowhand over on the Nueces one time roped and branded a razor-back hog," Simms commented.

"Now, that ain't a-tall likely," Bean objected. "You ever try to dab a rope on a hog? He holds his head down too low. I'd say a man ropin' one of them razor-backs had his work cut out for him."

"There was a hand rode for King Fisher down around Uvalde would dab his rope on anything he could get his loop over. He roped a buzzard one time.

It had got so full of meat off a dead crittur it couldn't get off the ground."

"How many head we got up there?" Simms asked. "We must have half the stock in East Texas."

"There's a few hundred head," Duvarney said, cautiously.

"You countin' deer?" Bean asked. "We got four, five head of deer in among them cows."

Welt Spicer drifted in, pushing a few head, among them a huge red steer that stood all of seventeen hands high and carried a magnificent head of horns. He rolled his eyes and bobbed his head at them, but went on by.

"Any you boys want some exercise, you might try ropin' Big Red there. He don't take to it," Spicer said.

"Knew a cowhand one time over in the brush country," Lawton Bean said, starting to build a smoke. "He was a reliable man. You sent him out to do something, he done it, no matter what. Well, one time the boss told him to clean up all the stock south of the ridge, and when he came in that night he had a hundred and twenty-seven head of cattle, thirty sheep, three mountain goats, seven tom turkeys, a bobcat and two bears...and what was more, he'd branded ever' last one of them."

"I don't believe that part about the sheep," Jule Simm said mildly. "Seems unlikely a man would run sheep with cows."

Tap Duvarney looked around, and found a sheltered spot near some dunes, with the Gulf waters within view. There was driftwood about, and some brush. "We'll camp right here," he said, "and make a small fire. We'll take turns on guard tonight."

"You goin' on in tomorrow?" Spicer wanted to know.

"Uh-huh...right in. We'll hold the herd a few miles out and I'll go on in and make a deal." He looked around at them as they stripped their gear from the horses. "From here on in, you boys act like you're expecting Comanches. You'll earn your wages before we leave Indianola, unless I'm mistaken."

"How about the cattle? Will that water be shallow enough?"

"For them?" Welt Spicer grinned at the speaker. "Mister, those cattle don't know whether they'd rather graze on the prairie or the ocean bottom. They swim like fish. Shanghai Pierce calls his sea lions. You'll see why."

Jule Simms took over the cooking. Earlier in the day he had shot a deer, and they ate venison and the remains of the *tortillas* they had brought along, and drank coffee. Doc Belden strolled down to the edge of the water and for some time they could see his dark figure against the steel gray of the Gulf. When he came back, he said, "Let me have first watch. I'm not tired."

The fire died down, the men rolled up in their blankets, tired out with the day's work. Tap walked to the brackish pond and washed his face and hands. When he went back to the fire all the men were asleep but Doc, who was up on the side of a dune with his Winchester.

"What's the 'Doc' stand for?" Tap asked him.

"Courtesy title. I had a notion back when I was a youngster that I wanted to take up medicine. I read for it, worked four years with a doctor . . . a damned good one, too."

"What happened?"

Doc Belden glanced at him. "I was a kid. The girl I thought I was in love with married somebody else, so I pulled my freight. Away down deep I think that was what I wanted anyway. I wasn't cut out for a home guard. The army was recruiting, so I joined up. I did a year at Fort Brown, and then they transferred a few of us west. I was at Fort Phil Kearney when Carrington was in command."

After that they sat silent for a time, staring out to sea. The night was cool, the sea calm except for that slight persistent swell.

Tap indicated the Gulf. "I don't like the look of it . . . too quiet."

"I know nothing about the sea."

"That's where I started."

Tap continued to stare seaward. It was a lovely night, with a young moon high in the sky. "There's something going on out where that swell comes from."

He got to his feet. "If there's trouble, I'll be sleeping yonder, and I'm a light sleeper."

He went down the dune, checked the coffeepot, and added a little water and a little coffee for the guards to come. The cattle had wandered off toward the north, and only a few were in sight. There was grass up where they had bedded down, and he doubted if any would start back before daybreak.

He checked his gun, then peeled off his coat and sat down, tugging at his boots. How many times had he slept out as he was sleeping now? And how many times would he do so in the future? Belden was one of those who did not fit...he was a square peg, and content to be so. Was he, Tap Duvarney, a square peg? If so, he was not content. He wanted a home... and he wanted Jessica.

How long he had been asleep he did not know, but when a hand touched his shoulder gently, he opened his eyes at once, his fingers already closing on the butt of his gun.

It was Lawton Bean, who was to stand the third watch. Tap's mind put that together, and he noticed the position of the stars...it was within an hour of daybreak.

"Major," Bean said in a low tone, just loud enough for Duvarney's ears. "There's somebody out there... somebody on a horse."

CHAPTER 7

TAP DUVARNEY THREW back his blanket and got to his feet. For a moment he listened, hearing nothing. He glanced toward the fire, now a bed of red coals. The scattered sleepers were all hidden from sight in the deeper shadows. He sat down again and tugged on his boots, then thrust his gun down into his belt, and picked up his gun belt and holster.

"South?"

"Yes . . . close by."

They walked away from camp, keeping to the brush shadows. To the south there was an open space of about three acres, all grass well eaten down. Farther to their right, which was the inland side, there were tall reeds along what was called Pringle Lake, which was actually an almost landlocked cove.

The approach from the south was difficult, which was one reason for Duvarney's choice of the position. The night was clear and the stars were out, but the moon was now low in the sky and not of much help. However, the sea and the sand reflected enough light to make anyone hesitant about attempting an approach.

The two men stood there together, waiting. After a moment or two they heard a sound, the same sound Bean had heard before. It was the whisper of brush over coarse denim . . . and then the slightest jingle of a spur. A rider was coming up from the south, walking his horse.

Lawton Bean watched the shadow take shape. "It ain't the same one, Major, I'll take an oath."

"I believe you." He hesitated. He had a pretty good idea who it was now; he even believed he could see the horse. "You go back on watch, Bean," he said. "Keep a good lookout."

Tap waited, standing there alone, watching the rider come nearer. When the horse was still a little distance off he spoke. "Come on in, Tom, with your hands empty."

Tom Kittery rode on up, reining his horse in as he neared Duvarney. "Hey, you mean it!"

"Yes, I mean it, Tom. Some of your boys are after my scalp."

"*My* boys? You're crazy!"

"They want to fight, Tom. They want to push that feud. They also want me out of the way, because they think I'm blocking them."

Tom Kittery chuckled. "Well, ain't you?" He pushed his hat back, curled a leg around the saddle-horn, and started to build a smoke. "You can't blame them, Tap. They've lost people to the Munsons, same as I have. They figure you're an outsider."

"You tell them to lay off. Tell that to Lubec and Breck, and whoever. I haven't got time to fight, but if they push me, they can get it."

"You surely ain't changed," Kittery said. "You always was a right smart fightin' man, Tap. They got that to learn."

He glanced around. "You're pushing north?"

"Uh-huh...I'm going to sell cattle in Indianola while they're watching you at Horseshoe Lake, or about there."

"Canny...you always was a canny one. How many head you got?"

"Eight, nine hundred. Mixed stuff."

Tom drew on his cigarette, and the end glowed in the darkness. "Sorry to say this, boy, but you got to go back. There's no trail across the swamps."

"There's a trail. Just don't you say anything about this when you get back to camp."

At Tom's odd look, Duvarney added, "You've got a spy in camp. Or somebody who comes to camp now and again. They almost had us in Refugio, and they knew we were coming."

"One of my boys?" Kittery shook his head. "I won't take stock in that, Tap. I know my outfit. They've been with me for years."

"They haven't been with me, and I *don't* know them. No matter...Those riders had to run their horses half to death to get to Refugio in time to meet us."

Tom Kittery said nothing, but Tap knew he was irritated. Tom trusted his friends, and he wanted to hear nothing against them.

Tap changed the subject. "How does it happen you ride in here at night? Is something wrong over yonder?"

"Mady's lit out. Her pa came into camp just a-foamin' and a-frettin'. Figured she'd come to me, but she sure enough hadn't, so I came over here."

"*Here?*"

Tom rested his left hand, holding the cigarette on his knee, which was still around the saddle horn.

"Heard you was with her in Victoria," he said mildly. "I figured maybe you two had somethin' goin'."

"Don't be a damn fool, Tom, and don't try snapping that cigarette in my eyes when you go for your gun, because it won't work."

Tom gave another chuckle. "Canny...that's what I said. She ain't here, then?"

"She wouldn't come here, Tom. We talked a little, that was all. I'm an engaged man, Tom, and I take it seriously. I wouldn't start anything with the girl of a friend, anyway."

"All right. You say that, but what about Mady? She's forever talkin' of city folks and their ways... and you especially, ever since you came."

"Well, she's not here, Tom. Forget it, and let's go have some coffee."

They went into camp together and took their cups to the fire. The coffee was black and strong.

Hunching down by the fire, Duvarney studied Tom Kittery carefully. The man looked thinner, harder. He looked like a man with an edge to him, a man ready to strike out suddenly, violently. And Tom Kittery, at any time, was a dangerous man.

"Let's get some sleep." Tap drained his cup and threw the dregs into the fire. "You can use Bean's bed."

"I got one." Tom got up slowly. "If you ain't seen her I just don't know where to look."

Tap sat down and started to tug off his boots. Then suddenly he went cold and clammy. That other sound—the one Lawton Bean said he had heard before...

Tom Kittery would never believe Tap had told the

truth if Mady Coppinger rode into camp. Or if he awakened to find her there in the morning.

Tap sat there, feeling the damp chill, holding a boot in his hand. Across the camp he could see Tom Kittery unrolling his blanket and tarp.

Behind him, Tap heard something stir in the sand.

Inwardly he cursed, suddenly, bitterly. Leave it to a woman to get a man killed. What had she run away for, anyway? Some fool notion about going to the city, as if that was the answer for everything. In a city, without family or connections or money, there was only one way for a girl to go.

He was tired, dead tired, but he'd be damned if . . . Behind him he heard a faint whisper. Or had he imagined it?

Deliberately, he got up and crossed to the fire, filling his cup at the pot. The coffee was strong enough to stiffen the hair on a man's neck, and hot enough to scald. He tasted it, then put the cup down.

He had no intention of being killed or of killing anyone over Mady Coppinger. If that had been her back there . . . but suppose it was somebody else? Some wounded man, trying to reach him? He shook off the idea, and picked up the coffee cup. He needed sleep. He was desperate for it.

He sat quietly and now sipped the coffee. At last he put the cup down and, after rinsing it, he walked back to his blankets and crawled into them, boots and all. Almost instantly, he was asleep.

When he awoke it was broad daylight and the camp was still. He sat up, blinking and looking around. His horse was saddled and tied nearby, the coals were smoldering, and the coffeepot was still on the fire. Everyone was gone.

He got up, shook out his blanket, and rolled it in his tarp. Under a stone beside the fire there was a note, hurriedly written.

Figgered to let you sleep. Else you ketch up, we will hold this side of Bayucos. K still around.
                                            Spicer

Getting some jerked beef and hardtack from the saddlebag, he squatted on his heels and chewed the beef, ate the hardtack, and swallowed the coffee, which was bitter as lye. But it was hot, and he enjoyed it.

Finally he took the pot off the coals and covered the fire with sand. While the pot cooled off, Duvarney looked about the place where his bed had been. He could not be sure, but it looked suspiciously as if somebody had come up behind him in the soft sand.

He packed the coffeepot, then swung into the saddle and started north. The sand was so chewed up by cattle tracks that there was no possibility of reading sign.

He took his time. The occasional glimpses he had of the sea worried him. The swell had grown larger rather than diminishing, and the water still had that same glassy appearance. The sky was vague, the horizon indistinct.

The western side of the island grew more and more boggy, and the line of cattle slimmed down until at places it was moving almost in single file. Twice he saw places where animals had been dragged from the swamp. Where they had held closer to the Gulf side of the island, they had moved steadily along.

They were nooning and had a fire going when he rode up to them. "By Jimminy," Simms said, "there's our coffeepot!"

"Thanks, boys. I enjoyed the coffee."

"I crossed up yonder," Lawton Bean said. "It ain't bad a-tall. There's a few young uns we may have to pack over on our saddles, but otherwise it's a cinch."

"You boys go ahead. I'm going to scout trail."

He rode on, leaving them around the fire, and pushed through the cattle and crossed to the mainland. At this hour there was only one place where his horse had to swim, and the water was lower than his chart had told him. He was riding up on the shingle when he saw the tracks.

A horse had come this way not long after daybreak, to judge by the tracks—a freshly shod horse with a smaller, neater hoof than Bean's horse.

There were some windblown trees back from the crossing place, and he headed for them, wanting to take a sight over the route that lay ahead. After all, his chart was not new, and swampland could change. He had gambled on that trail.

Suddenly he glimpsed a horse and rider among the trees ahead. He turned his mount to weave around some small brush, and when his gun hand was on the side away from the trees he slipped the thong. He planned to use the gun he carried behind his belt, but a man never knew.

His horse scrambled up the sandy slope and into the trees, and he saw that the rider was Mady Coppinger.

"Tap," she said at once, "you've got to help me."

He pulled up six or seven feet away, his eyes scanning the brush behind and all around her. "What can I do," he asked, "that Tom Kittery can't do?"

"You can help me get out of here. I want to go to New Orleans."

"It's no place for a girl without family or friends," he said. "How could you make a living?"

"Oh...oh, I'll find a way!" She was impatient. "Tap, I just can't stand it any longer! I can't stand everybody going to bed when the sun's scarcely out of the sky. I want to go somewhere where there are lights and music, and something is happening. I'll just die here!"

"Have you talked to Tom about it? He's figuring on getting married. He wants to live in this country; and besides, it's the only life he knows."

"I don't care about Tom." Her chin went up. "I'm finished, Tap. Do you hear? Finished!" She swung her horse nearer. "Tap, if you'll take me to New Orleans I can go. I'll...I'll do anything you want."

"You've got a good man," he said roughly, "and no town is like you seem to think it is. They're all the same unless you have money; and going the way you are talking of, you simply wouldn't have any.

"Anyway, what makes you think you'd see any of the life you're thinking about if some man took you to New Orleans; or anywhere else? He might rent a house and just leave you there to visit when he pleased. He might not take you anywhere."

"I'd leave him!"

"For somebody else like him? Mady, you're too smart a girl to do anything so foolish. You've got something here—a good man who wants you, a recognized position, with family and friends around. You'd be throwing it all over ... for what? To live in a city where all the doors that mattered would be closed to you. Stop being a damn fool and go home."

She stared at him, her face white with anger. Her lips curled. "I thought you were really something! I thought you were the man I wanted, you with your city ways and your style! You talk like a preacher!" Her tone was thick with contempt. "I've had too much of that at home. I wouldn't go with you now if you begged me!"

He reined his horse around. "I haven't begged you, Mady. I haven't even asked you."

Ten minutes later, he came to the spot marked on the chart for the trail's beginning. It was overgrown with grass, but it showed evidences of recent use, more than likely by Indians going to the shore for the fishing, for there had surely been little other travel this way.

He tied his handkerchief to a bush to mark the opening, then rode out along the trail, scouting the way. At this time of year the swamp did not look bad, and it was possible there might be several routes that would take them through. Nonetheless, he held to the trail, emerging from it several miles farther along, near the head of Powderhorn Lake.

He found a place among the willows near the lake and made a concealed camp there, starting a small fire. This spot could be no more than five miles from Indianola, and it would be easy travel from here into the port. Yet he felt worried and restless. So far all had gone well, and his ruse might have taken the

Munson men out of the port city, but there was no certainty of that.

Tap Duvarney knew what remained. He must ride into town with at least one man who would know the Munsons when he saw them. That man would be Spicer. He might take one other. He would try to make a quick deal, then when they got their cash the lot of them would move out to join Tom Kittery and the main herd.

The cattle started to come, and he rode out to intercept the leaders and turn them. The grass was good at the head of Powderhorn, so the cattle settled down to grazing. Lawton Bean was the first man to appear. Together they held the cattle while the rest of the herd streamed in from the narrow trail. There had been no trouble. It was all too easy; and to Tap Duvarney, to whom few things had come easy, it only served to worry him still more. Something had to be wrong, or to go wrong. Things simply didn't happen this way.

"I was glad to get off that island," Doc Belden commented as he drew abreast. "You should see the way the sea is breaking out there. Smooth as glass, but great big swells . . . biggest I ever saw."

"Doc," Tap said, "I'm going to leave you in charge of the herd. They'll be uneasy, with the weather changing, so you'll have to hold them close. I'll take Welt Spicer and Lawton Bean."

Doc Belden tamped his pipe thoughtfully. "Spicer should know the Munsons. He's been around long enough, but you be careful."

"I'm going to turn a fast deal if I can. It may not be the best one, but it will be fast and it will give us some more working capital.

"Doc," he added, "Mady Coppinger is around. She's Tom's girl, but she's got some fool notion about running off to New Orleans. Tom's hunting her, and she's ready to jump at any chance to get away from here. Be careful . . . it's a killing matter if she's found with anybody.

"I told him I hadn't seen her, and I hadn't then, but now she's been close to camp and I've talked with her. She's mad enough to bite nails."

"Leave it to a woman to cause trouble," Doc Belden said. "All right, Tap, you go on in when the boys get here. We'll watch things here. Only don't be gone too long. I don't like the looks of the weather out there."

It was a short ride to Indianola.

CHAPTER 8

JACKSON HUDDY DID not leave Indianola when the others did.

Deliberately, he remained behind, disliking to trust his safety to such a group, with its accompanying noise, idle talk, and carelessness. He preferred to depend on his own sense, his own instincts.

His were the feelings of a prowling carnivore. He preferred to travel alone, to hunt alone. In the presence of others he was stiff, stilted, and cold, but out alone in the night, in the wilderness, he was strictly a killer.

A solitary man by disposition, he had much in his nature to make others uncomfortable. Faultlessly neat, he wore the plainest of clothes, always carefully brushed. His thin hair was combed close to his scalp; his jaws were never unshaven. He had never been seen to tip back in a chair, lean against a wall or a post, or to make any careless gesture.

None of the Munson riders were at all unhappy he chose to remain behind and follow along later. His presence put a damper on idle talk, and it was well known that he disliked profane or obscene language. His standards and morals were largely those of the hard-shell Baptist family in which he had grown up, and had he discarded his guns there was nothing in his conduct to which they could have objected. He was a man with a single, deadly vice.

The usual conceptions of fair play were foreign to him. He killed his enemies when and where he found them, and at his own convenience. He wasted no efforts, and wasted no lead. He disliked gun battles in streets or saloons, avoided any display of temper on the part of others, and showed no emotions of his own. His peculiar walk and his high-shouldered, erect bearing drew attention; otherwise he was colorless.

His mother had been a Munson, an Alabama cousin of the Texas family. The Texas family had, several generations back, migrated from Germany to Mexico, and had moved to Texas some years later. Jackson Huddy heard of the Munson-Kittery feud in Missouri, and rode south to help his family. The first Kittery he killed was a pleasant young man, Al Kittery, who rode in from El Paso to visit his kin. He commented, in a saloon, that it looked as if the family might need his help.

When Al Kittery left the saloon and went into the street, Jackson Huddy followed.

Al Kittery, it had been said, was quite a hand with a gun, but he had not killed anyone. Loafers in the saloon heard two shots that sounded almost as one, and going out, they found Al Kittery's hand on his half-drawn gun and two bullet holes in his heart. Jackson Huddy was gone.

Now, standing on the street in Indianola, Huddy watched the stage arrive. He was waiting for Every Munson, the only one of the family to whom he was in any way close. Ev Munson was as completely opposite in appearance to Huddy as a man could be—young, handsome, reckless of bearing, inclined to the flamboyant in dress and manner. Only in one thing were they alike, for when it came to killing, Ev was as cool and efficient as Huddy himself.

Every Munson would not be on the stage, but he would be riding up that same street within minutes, if he was on time, and he usually was. This was another reason Jackson Huddy had let the others ride on ahead...he wanted to see Ev without the others.

The stage rolled in and came to a stop; the dust cloud that trailed behind it caught up and settled over and around the stage. The first man out was a fat drummer, his vest buttons spread so wide over his stomach that glimpses of white shirt showed between them.

The second person to get down was a young woman, and when the drummer turned and held out his hand to help her, she took it and stepped lightly into the street, and all Indianola stopped in its stride.

Jessica Trescott, of the Virginia and New York Trescotts, stepped down onto dusty Main Street of Indianola and looked about her, in no way disturbed by the shabby little western town. She had dignity as well as elegance and charm, and no amount of heat, dust, or travel could wilt any of it.

There were a dozen women along the street, and each paused, some of them peeking around parasols, some frankly staring, for Jessica's clothes had come from Paris. Not Paris of last year or two years ago, but the Paris of today, almost of tomorrow. She wore an all-beige dress with black pleated ruching at the hem, on the caught-up apron part, and the tight-waisted jacket. The straw hat was worn well back on the coiffure which was done with a chignon. There was an embroidered veil and a small velvet bow on the hat.

That was the moment when Mady Coppinger rode up to the hitching rail and swung down. She turned, and found herself facing the vision of all she had ever wished to be, and she stared, resentfully admiring.

Jessica Trescott smiled. "How do you do? I am Jessica Trescott. That hotel over there...is it a good place? I mean a clean place, and a respectable one?"

"Yes, it is," Mady answered. Then she added in a tone that sounded sullen, "I am Mady Coppinger."

"Mady—! But of course! You are Mr. Kittery's fiancée. Then maybe you can tell me where I can find Tappan Duvarney?"

Mady Coppinger's interest in the question did not seem very marked. "He's coming up the trail now," she said. "He should be in town before sunset."

"Do you know Tappan? I mean, if you know him—"

"I know him, and you can have him."

Jessica smiled again. "That's the general idea, Mady. Why else would I come here?"

"I can't imagine," Mady said, "why anybody would come here who could be anywhere else."

The porter from the hotel had crossed to pick up Jessica's carpetbag and small trunk. The men from the stage office were handing down still another trunk, and then a third.

"Are those all yours?" Mady asked.

"All mine. After all, you can't expect a girl to come unarmed and defenseless into a country like this, can you?" She turned to follow the porter. "Mady, I'm going to freshen up, and then I wish you'd join me—I am going to have tea, or something. Frankly, I'm famished!"

Then she was gone, leaving a faint scent of perfume behind her, and Mady looked after her enviously. Turning toward the boardwalk, she stopped abruptly. Ev Munson was standing there, grinning at her, his dark eyes dancing with amusement.

"That's quite a woman, Mady," he said; "quite a woman."

Mady replied sharply. "She's Tap Duvarney's girl, if you want to know. They're to be married."

He still grinned at her. "Young to be a widow," he said, "and she's goin' to be one before she's ever a wife!"

Mady stepped up on the boardwalk. "You got anything to tell me, Mady?" Ev Munson asked.

She hesitated, her eyes straying after Jessica, who had paused in the doorway to glance back. She made a move as if to draw away from Ev, then stopped. After all, Jessica had no idea who Ev was...what could it matter?

She stayed there, still looking across the street, standing near Ev but not seeming to be talking to him. "Duvarney's coming into town tonight," she said, "...with a herd."

"A herd?" Ev Munson was incredulous. "They're makin' their gather down to Horseshoe Lake. We already seen them. Our boys are on their way down."

"Have it your way, but you be around tonight and you'll see the herd come in. This is just a part of it that Duvarney brought over from Matagorda Island."

"How many's with him?"

"Three or four, I think. They're all strangers except Welt Spicer."

"Strangers?" There was disappointment in Ev's tone. "Are you sure?"

"Ev"—Mady looked around at him for the first time—"I want my money now."

"Money?" Ev said. "Now look, honey, you know damn well—"

"I want my money, Ev. You promised. You promised me two hundred dollars if I'd tell you where they all were and what they were doing. You promised me that two months ago."

"Sure, honey. Now you just wait—"

"I'm not waiting, Ev. I want my money, and I'm going to have it. I'm going to New Orleans."

He gave her a wicked smile. "Suppose you don't get it? You goin' to tell Tom on me? Or that Duvarney fella?"

"No, Ev." Her eyes sparked. "I'll tell Jackson Huddy!"

The taunting smile vanished. "You'll do nothin' of the kind, damn you! You'll—"

"I want my money, Ev," she repeated. "I want it tomorrow. No," she said with sudden anger, "I want it tonight, and I want every last cent of it. What I've been doing is a pretty mean thing, but I need that money, and if I don't get it I'll go straight to Jackson Huddy and tell him. You know how he is about breaking your word; and above all, how he is about women. He'd kill you, Ev."

"Like hell!" Ev's eyes slanted up the street. "I think I could beat him, anyway. I'm faster than he is."

"Want me to tell him that, too? Anyway, it doesn't matter how fast you are, he would kill you. He would kill you whenever he was of a mind to and you'd never know he'd done it."

Ev swore under his breath. "All right, I'll get your money. You just wait. I'll bring it by the hotel tonight."

She walked away, and Ev stood there staring along the street, eaten by anger and hatred. He had been top man among the Munsons, top man with a gun at least, until Jackson Huddy came along. Since then he had taken second place, and he did not like it. At the same time, Jackson Huddy was all that kept them going, for a good half of the Munsons wanted no part of the Kitterys. It was only the fact that Huddy would do most of the killing and take most of the risks that held them together.

Tom Kittery was supposed to be fast, but it was not Kittery who worried Ev Munson, it was Jackson Huddy. Huddy gave no man a fair chance, but Ev did not dare try to kill him, for without Huddy the Munsons would have to back up and sit down and shut up. Jackson Huddy's reputation and the fear that ringed around him gave them all a sort of courage.

ONCE IN HER room, Jessica did not take time to change. She freshened up a bit, brushed her hair, and replaced her hat. But she did take time to open her trunks and hang out some of her dresses to get the wrinkles out of them. She would have to see if she could hire somebody to do some pressing for her, and some laundry. If not, she would do it herself. She never had, but she could.

Thoughtfully, she considered Mady Coppinger. Why had she turned away so guiltily when Jessica saw her with that man? Because Jessica knew she was spoken for by Tom Kittery? Or was it something else?

She thought of how the man looked—dark, handsome in a tough, daring sort of way, but dirty, actually unclean. He had passed near her and she had seen the collar of his shirt was shiny with dirt. She shuddered. Her father had warned her that the world she was coming into was like nothing she had ever known. She had tried to learn about it, going more than once to the blacksmith down at the Corners, who had lived in Texas, and knew all about it. He came from Goliad, which was not far from this town. He had even known about the Kitterys and the Munsons. It was, he said, a bitterly fought feud.

Well, she would go to the dining room and eat... she had never been so hungry. After that she would return here and keep a watch out for Tap. She had forgotten to ask where he was coming from, but there were only two possible choices, unless he was planning to swim the cattle in. She smiled at that, for Tappan Duvarney was just the sort of man who might.

She thought again of the man Mady had spoken to... it was almost as if she did not want to be seen talking to him. Still, in such a country as this she must know all sorts of people. As far as that went, Jessica herself had known all kinds. The Judge, her father, had not exactly sheltered his only daughter. Since her mother died they had been very close, and she had often ridden into the country with him when he was buying stock or was riding to some other town to hold court.

She picked up her purse and left the room, and found her way to the dining room. She had been there only a few minutes when Mady Coppinger came in and joined her.

Mady looked across the table at her, enviously. "You look so...so *right*. I wish I could look like that."

"It isn't that difficult," Jessica said. "And why look as I do? You're beautiful enough as you are. Mr. Kittery must think so."

"Oh...*Tom*. Tom's all right—he's a grand fellow, but he doesn't have any ambition. He doesn't want to *go* anywhere."

"Go?"

"I mean he wants to stay here. In the West, that is. All he can think about is cattle. Sometimes I think that's all he knows."

"Maybe it is, but if he's a good man and he loves you..." Jessica paused. "And if you love him. You do, don't you?"

"I think so. I don't know. I just wish he'd take me away from here. I don't want to spend my life on a cattle ranch in Texas. Maybe...maybe if he loses out here he will go away. I mean if this deal falls through."

Jessica lifted her eyes slowly. "You mean his deal with Tappan? Do you think that will fail?"

"I don't know. It's just that it is such an awful gamble, driving cattle all that way. And if they do sell for a good price they will only buy more and do it all over again."

Jessica was thoughtful. She ordered a small meal, but most of all, she listened. She had heard discontented women before this, but never one who seemed quite so desperate. What it was Mady wanted from life Jessica could not decide; but whatever it was she did not expect to find it here. To her the "city"—a vague, rather unreal conception of the actual thing—was where she wished to be...and if Tom did not take her there she would go anyway...anyhow.

"How could he make a living there?" Jessica asked in a mild tone.

"Tom? Oh...oh, he'd find something. Men always do."

"It isn't that easy, I'm afraid. I mean without some special ability."

Mady refused to accept that. "He could find something. He just won't try."

"Why should he? He has a place here, people know him, respect him. He owns cattle. He owns land. If I were you I'd grab him quick. He sounds like a catch."

"Tom?" Mady was astonished. "He'll never be anything but a cattleman."

Jessica changed the subject then, talking lightly of other things—of the East and, although she disliked to mention such matters, of how much things cost in the cities. Mady's discontent was obvious, so what Jessica hoped to do was to indicate that the grass on the other side of the fence was no greener.

Finally, when Mady left her, Jessica relaxed and ordered coffee, genuinely relieved that the other girl had gone. From where she sat she could look out on the street, see the horses along the rail, and watch the people come and go along the boardwalk.

One of the men she saw was the man who had been talking earlier with Mady, and he was with a tall, austere-looking man. Once the latter caught her eyes upon him and he lifted his hat. The other man noticed and made some remark, at which his companion turned to look at her again with curious, penetrating attention.

"More coffee?" The waitress was at her side.

"Please. Most of the men out there ... are they cattlemen?"

"Them? Loafers, most of them. There's some cattlemen, buyers, and a few shipping men. But mostly they're trash."

"The dark one with the red-topped boots—is he a cattleman?"

"You could call him that. He's one of that Munson outfit. You know, the ones that have the feud. They do run cattle, but they're usually too busy hunting Tom Kittery or boozing it up, to do any work."

"Munson? I've heard the name."

"That's Ev ... he's ringleader since the old man was killed. Him and Jackson Huddy."

Jessica sat a little straighter. What was Mady Coppinger, Tom Kittery's girl, doing talking to Ev Munson, a leader of the opposition? Jessica was young, but her years had been lived closer to the business and the courts of the land, so she was acquainted, at least by second-hand, with the perfidy of the world. If one thought of Mady's feverish desire to escape from Texas and the cattle range, and you coupled that with her whispering to Ev Munson ...

Surely she was imagining things. Nevertheless, she was worried, and she remained by the window until the supper crowd started to gather. Then she went to her room, put on a black cloak, and went back down the stairs.

"Ma'am?" The clerk was a kindly, elderly man. "I'd not go out on that street if I were you. We've got good folks hereabouts, but there's riffraff, too."

"Just for a breath of air. I won't leave the board-walk."

She stepped outside. The wind off the Gulf was light and cool. The night was very still. Only a few stars were out, and a vague light lingered in the western sky.

At first she thought there was nobody on the street but herself, and then, not sixty feet away, she saw a tall, slender figure. It was that man with the odd, high-shouldered appearance, and he was coming toward her.

CHAPTER 9

H E STOPPED IN front of her, not quite blocking her way, and when he spoke it was in an odd, almost hesitant way.

"Ma'am?" He cleared his throat. "I would not be out on the street if I were you. There ... there is often trouble ... rough men ..." His voice trailed off, then seemed to gather power as he added, "Sometimes even shooting."

"Thank you. It was very close inside," she said quietly, "and I wanted a breath of air."

"Yes, it must be stuffy inside. I think there's ..." He hesitated again. "I think there's a storm ... change in the weather." He lifted his hat. "I am Jackson Huddy, ma'am. You take your walk, and if you are bothered ... if anyone stops you, tell them I am near."

"Thank you, Mr. Huddy."

He bowed and stepped aside, and she walked on. He had seemed embarrassed, almost frightened by her, and her curiosity was aroused. She remembered hearing the waitress mention Jackson Huddy as a man who was a leader among the Munsons.

Jackson Huddy and Ev Munson were in Indianola, and the herd was due to arrive tonight, she was thinking. Tappan Duvarney might be coming up that road at any time.

She walked on to the end of the street, then crossed

over, holding her skirts up a little to keep them from the dust. Far down the street she could see Jackson Huddy, and she was about to start back when she heard the muffled footfalls of a horse walking in the dust.

She stood very still listening. There was more than one horse, and they were coming up an alleyway between the buildings. When they appeared at the edge of the line of buildings they drew rein, and she could see their heads thrust out to peer down the street.

Then one of them spoke. "Too quiet. I don't like it, Major."

"Where's the hotel where Brunswick will be staying?" It was Tappan's voice.

She stepped forward and said quietly, just loud enough for them to hear. "He is at my hotel, Tappan."

The heads jerked around, and Tap Duvarney said, "Jessica! Is that you, or am I going crazy?"

She walked toward them. "Yes, Tappan, I am here.... Be careful, Tappan. Huddy and Ev Munson are still in town, and they know you're bringing in some cattle."

"Now, how the dev—?" Tap began, then went on, "How did you know that?"

"I met Mady Coppinger, and she told me. I think she also told them. She was on the street, standing very close to Ev Munson, and I think she was whispering to him."

"How long have you been in town, Jessica?"

"Several hours," she said.

"And you know all that? And you know who Ev Munson is?"

She smiled brightly. "I also know who Jackson

Huddy is, and if I don't keep moving he will be up here to see what's wrong. He told me that if anybody bothered me, to mention that he was near."

"Jackson Huddy?" Tap was incredulous.

"He's like that about womenfolks," Spicer said. "He's almighty respectful to them, and I think a mite scared of them."

"Do you want to see Mr. Brunswick?" Jessica asked. "I heard him named at the hotel, and if you want me to, I could speak to him and arrange it. When I came out he was reading a newspaper in the lobby."

"Could you do that? We'll be at the corral. No," Duvarney said, changing his mind. "Ask him to go to his room. I'll see him there. Welt, you and Bean stay off the streets."

"We'll wait in the barn, yonder. You watch your step, Major. That Jackson Huddy is pure poison, and Ev Munson is hell on wheels with a six-gun. He's killed eight or nine men I know of."

"Jessica," Tap warned, "you be careful."

"You, too. I can't wait to have a talk with you. Later, at the hotel?"

"If I can. This is touch and go."

She walked away, taking her time, and when she passed Jackson Huddy he looked at her, then looked away quickly.

"Good night, Mr. Huddy," she said. "And thank you."

"Yes—yes, ma'am." He spoke so quickly he almost stuttered.

When Jessica got back to the hotel, Bob Brunswick was no longer in the lobby. She stopped at the desk to get her key, and as the clerk was not around, she glanced at the register. Brunswick was only three rooms down the hall from her own. She went up the stairs, opened the door of her room, and put down her key. Then she walked down the hall and tapped lightly on Brunswick's door. He opened it slightly, then wider.

He was a large, portly man with a black walrus mustache. He was in his shirtsleeves; a heavy gold watch-chain with an elk's tooth was draped across his stomach. His expression now was startled.

"Mr. Brunswick? I am Jessica Trescott, and I would like to speak to you." She smiled slightly. "I am a lady, Mr. Brunswick."

He flushed. "I can see that, ma'am. The lobby, then?"

"No, it must be here...now...and quickly."

He stepped back, and when she had entered he closed the door. Taking his coat from the back of a chair, he put it on. "Sorry, ma'am, for the cigar smoke. I wasn't expecting a lady."

"Mr. Brunswick, you are a cattle buyer. My fiancé, Mr. Tappan Duvarney, is right down the street. He is bringing in a herd, and they will arrive very soon, I believe. Jackson Huddy and Ev Munson are on the street, too, and Tappan does not want trouble. He wanted me to ask you to stay in your room and wait for him."

"Whose cattle are they?"

"He is in partnership with Tom Kittery, who is, I believe, holding another herd somewhere south of here."

"All right, I'll wait." He took up his cigar, started

to smoke, then rubbed it out. "Ma'am...Miss Trescott, if I were you and I loved that man I'd get him out of here—fast."

She smiled. "Mr. Brunswick, you would do no such a thing...not if you were me. Tappan is a man, doing a man's work. It is the work he chose to do, and I would never interfere. As for danger, I suspect there are many men in danger right now, in a lot of ways. I might tell you something about Tappan, Mr. Brunswick.

"He is not a man I could persuade to leave here; and if I could, I wouldn't want him. Nor is he a man to be intimidated. Major Tappan Duvarney," she said, lifting her chin a little, "is a veteran soldier, sir. He has been in campaigns against the Kiowas, the Apaches, the Sioux, the Cheyennes and the Modocs. Also, there was a western town, Mr. Brunswick, with a very bad reputation, which was near Tappan's post, and he was deputized to clean it up. He did so, Mr. Brunswick, in just three days. I believe there were several altercations."

Brunswick smiled warmly. "Ma'am, whoever he is, he must be quite a man to deserve you. I'll wait for him, right here." He opened the door. "And you know something? I'm not going to worry about him—not a bit."

Jessica went back to her room and removed her hat. She sat down in the rocker, but she could not remain still. Tappan was out there in the night...and he was in danger.

She should, she decided, be frightened. Yet she was not. Always when traveling with her father she had a feeling of being a bystander, of observing the courts in action, of witnessing violence after the fact. She had always had more confidence than other girls, always was more assured. Now, instead of being depressed by the impending danger, she felt exhilarated. She was frightened, yes, and she was worried. Part of her mind admitted this, but the other part was enjoying the sense of being part of things.

She knew exactly why she had come to Texas. She had faced her father with it several times in the weeks before she left. Tappan Duvarney was, she said, the only man she had ever wanted to marry; but Tappan was fiercely proud, fiercely independent. It would be just like him not to come back if things did not go well for him, and she had no idea of taking that risk.

"I'm going after him, Father. I'm going to Texas," she had said.

Some fathers would have been furious, some would have refused to permit any such thing. Hers was amused, and interested.

Judge Trescott had enjoyed the company of his daughter for longer than he had expected, and he had watched her grow and develop in personality and character. She was much like her mother, even more like himself, and she was somewhat like her grandmother on his side. But most of all, she was somebody new; she was herself.

He had not done as much for her as he would have liked, but he had tried to offer a guiding hand, and friendly advice. Youngsters invariably began by thinking their parents were "old-fashioned," "out of date," or "back numbers," and they usually ended by admitting how right the parents had been, in most cases.

Jessica had traveled with him, had taken care of him, scolded him, admired him, and had been not only his daughter but his friend. But until Major Tappan Duvarney came along he had seen no one he thought worthy of her. He had admitted none of this to her, merely watching from the sidelines. He knew that a lot of the old ladies, both male and female, had deplored his taking his growing daughter around the country with him, and had been shocked at his permitting her to sit in the courtroom while he tried his cases. Many of these were civil cases, but many were criminal, so that Jessica at nineteen had few illusions about the kind of people there were in the world, and about the situations with which she might be faced.

He had listened to her talk of Tappan Duvarney and he was pleased with his daughter. He agreed that Tap was just the sort to remain away if he did not at first succeed.

"All right," he said, "if you love Tap, go get him." He smiled at her.

Then, just as she was packing he had come into her room carrying a pistol. It was a Colt five-shot, .41 caliber House Pistol. "Put this in your things," he said, and with it he gave her a small sack. "There are fifty rounds there. If you need more," he said with a smile, "you'd better get a bigger gun."

Her eyes met his. "Do you think I'll need that, Father?"

"I doubt it, but let's say it is insurance. Texas is a country where they respect women, but I can't promise that you'll always find it so."

She went to her carpetbag now and removed the pistol, which was loaded. The barrel was short; the pistol would fit into her handbag. Heavy, yes, but reassuring in its weight.

The dining room was open until ten o'clock. In a few minutes she would go down, eat a leisurely supper, and listen to what was happening. She tried to read ... but a part of her mind was alert to the outside sounds. She knew what she listened for, what she expected and feared—pistol shots.

TAPPAN DUVARNEY STOOD at the opening between the buildings and surveyed the street. Far down, he could see the tall, dark figure of a man. Other men were walking along the street, and occasionally one disappeared into or emerged from a saloon. There were lights along the street; a few horses were tied to the hitching rails, with here and there a buckboard. At this hour no wagons were in sight.

Tap stepped out and walked down to the hotel and entered. The clerk looked up and Duvarney asked for Brunswick's room, and disappeared up the steps. The clerk looked up after him, then glanced nervously at the door. He did not know Tappan Duvarney by sight, but he had heard him described, and this stranger looked like the description.

Tap knocked lightly on the door, and Brunswick opened it, glanced at him, and stepped back. "Come in," he said. "You have cattle to sell? How many?"

"At a rough count, I'd say eight hundred and thirty head."

"What kind of shape are they in?"

"You've seen island cattle. This is a mixed lot, mostly big stuff, and they're in good shape. I'd say about half of them are steers upwards of five years old."

Brunswick chewed his cigar. "Those cattle on the island are usually in good shape—lots of feed, and they don't have to go far to water; but beef prices aren't at their best now."

"I want a fast deal," Tap said quietly, "and I've heard you're a fair man."

Brunswick rolled his cigar in his lips. "I've got to ship to New Orleans. There'll be some loss at sea." He took a good look at Tap, and said, "I'll give you twelve dollars a head, right across the board."

"Twelve dollars? Brunswick, there's some steers in that lot who'll weigh fifteen hundred pounds."

"Sure there are. And there's probably forty, fifty head in there won't weigh more than a hundred pounds. That's mixed stuff."

"Make it sixteen?"

Bob Brunswick shrugged. "Fourteen; and I'll be lucky not to take a loss."

"All right, I'll go along. You make the check for eight hundred head. If there's less, I'll make it up, and if there's more—and there is—you can have them."

Brunswick sat down at the table and wrote the check and handed it to Duvarney. "There you are, Tap, and my regards to the little lady. She's got sand, that girl."

"Thanks." Duvarney hestitated. "Brunswick, you've been fair, so I'll give you a piece of advice. Either get those cattle loaded and out to sea, or drive them inland—ten miles inland."

Brunswick took the cigar from his mouth. "What are you telling me?"

"That's hurricane weather out there. I can smell it."

"All right." He paused. "Duvarney, your boys are moving those cattle. What do you say if you keep right on moving them? Start them toward Victoria, and hold them somewhere along Placedo Creek."

Tap considered. He had hoped to get his men right out of town to avoid trouble, yet he could scarcely leave Brunswick in the lurch, and finding cowhands at this hour of the night, or even tomorrow, would be difficult. Yet this might be the very best way...or it might be the worst.

"I could hold them here," Brunswick said. "If I get them penned up they can't stampede."

"Have you ever seen a hurricane, Brunswick? I was a seaman in the West Indies and along the Atlantic coast for several years. This storm started some place far south of Cuba, maybe off the coast of Brazil, and she's been moving north. Those winds will be blowing hard enough to flatten anything around here, but the whole storm won't move more than fifteen miles an hour."

"That doesn't make sense."

"The winds blow in a big circle, ten or twenty miles across. I don't know that anybody ever measured one, but I'd guess a couple I ran into were that big."

Tap paused. "I'd move them," he said again. "Somewhere back on the prairie, this side of Victoria."

"They'd have to go right through town. Have you ever seen cattle go through a town?"

"They're tired. I think they'd handle easy. You want to try it?"

"Well . . . you've got my money. You made your deal. You've no reason to stay on unless you want to."

"I've already agreed. You pay the boys what you think the job is worth." He pocketed the check. "Let's go, then."

"You'd better see that little lady before you go. She's worried."

Tap opened the door and glanced up and down the hall, then he stepped out. Almost at once, Jessica's door opened.

"Tap . . . oh, Tap!" He went to her, caught her hands.

"You shouldn't have come here," he said. "But now that you have come, you should get out. There's going to be a storm."

"You go on. I'll be all right."

She listened while he explained about moving the cattle. "If the storm looks bad, I'll come back for you, but don't wait here for me. If it starts to blow up, go to the courthouse. It's on a knoll in the center of town, and the building is solid. If anything in town comes through all right, the courthouse will."

"Don't worry," she said. "I'll be all right."

He went down the stairs and walked across the lighted lobby. Stepping out onto the walk, he came face to face with a tall, lean man.

It was Jackson Huddy.

CHAPTER 10

I N WESTERN TOWNS where the work begins at daybreak or earlier, supper is eaten early, and most good citizens are in bed before ten o'clock. It is only along the main streets where the saloons and the honky-tonks are that people drink and gamble far into the night.

Indianola was in bed or preparing for it. The night was still and the air seemed close; there was something in the atmosphere that made animals restless and men irritable. There lay over the town and the flatlands beyond a breathless hush that seemed like a warning.

The truth of the matter was that Indianola had not long to live. Here, within the space of a few hours, a town was to be destroyed, a way of living wiped out. And nobody was aware of it.

Down along the two piers that thrust their long fingers into the bay waters, the masters of the few ships in port were nervously running out additional lines. The swell breaking on Matagorda Island had already become so great that getting through the channel would be a doubtful matter...nobody wanted to try it. And few seaports anywhere seemed more sheltered than Indianola.

When Tappan Duvarney stepped out on the street and came face to face with Jackson Huddy there was a moment when neither man moved nor spoke. Then Jackson Huddy said, "You are driving Rafter K cattle."

"Some are Rafter K, some wear my own brand, but I am a businessman, Mr. Huddy, doing business in cattle. I have no interest in the Munson-Kittery feud, as I have said before this."

"How long before you'll be drawn in?" Huddy asked.

"That depends on the Munsons. If they move against me or my men, they must accept the consequences. If they do not move against us, they have nothing to fear."

"We do not fear, Major Duvarney."

"Do not disregard fear, Mr. Huddy. A little fear inspires caution. I have learned there is a little fear and a little caution in every victory. And from what I have heard of you, I had suspected you to be a cautious man."

"And what have you heard of me?" The small blue eyes were probing, curious, yet somehow they were strangely empty.

"That you take no unnecessary chances; that to you victory is the result to be desired, and the method is less important."

"You do not like that?"

Duvarney smiled. "Mr. Huddy, I cut my eyeteeth on the Apaches, the greatest guerilla fighters the world has ever seen, and I have had some dealings with the Sioux and the Cheyennes, too. I found their methods very useful to me, and easily understood. As in all things, Mr. Huddy, the number of possibilities of attack is limited. One considers those that are manifestly impossible. They are eliminated, and the others prepared for. We killed or captured a lot of Apaches."

"Is that a threat?"

Duvarney did not answer the question, but said, "Mr. Huddy, you have a certain reputation. Why risk it against a man who is not your enemy?"

Deliberately, he walked past him and on down the street, moving easily, stepping lightly, ready to throw himself to right or left if the need arose, and picking one vantage point after another as he walked along. He had no idea that what he had said would matter in the long run, for Jackson Huddy would move as the situation seemed to dictate; yet he had to say what he could in an effort to prevent a gun battle that could kill good men and serve no one.

———

DOC BELDEN HAD reached the rendezvous point. The cattle were still moving, however. Tap rode out to swing alongside of him, riding point.

"I've sold the cattle," he said to Belden, "and we're going inland, away from the storm. We're taking them right down the main street."

"You're taking a chance. If they stampede in town they could bust up a lot of stuff."

"They're tired," Tap said. "Also, I think they're ready to turn away from the sea. There's a storm coming."

He paused, then added, "Pass the word along. Every man is to ride with the thong off his pistol. He must be ready to fight, if need be."

In the southeast the stars were gone, and the night

sky showed a bulging, billowing mass of cloud that seemed to heave itself higher and higher against the sky as the moments passed. The cattle broke into a half-trot, settled back into a walk, and then began to trot again. Belden and Tap swung the point into the street.

At the muffled thunder of hoofs, lights suddenly blazed and doors opened. A murmur, then a growl ran along the street, but though the cattle were tired, they were intent on moving, and they went silently, except for the beat of their hoofs in the dust, and the rustle of their sides against one another. Here and there horns clacked against each other; a cowboy, moving up on some recalcitrant steer, called "Ho!" They moved steadily on, keeping to the street.

The people, watching, became silent. A few came out on the boardwalk to look at the sky when there was a far-off rumble of thunder.

A gust of wind blew along the street, creaking signs, rattling shutters. A brief spatter of rain fell, then subsided. The night was perfectly still.

The last of the cattle passed, and they vanished up the street.

Jessica, standing in the dark by her window watching the street below, breathed softly in relief, scarcely believing it had been done. Then a door nearby opened and a tall man came out on the street, and she saw that it was Jackson Huddy. He was followed by another, a man with a slouching, lazily affected walk, who leaned against a post by the boardwalk and tood there with thumbs behind his belt. Out of the night two other men came up the street and joined them.

Her light was out, her curtain unmoving, but

Jackson Huddy twice turned his head to look up as if he felt the impact of her eyes. No matter what they planned, there was nothing she could do now—she could only wait.

And then the wind came.

It began with a wall-shuddering blast, and a quick spatter of rain. Jessica opened her window and pulled the shutters together and fastened them. She could hear others doing the same, and through a crack in the shutters she could see men on the street in their nightshirts or in hastily donned Levis putting up shutters, and in some cases nailing them down.

She had not undressed, and suddenly she decided she would not.

The old building creaked under the weight of the wind, and somewhere something slammed against a building and fell heavily against the boardwalk— probably one of the street signs. Looking through the cracks in the shutters, she could no longer see any lights, and suddenly she realized it was because of fear of fire.

———

OUTSIDE, LIGHTNING NOW flashed almost continuously, lighting the sky weirdly. The bulging clouds were lower than she had ever seen clouds before. She was frightened, and she admitted that to herself. But she remained calm, considering the situation.

Nothing can be done about a storm. One takes what precautions one can, and then waits. Now Jessica lighted her lamp and placed it, turned low, on the floor, so that it could not be knocked from the table. Propping her pillows against the base of the bed, she got out a book of poetry and sat down to read, but after a minute she gave up. The roar of the wind was now terrific.

Suddenly someone banged on her door and she went over to it, hesitating only a moment, to be sure she had the gun. Holding it in the folds of her skirt, she opened the door.

Mady Coppinger stood there, soaked to the skin, gasping for breath, and wild with fear.

"Please! Let me come in!"

Jessica stepped back, and when Mady was inside, she closed the door and stood with her back against it.

"Oh, I hope you'll forgive me, but I had no place else to go!" Mady's voice shook. "It's awful out there—awful!"

"You must get out of those clothes," Jessica said practically. "I have some dry things you can wear."

Mady sat down, trembling. Her shoes and ankles were muddy, and she herself was literally drenched. Her hair had come undone and hung about her face and shoulders.

Jessica asked no questions, offered no comment. She gave Mady towels, and when it did not appear that those she had would be adequate, she went across the hall to an empty room and took the towels she found there.

Slowly Mady began to calm down. "It's awful out there," she repeated, almost to herself. "I've never seen anything like this."

"You'd better change. We may have to leave the hotel. Tappan said we should go to the courthouse."

"It's on higher ground," Mady said. "Yes, I think we'd better."

She dressed hurriedly, but as she did so she was admiring the clothes she was putting on.

Jessica listened to the wind. She went to the closet and took out her warmest coats, a mackintosh and an ulster. The mackintosh was rainproof, or close to it; the ulster was heavier, and warm. She was trying to decide, even as she took down the coats, what was the best thing to do. Tappan's advice was clear in her mind, but wouldn't they say she was just a silly woman? And suppose the courthouse was closed?

It was raining now, if one could call it that: a tremendous sheet of water was smashing down the narrow street, and she could feel the weight of it against the wall of the building. Even as she put on the mackintosh and prepared to leave the room, one part of her mind was wondering where Mady Coppinger had been and what she had been doing on such a night . . . And had her terror been only the terror of the storm?

They went down the stairs, feeling the straining of the building, and into the lobby. They found themselves in a tight group of people. A few were whimpering in fear, but most were silent, listening to the terrible sound outside, hearing the thunder of the storm.

Jessica pushed her way through them and they gave way, staring at her blankly.

Near the door she saw the clerk standing with Mr. Brunswick and two other men, both of whom were solid-seeming men, those who are among the leaders in any community.

"Mr. Brunswick?" He turned impatiently, then removed his hat. "Mr. Brunswick, can you let us out?" Jessica said.

"In this? Ma'am, I wouldn't let anybody out in a storm like this. There's water almost knee-deep in the streets right now."

"Tappan...Major Duvarney...advised me to take shelter in the courthouse if the storm got worse. I believe we should go while we can."

"What's Duvarney know about storms?" The speaker was an austere-looking man with a permanently disagreeable expression.

"Major Duvarney was a seafaring man before he went into the army," Jessica replied stiffly. "He was an officer on ships in the West Indian trade. He knows the sea, and he knows hurricanes."

Worriedly, the gray-haired man beside Brunswick asked, "Did he think this was going to be a hurricane?"

"He told me there had been great swells breaking on Matagorda Island for several days, and such swells come only from a great storm at sea." While she answered him her eyes looked at the street.

Through the front windows, where some of the shutters had been blown away, she could see outside. The water was surging out there, and it was deep. Signs were down, and there was a scattering of debris lying across the walks. Even as she looked, some flying shingles whipped past the window.

"I've never seen it this bad," Mady said.

The thirty or more people gathered in the lobby were staring at the storm. Only a few of them were dressed for what must lie ahead.

"All right," Brunswick said, "we'll try it. We'll have to stay close to the buildings where we can, and hang onto each other."

Suddenly there was a tremendous blast of wind that ripped the few remaining signs from the buildings along the street, and sailed them before it. At the same moment a great rush of water tore by, ripping up a part of the boardwalk and filling the street with a deeper rushing torrent.

Now all lights were out. The town stood in darkness, all sound drowned out by the whistling roar of the hurricane. Somewhere a sound did break through, a sound of splintering wood; and then the wall of a building hurtled past. The corner hit the door of the hotel and smashed a panel before the force of the water tore it free and sent it on.

"We'll never make it now," the gray-haired man said solemnly.

"We can make it, Crain," Brunswick replied. "Let's wait until this spell is over."

"If it ever is," Mady said.

Jessica was silent, thinking about Tappan. He was out there somewhere in that roaring world of wind and water. He was out there moving cattle in all this . . . or he was dead.

————

IT WAS TEN o'clock at night when the storm first came to Indianola, and by the time the full force of the wind was beginning to smash the town Tap Duvarney had his cattle several miles west of the town and was driving them hard.

To the east, out over the Gulf, lightning flashed

intermittently, showing great masses of wind-torn clouds.

From out of the night, violence and the storm, and the vast thunder that rolled on and on, each enormous crash followed by another. From out of the night a moving wall of slashing rain, a wall of steel. The roof of clouds seemed only a few feet above the heads of the frightened cattle and the straining riders.

Tap Duvarney had turned to look back, and was appalled. He could see the storm coming upon them. At the bottom it was a ragged cloud and the steel mesh of the rain; above, the massed black clouds were laced with lightning.

"Look, Doc," he said. "Look at that and you can tell them you've seen hell with the doors open."

Belden's face was pale. "What do we do?" he asked.

"Try to hold them in a bunch. That's all we can do. It can't last forever."

Lawton Bean pulled up alongside them, his face strangely yellowish in the odd light. "I wonder what's happening back there in town," he said. "One time when I was a kid I lived on Matagorda. I seen the sea break clean over the island. Dad and me, we made a run for it."

"You made it, looks like," Belden said.

"I did . . . Pa didn't."

Hunched in their slickers, they watched the backs of the cattle as seen in the flashes of lightning. The rain hammered on the animals until they were almost numb from the beating.

"We've got to get shelter," Tap called out. "Keep your eyes out for a good bank that will keep us out of the wind!"

They had been moving steadily with the cattle at a trot a good part of the time. Tap thought for a moment of Lavaca Bay, which lay somewhere to the east . . . but that would be too close to the path of the storm. He yelled at Belden and Bean, then started along the flank of the herd. At the point, with steady pressure, yells, and lashes with coiled lariats, they edged the herd to the west.

The cattle needed no urging, seeming to realize that the storm was behind them, and that safety, if there was any, would lie somewhere in the darkness ahead.

Slowly, the riders bunched. Welt Spicer came around the drag to join them, followed by Jule Simms.

"You seen Lon Porter?" Simms asked.

"Lon? He's over with Foster," Belden replied. "Or should be."

"Well, he ain't. He come up to me just as we were headin' into town. Had a message for the Major."

"I didn't see him." Tap Duvarney edged over toward Simms. "Did he say what he wanted?"

"He was huntin' you. Seems they had no trouble with the cattle . . . most of them were already moving off the peninsula . . . just like they knew this storm was headin' in. Lon told us that, then took off for town, a-huntin' you."

They were bunched now in the doubtful lee of a cluster of cottonwoods, and for a moment there seemed a lull in the storm.

"The feelin' I got," Simms said, "was there'd been trouble below . . . some shootin', more'n likely."

Why hadn't Lon Porter found him, Tap wondered. He had been in the hotel or on the street much of

the time, and it would not have been difficult to locate him.

They rode on after the cattle, closing in around
them, keeping them bunched, until in the gray light of
a rain-lashed dawn they circled them at last on a
small piece of prairie shielded by brush, mostly curly
mesquite and tall-growing clusters of prickly pear.
Here and there were a few small clumps of stunted
post oak or hickory.

The exhausted cattle seemed to have no desire to
go farther, and they scattered out, some seeking shelter in the brush, but most of them simply dropping in
their tracks. A few tried aimless bites at the coarse
bunch grass, ignoring the sheets of rain and the wind.
One clump of the mesquite and post oak had made a
cove of shelter against the wind, and the riders rode
in and dismounted.

Under the thickest of the brush they found a few
leaves that were still dry, and they gathered some
dead mesquite. After a brief struggle they had a fire
going, half protected by a ground sheet stretched
above it.

Jule Simms came up with a coffeepot, and soon
there was water boiling. Lawton Bean, a limp cigarette trailing from his lips, hunched close to the small
fire, nursing it with sticks. It gave off only a little
heat, but it was comforting to see. The riders sat
about, hunched in their slickers, staring dismally into
the fire.

"How far did we come?" one of the men asked.

"Maybe twenty miles," Belden said. "We've been
moving seven or eight hours, and faster than any trail
herd ought to travel under ordinary conditions."

Tap got up and rustled around in the brush, where he found an old mesquite stump that he worried from the muddy ground, then some dead mesquite branches and a fallen oak limb. He brought them back to the fire and started breaking them up.

"Lon was a good man," Lawton Bean said suddenly. "He was a mighty good man. I crossed the Rio Grande with him a couple of times, chasin' cow thieves."

"You think he's dead?" Tap asked.

"Well . . . look at it. You surely weren't hard to find in that piddlin' town, but he never showed up. He didn't have much of a ride to where you were, and he was hale an' hearty when he left us. I figure somebody killed him."

"If anybody killed Lon," Simms said quietly, "he's got me to answer to."

Lon might simply have got tired of the rain and taken shelter in a saloon. Yet he had a message so important he had ridden some miles to deliver it. To give up was not like Porter, and he was too recently from the army not to pay attention to duty.

"What do we do now?" Doc asked.

"You hole up and wait out the storm," Tap answered. "It's no use trying to push on in this. We've come to higher ground—"

"Not much higher," Bean interrupted.

"Probably thirty or forty feet higher," Tap said, "and we've come inland a good piece. We'll hold them here and keep a sharp lookout for Munsons. We're not out of the woods yet."

"You think they killed Lon?"

"Who knows? I agree that he could have found me

easily enough. The way I see it, he would ride to the stockyards, and if he didn't find me there he'd come on up the street. I'm going to look around the yards for him first."

They stared at him then. "You goin' *back?*" Spicer said. "You're foolin'!"

"Lon was riding for me. I want to find him, or find out what happened to him. I want no part of this Munson feud, but if they've killed a man of mine, that's something I'll take care of."

"I'll go along with that." Doc Belden got up. "All right, if you're going, let's go."

"I'll go alone."

"Now, that's foolhardy," Spicer said. "If anybody goes it should be me. I know them boys, every last one of them."

Tap did not move, but stared at the fire, considering the situation. "If Lon came running for me in this weather," he said after a moment, "there was trouble, real trouble. So you better keep a sharp lookout."

"You think the Munsons would move with it blowing like this?"

"Most of them wouldn't. They'd be more likely to sit it out in comfort, but that isn't Jackson Huddy's way. It would be like him to use this storm to end the feud once and for all. You see, because of the drive he's got all the Kittery outfit bunched up where he wants them."

Still Tap lingered. He was no more anxious than any other man to leave even the small comfort of that fire for the storm outside. He looked around at the campsite. It was almost surrounded by the wall of mesquite, prickly pear, and post oak, but on one side it opened on the small parklike area where the cattle slept. Seeking shelter from the storm, they had also found a position that could be defended if necessary.

It was a dawn of rain and dark clouds, so low they seemed scarcely higher than the brush, and above all was the sound of the roaring wind. There was no question of escaping the rain; one could only hope to avoid the worst of it. The wind drove through the brush, bending the stiff branches, bending even the stunted trees until it seemed they must break or be uprooted.

They huddled together a minute or two longer. "You watch yourself, Major," Belden said quietly. "This here is one helluva storm. I never saw its like."

Tap wiped the water from the horse's back, then saddled it once more. Welt Spicer came up, a small bit of rawhide tied over the muzzle of his rifle.

There was a minute or two when the horses fought against facing the wind; then reluctantly they started, bending their heads low, pushing against it, moving forward with straining muscles.

CHAPTER 11

DAWN CAME TO Indianola with a weird yellow light, revealing the gray faces of the rain-hammered buildings, the dark, swirling water, ugly with foam and debris, rushing through the street. A lone steer, moss trailing from one great horn, came plunging and swimming along, a straggler from the herd, following blindly.

Somewhere up the street there was a crash as a wall gave way ... more wreckage went by.

Jessica had risen from her seat in the old leather armchair. "Mr. Brunswick," she said, "we've got to chance it. I think everything is going to go."

Reluctantly, he agreed. "All right." He looked around at the stunned, frightened people in the room. "We've got to get what blankets we can, and whatever food there is. There's no telling how long we'll be caught there."

"Major Duvarney will return," Jessica said. "He knows I am here."

"If he can," Brunswick responded grimly.

"Oh, no!" The words came from Mady in a low, tortured cry. Jessica looked out at the water. Something else was swirling there, hanging for a moment against the smashed boards of the walk. It was a body, the body of a man, and it needed only a glimpse to see that no flood waters had killed this man. He had been shot...shot in the back of the head, and one side of his head was blown away.

For an instant nobody moved, then Brunswick and Crain lunged for the door, catching the body before it could be washed away, and getting it onto the solid part of the walk. Huddled over the body, they searched it for clues, and then stumbled back inside, Brunswick holding a small handful of money, some water-soaked papers, and a gun belt.

"His family might need this money," Brunswick said. He straightened the papers. One was an envelope addressed to Lon Porter, in care of a hotel at Brownsville, Texas. "Don't know him," he muttered.

"That man was murdered," Crain said sternly. "He was shot in the back of the head, at close range."

"There's twenty-six dollars here," Brunswick said. "Ma'am, will you see that this gets to whoever should have it? This letter here—I think you can make it out...that might help some."

"Yes." She took the money and the letter. She was thinking that this might be one of the men Tappan had hired. Brownsville...Fort Brown...yes, she was sure of it.

Something else occurred to her.

Mady...Mady had come to her room drenched to the skin and frightened, and there had been mud on her shoes. That was easy enough to get, even by crossing the street, but it had looked like the dirt from a stable or a corral. And Mady's sudden exclamation just now...was it only at seeing a man's dead body? Or was it because it was this particular man?

Jessica turned to look, but Mady had withdrawn and was working her way toward the back of the group, as if to avoid the accusing face of the dead man.

Jessica suddenly remembered their critical situation. "Mr. Brunswick," she said, "we've got to go. We've got to move right away."

Crain suddenly spoke up. "My God! We have prisoners locked in the jail!"

"Bill Taylor's in there," somebody said.

Just then two riders turned into the street, their horses almost belly-deep in the rolling water. Both men were bundled in slickers, and both had their hats tied under their chins, but she recognized Tappan at once.

She stepped to the door and Brunswick tried to restrain her. "Wait! We'll join hands! We can make a human chain, and the first ones who get to the courthouse can help the others."

"We'll have help," Jessica said. "There's Tappan Duvarney."

He rode up, facing his horse into the current. He saw her, started to speak, and then he saw the body of Lon Porter.

Instantly he swung to the hotel porch, which tilted badly under his weight, water sloshing over it. He bent over the body, turning the injured head gently with his fingers. Then he looked up. "Did anybody see this happen? Who shot him?"

Nobody answered, but involuntarily Jessica looked at Mady, whose face was taut and pale. Mady's stare was defiant, but she said nothing.

"His body floated down here," Brunswick said. "He must have been shot somewhere east of town."

"He was looking for me," Duvarney responded.

"Somebody did not want him to see me, or else killed him because he was herding Rafter K cattle."

"We were going to make a try for the courthouse," Crain said. "I've got to go to the jail. If you could—"

Tap stepped back into the saddle and took down his rope. He shook it out. "Grab hold," he said, "and hang on."

People rushed to catch the rope, but Welt Spicer was doing the same thing. Just then four riders turned into the upper end of the street.

"Look out, Major!" Spicer spoke quickly in a low tone. "Those are Munsons."

"Let's go!" Duvarney shouted to the crowd. "Let's go and keep moving!"

Crain, also mounted, was riding toward the jail. Tap caught a glimpse of him, and then could pay no more attention, for he needed every bit of his awareness. His horse started well, but the footing was bad; once the horse slipped, going almost to his knees, and it was only Tap's strength on the reins that pulled him up.

Half the people clinging to the rope were elderly. The wisest ones had managed to take a turn of the rope around their arms, for even if it was pulled taut and caused pain, it would at least hold them.

Only two persons were still at the hotel when Tap looked back. One was Bob Brunswick, and the other was Jessica. He almost pulled up when he saw her there, but she waved him on, and he lifted a hand and then spoke to his horse. "Steady, boy," he said. "Steady now."

A barn door went swinging by, narrowly missing the horse's legs. Tap squinted his eyes against the rain and stared ahead. At the corner, where two currents met, there was a swirling whirlpool. Somewhere along here the street was lower than farther back... but where?

The four riders were coming nearer. He reached back and under the guise of straightening the rope, slid the thong from his pistol butt.

He felt the drive of the rain, and knew the sea was rising, rising with the wind. He looked back along the black swirling river of the street, and saw the collapsed buildings, the gutted stores, all torn and spoiled by sea and wind. His hat brim flapped against his brow; the wind tugged at the drawstring that held his hat in place, and flapped his slicker against the flanks of the horse.

"Steady, boy. Take it easy now."

The rocks that had washed from the makeshift foundations were slippery, mud coated, and mud was deep in the street. He held to the side of the street for doubtful shelter from the wind. Always his eyes looked ahead, watching the wreckage as it hit the whirlpool at the corner, studying the currents, to move with them when crossing.

Actually, he was only supposed to be guiding the people, giving them something to cling to, but in effect he was hauling them along through the water, for many were too weak to do more than struggle feebly. Water had soaked their heaving clothing and weighted them down.

A cry rang out behind him...somebody was down. He drew up, giving his horse a chance to breathe. A woman had lost hold of her valise and her cry was one of anguish. No doubt the valise contained those keepsakes that a woman holds of most value, and she let go her hold on the rope and grasped frantically for it.

Instantly the swirling waters swept her from her feet. She struggled, came partly erect once more, then was knocked down by a piece of wreckage.

A tall, fine-looking man, roughly dressed and un-shaved, broke from his shelter near the side of a house and caught her sleeve, helping her up. Looking past her, he saw the valise had brought up against a step, and he struggled across the street, almost breast high in the center, retrieved the valise, and brought it back. With one arm around the white-haired woman, he helped her on toward the courthouse, holding the handle of the valise in the other hand.

"That's Bill Taylor," somebody said. "Crain must have let them out of jail."

Duvarney headed his horse for the courthouse steps. Turning in the saddle, he glanced at the Munson riders. Two of them he knew, the two on the wharf at Indianola on that first day. They were look-ing at him, and the grin on their faces was not pleasant.

"Go ahead, Majuh," one of them said. "You get free of what you're doin'. We can wait."

Four of them ... and there was just Welt Spicer and himself.

It was to be a fight this time, storm or no storm. Duvarney watched them sitting there in their saddles, water washing their stirrups, making no effort to help. Taylor had been a feudist, too, imprisoned for the killing of Sutton and Slaughter on a steamboat alongside the dock in Indianola; but Taylor was a gentleman and a Texan. The Munson crowd were a rabble; few of them now were even of the family, most were just a gang gathered together, fighting for whatever they could win.

"Better get inside," Duvarney said to a man who stopped at his stirrup to thank him. "I've got to go back after Brunswick and that girl."

"She gave up her place," the man said. "She stepped aside."

"She would," Duvarney said; "she's got the backbone to do it." And to follow him here, to leave a comfortable and beautiful home...she had come here to this and, knowing her, he knew that she would have no regrets.

He turned his horse as Welt closed in beside him. "Well, here it is, Major. We've got our fight, whether we want it or not."

"If they killed Lon Porter," Tap said, "I want it."

He swung his horse and rode toward them. Out of the corner of his eye he could see Jessica standing with Brunswick on the end of the boardwalk. He wanted to go to them, but if he did he would expose himself to the fire from the Munsons...and he knew they would wait no longer.

He rode right at them, his horse buck-jumping through the water. Welt had kept a little behind and on the right, working toward their flank, and they didn't like it.

"Which of you killed Lon Porter?" Tap spoke mildly.

"That gent over back of the corral who was huntin' you?" one of them asked. It was one of the men from the wharf who spoke. "I missed out on that. Didn't git there soon enough. Know what he was fixin' to tell you? We hit ol' Tom Kitt'ry t'other day an' knocked him for a loop . . . scattered his cows, shot up all those folks he had with him. Ol' Tom's either dead or hidin' in a swamp somewheres. Maybe he's drowned by now."

"We come after you," the other one said. "We heard tell ol' Jackson had staked you out for hisself, but that ain't fair. We figured to owe you somethin' for that mix-up down to the dock."

"Now, look, boys." Tap's voice was still mild.

He went for his gun.

Both Munsons had been holding guns under their slickers, drawn and ready, but they were talkers, and they wanted to tell him what they had done, and what they planned to do.

Duvarney's gun came up fast, the hammer coming back as the gun barrel swung up; then the hammer dropped and he was thumbing it in a steady roll of sound. The tallest Munson grabbed his stomach, swinging his pistol to bring it to bear, but the gun would not fire. Evidently Tap's bullet had hit the hammer or the trigger of the gun as Munson held it across his stomach under the slicker, and the gun was jammed.

The bullet had glanced upward, inflicting a wound . . . Tap could see the blood, bright crimson before the rain hit it, even as he fired his second and third shots.

His second shot caught Munson in the chest; the third was directed at the second Munson. He heard guns hammering, knew Spicer and the others were fighting. He saw the tallest Munson drop, heard the *whiff* of a bullet by his face, and saw the second weaving in his saddle. Even as he shot, he saw that these men were not fighters, they were killers, an altogether different thing. It is one thing to shoot a man from ambush, or when outnumbering the enemy; it is quite another thing to stand up face to face with a man who also holds a gun, and will shoot.

Tap turned toward Spicer, but Welt had been smarter than he, for Welt had stayed off some thirty yards and used his Winchester. In the driving rain, at thirty yards he was not a good target for hasty six-gun shooting. He had shot his first man, cold-turkey, and had his Winchester .44–40 on the other when the man threw down his gun and lifted his hands.

"You all right, Welt?" Tap asked.

"Sure. You?"

"Hold that man, Welt. I want to talk to him." He walked his horse slowly through the water, keeping to the side where it was not more than stirrup-deep, and rode to where Jessica stood. Her face was very pale, her eyes unnaturally large.

"You came to a rough country, Jessica," he said.

She looked up at him, holding up her skirt in one hand, "My man was here," she said simply.

CHAPTER 12

H E BENT OVER, offering his hand, and, gathering her skirt a little more, she stepped a toe into his stirrup, and he seated her before him.

"Tappan...those men...the ones you shot? Did you kill them?"

"They fell into four feet of water, Jessica, and I am not wasting time looking for them. When I got off the ship, two of them were on the dock and picked a fight with me simply because I was a well-dressed stranger. Now they've brought me into a feud I wanted no part of. What happened to them ceases to be my concern."

They had reached the steps of the courthouse, and he let her down gently, water swirling only inches from the step. "Better stay inside," he said. "I think we haven't seen the worst of it."

"Where are you going?"

He smiled at her. "First, I'm going to get Brunswick over here. Then Welt Spicer and me will ride back to our cattle. Will you be all right?"

"Of course, Tappan. Don't worry your head about me."

He bent over and kissed her lightly. "I'll be back," he said.

Welt Spicer took the lead. The rain had eased a little, and there seemed to be a lessening of the wind. Duvarney was sure what they had seen was only an outer edge of the storm, and the worst was yet to come. This was not the eye of the storm, but one of those curious gaps in the wind, an island of calm in the midst of fury... or relative calm, for rain still fell, and the wind still blew. He also knew there was little time to do what must be done.

There was no better place to stay than the courthouse. It was a strongly built structure on higher ground, and so was above the rising water, and it seemed able to withstand the wind.

Welt dropped back beside him. "Major, you'd better start considering Jackson Huddy. You'll have him to contend with."

"I know."

He had been thinking a lot about Huddy, and knew what he must do, if he could. He must find Huddy and force him into a fight. If given time, the man would surely plan an ambush and kill him in his own time, on his chosen ground. The only way to fight such a man was in the way he did not want to be fought—in the open and man to man. To do that, he must stay on Huddy's trail, find him, and either push the fight, or stay with him until Huddy had no choice.

It was easy enough to consider such a plan, but it was something else to bring it to a conclusion. It was like serving a bear steak. First you had to catch a bear.

"Hey!" Welt exclaimed. "Look over there!"

On a low ridge off to their left was a dark mass of cattle and horses. At least twenty acres of the long ridge and its flanks were above water, and they could see several riders around a fire.

Duvarney turned his mount toward them. "If they're friendly, maybe we can get some fresh horses."

They could see that there were three men and a spindling boy of fourteen or so. One of the men stood up, waiting for them.

"Hell of a storm," Duvarney said, "and there's more on the way."

"You think so? We'd about come to the notion it was over."

"Don't you believe it. Hold your stock right here. You'll see all hell break loose within the next few hours. Worse than it has been."

"Light and set," the man suggested. "You boys look played out."

They swung down and edged up to the fire, where a cowhand with a square, tough face gestured at the pot. "Help yourself," he said. "It's hot and black."

It was, hotter and blacker than the sins of the devil himself. But it tasted right.

Duvarney glanced over at the man who had spoken first, the oldest of the lot. "You want to sell some horses? Or swap? We're going to need some horses that can stand the gaff."

"You runnin' from something?" The old man eyed them sternly.

"Runnin' at it," Spicer said. "There's been some shootin', and there's like to be more."

"You ain't Taylors?"

"No, but we saw Bill Taylor in town. They freed him from jail, and he risked his neck helpin' women-folks to the courthouse." Spicer looked at them over the brim of his cup. "I'm thinkin' you've seen the last of Indianola."

They stared at him. "Half of it's floatin' in the street now," Spicer went on.

The boy was interested. "You said there'd been shootin'?"

"This here's Major Tappan Duvarney," Spicer said; "he's partnered with Tom Kittery. We were taking no part in the feud, but they murdered one of our boys, and when we were helping womenfolks to get to the courthouse they came up on us. Four of 'em."

"Four?" The short puncher looked doubtful.

"The Major here, he taken two of the Munsons, shot 'em right out of the saddle. I taken one of them with my Winchester, and the other was of no mind to fight."

Welt turned suddenly. "Major, we done forgot all about him. He must've slipped off!" Spicer swore. "Major, that was my fault. I was s'posed to watch him."

"Forget it. I don't know what we'd have done with him anyhow."

"You can have the horses," the stockman said. "You want two?"

"Six," Tap said, "if you can spare them."

Over coffee and corn pone with sow belly they worked out a deal. Welt Spicer roamed restlessly, his eyes on the country around. Much of it was above water, but was a sea of mud. Water swirled in all the low places, dark brown under the somber sky.

When the bargain had been made, and Tap had paid the money, the rancher filled his cup again. "Major," he said, "ain't you the man who is driving north with a trail herd?"

Duvarney explained about the herd he had sold, and where it was, then added that Kittery's cattle had been scattered by the Munsons . . . or so he had heard.

"My name is Webster, Major, and I'm holding about two hundred head here, and I've got about thirty head of saddle stock. How about me throwing in with you for that drive?"

Tap considered. Undoubtedly, if the Munsons had told the truth, his herd was scattered, yet some might still be together, and despite the conditions he was in no mood to quit. The check he had in his pocket represented a part of his investment, but only a part. If he could round up some of the cattle—and those alive would surely be bunched on high ground and easy to find—he could start a drive anyway.

"Fine!" he said. "I'll tell you what, Webster. When the water is down enough to move, you start for Victoria. Camp on the first big bend of the Guadalupe above the town, or as near there as practical, and we'll join you there. I've an idea I'll be driving Brunswick's cattle, too."

The day was nearly gone when they moved out again, holding to high ground and scouting for cattle. Here and there they found a few Rafter K steers, and several bearing Duvarney's own brand. Moving them on, he was driving about thirty head of steers when he drew rein about a mile from camp. Against the dark clouds he could see a thread of pale smoke mounting... the camp was there.

Welt rode up beside him and began to build a smoke. The hills were dark with evening, the low-hanging clouds turning all the shadowed hills and hollows into black and gray. The cattle were concealed in the brush and so could not be seen; the brush itself was all a uniform blackness.

"You know, Welt, take a man like Jackson Huddy,

now. He'd be apt to scout around hunting us out. He could find that herd now, couldn't he?"

"I reckon so."

"And being the kind of man he is, what would he be likely to do? Figuring you were him, with his makeup, what would you do?"

Welt Spicer's cigarette glowed in the dark. After a moment, he answered. "Why, I'd locate the cattle and leave them be. In this sort of weather, they ain't goin' no place I couldn't find 'em. So I'd move out somewhere and hole up and wait for you. After all, you're one of the men I'd want to kill."

"That's what I was thinking," Duvarney said. He studied the terrain ahead of them. "Being that kind of man, where would you lie up to wait?"

In the light that remained, they studied the layout of the country around. The low ground between the ridges and knolls was flooded, the small lakes like sheets of polished steel in the gray light. Trees and brush merged together into the darkness of the land.

The camp could be anywhere out there—not in the flooded lowlands, but on the slopes. Suddenly he made up his mind.

"We aren't going in, Welt. We'll bed down and wait right here."

"It ain't far," Welt said. "I had my mind set on hot coffee and a meal."

"I picked up some grub from Webster back there," Tap said. "We'll stay here. My theory is, never walk into an opponent when he's set. It's better to circle around and get him out of position. In this case he can come to us if he wants to."

The place they found was ideal. It was on an open

slope under a brow of sand. Sixty feet out from the bank they built their fire. The sand ridge had been scoured by wind until the overhang seemed ready to collapse at any moment, but the site they chose was just beyond the limits of where the sand would come if it did fall. Certainly nobody could approach the edge of that bluff without sending the sand, and himself, tumbling down the bank, and that insured them of safety from behind.

Before them the slope fell away, covered with sparse grass for the hungry horses and cattle. Most of the night they would be moving about on the slope between the fire and any approach from below, effectively blocking any attack from that side.

The fire they built was small, and was partly shielded by a mound of wet sand they built up for the purpose. There they made coffee and fried bacon. They had little enough, but they were hungry, and when they had eaten the bacon they wiped up the grease with chunks of bread that Webster had given them.

"You sleep, Spicer," Duvarney advised. "I'll call you after a bit."

Welt hesitated. Tap had seen that Spicer was half dead from fatigue, so he blocked any protest by adding, "I'm not tired yet, Spicer, and I've got to do some thinking. You get some sleep."

When Spicer was asleep, Tap added a few sticks to the fire and moved back from it to a spot partly sheltered by a hummock of sand and brush. The truth of the matter was he was half dead from weariness himself, but he did have thinking to do.

His plans had been shot to pieces by feud and

storm. If he hoped to save anything from the wreckage, he must have another plan. Brunswick could no longer make a shipping from Indianola, and the chances were that all the Gulf ports had suffered. The thing to do, he knew, was to make a drive to Kansas, as originally planned.

The only way he could do that, even with Brunswick's help, was to strike south quickly, round up all the cattle he could find that wore his brand or that of Kittery, and then start north at once. This country would be weeks if not months recovering from the disaster, and if he moved swiftly he might even get away before any more serious fighting developed.

But, whether he liked it or not, he had to get Jackson Huddy before the killer got him. For one thing was certain: Huddy would try. Duvarney was no longer an outsider, for now he had killed Munsons.

He carefully considered every move, and then when the skies were thickening again, he shook Spicer awake.

"Can you spell me? I've about had it," he said.

Welt Spicer rolled out and slipped on his slicker. He took his rifle and slung it, muzzle down, from his shoulder. Duvarney rolled into a half-wet blanket under a tarp, and was almost instantly asleep.

Awakening suddenly, feeling the tap-tap of rain-fingers on the tarp, he lifted the edge ever so little, inhaling deeply of the fresh, rain-cooled air, and listening. He could hear the hiss and crackle of the small fire, but unless he moved he could see only the light cast by the flames, not the fire itself. He felt a curious reluctance to move, as if some subconscious warning had come to him in his sleep, awakening him.

He slid his pistol from its holster under the tarp and hooked his thumb over the hammer, easing the gun up, chest-high and ready for firing.

His ears captured no sound, his eyes could see nothing but the firelight. The wind, which had almost died away, suddenly guttered the fire, and rustled among the leaves of the brush. Ever so slightly, he tilted back his head and opened the tarp a little more. A cold drop of rain fell from the edge to his arm and trickled from his wrist toward his elbow.

Welt Spicer was seated at the fire, just far enough back to be out of its light, and his head was hanging down. Even as Duvarney saw him, Spicer's head came up. He shook it, trying to clear it of sleep, and stared all around him, holding his eyes unnaturally wide as a man does in trying to ward off sleep. He eased his position, and soon his head lowered again.

At that moment, and for no apparent reason, Duvarney glanced up toward the rim of sand that hung above their camp. His bed was made so that his feet pointed toward the bluff, and now, as he looked, he saw something round and white rising above the rim. A gleam of light appeared and vanished... a rifle barrel?

The spot of white lifted, and now he could make it out better. There was just enough light from the fire to reflect from the face of the man who was some yards off on the rim of sand.

For a man was there, rising up to his knees to aim his rifle into the camp. But his position was not quite what he wanted, and he hitched one knee forward. The movement was his undoing.

He was already on the very lip of the sand, and the move put his knee down on the overhang. Instantly the sand gave way and the man came tumbling down, accompanied by a great mass of sand. He hit bottom floundering, and as he struggled to his feet Duvarney lifted himself on one elbow and shot him.

The fall of sand made only a heavy *whush* in the night, but the shot startled the animals to their feet and brought Welt Spicer up standing.

"Watch yourself, Welt. There may be more of them."

Where Welt had stood, there was emptiness, then his quiet voice came. "Sorry, Major, I must have fallen asleep."

"You were dozing. It's all right, I was awake."

"Who was it?"

Duvarney pointed. "He was drawing a bead on you from the rim, but he changed position a mite, and it toppled with him. I took his action as unfriendly, so I put the brand on him."

Duvarney remained where he was, but after a moment he ejected the empty shell from his gun and reloaded.

"I figure this man was scouting and saw his chance. Now, they heard that shot but they don't know whose it was—he might have shot one of us, or we might have shot him."

"They'll think he got one of us," Welt said. "They might not even know there was two of us here." Welt was close by now, only a few feet from Duvarney. "They'll be expectin' him back, you know."

Tap considered that. It would give a man a chance to walk right up on their camp. He could work near to it in the darkness, then just stand up and walk in. If he came right up to their fire they would be sure it was their own man, returning from whatever he had set out to do.

"I'm going down there," Tap said, "and see if Huddy is around."

"You want comp'ny?"

"They'll be expecting one man. You sit tight, . . . and take care."

Duvarney took his rifle and went down the slope. When he found their fire he saw that there were five men seated by it, or lying around, talking. They seemed unworried about the possibilities of attack, which meant they had hit Tom Kittery hard.

He went on down, making no pretense of being quiet. At the edge of the fire he saw seven saddled horses.

They looked up as he came near, and one man started to speak; then he saw Duvarney. "Sit tight, boys," Duvarney said. "I don't want to kill anybody unless I have to."

One of them was the man who had escaped from them in Indianola. "Do what he says," this man said. "This is Duvarney . . . the one I was tellin' you about."

Suddenly Tap's mind registered the significant fact that there were five men here. He had killed one up at his camp, and yet there were seven saddled horses . . . *where was the other man?*

"Where's Jackson Huddy?" he asked.

One of the men grinned. "Don't try to find him. He'll find you."

"I hear he's something of a manhunter," Tap responded, "but as near as I can find out he never met anybody in a fair, stand-up shooting match. Anybody can run up a score hiding out in the brush."

It was a deliberate taunt. He wanted Jackson Huddy to hear it. He wanted to anger him, to jar him out of his usual pattern. He wanted that slow, meticulous, careful man to be jolted into acting quickly.

"Man, you're askin' for trouble!"

"I shouldn't really ask, I expect," Duvarney said carelessly. "From all I hear, he's so used to crawling on his belly in the grass that he wouldn't know how to stand up and fight."

"Jackson Huddy never went after a man yet that he didn't get," one of the men said. "You'll be the next, mister."

"Well, you just tell him I was around. And don't forget the name. I wouldn't want him to miss seeing me. . . . And you tell him that if he doesn't want to meet me face to face I'll do a little stalking myself."

He backed off into the darkness, still holding the rifle easy in his hands.

Returning to his own fire, he told Spicer briefly what he had done, and doused water over the coals.

"I want to get him out of the brush if I can, but I'm not going to wait. I'm going after him . . . now. He'll be over there somewhere near our camp, but let's scatter those other boys, anyway."

They rounded up the small bunch of cattle they had. He let out a whoop and fired his pistol. It needed only that to start them running, and he headed them toward his other camp, right across the slope where the Munson fire was.

They heard the cattle coming, and in the dim light Duvarney saw them scattering, horses and men. Only one shot was fired, and then the cattle went storming through the camp, churning the fire into the ground, and men and horses fled.

One man had caught up his rifle, and now he tried to swing it around to bear on Duvarney, but Spicer rode down on him. Too late, the man tried to wheel to fire at Spicer, and then the charging horse hit him and knocked him rolling in the mud.

They went up the slope on the run, and Duvarney's riders came rushing out, ready for a fight.

"Mount up," he said, "and keep moving." Crouching low in his saddle, he skirted the dark brush, hunting in the gray light for tracks where a man might have gone in.

If the seventh man was Huddy, as Tap suspected, he had to be hidden somewhere in the brush where he could wait for a shot at Duvarney. It would be natural for Duvarney to return to his campfire and his men, and a man might by searching find a good spot from which to shoot at his target.

A moving target would be something of a problem, for any hiding place that Huddy might crawl into that would allow him to get in sight of the camp would be in dense brush where swinging a rifle would be difficult, and finding a clear field of fire in more than one direction would be impossible.

Twice Tap stopped on the windward side of the brush and, digging beneath the surface of the leaves, sought for some dry enough to burn. He did not hope for a real fire, wet as it was, but for a good smoke, a smoke that might drive him out.

"He's afoot, anyway," Lawton Bean commented. "The way you scattered their horses, that whole outfit is afoot."

The fire smoked and, blazing a little, ate away at the edges of the leaves, fighting against the dampness. The smoke drifted through the brush, as he had hoped it would.

Duvarney considered the situation, and liked none of it. The rain would undoubtedly put out the feeble fires he had started, probably before they had developed sufficient smoke to drive Huddy, if it was Huddy, from concealment. The smoke might cause him some discomfort, but nothing more. In the meanwhile, it might be a long wait, and Huddy might find a place where he could get a good shot at them. And all this time Tom Kittery was in trouble to the south, and that was where the cattle would be.

From the very beginning, he was thinking, nothing had gone well. He had hoped to land in Texas, find a gathered herd ready to move, and start at once for Kansas. Instead, he had found his partner involved in a killing feud to the point where all business had been neglected; and to be on the safe side Tap had had to recruit his own men. They had gathered cattle, only to be interrupted by the storm, yet he had sold cattle and had the check in his pocket.

Now, like it or not, he was involved in the feud. One of his men had been killed; he himself had been attacked, and he had killed in return. Yet he wanted nothing more than to be on the trail to Kansas.

The cattle would be, he surmised, on high ground. Bunched by the storm, they would be ready for a drive. He was torn between the need to find Kittery, to round up a herd, and to locate Huddy and force him into a show-down.

He made up his mind. He would have to chance Huddy. First things must come first; and he must find Tom Kittery, and get a herd on the trail to Kansas.

But even as he turned away, he was haunted by fear. Jackson Huddy was no man to be trifled with, and Jackson Huddy would be hunting him like a wolf trailing for a kill.

From now on, no moment, waking or sleeping, would be without fear.

CHAPTER 13

BUNCHING THE CATTLE, they started them westward. Driving them down off the ridge, they waded them and swam them until they had put a good mile behind them. Then they found the ground above water, but soggy and miserable.

The cattle moved sullenly. The rain had ceased, but the sky remained dark and heavily overcast, and they could hear thunder in the distance. The wind was rising.

During the incessant blowing of the past two days the wind had become almost a part of their lives, and the time before that was wiped out, almost as if it had never been. To Tap Duvarney it seemed as if he could not remember a time when he had not been wet and cold, and harried by wind.

Leaving Belden in charge, he took Spicer and Lawton Bean and they headed south.

"In this weather," Bean said, "we ain't got a chance of findin' them. They'll be holed up somewhere, if they're alive." Every word had to be shouted to be heard above the rising wind.

"We've got to try," Tap yelled, and they kept on.

The earth was black beneath, the sheets of water like steel under the heavy sky, and the dark slim trunks of the few trees were like prison bars.

At noon they came to a cabin where there was a

corral, and a lean-to stable half hidden in the brush. A thin line of smoke was rising from the cabin, and with rifles ready, they hailed the door.

It opened a slit, and a thin, mustached face peered out, saw the rifles, and started to close the door, but Duvarney rode forward. "Hold it, there! We're ridin' the grub line—how about some coffee?"

The door opened wider. "All right, put your horses up and come on in, but come peaceful. I'm holdin' a Colt revolvin' shotgun."

The cabin was snug, overly warm, and dry. The squatter had not lied...he had the shotgun right at hand, and he was wearing a six-shooter.

"Never turned away a hungry man yet," he said, "but you boys rode up holdin' a lot of shootin' power."

"We're hunting some friends," Duvarney told him. "Hear anything of a fight down this way?"

"I heard it...seen some of it. That was eight, maybe nine mile southeast of here. I'd been down to Refugio after grub...had a couple of pack mules. I was nigh to Horseshoe Lake when somebody busted loose with a war right close by. I pulled off into the brush and kept quiet. It was quite a scrap, by the sound of it."

He was a talkative man, as men who live alone are inclined to be when company shows up. He moved about, dishing up beans from a big crock, getting out some homemade bread, and putting on the frying pan. "You boys just set still an' don't go to pullin' leather. I'll roust you up some grub."

He squinted at them with inquisitive blue eyes.

"You boys don't have the Munson look. Must be kin of the Kitt'ry's."

"I am Tappan Duvarney, Tom Kittery's partner."

"Figured you was kin or somethin'. Well, you won't find much left...cattle scattered hell to break-fast...Roy Kitt'ry's dead...Joe Breck is dead."

"How about Tom? How about Lubec and the Cajun?"

"Hid out, more'n likely. Looks like them sorry Munsons got the upper hand. Ain't been a Munson killed in quite a spell."

As they ate, the old man told them of several small herds of Rafter K cattle and where they could be found.

"How are you fixed for horses?" Duvarney asked. "We could use some."

"Fix you up, all right." He gestured toward the corral. "Go have a look."

Duvarney got up slowly, surreptitiously watching his host, who was busy over the fire...too busy. Tap stretched, yawned, and glanced out the window at the corral. It was close to the brush on one side, where some post oak provided shade for the stock. He could see several horses in the corral, and he glanced around at Spicer.

Welt was smiling, and he had a Colt in his hand. "You go have that look, Major, and if I hear a shot, I'll kill the cook."

The old man stiffened up, turning, half ready to reach for his shotgun, but Lawton Bean had it, and he was smiling, too. "How about it, old man? You still want the Major to look at your horses? It's all right with us—on'y at the first shot we're goin' to cut you in two."

"What else could I do?" the old man said. "If I warned you, they'd shoot me. An' that there Huddy, he'd come after me. And like I said, you boys are losin' the fight."

"Don't be too sure," Bean drawled. "The Major here, he taken two Munsons just yesterday. He killed Eggen an' Wheeler Munson. Welt Spicer here, he nailed another one of that outfit. And last night one of 'em tried to dry-gulch us an' he cashed in his chips mighty fast."

The old man looked from one to the other. "I ain't no coward, and I don't like Munsons, but what can I do? I'm alone out here, an' with that Huddy around..."

"He won't be around long," Spicer said.

"What's out there?" Duvarney asked quietly.

"Three of 'em. They stopped by to get out of the storm but when they saw you comin' they headed for the brush, figurin' to lay out an' pick you off, easy like."

Duvarney stood well back inside, but he was looking out the window, studying the environment with care.

"One of them is Pinto Hart," the old man offered, "an' he ain't no schoolboy."

"They call him Pinto because of a scar on his face," Spicer said. "He's a brother to Jim Hart, and they're two of the top men in the Munson crowd."

Tap went from window to window, looking at the surroundings. When he had found what he was looking for, he turned back to the room. He gestured toward the moccasins the old man wore. "Have you got another pair of those?"

"I might have."

"I'm buying them," Tap said; "get them out."

The old man opened a chest and removed several pairs of trousers, some shirts, and then the moccasins. "I traded 'em off a squaw. They're new...never worn."

Duvarney dropped a silver dollar on the table. "You probably didn't give her half that," he said. Then he sat down and slipped off his boots and put on the moccasins. They were a surprisingly good fit.

"You boys sit tight," he said to the others. "Keep an eye on that bunch out there, and if Dad here gives you any trouble, tie him up."

"Now what kinda talk is that?" the old man complained. "I'm no Munson, and I'm not huntin' trouble." He paused, watching Duvarney hitch his bowie knife around, ready to hand. "Did you hear me right? There's three of them out there...an' Pinto's worth two or three all by himself."

Tap ignored him; then, like a ghost, he slipped from the door. Outside, the wind was blowing and a light rain was falling. He went around the cabin to get it between himself and the hidden men, and dropping to a crouch, moved behind a bush, hesitated a moment, and slipped beyond to a tree.

He had fought too many Indians and stalked too much wild game not to know how it was done. The moccasins could feel of the earth beneath, avoiding any stick that might break...He moved deeper into the brush. He carried no rifle, preferring to depend on his two pistols and the knife.

He scouted wide, moving with the wind to cover any sound, his eyes watchful. The trees bent under the wind, and a spattering of huge drops fell on the leaves, and on his head and shoulders.

It was a game of death he was playing, but a game he had played before. These men, so far as he knew, were cowhands, men who rode horseback. They were not woodsmen in the sense he had been. Now, if the Cajun were out there . . . He had a feeling about the Cajun . . . *there* was a dangerous man.

There was a weird, yellowish light in the trees. This was a fairly large patch of ground, covering fifteen to twenty acres, part of it running down to a streambed. He took his time, knowing that death awaited a careless hunter, but he moved in closer.

Suddenly he stopped. Not far ahead he could see the light beyond the trees, and knew that he must be somewhere within a hundred yards of the men he hunted—very likely much less than that.

He had paused behind a bush, with two trees in line behind him, and another one only inches to the left. No one looking in his direction would guess that a man stood there. He studied the leaves and the brush about him with care.

His eyes scanned the woods ahead of him, looking across a leaf-filled hollow where the slow drops fell from arching branches above, when he saw them. They were bunched as he had hoped they would be, and were seated where they could watch the cabin and anyone who approached the corral.

They were closer than he had thought—only about twenty-five yards away. The gun he carried in his holster was a Smith & Wesson Russian .44, the straightest-shooting gun in the West at the time. At that distance he had often scored high at target shooting. This was not so easy, for the background made it difficult, the men and their clothing merging well with the trees and brush.

He moved a step forward, putting his foot down with the utmost care, and letting it sink into the wet leaves. Then he took another step. As he moved, his mind was telling him that at that distance he would probably do better than they could, for though they were used to guns, they were not likely to have had as thorough a training as he had had, nor the experience in the cavalry.

He took a third step—each step was a short one. They would turn soon, and that was the way he wanted it. He did not want to surprise them into shooting. If possible, he would take them without any shooting, and without killing.

He stood now beneath a huge pecan tree and looked at the three men across the small hollow. They were talking quietly, and smoking. He smiled at that. An Apache would have smelled that smoke—as he had—long before he saw them.

One of the men knocked out his pipe against his heel, a sound that would carry too far . . . these men were not the sort he was used to dealing with. The man started to put his pipe in his pocket, and he turned just a little as his hand reached back for his coat pocket. With that motion his head turned slightly to the right, as it often will with such a movement, and he saw Duvarney.

He froze with the movement half completed, staring hard, obviously unwilling to believe what he saw, or unsure of it. The position in which Duvarney was standing would be even worse for them to see clearly than was their position for Tap.

"Pinto," he said. "Pinto...*look*."

When Pinto turned his head Tap saw the scar...a bad powder burn, he would guess, although it was impossible to tell at that distance.

"You boys waiting for me?" Duvarney asked in a conversational tone. "There doesn't have to be a shooting, you know. You can just shuck your guns and back off. I'm down here on business—I'm not trying to run up a score."

They looked at him, unwilling to believe that he was actually there, that he had moved up behind them without their knowing it. It offended their pride...after all, they were fighting men.

He held the Smith & Wesson in his hand, the muzzle down slightly, but ready.

"You'd better do that," he added. "Just loosen your gun belts and let them fall."

Pinto Hart was getting slowly to his feet—slowly and carefully. Tap watched them all without any partiality, and he could catch any move. When Pinto was on his feet, he said, "I'll be damned if I will."

"You boys better talk to him. I shoot pretty straight, but at this distance I might nail any one of you. I'll surely get him, but one of you might get hurt."

One of the two men sitting there had a rifle across his knees, but he would have to swing ninety degrees to bring it to bear...it would take too long, and the man knew it. The other man was the one who put the pipe in his pocket, and his hand was still there, clutching the pipe. Nobody wants to die, and this man knew he had a good chance of not living out the next two minutes, and he was sweating.

"Talk to him, boys," Tap said again, "or pull him down. He'll only get you killed."

"Pinto?" The man with the rifle was speaking. "I think—"

Pinto took a step back and went for his gun. Tap hesitated a fraction of a second to see what the others would do, and then shot Pinto Hart through the lower right corner of his breast pocket. He fired only once, then held his fire.

"How about it, boys? What's in it for you that will weigh as heavy as a bullet in the head?"

Very carefully the man with the rifle pitched it from him, and unbuckled his belt. The other man moved gingerly to do the same.

"Why don't you boys just head for Refugio and take the stage on west? Arizona's a good country. So's New Mexico."

They turned with great care and, stiff-backed, walked away as Duvarney followed them. He glanced once at the body of Pinto Hart. A tough, reckless man, and a game one. It was a pity, but he had thought of himself as a good man with a gun, and that kind of belief can get a man killed. A reputation for being tough can give a man some standing with his fellows, but there always comes a time when he has to back it up...and the same men who praised your skill will sneer at it by comparison with the man who shoots you.

"We got to get our horses," one of the men said.

"Walk," Duvarney said. "A good walk in the rain and the wind will give you time to consider your ways. And boys—be sure you take that stage. If I saw you around I might just think you were waiting for me, and I'd have to shoot on sight, I wouldn't want to do that."

He watched them go, and then he walked back to the cabin and went in the door.

The old man was tipped back in his chair, and he let the chair legs down hard when Duvarney came in. Welt Spicer merely gave Tap a satisfied look, and Lawton Bean stretched.

"Two of them are walking to Refugio," Duvarney said. "It will cool them off a bit."

"Pinto?" the old man asked quickly.

"Pinto's out there. Will you take care of him, *amigo*? We'll take those horses, too," he added. "I think we're going to need them, the way the weather is."

"You killed Pinto Hart?" The old man could not find it in himself to believe it could happen that way.

"He killed himself," Duvarney said. "He made an error in judgment."

They rode to the south and then east, and within a few miles they began to see Rafter K cattle.

CHAPTER 14

JESSICA TRESCOTT HUDDLED in her mackintosh, half asleep. The wind filled the day with a dreadful roaring, like nothing she had ever heard. Outwardly, Jessica was calm; inwardly, she trembled. It was a trembling down deep inside her, the trembling of a fear such as she had never known.

The others were gathered about her, together yet alone; for in a terrible storm each person is alone within their minds, cowering with their own private fears, their uncertainties. There is no isolation like that brought on by storm, for the voice cannot rise above the wind, nor can it reach that private place within the head where man hovers in the midst of all that he is and has been.

Jessica's hands were thrust deep in her pockets, her shoulders were hunched, as much to shut out the sound as to bring warmth.

The courthouse was of concrete, and it was strongly built. The rise of ground on which it sat lifted it somewhat above the waters.

And now, for the first time, the great waves began to break over the island.

Up to now the wind had driven the waters of the bay upon the shore, had driven great volumes of water through the passages between the islands, and the swells had pounded the outer islands, but only now had the sea begun to roll its swells clear across the island and up on the low shores.

It began in the town with a mighty wave that sent a rolling wall of water up the street. This was almost immediately followed by another. The outer buildings of the town, battered by the gigantic winds, now crashed before the onrushing sea.

"Ma'am?"

Jessica looked up to see Bill Taylor standing beside her, hat in hand. "Ma'am," he repeated, "you got to see this. Maybe you'll never see the like again."

With Mady and Bob Brunswick, she followed him up the stairs to the second floor. Up there she was conscious only of the mighty sound of the wind. The building seemed to give before the weight of it pressing against the walls. It even seemed to suck the breath from her lungs, causing her to gasp for each breath. When he led her to a window with a broken shutter, she looked out over Indianola and was appalled.

As far as her eyes could see, in the intervals between the gusts of wind and rain, there was only water. The rushing waves were smashing the buildings now, floating the less securely anchored, sending them crashing one against another with tremendous, splintering force.

There was no longer a harbor, no longer any piers to be seen, or any land at all. Here and there a tree, rooted more deeply than the others, still held its place, almost drowned by the rising water.

The boardwalk where she had stood not long ago was gone, and the hotel itself canted over weirdly. For a moment she thought of her clothing there ... of the pictures of her father and mother, her diary . . . all would be gone, carried away by the flood.

Mady was thinking of those dresses, too. "All those beautiful gowns!" she wailed.

Jessica glanced at her, and said wryly, "I don't believe those clothes have much to do with what is really worthwhile, and I doubt if Tappan will even realize they are gone."

"I wish I had them."

"The only things I regret are a few personal keepsakes and my books, and I haven't really lost them, I suppose. Once you have read a book you care about, some part of it is always with you."

She looked out at the frightful havoc of the storm. A town was dying out there, being wiped from the earth, but guiltily she realized that all she could think about was Tappan. Where was he? Was he safe?

The worst of it was, there was nothing she could do. Those who could reach the courthouse were there. Bill Taylor and a few others had performed amazingly, rescuing men, women, and children, and getting them all inside. Taylor, awaiting trial for his part in a shooting, had worked harder than anyone in getting people to safety.

She went back and sat down. The water was over the steps now, and the town was simply caving in under the combined attack of sea and wind.

Here and there clusters of men bunched together. Once Taylor came over and squatted near by. He knew Mady, of course, but it was to Jessica he talked. "Stories are going around," he said, "that there's been more shooting south of here. But don't you worry; that man of yours is a good hand. I watched him out there against Eggen and Wheeler. He'll take care of himself."

He did not look at Mady or speak to her. Once she started to address him and he pointedly looked away. She flushed.

"Tom Kitt'ry," Taylor said, "ran into a bunch of trouble. Seems they knew right where to find him, and they did. Feller rode into town...he's downstairs right now...he heard Pete Remley and Joe Breck were dead...Roy Kitt'ry, too. Tom's hurt, an' he's hid out. Somebody wished him no good," Taylor added insinuatingly, "and folks know it. If there ever was a talker, it was that show-off, Ev Munson."

From the corners of her eyes, Jessica looked at Mady. Her face was shockingly white and pinched. She seemed shrunken, somehow, and she stared straight ahead in a kind of stark shame.

"Tom's goin' to win now. That man of yours, Duvarney—he makes the difference. Those men he's got, they're good ones, but it's Duvarney...he's outguessed them every turn."

After a while, Taylor moved away, and the two girls sat silent. Finally, Jessica could restrain herself no longer. "Mady...why did you do it?"

"Oh...you! You think you know so much! How do you know how it is to live in a place like this, year after year? I wanted Tom to leave. I wanted him to get out. And I knew he never would as long as that crazy feud was going on! Anyway, I had nothing to do with what happened."

"I saw you talking to Every Munson, Mady."

"What if you did? I've known Ev Munson all my

life. I never cared about their silly feud. All I wanted was for Tom to take me away."

"Away from all he knew? Did that seem wise, Mady? This is Tom's life. He knows cattle. He knows the range, the people. In the city he would be just another man struggling for a living among men who had grown up in a life he had never known."

"Tom would do all right," Mady said defiantly.

"And so you betrayed him?"

Mady turned on Jessica, her eyes hot with anger. "I did no such thing!"

"I think you did, Mady. I also think you were there when Lon Porter was killed."

Mady was silent. After a moment she said, "I did see that, but I had nothing to do with it. When I got to the corral Lon Porter was tying up his horse and asking for Major Duvarney. He said he had a message from Tom.... Well, he talked too loud and Jackson Huddy heard him."

"Did Jackson Huddy kill him?"

"Yes, he did. He shot him through the back of the head, and I saw it. Oh, he didn't see me, and I was so scared I couldn't move if I'd wanted to! Jackson Huddy wasn't more than thirty feet from him, and Lon Porter never knew anybody else was around, and you can just bet that hostler isn't going to tell of it."

The wind was rising, and talk was becoming impossible. Sheets of rain battered the walls, seeping through around window casings and falling in huge drops from the ceilings. Outside, almost nothing could be seen, and nobody wanted to risk standing near enough to a window even to try.

All of those on the ground floor had now climbed

the stairs, for water was coming through under the doors, and one of the windows had been smashed by the wind. The wild banshee howling of the storm was maddening, and Jessica crouched on a bench, her legs drawn up under her, her head sunk behind the collar of her mackintosh, and her hands over her ears.

Once, Taylor caught her shoulder and pointed. A window had smashed and water was pouring in, blown by the howling wind. A momentary lull gave them a glimpse of the town . . . only there was no town, only a torn and ravaged sea, littered with wreckage and the hull of a bottom-up ship. Then the streaming rain and blown spray shut out the sight again.

Cowering on her bench, Jessica could only clutch herself and wait.

TAPPAN DUVARNEY AND his men were scattered widely when the wind came. Duvarney himself had found some thirty head of cattle on a slope and started moving them inland. Soon he had come upon a dozen more, all steers in this lot, bedded down on a long ridge.

He had driven them no more than a mile when Lawton Bean appeared, driving thirty-odd head of mixed stuff. Some distance off they could see a long ridge running roughly north and south, and they started for it, picking up a few head from the country between.

Welt Spicer came up driving a small herd, and they bunched them on the ridge, somewhat in the lee of the rocky crest that was tufted with stunted trees and low brush. There, under a deep hollowed-out space in the rock, they found where men had occasionally taken shelter. A crude wall of piled-up stone had been built to offer even more shelter, and when the wind came they brought their horses under the overhang.

Thunder was now an almost continuous sound, and lightning flared again and again, lighting up the deep shadows under the overhang. The darkness was like late twilight. The rain roared down, slashing at the skin like cutting knives whenever one got within its range.

Spicer sat in the farthest corner of the cavelike space and stared out at the storm. All the men, for fear of lightning, had placed their guns some distance away from them. Suddenly Bean looked around at Tap. "I thought I heard a yell!" he shouted. *"Listen!"*

Duvarney went close to the mouth of the cave and waited, but for several minutes he heard nothing; then faint and far off, he heard what sounded like a shout.

"Somebody is out there needing help," he said. "You sit tight, and I'll have a look."

"Don't be loco," Spicer objected. "A feller often hears such sounds in a storm."

Drawing the string under his chin a little tighter, and turning up his collar again, Duvarney hesitated only briefly, then plunged into the wall of water outside. His heels skidded on the muddy surface, and he almost fell, then he turned and started to clamber up the slope toward the crest of the ridge, clinging to the brush to help him climb.

He could see that on the top of the ridge the trees were bent at an impossible angle, their roots still holding but the trunks almost parallel with the ground beneath. He clung to some brush, half crouching, and looked at the top of the ridge.

No man could stand erect there. The wind would blow him right off. He turned and looked all around. He could see nothing but the driving rain. Below the ridge all was a swirling mass of water from the swollen creeks. The cattle were huddled just under the crest of the long ridge, taking what shelter they could from the onslaught of the storm.

A feeble shout made him turn his head again, and he saw them. Past the point of the ridge where the slope fell away to the creek bottom a man was struggling with a mired horse, a horse that carried a dark, humped bundle on its back.

Duvarney fought his way along the ridge through the brush. One look and he could see that the man was staggering with weariness. Once he fell to his knees and could barely struggle up. Duvarney yelled and ran to him, stumbling and falling himself, skidding on his knees. He got up, reaching the man just as he was about to fall into the water.

It was Tom Kittery.

Tap led him back to the slope, where he made him sit down, and then he caught up the reins on the horse. "Come on, boy!" he called. "Let's get you out of here!"

The horse needed little help, only a little more than Tom Kittery was able to give in his exhausted condition. He struggled, forefeet clambering at the bank, but with Duvarney's help he struggled free. It was only then that Duvarney looked to see who was on his back. Two men . . . or bodies . . . wrapped in their slickers so as to shelter their heads, and tied to the horse's back.

Grabbing Tom by the arm, Duvarney pulled him erect. Just then he saw Lawton Bean and Spicer coming toward him in a tumbling run.

"Wondered what was keepin' you!" Spicer yelled.

With Bean supporting Kittery, and Spicer walking alongside, they got back to the shelter of the overhang. Once they were out of the immediate roar and rush of the storm, it was like a reprieve from some ghastly hell, or from a wind-tortured world where one gasped for every breath, struggled to make every step.

Duvarney untied the men on the horse, and saw that they were the Cajun and Lubec. Both were wounded. The Cajun was stretched out on his slicker, and Lubec helped himself to a corner and leaned back, breathing hoarsely. One of Lubec's arms was clumsily bandaged and in a crude splint.

"What happened to that?" Spicer asked.

"Horse fell on me," Lubec grumbled. "Slipped on a bank." He indicated the Cajun. "That one's been shot. Caught two slugs."

A long time later, with the wounded men cared for and Tom in an exhausted sleep, Tap Duvarney slept, too.

Outside the storm still raged, thunder crashed and reverberated against the hills, but he slept.

CHAPTER 15

WHEN THE MORNING came, the storm was gone. A few scattered clouds, ragged with a memory of yesterday's winds, still remained in the sky. Only a small wind blew, and there was no rain.

Tappan Duvarney stood at the opening of the overhang and looked out across the rain-soaked landscape. Everywhere were evidences of the hurricane's passing. Trees were down, streams still rushed bankfull, and great pools of water were everywhere over the land.

He went outside and looked along the ridge. The cattle were up, beginning to move around, seeking out the sparse grass. Half a mile away he could see another slope, also dark with cattle.

Welt Spicer came out, hitching his gun belt into place. "What's up, Major?"

"We're going to move cattle," Duvarney said grimly. "When we get some chow we're going to check out that bunch yonder. If there's any Rafter K stuff there, we'll drift it north along with what we have."

"What about them?" Spicer motioned behind them.

"The Cajun's got to have treatment. If we can find that buckboard—"

"I know where it is. Come across it t'other day. Do you want I should ride up there and get it?"

Duvarney checked his watch. It was not yet five

o'clock in the morning. There were several hundred head of cattle on this ridge, and nearly as many on the other. He went to his saddlebags for his field glasses and climbed to the top of the ridge. From there, studying the terrain, he saw that, as he had suspected, there were cattle and occasionally horses on every rise within sight. Some of those must be from the scattered herds or ungathered cattle wearing the Rafter K brand.

Spicer had coffee boiling when he came back. The Cajun was lying on his back, half reclining against the wall.

"A man would think you'd been hurt," Tap said, grinning. "You mean it only took two slugs to put you down?"

"Maybe I'm gettin' weak in my old age." The Cajun's eyes searched his. "You find many cow, yes?"

"Plenty. Can you sit it out here while we round them up? Then we'll get the buckboard and you can ride in that when we drive them."

"I be all right. You go along."

Tom Kittery was on his feet. "I'm ready to ride if you are, Tap," he said quietly. "I'm beginning to think you're right. We should be in the cattle business."

"How about you?" Duvarney looked over at Lubec.

Johnny Lubec had changed none at all. "I'll handle as many cows as any of you, busted arm and all, but I'd rather stay and fight."

"Welt, you ride south with Johnny. Start all the Rafter K stock north and west. If you see trouble coming, come on back this way and we'll meet it together. But if you see Jackson Huddy, come running for me, fast."

They looked at him.

"I've staked him out," Tap said quietly. "When he killed Lon he killed a man of mine; and besides, he's the one who's out to stop us. When we get this drive started I'm going to cut out and go after him."

"Who's huntin' trouble now?" Lubec said.

"It's a safety precaution. If there was any other way I'd leave him until later. But I'm going to hunt the hunter."

"He'll kill you," Lubec said.

"Well," Tom said, "Huddy ain't never got me, and Tap here took me alive ... although," he added, grinning, "I don't believe he could do it again."

Bean worked east, and Tom Kittery with Duvarney himself rode north. By noon they had brought the cattle down off the high ground, and had then waded them and swum them until they could get them to still higher ground west and north of Horseshoe Lake.

Lawton Bean was the last man to come along. None of the cattle were in a mood to cause trouble. After the fury of the storm, they seemed to welcome the presence of men and drifted ahead of them as if they realized they were driving them to safety.

It was almost sundown before Bean came in. He was riding with his rifle across his saddle.

"Picked up some sign back yonder," he said to Tap. "I think we're goin' to have comp'ny."

"How many?"

"One man ... it's Huddy, all right, and he's ridin' his killin' horse."

When Duvarney looked his question, Bean added, "Folks down here tell me when Jackson Huddy goes huntin' he rides a blaze-face roan. Good, steady horse . . . hard one to see . . . lots of bottom, and quiet."

"That's a good horse," Kittery agreed. "I know him."

"I picked up some hairs off a tree where he'd been scratching himself." Bean looked at Duvarney. "Since the rain stopped."

"You didn't see him?"

When Bean shook his head, Kittery said, "I'll lay five to one he saw you. And that means he trailed you back here."

"Tom," Duvarney said, "I've got Belden and some of the boys holding a herd on the Guadalupe just west of Victoria. Most of them are cattle I sold to Bob Brunswick, just before the storm." He touched his shirt pocket. "I've got the check right here."

"You moved fast."

"We had to, with the storm coming, and then I moved the cattle for Brunswick. What I'm suggesting now is that you push this herd on to join those cattle."

"What about you?"

"I'm heading for Indianola. My girl's there. Also," he went on, "I want Jackson Huddy to follow me."

He had been thinking as he talked. Riding with a herd would not only make him a sitting duck, but would endanger the others. What he must do was lead Huddy down the trail, and it was a trail that Duvarney now knew pretty well himself . . . and somewhere along that trail there might be a show-down.

He already had part of his route planned. He would ride right out in plain sight, but where there was no cover for Huddy, and then when he got to where there was cover, he would ride right into it.

"You're buckin' a stacked deck," Tom said. "I think we'd best stick together."

"No, I want him to come for me."

"Don't worry," Lubec said, "he will!"

Duvarney left the herd on a bare hill with no cover for several hundred yards in either direction. He decided that he could take it for granted that Huddy was a good shot with a rifle, but he would also remember that Huddy, now at least, was not a gambler. Huddy would study his victim, stay with him until he got within easy range, then shoot him down. From all he had heard, Huddy was a one-shot killer...it was even a matter of pride with him.

That meant Duvarney must not give him that one shot until he was ready to do so.

He rode north, scouting the land and the possible routes that Huddy might take, and then he began a bit of mental warfare. Huddy would be looking for a pattern, and for a time he must not find one. Duvarney felt that first he must shake Huddy's overweening confidence in himself. He must worry him into acting as he had not planned.

For two miles he kept to open country that offered no concealment. Dropping behind a screening ridge, he wheeled his horse and raced back a quarter of a mile in the direction from which he had come, then rode down into a sandy wash. He followed it for half a mile and, climbing out of it, went to a thicket of mesquite, prickly pear, and oak. Doubling back, he scouted his earlier trail with care, finally emerging upon it.

Sure enough, another horse had been along here. He rode on across his trail without a stop, went over a low saddle, and headed back in the original direction, paralleling his old trail. Finding a long, shallow pool of muddy water, he rode into it and followed it along for a few hundred yards, then deliberately he cut across it.

A pursued man will usually emerge from a stream on the same side on which he entered; knowing this, he did the opposite. Mounting a low hill, he crossed over it and left his horse tied to a small shrub while he crept back to the crest of a ridge where there were a few scattered stones and some low brush. Lying there, he settled down to wait.

He had his back to the sun, and so could use his glasses without fear of being seen. He was lying there watching when he saw, far off, a rider approach the place where the trails crossed. He smiled, but he continued to watch, knowing he must understand this man and his thinking if he expected to remain alive.

Jackson Huddy seemed to be a man of little imagination—hard, dangerous, and tenacious, and above all a man of enormous ego, completely confident of his own ability. But always before Huddy had been the hunter, never the hunted. By now he realized that Duvarney had circled around, and knew he was being followed.

Jackson Huddy sat his horse for some time, then followed the trail. When he reached the pond he rode along the edge, then circled it until he discovered where Duvarney had emerged. When Huddy finally saw where Duvarney had left the water, he was scarcely three hundred yards off, and Duvarney took up his rifle and drew a careful bead on the dirt right in front of Huddy's horse . . . and fired.

It was muddy, and when the bullet struck it splattered mud, and Huddy's horse leaped wildly, and pitched hard until Huddy got him quieted down. Then Duvarney shot twice more; both were shots calculated to start Huddy moving.

Tap knew he should kill the man, yet it went against the grain to shoot from ambush, even though that was the policy of his enemy; moreover, he took a wicked satisfaction in putting the man in the place of his victims.

Huddy, out in the open with no cover, slapped the spurs to his mount and went away from there as if somebody had set fire to his coattails.

Tap mounted up and rode at a canter, heading back toward Indianola. Huddy, shaken, would be wary about picking up the trail, and that would give Duvarney time.

As he rode, he studied the country, and an hour later he found what he wanted—a small hollow in the hills, ideal for a nooning, which could be looked into from only one direction. On the crest of a low rise there was a small clump of brush and trees.

Taking a branch of one of the trees, he bent it down in such a way that if one wanted to look down into the hollow, the branch must be moved. Then he cut a branch, took a piggin string from his belt, and bending the branch, made a small, crude bow of it. He sharpened a stick for an arrow and set the bow in position, the arrow drawn back and ready.

If the branch was moved, the arrow would be released and might hit the hunter.

It was a crude, hastily contrived trap that Duvarney did not expect to cause any damage. All he hoped to do was to shake Huddy's confidence, to make him feel he could trust himself nowhere.

Going down into the hollow, Duvarney built a small fire; then back at the edge he gathered enough brush to make a large armful and tied another piggin string around it. Looked at from above, it would create a shadow, and might give the appearance of a man in hiding. At least Huddy would want to take time to study it.

Time was running short now, and Huddy might appear at any moment, so Tap rode away swiftly, but watched the hills around, careful to avoid any place that might offer Huddy a good field of fire.

Hours later he crossed Black Bayou and made camp in a clump of trees and brush northeast of Green Lake.

Before daylight he was up, and for half an hour he studied the country around. Then he left his camp and went back for half a mile in the direction from which he had come, circling wide around before riding for Indianola. He saw nobody, found no tracks leading toward Indianola.

He rode on, seeing on every side the havoc created by the storm—trees uprooted, buildings smashed flat, the earth a sea of mud, with water standing in the low places. Here and there he saw the bodies of dead cattle or horses.

When at last he rode up to Indianola he knew it only by the courthouse.

Where the town had stood there was now mud and sand, with scattered debris brought in by the sea, smashed boats, and the foundations of the buildings.

The town was gone ... wiped out.

People were moving around, searching for bodies or prowling among the wreckage of the saloons for unbroken bottles or whatever might be found.

Smoke was rising from the chimney of the courthouse, and when he walked inside he walked right into Bob Brunswick. "She's in there," Brunswick pointed. "We're trying to feed everybody, at least."

Duvarney explained about the cattle. "We've got a bunch together, and we're going to drive to Kansas. I figured you'd want your stock to go along. A man named Webster is throwing in with us, and we'll have a strong party and about fifteen hundred head, or more."

"Take them along. You going to Dodge?"

"Yes. I'll meet you there, or leave word if we've gone elsewhere. It doesn't look as if you'll be buying stock in Indianola for a long time."

Suddenly Jessica appeared in the door. She ran to him, caught him by the arms. "Tappan! Oh, Tappan!" was all that she could say.

"We're leaving," he said. "We're getting out of here right now. Jackson Huddy will be along, and I don't want a showdown here."

She wasted no time, but when she came back Mady Coppinger was with her. "Can Mady come?" Jessica asked.

"Sure." And then he added, "Tom's with the herd."

"I've got some saddle stock out of town," Bob said, "and you'll need horses going up the trail. Leave the bay gelding with the three white stockings for me, and take the rest along."

He stepped closer and said to Tap, "Be careful.

Every Munson is somewhere around." Then he went on, "You hear about Bill Taylor? He and some other fellow who was locked in the same jail, they stole the sheriff's horse and lit out. I don't think anybody minded too much, not even the sheriff. Bill proved himself pretty much of a man in this shindig."

By the time Tap had managed to get a couple of saddles and mounted the girls on the horses, it was well into the afternoon. He was growing more and more worried. Curiosity might take Huddy on into Indianola, but he would be on their trail soon, and he might be lying in wait for them somewhere to the west.

Tap wasted no time. He rode with his rifle across his saddle bows and he held to a good pace. They were leading six extra horses. All of them seemed glad to go, to be anywhere but around the storm area.

Nobody talked. Tap grew increasingly jumpy, and was ready at every sound. He changed direction again and again, trying to establish no pattern with his changes.

Around Chocolate Bay the scene was desolate. There had been a few cabins there, and some fishing boats. All these were gone. The shore was littered with debris.

At last, long after dark, he led them into camp in a corner of the Chocolate Bayou. It was on a bench above the stream, and taking a chance, he built a small fire. They made coffee and ate a little, and he prepared a place for the girls to sleep. As for himself, he drew back into the trees and bedded down in thick brush. He slept little.

At daybreak they were in the saddle once more.

CHAPTER 16

VICTORIA WAS PICKING up after the storm. Tappan Duvarney had no wish to ride into the town, but they needed food, and both of the girls needed clothing.

By now Jackson Huddy would have decided where he was going, and would undoubtedly be on his trail, or perhaps be in town waiting for him.

They had seen few travelers, and most of these were going in the same direction. Everybody who could move seemed to be leaving the coast.

Not even the havoc created by the storm could rob Victoria of its quaint, Old World beauty. They came into the square, Tappan Duvarney riding warily. It was a lovely place, with roses everywhere—a charming town, but it might be a deadly one for him.

He dismounted, keeping his horse between himself and the street, which he studied with careful eyes, paying attention to the roofs, the windows, the people along the street.

"You'd best go to your folks," he said to Mady, "or else get what you want and meet Jessica and we'll take you to Tom."

She hesitated a moment, obviously not liking the alternatives. "All right," she said.

When Mady had moved away, he spoke softly to Jessica. "I'm going to move the horses soon. They will be over in back of that building at the end of the street. Don't mention it to Mady, but if she's coming with us, you can meet me there in an hour."

When he left her he paused at the corner of a building, again studying the street. Then he went to a store, bought new clothes, and going out of the back door, took them to his horses, and led the horses off the street. He bought groceries and other supplies, always moving with caution.

He had gone into the restaurant when suddenly he saw Harry and Caddo, the two men he had seen with Mady in the buckboard that day beside the trail. He crossed to them. "Hello, Harry," he said.

The man turned and looked at him with careful eyes. "You have the advantage of me," Harry said.

"I am Tappan Duvarney. I know your name because you were with Miss Coppinger one day. I was close by, just off the trail."

Caddo grinned. "Now, I figured that. I really figured it," he said.

Harry held out his hand. "Heard about you," he said.

"Mady's in town. She's with my fiancée, Jessica Trescott. She may be riding out with us to join Tom—I'm not sure."

He heard someone coming up behind him and he turned slightly. It was Lin Stocker, who also rode for the Coppinger outfit. Duvarney remembered him with no liking.

"Jackson Huddy's huntin' you," Stocker said, with a hint of malice in his tone. "Looks like you won't be with us long."

"No. I'm going out with a trail drive."

"I didn't mean that, I meant—"

"Shut up, Stocker," Harry said shortly. "He knows what you mean...so do I."

Abruptly, Stocker turned and strode from the room, but when he was at the door Duvarney called after him. "Don't forget to tell them where I am, Stocker. Just don't be with them when they come hunting me."

Stocker started to speak, but he stopped, and went out.

"Most of our boys favor Tom," Harry said, "and our money is ridin' on you."

Caddo spoke suddenly, quietly. "You want help, White Man? I can use a gun."

"No...thanks. This is my fight."

Out of the corner of his eye he had seen Stocker start diagonally across the street. He went to the window and, standing well back, watched him cross the street and go into a saloon. In a moment he came out and started on up the street.

"If you boys will excuse me?" Tap said, and stepped out of the door.

He watched Stocker until he disappeared into another saloon farther up the street, and then he came back inside the restaurant. Harry and Caddo had gone, but he found a table in a corner where he could watch the street, and ordered a meal.

It was only a few minutes later that he saw Caddo ride swiftly out of town.

"Do you mind if I join you?"

He had been so intent on watching the street that he had not noticed Jessica approaching his table.

"Mady will be along soon." She sat down in the

chair he held for her, and when he was seated she asked, "Is there going to be trouble?"

"Yes."

"You would rather I was out of the way, wouldn't you?"

"Of course, but they'll wait until I come out on the street. They know where I am sitting by now, and there is no way they can come in here without exposing themselves. And you're here. So they will wait until I come outside, and I'm going to let them wait."

She searched his face. "You aren't afraid?"

He shrugged. "I expect I am, a little. Fear sets a man up sometimes for what he has to face. A little fear does no harm, just so it doesn't put a man on the run."

A man was walking across the square, a big, narrow-shouldered man with wide hips. It was Shabbit, and he was carrying a slicker wrapped around something...probably a rifle or a shotgun. Considering the man, it was probably the latter. He stopped on a corner just across the street that left the square alongside the restaurant. From there he could cover the door easily.

Up the street another man with the Munson look about him was leaning on a wagon wheel, smoking a cigarette.

Following his eyes, Jessica said, "You could go out the back door."

"They will have men out there, too," he said lightly.

They ate, talking only a little. He enjoyed sitting there, making them wait in the hot sun.

Suddenly the door opened and Ev Munson came

in. Shabbit was with him, and another man. It was Lin Stocker.

"You comin' out?" Ev asked him. "I'm gettin' kinda tired waitin'."

"You...or that army it's going to take to help you?"

Ev's features flushed with anger. "I don't need no help. I never saw the day I couldn't take you, an' three like you."

Duvarney looked up at him, smiling a little. "All right, Munson, let's just talk about me. Do you want to take me? Out in the street right now?" He glanced at the others. "I mean without this carrion to help."

Stocker started to step forward, but Ev waved him back. "Sure," he taunted, "if you can get out from behind those skirts, I'll meet you outside, right now!"

Tap Duvarney got up. "Will you excuse me, Jessica?" Deliberately he raised his voice so that the three men striding to the door could hear him. "This won't take long." Under his breath he added, "Get back in the office, out of range."

He loosened his gun in its holster. He had not really thought much about a fast draw since the time he cleaned up that tough town out west, when he was sent by the army to do it, as the marshal's deputy.

He walked to the door, keeping to one side. Every Munson was out there, waiting. He had an idea Ev would hold the others off so he could make the kill himself. At the same time he knew that if he killed Every Munson they would shoot him down where he stood...unless he moved very quickly indeed.

Tap reached over with his left hand and turned the knob, releasing the bolt, but leaving the door almost closed. He took a short step forward, put his left hand on the door, slamming it open suddenly.

He knew what would happen. At the sudden slamming of the door Ev Munson's hair-trigger nerves would react and he would draw, and that was just what happened.

The startling slam of the opening door triggered Ev Munson's gun hand and it swept down for the six-shooter. Tap took one long step through the door and drew at the same instant. His gun muzzle came up, he saw the reckless, black-clad young man with the wolfish smile, and he fired.

The wolfish smile vanished in a sudden blotching of blood, and Tap shot again, holding the gun lower, and saw Ev Munson stagger one hesitating step forward and go on his face.

At the same instant, he switched his gun and shot at Lin Stocker, who was a few yards to the right. He shot too fast, and the bullet hit Stocker in the knee and he pitched over, losing his grip on his gun.

Tap quickly stepped back inside, jerking the door to, and wheeling, he raced up the steps. In his mind he had rehearsed every move that was to follow, and he performed them smoothly now. As he reached the top of the steps he took three long strides down the hall, grasping a chair as he left the landing, and putting it down under the trapdoor that led to the roof.

He stepped up on the chair, jumped, and grabbed the edge of the opening. Holding himself with one hand, he pushed back the trap, then hoisted himself through.

He took a quick step, and was under the trap to the roof itself. He released the latch, pushed open the door, and after a quick look pulled himself through to the slanting roof, where he was hidden from the street by the false front of the building. He ran along the roof, jumped to the flat roof of the next building, and went quickly to the front of it.

The man at the wagon whom he had seen earlier was standing there holding a pistol; a few feet away, Shabbit held a shotgun. Both were waiting for him to show himself. He took a careful sight along the barrel of the Smith & Wesson and shot the man by the wagon through the shoulder. He dropped the rifle and whipped sharply around.

Running to the rear of the building. Tap leaped to the roof below, then dropped into the space between the buildings. There was a door there, and he ducked through it just as a bullet smashed into the door jamb, inches from his head, stinging his face with splinters.

Instead of going out the front door, he ran across, seeing a window open, and leaped through it into the alley beyond.

At that moment there was a sudden burst of firing in the street, and he paused, gasping for breath, and puzzled. Suddenly he saw Shabbit running, and he ducked into the same narrow alley in which Duvarney stood. There was blood on Shabbit's shoulder and his face was white and frightened. He started to run, then brought up short. His shotgun started to lift, and Tap Duvarney shot him through the second button of his shirt, shot twice.

Surprised at the shooting from the street, he started back that way, picking up the shotgun as he stepped around Shabbit. At the opening into the square, he paused, looking out.

The shooting ceased.

On the far side of the square a tall man was sitting quietly in his saddle; nearer by he saw another. Other riders were coming along both sides of the square, their guns ready. Doc Belden . . . Lawton Bean . . . Welt Spicer . . . they were all there.

He stepped out, and half a dozen guns swung to cover him until they saw who he was.

"You know somethin', Major?" Lawton Bean said, grinning at him. "Those boys weren't much on the fight. I was some surprised. Figured they'd hold up better. Why, this here shindig hardly got started until they all taken out runnin' . . . all that was able."

Doc rode up. "Are you all right?" he asked.

Tom Kittery came walking across the square. "You tryin' to hog all the fun? I almost missed out on the endin' of my own feud!"

Tappan Duvarney looked around carefully. "All right, boys," he said. "We've got some cattle waiting. Shall we get back to them?"

———

IN HIS ROOM on the second floor of the hotel Jackson Huddy held his rifle easily in his hands and looked down into the square. He could see Duvarney's shoulder . . . just a *little* more now, and . . .

"Mr. Huddy?"

He turned sharply. Jessica Trescott was standing within ten feet of him and she was holding a very steady Colt House Pistol aimed at his stomach. "Mr. Huddy, I would take it kindly if you would just put that rifle down, then unbuckle your gun belt, very carefully."

"I never shot a woman," Huddy said. "I never would."

"The reverse is not true, Mr. Huddy. This woman has never shot a man, but believe me, she certainly would. Also, I am somewhat nervous, and if I start shooting it is likely I will empty this gun into you.

"You see, Mr. Huddy, I came west to marry Mr. Duvarney. I came out here because I love him and I want to bear children for him and to live out my life with him, so if you think I am going to let a man like you come between us with a bullet, you are wrong. I will kill you, Mr. Huddy, if you do not come away from that window, get on your horse, and ride right out of our lives.

"Mady Coppinger told me you came from Alabama, Mr. Huddy. The only city in Alabama that I know is Mobile. It is very lovely at this time of year. Would you go now . . . please?"

He looked at her, and then he looked at the gun. The hand that moved was only to lift his hat. "Your pleasure, ma'am," he said, and walked from the room and down the back hall.

She followed and stood by the door, watching him ride away, sitting very straight in the saddle.

Tom Kittery stood with Tappan when she reached the street. "Mady is here," she said.

"I saw her," Tom said. "I . . . I borrowed money and loaned it to her. She's gone off to N'Orleans. I reckon I'll find somebody else, somewhere on up the trail."

"You will, Tom. I'm sure of it." Jessica turned to

look up at Tap. "Come on, Tappan. Those cattle are waiting."

"And we'd better find a sky pilot," Tap commented. "We might as well make it legal while we're at it."

"Yes, that, too," she said.

"You're forgettin' somethin', Major," Spicer said. "What about Jackson Huddy?"

"Oh, don't worry about him," Jessica said. "We had a talk and he decided to go back to Alabama. If you doubt it, look in the room up over the door. You'll find his rifle and pistol there."

Tappan Duvarney looked at her quizzically. "You know, Jessica, that's a story I would really like to hear."

"I'll tell you...sometime." She reached in her purse and took out the Colt. "Tappan, would you carry this for me ? It is getting very heavy."

THE FIRST
FAST DRAW

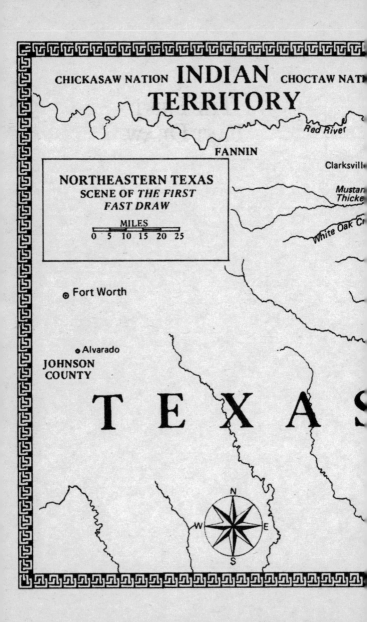

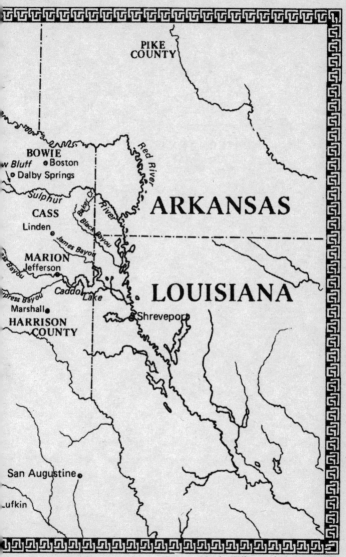

PIKE
COUNTY

ARKANSAS

LOUISIANA

BOWIE
w Bluff   Boston
Dalby Springs

Sulphur

CASS
Linden

MARION
Jefferson

Red River

Baker CJ River

Black Bayou

James Bayou

Bayou

press Bayou   Caddo   Lake

Marshall

HARRISON
COUNTY

Shreveport

San Augustine

ufkin

Map by William and Alan McKnight

CHAPTER 1

WHEN THE SHELTER was finished, thatched heavy with pine boughs, I went inside and built myself a hatful of fire. It was a cold, wet, miserable time, and nowhere around any roof for me, although here I was, back in my own country.

Hungry I was, and soaked to the hide from a fall my mule had taken in the swamp, but I kept my fire small, for I'd come home by the back trails, figuring to attract no notice until I could look around and take stock.

They'd given me nothing here in the old days, and I'd given them a sight less, and the only memory they would have of me would be one of violence and anger. Yet hereabouts was all I had ever known of home, or was likely to know.

The woods dripped with rain. Sometimes a big drop would fall from the thatch overhead and hiss in the fire, but other than that and the soft fall of rain in the twilight forest, there was no sound. Not at first.

When a sound did come it was faint. But it was not a sound of the forest, nor of the rain, nor of any wild animal or bird, for these were sounds I knew and had known since childhood.

It was a rider coming, maybe two, and nobody I wanted to see, but that was why I'd put together my lean-to back over the knoll and hid down deep among the rain-wet trees.

This was a rider coming and I could only hope the rain had left no trail they could find, for if trouble was to come to me here, I wanted it to wait, at least until I had walked the old path to the well again, and seen where Pa was buried.

Standing there like that with the rain dripping down, me in my shabby homespun, wore-out clothes, I tried to figure if there was anybody hereabouts beyond a few Caddos whom I could call friend. I couldn't think of anybody.

For a long time then there was no other sound but the rain, a whisper of rain falling among the leaves, and a far-off stirring of wind. And then I heard that sound again.

Behind me the raw-boned mule lifted his head and pricked his ears against the sound, so it wasn't only me heard the sound. No matter, the buckskin mule was ga'nted some and it would be a few days of rest he'd need before I could move on anyway, and maybe I just wasn't feeling right to move at all. Maybe I had come home to stay . . . whether they liked it or not.

Rising, I could just see across the top of the knoll in the forest, and the place I'd chosen to camp commanded a view of the trail at intervals along its course through the swamp woods.

When at last they came in sight there were two riders and they rode as tired men ride, and there was that about them that was somehow familiar. Maybe it was only that they were mighty near as shabby as me, unkempt and lonely as me.

Two riders walking their horses, two riders hunting something. That something could be me.

My Spencer carbine was behind me and so I reached a hand back for it and pulled it close against my side for shelter from the rain. It was a new Spencer, caliber .56 and she carried seven shots—I'd picked it off a dead man up in the Nation. A brand-new, spanking-new, mighty slick piece of shooting iron.

Right there I stood with no notion of moving. Place I stood was a hidden place where a body might pass within six feet and never see it was there. Man like me, in unfriendly country, he can't be too careful. These past years I had seen almost nothing but unfriendly country. Maybe it was my own fault, for I was a man rode careful and who kept a gun to hand.

When I saw them first through the farthest gap in the trees, I'd seen nothing but a couple of men hunched in their saddles, one wearing a ragged poncho, the other a gray Confederate greatcoat.

A moment only, a glimpse, and then they were gone from sight among the trees that lined the trail below, but at the nearest point they would be no more than thirty yards away. So I waited where I was, trusting not to be seen, but keeping the Spencer to hand in case of trouble.

This was a place I knew, an arm of the swamp to protect my right flank, an almost impassable thicket of brush on my left, and the main swamp close in behind me. There was a trail came from the swamp into the trees behind me, but anyone using that trail was likely to be a Caddo or someone as averse to trouble as myself.

The brush on my left could be got through, no question of that, but not without a sight more noise than anybody was likely to make, coming easy to a strange camp.

The people of this northeast corner of Texas had not liked me before, and with times what they were they had no reason to be friendly. The War between the States was just over a few days past, and it was a wary time for strangers.

In the old days when a boy I'd taken nothing from them, nor given them anything they could lay hold on, they disliked me from the start because I wouldn't knuckle under to the town boys, and I'd met dislike with dislike, anger with anger, fist with fist. Despite the war that intervened they would not have forgotten.

Yet it was to this land that I'd come home, for it was as much of a home as I could claim, and despite the hard ways of the people toward me, it was a land I loved. From the deep silences of the forgotten swamp lagoons to the stillness of the fields at evening with the mist of night laying low along the fences, it was a place that belonged to me. There was a feel of things growing here, of a rich, dark soil bursting with eagerness to grow beneath my feet.

Those riders came along...there was something seemed familiar about them, but this corner of Texas had been a bloody country filled with black angers and feuding families, and now to the old hatreds there would be added the feeling left by the war just now ended. It was no country for a man to step out and go hailing strangers—least of all for me.

My tiny fire was over the top of the knoll from them and behind a great dead log, the side of the log serving as a reflector to throw heat back into the lean-to. It was snug and tight, and should have been, for I'd lived most of my life like this, and it was most two years since I'd slept beneath a roof of any decent kind. What little smoke the fire gave off lost itself among the leaves overhead, yet a knowing man with a keen nose might catch a whiff if the wind was right.

They drew up in the trail below, in plain sight and an easy shot for my rifle, and they talked there, and one of their voices had an old, familiar ring. So I stepped out of my shelter and strolled down the slope of the knoll toward them, walking soft on the dead wet leaves underfoot. The carbine was in my right hand and in my belt was a Dragoon Colt, within easy grasping.

"Bob Lee," I said aloud, and no louder than needed.

They turned sharp around, but it was to the more slender of the two whom I spoke. He looked at me, measuring me, then making up his mind.

What he was seeing wasn't much. A battered black slouch hat, a shabby buckskin jacket, squaw-made by a Ute west of the big mountains, with cabin-spun shirt and pants, mighty worn. My boots were Army issue, and the man in them a lean, dark young man standing two inches more than six feet in his socks, and weighing nigh two hundred pounds, but with the face of a man who had known much trouble and little of softness or loving—the face of a man born to struggle and the hard ways.

"Cullen, is it? Damn it, man, it's been years!"

"Three."

"I'd have guessed it longer. Bill Longley, meet

Cullen Baker, such a man as we need right now in this country."

"I'll take no man's word for that," I said. "They'd no use for me before."

"You were a hard lad, Cullen. And once the trouble began you believed we were all against you, all over the five counties."

"Coffee yonder." I turned away, walking back up the knoll not wanting them to see how it moved me, the friendly way of them to a man just back in his own country, but where he'd expected nothing.

Bob Lee was a gentleman, a man of some book learning, a thin-faced man, and proud. He came of a family known in the South and respected, and the temper he had along with his skill with weapons and readiness to use them won him another kind of respect from another kind of man. Yet whatever anybody said of Bob Lee, nobody said anything except that he was an honorable man.

Bill Longley? He was eighteen then, a tall, raw-boned young man who in his time was to be known as one of the most feared of Texas pistol fighters, but that time was yet to come, and I'd only heard his name first up in the Nation, and I could not remember what had been said of him.

Hunkered down beside the fire, I stirred the coals and got out my cup. Each of them dug a blackened cup from among his gear and we shared the coffee in my beat-up old pot. Long ago Pa taught me to share what I had with guests if it was the last I had, although few had done the same for me.

"You're returning at a black time, Cullen. The Reconstruction people are in, confiscating property and raising hob generally with anyone who fought for the South. If they've not taken your place already, they'll be after it."

"They will buy trouble, then."

"Trouble is what they want, I'm afraid. They have the Army here, and more of it coming, and they've friends from about here to tell them the choice land."

"You've got to jump to their tune or you'll have to fight," Longley said.

"I've had enough of fighting," I replied. "I want no more of trouble from any man."

"Your wishes won't chop much cotton, Cullen. If you have what they want, they'll take it. And if you don't accept their rule with a tight mouth, you'll have trouble." Bob Lee glanced at me. "It has come to me already."

Rain fell among the leaves, and I'd a sorrow on me, and a deepening fury, too. Could a man not be left alone? There had been small chance in the old days for me to be anything but a bad one, although the Good Lord knows I'd wasted little time waiting for the invitation. When they came to me with trouble in those years, I was out there to meet them halfway.

A boy can be that way, but I was a man grown now, with a man's hard judgment, and some long miles behind me of riding with a gun for companion, through bitter, lonely days and more miles than I rightly could remember.

There was deep within me a love of the land, of a rich soil and what a man could grow, and over all those dry miles in the West I'd thought of the greens and beauties of this corner of Texas. I was back wanting no troubles left over from a war I'd never fought, nor had sympathy for, on either side.

Longley brought fuel to the fire and went off into the dark to strip the gear from the two horses and bring it under the shelter. Under the branches of the huge cypress where I'd picketed my mule there was room enough for a dozen horses, and mighty little rain came through the thick tangle of Spanish moss, leaves and branches. The horses would be dry enough.

The coffee smelled good, and the sound of rain was friendly now. Sitting there smelling the coffee I got to thinking how strange it was that Bob Lee, of all folks, should be a friend of mine. Not that we'd ever been close, only from the first he'd seemed to understand me. Maybe it was because we'd both had our fighting troubles.

Only he had education. His folks had wealth, and many friends. Time to time I'd heard talk of him during the War—he'd become a colonel, and a good officer. Now that he was home I could see it would not be easy for him with his fine pride, and even less easy for me.

Folks would not have forgotten Cullen Baker. They would remember, and that was handicap enough without trouble shaping up with Reconstruction soldiers and carpetbaggers. The ones from Texas could be the worst, poor whites and such; now they had their chance to strut and talk up, they'd use it.

All the way home I'd seen them coming like locusts into a cornfield, the poor kind of men quick to jump on the band wagon once they'd heard the music and knew which way the parade was going. In every community there are those quick to take advantage, just as there are those who have no loyalty except to their property and their skin's safety.

Sitting there, huddled over our small fire, we yarned the hours away, with Bob Lee telling about the war and the State of Texas, and what had happened and what he figured was going to happen. None of it shaped up as likely for a man named Cullen Baker, who'd be caught fair in the middle.

I'd no family awaiting me. Ma died long ago when I was a youngster, and Pa died while I was gone west. Nobody cared whether I came or went, but here I owned property, and here I aimed to stay, to raise me a crop, and to try to make something of myself.

This time I'd try to make it different than when we first came down from Tennessee. Maybe I could have avoided the first trouble, but I was a youngster then, and too proud. A really tough man never has to prove anything to anybody, he knows what he can do and he doesn't care even a mite whether anybody else knows or not. With a youngster it's otherwise. He figures he's got to show everybody how tough he is or nobody will believe it, so he winds up in plenty of grief.

When the Civil War broke out I was west of the Rockies. When most folks got worked up about it the whole shebang seemed far away and mighty unreasonable to me, and I couldn't get wrought up. Never being sure which side was right I lost no sleep over it, and out there in Utah it seemed far away. When I did come east it seemed that being from the South I should join up, and Quantrill being the nearest to me, I joined his outfit.

From the first I didn't shape up with that crowd. They were a lot of murdering, drunken thieves, burning down farms or attacking unarmed folks—didn't seem right to me. I had come east to fight a war, not to rape farm women and burn barns. Right after the first shindig I decided I'd bought myself a ticket on the wrong train.

Cap'n Weaver—he was my boss with that outfit— was a thick-set man with a rust-red beard and a blustering loudmouthed way about him. He shaped up like a man who was all noise and bluster, and no kind of man in a scrap. He had with him a kid horse thief they called Dingus who had a Bible-toting brother. I liked none of them.

Morning after that fight I rode up to Weaver. "I don't like this outfit. I'm riding out."

He set there staring at me and those two brothers they set there, and then Weaver says, "You can't go nowhere thout permission, an' permission you ain't about to git."

"Ain't asked for it. I'm just a-leaving. I don't cotton to the way you do things in this outfit, destroying crops, burning up farms, and attacking womenfolks. I worked to raise a few crops myself and I won't have no part of such carryin' on."

Well, sir, his face was a sight. Behind those dirty whiskers he began to swell up and flush up red like a country girl caught in the back of a farm wagon with a boy. There for a minute I thought he'd bust a gut. Then he spoke up real big. "You got two minutes to git where you b'long or you'll be court-martialed for refusin' duty."

Most accidental-like my carbine was lyin' across

my saddle and pointed right at his heart, and my hand was right over the trigger guard. But I wasn't leaving those brothers out of my sight, either. "You better get on with whatever you've a might to do," I told him, "or I won't be around to see the fun."

Weaver, he made a start for a gun but the *click* of that cocking Spencer stopped him. I never did figure him to have belly enough to stand up to a man. "Now you looka here!" he began to loud-mouth it. "You cain't—"

"I already have," I told him, and rode out of camp.

Of course, once I had the camp behind me I lit out of there like who flung the chunk, and when I was well down the trail I lost my tracks in those of the night before, and then cut off across the country.

That was miles ago and weeks ago, and now I was back, almost within hollering distance of the home where I was brought up, the only one I could rightly recall.

Not that it had ever mattered to anybody but me. Those days I was a lonely youngster, shabbier than anybody else and too proud to try to make friends after that first trouble. That was why I started going to the swamp. When a man has no friends he makes up for it sometimes by learning a lot, and I learned a-plenty in those Sulphur River bottoms, and knew all that country away down to Caddo Lake. I knew places even the Caddo Indians didn't know.

Those days I wandered the swamp trails, hunted and trapped for fur, and I knew where the solid ground was, and the passages a man could go through in a dugout canoe, and the hide-outs of the Indians and a few runaway slaves.

Now I was back. The farm would be there; most folks called it a ranch. There would still be the orchard and the cabin would be standing, and there was land belonging to me that stretched away down to the Big Thicket. Only those days land was not worth much, and everybody had a-plenty of it.

Lying awake staring up into the dark where the rain dripped from the cypress trees, it felt good to be back home. There was nobody anywhere who cared whether I came or went, but I knew the soil, and I knew what I could do with it, given a chance. And I'd been as homeless as a worn-out saddle pony for so long.

My plans were clear and proud. First off I'd break ground and put in a crop, and once I'd earned some cash from selling my crop I'd buy a brood mare and start raising blooded horses. Maybe a man could find a stallion with good lines; there was money to be made with a well-bred stallion.

As a boy in those East Texas swamps and thickets I'd almost never seen anything like a really good horse. Of course, there were some good horses around, but not much of it ever came my way and the horses folks up there had were a rugged bunch, tough stock, and good for working cattle in the brush, but I wanted some horses.

Time had been, right after I took off from home, I'd gone north through Virginia and Kentucky. Talk about horses.

Most of the breeders in the South had been put out of business by the war, so a man with a good stallion, good mares and pasture, a man set up like that could do all right.

Boylike, I'd figured to be rich some time. Every boy at one time or another wants to be rich. He wants to strut it around and make smart with the best clothes and have the girls look him over. He figures with enough money showing the girls will all get round heels when he comes around.

One thing I'd learned was it mattered mighty little how much money a man had as long as he was contented. Me, I wanted enough to eat, my own roof to sleep under, and my own place with crops and horses growing.

Some time maybe I'd find me a woman. Not in this country. I'd go away for that. Hereabouts the name of Cullen Baker was a bad name and nobody was likely to want me.

There would be trouble enough, but trouble begins with people and I would stay shut of them. None of them had any use for me, anyway, and that would make it a simple thing. Run down the way the place was sure to be, I'd have my work cut out for me without traipsing off to town, tomcatting around and maybe getting my tail in a crack.

Longley got up quietly when I figured he was asleep, and rustled an armful of dry wood. If a man can find dry wood after three days of rain he's a man to ride the river with.

Bob Lee turned over and sat up, reaching for his pipe.

Longley squatted over the fire. "Seems quiet," he said. "Bob, you reckon them carpetbaggers from up the state at Boston will come into the swamps hunting us?"

"Not unless they're crazier'n they look." Bob Lee

turned to me. "You awake, Cullen? We should have explained it to you. We had a difficulty up to Boston. Shot a man."

"Needed it, I reckon. You always were a proud man, Bob Lee, but I never knew you to shoot too quick nor to kill a man who wasn't asking for it."

We talked it over some, and they told me more about the country I'd come back to, and none of it looked very good for my plans. There was one thing they forgot to tell me, but I learned it soon enough: my worst enemy was back there, and he was a big man around the country. He was a Southern man but he was thick with carpetbaggers. I would never have believed it of him.

Some time about then we all went to sleep. Bob Lee was right. Any carpetbagger who followed them into the swamps would be crazy. Both men were tired, like men are who have spent sleepless nights of running and riding, and if a man like Bob Lee could be on the dodge, with folks everywhere around, how could I hope to stick it out?

Nobody talked much when we saddled up come daylight. I told them about the trail into the Sulphur Swamps. Unless you know it, I'll tell you. That Sulphur is a might twisty stream, and there's bayous running off from it and a good bit of swamp, and those days the thickets were bigger and came closer to the Sulphur. Only a little way south was Lake Caddo, and nobody knew much about the lake but the Caddos and me.

We parted company at the Corners. "Better come with us, Cull," Bob Lee advised. "You won't find anything but trouble and knowing you like I think I do, you won't stand still for it."

"I'm a man wants to sleep under his own roof."

"You fight shy of that widow woman. She'll make you more trouble than all them Union soldiers!" Longley said, grinning.

When they had dusted out of sight I turned that buckskin mule down the grass-grown lane. This was a mighty good mule and he could run the legs off most horses. Maybe he wasn't so fast for a sprint but he could hold a pace that would kill most horses, and better than any watchdog at night.

Longley mentioned a widow. With the war over this country must be crowded with widows. Far as that went, this here was a widow-making country, and leave out the war.

No decent woman would be wanting to have any truck with me, and if one did it would surely come to a shooting matter with a father or brother. Cullen Baker was a known man, a trouble-hunter they used to say, and a man with a drive to kill, others said. They said, too, I was drunken, but I could give them the lie on that story. I'd little taste for strong drink, and when they thought me drunk it was only with fury.

Besides, there'd be no time for widows. It would take all my time to get a crop in, to work and even get my seed back; by now the whole ranch might have grown up to crab grass.

Drawing my Dragoon Colt I checked the loads— paid a man to be ready, although I was hoping never to use a gun again, except for wild game. Still, I've noticed a ready man is often left alone, and if it took that to have peace, then I should be ready, but it took no doing for me. I'd the habits of a lifetime behind me.

Right there in a secret pocket back of my belt there was the margin, a .41-caliber twin-barreled derringer which I carried for insurance. It was my margin of safety. Time was, a hide-out gun had been useful, and such a time might again come to me. Could be I'd never use either gun again, but I was no man to draw my teeth before I knew what the beef was like.

Turning the corner of the back lane along which I'd come, I drew up before the gate.

There it was, then.

Three years I'd waited to look upon it again, and the three years seemed like ten, or even fifteen. It seemed another lifetime, another world than this, and yet I was back. All was the same and yet nothing at all was the same.

The yard, which had been hard-packed earth there at the back of the house, had grown up to weeds and grass. The house itself looked older than it was, weather-beaten, blistered, baked and warped by sun and rain.

The sun, the rain, the wind let nothing alone, but they worry at it, smooth it and rough it again until it is their own. I was like that, myself. A man shaped by storms and hot suns, but most of all by the thousand storms I kept buried inside, all of them crowding at my lips and eyes for expression, working their way down into my quiet fingers, feeding anger through my veins that I'd had to fight back, again and again.

For what they said of me was true. I was a killing man, a man of frightful rages that all my life I'd had to keep back inside me. Once in a while when something would go against me, I'd tear loose and it frightened me, for I had no grudge against any man, nor did I know what it meant to hate. To be wary, yes, for I knew there were hating folks about, but for myself, I hated no man. Only there was a point beyond which I'd not be pushed, and when beyond that point the fury came up in me, cold, dangerous and mighty.

Swinging down from the saddle I opened the gate, taking my time, almost scared to go in, for opening that gate was opening the memories I'd fought back for a long while now.

It seemed any minute Ma was going to open the door and call me for supper, or Pa would come, holding out his hand to greet me. Only they weren't going to come out, and nobody at all was coming to that door, which had remained unopened these two years now.

Leading the mule through the gate I dropped the bridle reins and walked slowly forward, and in my throat there was a lump.

Nobody was there. The kitchen door hung on old strap hinges, dried and shrunk from the neat fit Pa had given it when he built the place with his own hands, me helping as much as I could. A boy then I'd known little of the slights a man learns by working with his hands, and all I'd had to help was a strong back and arms for lifting.

The boards on the stoop were warped and gray, and brown leaves had gathered in the corner between the stoop and the house. Only the iris still grew along the path where Ma had planted it, and the redbud tree Pa and me dug up from the river's edge was well-grown now and making like a tree more than a shrub like they usually are. These things can last, I think, the trees a man plants and the wells he digs... I do not know if the buildings last.

The door opened stiffly under my hand, and when I went through the door there were tears down my cheeks like I was a pigtailed girl.

Empty, the way it was, it looked like I'd never seen it. Everything a body could carry off had been toted away except the big copper kettle near the fireplace which was unhandy to load on a horse. The rooms were empty and here and there the chunking had fallen from between the logs in the log part of the house which we had built first. Later, Pa started to build the rest of it with planks, and he was fixing to give Ma a real home at last. He never done it though, and hard work caught up with Ma first; she'd never been real strong.

She was buried out there back of the orchard, where they'd put Pa...somebody told me that; I'd not been here myself.

An owl had been roosting in the kitchen and left his sign around the way an owl does. A body would think there was fifty of them rather than one. There was dust over everything, and when Ma had lived there never was dust. She never had much to do with, but she made out, and that place had been spic and span like I'd never seen another place. It had been a home blessed by care if not by money.

At the fireplace I could see where night-stoppers had left the remains of their meal—only the mice had been at it.

Outside again, not liking the hollow sound of my

feet on the board floors, I saw the weeds had grown up among the roses, and I could see there would be a sight of work to keep me busy.

"Well Pa," I said aloud, "what you wished it to be, that's what I'll make it."

When I went outside once more that old buckskin mule was cropping grass like it was the day before Judgment. Seeing he liked it so much, I picketed him there, and then took my Spencer and strolled down toward the swamp.

Ever go back to a place and walk down the paths you walked as a boy? The old paths, the unforgotten paths? The sun was hot on the green leaves and grass, the path was overgrown, and the blackberries had straggled over it and were choked with grass ... many a time I snagged myself on those briars, and tore my shirt, too. The biggest, blackest and juiciest berries always seemed to hang in the places hardest to get at.

Every step was a memory for me, and time to time I'd just stop and stand there, remembering. The mist used to rise off these swamps sometimes in the mornings. The tops of trees in the low ground would be like islands lost in a vast sea of cloud. Here was where the deer used to come to eat the green grass and get into Pa's corn—many a time I got me a deer down at the end of the cornfield.

It was warm and lazy in the sun and a big bumblebee buzzed fatly among the leaves. Folks are always talking about how busy a bee is, shows they never really watched a bee. A bee makes so much fuss with all his perambulating around that folks think they're doing a sight of work, but believe me, I've watched bees by the hour and I can tell you all that buzzing is a big fraud. The bees I've watched always buzzed in the sunniest places around the best-smelling flowers, just loafing their heads off fusting around in the play of sun and shadow at the swamp's edge. Busy? Not so's you could notice.

Used to be deer along the swamp edge but tonight my luck was played out, so I contented myself with a duck who got up lazy from the water, the dark, dark water among the lily pads. The Spencer took his head off just as he was clearing water so when I started back toward the place I had my supper. And then I heard voices and knew it was the sound of trouble.

Three mounted men at their horses in the yard, sizing up my mule. There was a tall man astride a mighty handsome bay gelding, and the next man was Joel Reese about whom I could remember nothing good, and the third man was a fellow with a face to remember—if a man was smart.

"Whose mule is that?" The man on the bay gelding was talking. There was authority in his voice, but my first impression was he was an empty man, impressed overmuch with himself, but knowing all the time there was nothing inside him. "You told me the place was deserted, Reese."

"Some rider-by or all-nighter," Reese explained. "The place has been abandoned for years and sometimes folks stop the night when passing through."

Looked to me like this was my time to talk up, for they had not seen me yet. "The place isn't abandoned and it is not for sale," I said. "I'll be living here myself."

They turned sharp around to look at me, and Joel Reese grinned at me, with a mean glint in his little eyes. "Colonel, this is that Cullen Baker I told you about."

The colonel had a cold eye, and there was nothing pleasant in his eyes when he looked at me, but I'd looked into eyes over a gun barrel that were colder than these.

It was that third man who was holding my attention. The colonel was no fighting man and Reese would only fight if he had an edge, a big edge. But the other man was a different kettle of fish. That third man was a full-fledged red-in-the-comb fighting man who had grown his own spurs. I knew the type.

"Seems I should know you." I looked directly at him for the first time.

"The name is John Tower. I've come into the country since you left."

"Were you ever west of the Rockies?"

Tower's eyes became suddenly alive. "Could be," he said. "A man gets around."

The colonel interrupted. "Baker, you fought with the Confederacy. You are known hereabouts as a troublemaker. We will have no trouble from you, do you hear? The slightest evidence of trouble from you, or interference with the Reconstruction program, and you'll go to jail. Also, we're going to take steps to confiscate this land from you as an enemy of your country."

"You'd better look at your hole card, Colonel. There's no record of me fighting on any side. I've been out West the whole time. Only fighting I've done was with Comanches, Utes and such like."

"What's that?" The colonel turned on Reese, his

face growing red. The colonel was a man quick to anger. "Reese, is this true?"

Reese was worried. "Colonel Belser, sir, I just know he fit for the South! Why, why, there just ain't no other way he could fight!"

"Joel Reese," I explained, "was always a yellow dog. He should be right ashamed to mislead you this way. If he knows anything at all he should know that I spent the war in New Mexico and Utah. Shortly after the war broke out I drove a herd of cattle east and sold them, and then three years ago I went back West.

"Reese hates folks around here because they'd no use for him. My advice would be to go easy on anything he may tell you. He'd be like to cause you trouble, getting even with folks he figured treated him wrong."

"I need no suggestions from you!" Colonel Belser was furious. He jerked his bay around...no way to treat a horse as good as that one, or any other horse, for that matter. "The records will be checked as to your service with the Confederacy. You will hear from me again."

"I'll be right here," I told him. "I'll be growing corn."

Tower lingered as the others started off. "You were in New Mexico and Utah? And California?"

"I had a horse liked to travel."

"Have we crossed trails before this?"

"I cut a lot of sign in my time," I told him, "and once I've seen the tracks a man leaves, I don't forget."

"You mean that if you'd ever cut my trail you'd remember? Is that it?"

"I'd remember."

John Tower touched a spur to his mount and rode away after the others, and of them all he was the only one who might be dangerous in the way a man was dangerous. Yet he would come at a man, face up to him, and those others would not. It was not until they were out of sight that I turned and saw the girl under the dogwood tree.

It is a nice place to see a girl for the first time, and it had been a long, long time since I had seen such a girl. For girls of her type do not come to the Cullen Bakers of this world, for I was a rough man, grown used to rough ways, and I had no fine graces to use in meeting such a girl.

She was taller than most girls, with dark hair and a fair skin, and she stood very still with one uplifted hand upon a dogwood branch. She wore a white dress, and she was young, but there was in her eyes none of the guilelessness of the child. Beautiful, she was. Beautiful and graceful as the dogwood beside which she stood, a dogwood covered with white blossoms, some of them fallen to the grass at her feet.

"Did I surprise you?"

"You weren't expected, if that is what you mean."

"I am Katy Thorne, of Blackthorne."

There was no reason for me to love the Thornes, or even to think of them, for my only friend among them had been Will, and Will had been the strange one among the Thornes, whether those of Blackthorne or the others. His cousin Chance had been my worst enemy. And I remembered no Katy Thorne.

"You related to Chance?"

"I was his brother's wife."

"Was?"

"He tried to be a soldier and charged very gallantly with Pickett, at Gettysburg. Were you a soldier, Mr. Baker?"

"No." Maybe there was bitterness in the tone. "I have been nothing that mattered, Mrs. Thorne. I have never been anything but Cullen Baker."

"Isn't it important to be Cullen Baker?"

"Maybe, in the wrong way. Maybe"—why I said it I'll not know—"maybe I can make it mean something to be me. But hereabouts folks have little use for me, and I've less use for them."

"I know. I saw it begin, Cullen Baker, I was there at the mill the day you gave Chance Thorne a hiding."

"You were *there*?" I was astonished.

"Sitting in the surrey with my father and Will Thorne. I thought Chance deserved everything he got."

It was one day I'd not forget, for I'd come as a stranger with a sack of grain to the mill for grinding. We'd been down from Tennessee only a few days, and I'd not been off the place. Soon as I showed up Chance started on me, and the boys around followed his lead. He started making fun of my shabby homespun clothes. They were patched and they were worn, but they were all I had. They had shouted at me and laughed at me but I'd taken my grain to the mill, and when I came out and started to hoist it to the mule's back they rushed at me and jerked my suspenders down and then they clodded me with chunks of dirt.

It wasn't in me to hurry. That was what made some of the men turn to watch, I think, for I heard somebody speak of it. The first thing I did, with clods splattering about me, was to pull up my pants and fix my suspenders. Then still with dirt splattering me, I hoisted my sack into place, and then I picked up a chunk of wood and started for them, and they scattered like geese, all but Chance Thorne.

He waited for me. He was a head taller than me, and some heavier, and he was dressed in store-bought clothes, which I'd never had and had only rarely seen. He looked at me and he was contemptuous. "Put down that club," Chance had said, "and I'll thrash you."

A dozen men were watching now, and none of them likely to be my friends. So when I put the club down he rushed me before I could straighten up, and he expected to smash my face with his fists as I tried to straighten, but in the Tennessee mountains a boy has to fight, and sometimes I'd fought men grown. So I didn't straighten, I just dove at his knees and brought Chance down with a thud.

He got up then, and I smashed his lips with my fist as he started to get up, like he'd tried with me, and my fist was hardened by work and it split his lips and covered his fine shirt with blood.

Maybe it was the first time Chance had seen his own blood and it shocked him, but it angered him, too. He walked at me, swinging both his fists, but there was a deeper anger in me, and an awful loneliness for there were boys cheering him on, and none of them with a shout for me. I was bitter lonely then, and it made the hate rise in me, and I walked into his fists driving with my own. There was nothing in him that could stand against the fierce anger I had, and he backed up, and there was a kind of white fear in his eyes. He sorely wanted help, he wanted to yell, but I ducked low and hit him in the belly, and saw the anguish in his face, and white to the lips I set myself and swung a wicked one square at that handsome face. He went down then and he rolled over in the dust, and he could have got up, but he didn't; he lay there in the dust and he was beaten, and I had an enemy for all my years.

Other men rushed from the mill then, Chance's father and uncle among them, and they rushed at me, so I backed to my club and picked it up. I was a lone boy but I was fierce angry with hating them and wanting to be away, and hating myself because I was afraid I would cry.

"Leave him alone!" I did not know Will Thorne then, a tall, scholarly man. "Chance began it."

Chance's father's face was flushed and angry. "You tend to your knitting, Will! I'll teach this young rascal to—"

He paused in his move toward me, for I'd backed to the mule and was set with my club. I was only a boy, but I was man tall and strong with work in field and forest. "You come at me," I said, "and I'll stretch you out."

He shook a fist at me. "I'll have you whipped, boy! I'll have you whipped within an inch of your life!"

Then I'd swung to my mule's back and rode away, but I did not ride fast.

And that was the beginning of it.

A few days later when I had come to town Thorne was waiting for me with a horse whip. When I'd started to dismount, he came at me with the whip, but seeing it coming I swung on the mule again and slammed him with my bare heels. Thorne was coming at me, but before he saw what was coming the mule was charging him. He drew back the whip too late, and the mule struck him with a shoulder and knocked him into the dust with half the town looking on. And then I had ridden out of town.

The next thing was worst of all, for the Thornes were good haters and they believed themselves the best in the community, with a reputation to uphold. We were working in the field, Pa and me, and four men came for me. Pa tried to stop them and one knocked him out with a club, and then they set on me with the whip. When they were through I was bloody and miserable, but not a sound did I make until they were gone. Then bloody and scarce able to walk, I helped Pa home and to bed, and put cold cloths on his head. Then I got down Pa's shotgun and started for town.

Haas and Gibson, two of the men who had done the whipping, were drinking their bonus in the saloon. When I got down from the mule it was past dark and the street was nigh empty. Up in front of the hotel I saw a man stop and look back, and then I'd stepped inside. Haas saw me first.

"Gib!" His voice was shaking. "Gib, *look!*"

Gibson turned and he reached for the pistol under his coat, and I shot, but not to kill. The shotgun was heavy loaded but I shot between them, close-standing as they were, and both men went down, both of them catching some shot.

They lay there shocked and bloody in the sawdust. "I done you no harm," I told them, "but you set on me an' Pa. Was I you I'd stay clear of us from now on, an' if Pa dies I'll kill the both of you."

Turning toward the door I stopped. "Don't you set

up to give this boy no beating again, because I got the difference."

That was the summer I was fifteen.

Folks fought shy of me the few times I did come to town and I didn't come except when must be. Most of the year I spent in the swamps along the Sulphur, hunting, trapping, staying away from people, except the Caddos. But that had been the beginning of it. From then on I'd the reputation of a bad one and folks kept their daughters away from me, and even the men stayed clear of me.

Pa worked on, but he was never quite the same after that blow on the skull. Maybe it wasn't so much the blow what did the harm, but the feeling that here where he'd planned to start over, to build something of a place for Ma and me, here he had failed to do so. It was no fault of his, but he lost heart then and the fire went out of him. After Ma died he just continued on and went through the motions, but Pa was gone and I knew it.

Katy Thorne had reminded me and it all came back, the sound of Ma mixing batter in a wooden bowl, the weariness in Pa's face as he came up from the field, the morning singing of the birds, and the sullen splash of fish in the still water, the sound of dogs raising a coon out there on a still moonlit night.

These things had meant home to me, but Ma and Pa were gone and the memories of hunting wild cattle in the Big Thicket to the south was an empty memory, and the smell of damp earth and the warm sun of planting time ... I had been a fool to come back.

"I've no cause to love the Thornes," I said, "only Will. I liked Will."

"I come here to gather flowers," she said. "I was surprised when I saw you."

Walking to the house I put my rifle down and started plucking the duck.

"You only fired once."

"There was only one duck."

She was silent, watching me as I worked. "A duck should hang for a while."

"He'll do his hanging inside me then. This is my supper."

"It's a small supper for a hungry man. Come to Blackthorne for supper. There's a baked ham."

"Do you know what you're asking, ma'am? Cullen Baker to come to Blackthorne? I could not do it without a shooting, and even if that was avoided people would speak no more to you. I've a black name along the Sulphur."

"You've been gone a long time, Cullen Baker. Blackthorne is deserted now, and has been since the war ended. It is Will's house that I live in, and which he left to me when he died. Aunt Flo is with me there, and you're not likely to see anyone but her."

"Chance?"

"He's in Boston, or wherever, and he does not often come to call, anyway. Chance likes the towns of Texas, not the plantations and ranches."

It would not be the first time I had been to the house of Will Thorne, for even as I made enemies that day at the mill, I had also made a friend.

Will Thorne, in my estimation, was a man worth the lot of them, perhaps less the sportsman than the others, and much less the talker, but a man of some attainments in his own way. He studied nature a good bit, and I who had lived in the swamps found much to learn from him, as he, I suppose, learned from me.

He did a sort of writing. I never knew much about that as I was a man who had learned to read but poorly, scarcely more than my name, which I could write, and no more. But he wrote some things for periodicals in London and in Paris, one was about a heron we have in the swamps, and another was on the beaver. I believe he wrote about butterflies and trap-door spiders, and a variety of things. It made no sense to me at first; I'd known about those things from a child, and he told me once that I'd knowledge in my head a naturalist would give years of his life to own.

We had walked in the swamps. The trails were known to none but the Caddos and me, though later I showed a few of them to Will, and sometimes we'd hunt for plants together, or for strange birds or insects. Usually I knew where to find what he wanted, for a man who is much in the woods acquires a gift for observation.

In Will I had a friend, and I never forgot his one question after I'd told him of some fight—there were others after the one at the mill, like the one at Fort Belknap when I killed a man—all he would say was to ask me, "Do you think you did the right thing?"

A question like that sticks in a man's mind, and after a while I judged everything by it, deciding whether it was the right thing, and often if there was no other way. I expect it was a good lesson to learn, but a man in his life may have many teachers, some most unexpected. The question lies with the man himself: Will he learn from them?

For a man to be at peace with himself was important, Will said, not what people say. People are often wrong, and public opinion can change, and the hatreds of people are rarely reasonable things. I can hear him yet. He used to say there was no use a man wearing himself out with hatred and ill-feeling, and time proved it out.

"Will used to tell me about you when I was a little girl," Katy said. "He said you were a fine boy. That you'd the makings of a fine man if they would just let you alone. But he said you'd the makings of a great clansman in the old days among the Highlands of Scotland. He said you'd dark blood in you, dangerous blood. But he always came back to saying you were the best of them around here, thoughtful, he used to say, and a gentleman at heart."

Despite myself, I was embarrassed at that. It has been rare that anyone has given me a word of praise in my life, and the last thing I'd thought of myself was a good man. But it worried me some, for Will Thorne was a man of few mistakes, and his saying that put a burden on me, his saying I was a good man almost put it up to me to be one. The idea was uncomfortable, for I'd been busy being Cullen Baker, and what he'd said about the black angers I could grasp, for it was proved too often in my life.

We sat in the kitchen to talk, and I liked the rustle of her skirts as she moved about, making friendly sounds with glass and crockery, and tinkling a bit of silver now and again. The fire made a good homely sound, too, and the water boiling in the pot. I was a man unused to such sounds, knowing the crackling of a fire from my own lonely camps and not from a hearth.

Aunt Flo was napping somewhere in the house while Katy got supper, and it was a rare surprise to me to see how sure she was about it, with no finagling and nonsense, but with deft hands and of one mind about what to do. I'd never thought to see a Thorne preparing her own meal, least of all a meal for me.

She put the dishes on a small table in a corner of a room, a friendly sort of table, and not like the long one in the dining room, which scared me to look at, it was so far from end to end. There she lighted the candles, and a soft glow they made, which was as well, for I'd had no chance to shave the day, and my clothes were shabby and worn from riding in all kinds of weather. I was shy about them, the big hulking fool that I was, and no man to be eating supper with such a girl.

Yet she was easy to be with, easier than any girl I'd met, and here and there I'd known a few, although not always of the nicest. The sort you tumble in the hay with, or take a walk with out in the grass away from the wagons. Yes, I'd known them, but some of them were good girls, too. Maybe it was wrong of me to walk out with them that way, but when the urge is on a man his conscience is often forgot.

"Tell me about the West," Katy asked me over coffee. "It has always fascinated me. If I had been a man, I should have gone West."

Tell her of the West? Where could a man begin? Where could he find words to put the pictures before her that he saw when she asked about the West? How could he tell her of fifty-mile drives without water and the cattle dying and looking wild-eyed into the sun? How could he tell her about the sweat, the dust, the alkali? Or the hard camps of hard men where a word was a gun and a gun was a death? And plugging the wound with a dirty handkerchief and hoping it didn't poison? What could a man tell a woman of the West? How could he find words for the swift-running streams, chuckling over rocks, for the mountains that reached to heaven and the clouds that choked the valleys among the high peaks? What words did he have to talk of that?

"There's a wonder of land out there, Mrs. Thorne," I said, "a wide wonder of it, with distances that reached out beyond your seeing where a man can ride six days and get nowhere at all. There are canyons where no white man has walked, canyons among the unfleshed bones of the mountains, with the soil long gone if ever there was any, like old buffalo bones where the buzzards and coyotes had been at them. There's campfires, ma'am, where you sit over a tiny fire with a million tiny fires in the sky above you like the fires of a million lonely men. You hover over your fire and hear the coyotes speaking their plaintive words at the moon, and you smell the acrid smoke and you wonder where you are and if there's Comanches out there, and your horse comes close to the fire for company and looks out into the dark with pricked-up ears. Chances are the night is empty, of living things, anyway, for who can say what ghosts may haunt a country the like of that?

"Sometimes I'd be lazy in the morning and lie in my blankets after sunup, and I'd see deer coming down to the water hole to drink. Those days a man didn't often camp right up against a water hole. It wasn't safe, but that wasn't the reason. There's other creatures need water besides a man, and they won't come nigh it if a man is close by, so it's best to get your water and then sleep back so the deer, the quail, and maybe a cougar can come for water, too.

"Times like that a man sees some strange sights. One morning I watched seven bighorn sheep come down to the water. No creature alive, man or animal, has the stately dignity of a bighorn. They came down to water there and stood around, taking another drink now and again. Tall as a burro most of them, and hair as soft as a fawn's belly. A man who travels alone misses a lot, ma'am, but he sees a lot the busy, talky folks never get a chance to see.

"Why, I've stood ten feet from a grizzly bear stuffing himself with blackberries and all he did was look at me now and again. He was so busy at those berries he'd no time for me. So I just sat down and watched him and ate my own fixin's right there, for company. He paid me no mind, and I paid him little more. When I'd eaten what I had, I went back to my horse and when I left I called out to him and said, 'Goodbye, Old Timer,' and lifted a hand, and would you believe it, ma'am, he turned and looked after me like he missed my company."

I was silent, suddenly embarrassed at having talked so all-fired much. It wasn't like me to go to talking like that. Shows what candelight and a pretty woman can do to a man's judgment of the fitness of things.

Aunt Flo had not come down, although I heard some stirring about upstairs. For me it was just as well. I'm no hand at getting acquainted with people in bunches. I'd rather cut one out of the herd and get acquainted slow-like so I can really know what the person is like. Never much of a talker, I'd little business with women. It's been my observation that the men with fluent tongues are the ones who get the womenfolks, and a slick tongue will get them even faster than money.

"If you loved it so much out there, Cullen, why did you come back?"

Well...there was that question I'd been asking myself, and of which I didn't rightly know the answer. There were answers I'd given myself, however.

"It's all the home I ever had," I told her, trying to make the words answer my own problem. "My folks are buried out there back of the orchard where Ma used to walk. The land is mine, and it is good land. Pa would work from daylight to dark out there, trying to make it pay. I don't know, maybe it was a feeling I had for him or just wanting to be some place familiar, and there was nothing out West that belonged to me. Maybe, rightly speaking, I'm no wanderer at all, but just a homebody who would rather be unhappy among familiar surroundings and faces than happy anywhere else."

"I don't believe that." Katy got up to clear the dishes. "And don't call me Mrs. Thorne. We're old friends, Cullen. You must call me Katy."

Standing up I seemed most too high for the little room where we'd been eating, so I fetched dishes to the kitchen and got my hat to go.

"Come again, Cullen, when you've a wish to talk

or want a meal cooked by other than your own hands."

At the door I paused. "Katy...ma'am, the light must be out when I go out the door. There's folks about would just as soon have a shot at me if the chance was there."

Outside in the dark I stepped to the side of the door and let my shadow lose itself in the shadow of the house. Caution becomes a man in strange country, and this country would be strange to me for a few days until the feel was in me again.

At night all places have a feeling of their own, and a man must be in tune with the night if he is to move safely. The sounds were different, and a man's subconscious has to get used to them again, so standing there against the outer wall of Will's house, I listened into the night, my mind far ranging out over the great lawns of Blackthorne, which were off to my left, and the orchard to my right, and beyond that to the swamps the river was bringing closer to Blackthorne by the year.

The frogs were loud in the darkness, a cricket chirped nearby. No coyote sounds in here, although there were wolves enough in the thickets to the south and west. Somewhere an owl hooted, and something splashed out in the swamp. The night was quiet so I walked to where the mule had been left and tightened the girth, then adjusted the bridle. It was quiet enough, but the mule was alert and I was uneasy.

Maybe it was the strangeness after so many desert and prairie nights, but turning from the path to the lane, I took a way that led back through the orchard and so across the fields. It made no kind of practical sense, going back the way I'd come—a man in Indian country learns things like that because it is back along the return trail they may be waiting for you.

The night had a different smell, a familiar smell. The clean dryness of the desert air, touched by the smell of sage or cedar, was gone. Here there was a heaviness of the greater humidity, and heavier smells of decaying vegetation, of stagnant water, and of dew-wet grass. The leaves of the peach trees brushed my hat as I rode through the orchard, taking my way from old experience toward a place where the fence was down. Sure enough, it had never been fixed.

When I walked the mule across the soft grass coming up back of my own house I knew there was someone else around, and drew up, careful not to shift my weight so the saddle would creak, and then I listened. Then an owl hooted and I had a feeling it was no true owl but one speaking for me.

Searching a minute in my mind I tried to recall what Bob Lee knew of our place and where, if it was him, he would wait, and was sure and certain it would not be the house itself.

There was a big old stump Pa had never been able to grub out, gigantic roots, big as small trees themselves, curled deep into the rich earth and without powder, which we could not afford then, it would be a long task to get it out. So we left it there, and it was a known place, used for a meeting on coonhunting nights. Bob Lee would remember. One of the few times he'd been on the place was to coon hunt, so I swung in a wide circle toward the stump, and when I was backed by the trees I hooted like an owl, but low down, so I'd sound farther off than I was...in the night a knowing man can do many things with sound.

The answer was plain, so with the Spencer in shooting position I walked that mule over the weed-grown field toward the stump. Two men arose from its shadow as I pulled up.

"Cullen?" It was Bob Lee.

"You've the name. What's the message?"

"Chance Thorne has learned you're here. He's sworn to drive you from the country. You were seen by someone in the lanes today, and then you've talked to Joel Reese."

"If he comes for me, he'll find me here. I've work to do."

"If the time comes you've a need of friends," Bob Lee said, "you'll know where to find us. We've means of learning things, Cullen, and friends about who'll feed us and hide us as well."

Crouched by that big old stump we talked an hour away, and they brought me up to date on much that had taken place, and things they'd just got wind of. Bob Lee was a man with friends as well as a big family, and such can be a sight of comfort to a man, times like this.

Bill Longley had little to say. He was stern for his age, a tall, quiet young man that took getting used to, but I liked him.

"You know what I think," Bob Lee said, standing. "I think we'll all be lucky if we add five years to our ages. I think they've marked us down for dying."

"Five years?" Longley's tone was almost wistful. "Bob, I'd settle for the certain knowledge of one year."

Bob Lee stood silent, a fine man, but with sharp-honed pride brought to an edge by family position and the anger in him that he had to run. I'd have said he would be lucky to last the year. As for me, I intended to fight shy of trouble. The carpetbaggers would pass as all things do, and I'd show my patience—although I'd little of that—and try to wait them out.

"We'll have small chance," Bob Lee said, "unless we're armed and ready. You'd better give thought to that, Cullen, and go to your plow with your Spencer in a scabbard on the plow handle."

"This land is mine," I said. "I mean to crop it, and I'll buy cattle when I can, and horses, too. I mean to breed horses here, when it can be safely done."

"There's wild cattle in the thickets, Cullen. We could get together and round up a bunch and drive them to Fort Worth. If you want, tell me and I can have fifty men for you in a couple of days."

"There's that many?"

"In the thickets? There's more, man. And they'll fight, if it comes to that."

"I want no fighting. It is peace I have come for, and it is peace I will have."

When they were gone I waited until the sound of their going had faded away, losing itself among the night sounds. What Bob Lee had said was true. If they came upon me in the fields it would be well to have a gun, for it was always better to talk peace with a solid argument at hand. The Spencer carbine was not too long, easy to swing into line, but I must have another Colt. It was a hard-hitting pistol with a good range.

Yet it was not of peace I was thinking when the trouble came. It was of Katy Thorne.

There was a faint whisper of a boot in the grass but

my mind was elsewhere and the warning was an instant late. A gun jammed hard against my spine and a hand wrenched the Colt from my belt and another hand, rising almost from the ground, grasped the barrel of my Spencer. The gun muzzle at my back was an insistent argument. I relaxed my hold on the carbine and stood quiet.

"Welcome home, Cullen." That would be the voice of Chance Thorne, and a fine voice he had, faintly mocking now. "I was afraid you had gone for good."

At the moment there was nothing to say, and certainly nothing to do. Lee and Longley would be deep into the swamp by now, and whatever was done I must do myself. So I stood very still and I think my silence began to worry them.

"Shall we take him back?" It was Reese speaking. "Or just leave him here?"

"The colonel wishes to speak to him, but the colonel is sure he will resist, so naturally he expects to see him in rather rough condition, and in a mood to answer questions."

Reese said, "What are we waiting for?" And struck out viciously. And as he struck I kicked him in the groin. He screamed out like an animal in pain, and then they closed in around me. My swinging fist smashed at a face and I had the savage pleasure of feeling the bone crunch, and then I plunged forward, punching with both hands, fighting to get clear of the circle. And then out of nowhere a pistol barrel caught me across the skull and my knees went rubbery and I fell, and then they closed in, kicking and striking as I rolled on the ground, trying to evade them. Their very numbers interfered with brutality.

Suddenly Chance parted the group and said, "I waited a long time for this!" And he kicked me in the head.

Only a quick turn of my head saved me the full force of that kick, but I pushed my face into the soft grass and relaxed as if unconscious, which I nearly was. There was a heavy throbbing inside my skull and I wondered if it had been cracked, and vaguely I heard someone say, "Throw him over a horse." And in the brief moment before consciousness slipped away, I felt a swift, savage exultation that so far they had not found my derringer.

Only I knew that I must live. Regardless of everything, I must live and make them pay. They had come upon me in a mob, too cowardly to face me alone, and no man deserves to be beaten and hammered by a mob, and the men who make up a mob are cowards. But cowards can die, and being cowards death is a bitterness beyond anything a brave man can feel.

"You take my advice," I heard Joel Reese say, "and you'll hang him now."

"Did I ask your advice?" Chance spoke contemptuously. "Did I ever take your advice?"

When they threw me over the horse I was only vaguely conscious, but when the horses started down the lane I knew I had a chance if they kept on along this route. It was a slim chance, but I'd no intention of taking any more than I'd had; as long as they believed me unconscious I had a chance.

The rider who rode the horse over which they'd thrown me had kicked me in the head when mounting, and the boot in the stirrup was beside my skull, and I could hear the slight tinkle of the spur. When they made the turn along the swamp it was my chance and it had to come now. Grabbing the boot I jammed the spur into the horse's ribs as hard as I could shove.

It was unexpected, the man's foot was easy in the stirrup, and the startled horse lunged in pain, plunging off the trail into the brush and grass, and when the horse plunged I went off the saddle into the edge of the swamp.

There was a mad moment while the rider fought his horse before he was aware of what had happened, and in that moment I reached my feet and made three fast strides, and then dove head-first into the brush, squirming forward. Behind me there were shouts, screams of fury, and then shots cut the brush past my head. The earth turned to mud and then water and I splashed through the reeds and rank water-grass and lowered myself into the dark water.

There was an instant when my hand slid along a mossy log and I shuddered, thinking it an alligator, and then I half-waded, half-swam over to a mud bank and crawling out, lay gasping with pain.

My skull pounded like a huge drum, every throb was one of pure agony, and my body was wracked with pain, bruised from the kicking, and bloody as well. And that blood would mean added danger in the swamp.

Yet I knew my position would be secure only for minutes, and after that, I had to move.

Behind me there were shouts and the splashing and cursing of the searchers.

This was my first night at home, and already I was a hunted man. Deep within me there was a pounding hatred of those who had done this to me. They had mobbed me, beaten me, and for no reason. Yet *they* had declared war, *I* had not. Be it on their own heads, I told myself. Whatever comes now, they have asked for it.

CHAPTER 2

AFTER A TIME my breath came easier, and I
lay very still, trying to plan. I had come no
more than sixty feet from that swampy shore, and I
knew this bank upon which I lay sprawled for I had
fished from it many a time. It was only a narrow, pro-
jecting tongue of swampy ground that reached out
like a pointing finger into the dark waters.

It was this vicinity that was favored by the huge old
'gator locally known as Ol' Joe, and reputed to have
eaten more than three men, yet it was this water I
must swim, and there was no other way out. It could
be no more than a minute or two before either Chance
Thorne or Joel Reese remembered the mud bar.

To walk back to the mainland was to invite capture, for already the search along the shore was nearing the connecting point. Getting to my feet I hobbled
across the mud bar to the far side.

There was a knifing pain in my side, and one leg
was badly bruised and probably torn. Ol' Joe was a
chance I had to accept, wherever he was he would be
sure to catch the scent of blood in the water. On the
other hand it would make the pursuers no more eager
to investigate until daylight.

Walking into the dark water until it was chest-
high, I struck out. Swimming was something at which
I'd always been handy, and I moved off into the water

making almost no sound. Despite the throbbing in my skull and the stiff, bruised muscles I must swim about two hundred yards into the swamp before there would be a place to land.

Taking each stroke by itself, neither thinking nor trying to plan beyond the other side, I swam steadily, keeping my mind away from Ol' Joe.

Behind me there was a shout of triumph and I knew they had found some tracks. Glancing back I saw lanterns bobbing along the swamp shore.

Somewhere out here, and my swimming should have put me in a direct line with them, were a few old cypresses standing in the water. They were heavy with Spanish moss and a tangle of old boughs and might offer a hide-out. A few minutes later my hand struck an underwater root, then feeling around, caught a low-hanging limb. Taking a good grip I pulled myself up out of the water.

The air was cold after the water and my teeth chattered. From limb to limb I climbed until there was a place on some twisted limbs where I could make a nest for myself. Removing my belt I belted myself around a branch of the tree and lay there in the darkness, teeth rattling with cold, mosquitoes swarming around.

The last thing I recalled was the lights along the shore line and then I must have slept or become unconscious for when I opened my eyes again the sky was gray in the east, and their campfires were large on the shore, waiting for daylight and serious search.

Something was wrong with one of my eyes and when I felt of it with careful fingers I found it swollen enormously, and fast shut. There was a great welt above one ear, and a wide cut on my scalp. Every muscle was stiff and sore, and my head throbbed with a dull pound. The flesh of my left arm was badly torn by the hobnails of a boot, and only the fact that it had been cushioned from beneath by grass and soft earth had saved it from breaking. No matter how I felt, I could wait no longer, for this place while good enough at night, would never survive a search by day.

Peering about, turning my head awkwardly because of the one eye I could use, I searched for some escape. And then I glimpsed a huge old log half concealed by vines. It was afloat, but hung up on a root of the very cypress where I was hiding.

There was movement around the fires and their voices carried to me as I climbed down the tree, every move painful, and my head feeling like a keg half-full of water, sloshing around and hard to manage.

By bending branches I got the log loose. By the sound of the voices I knew the searchers were drinking, which would make it worse for me if caught. Then pushing the log free with a broken branch for a pole, I started to move. The swamp was one of the arms of Lake Caddo, which nobody knew much about, and my guess was that a hundred years from now, folks still would not know all its tortuous sloughs and the hyacinth-clogged bayous of sluggish brown water. Yet around this lake with its bayous and sloughs, and the swamps along the Sulphur I'd spent most of my boyhood, and I figured to know this swamp country in both Louisiana and Texas as well as anybody.

Keeping that clump of cypress between the shore and me, I poled steadily, every bruised muscle aching, pushing deeper and deeper into the swamp. Where I was going now they would not follow me even if they knew of it, and I was mighty sure they didn't. I was going to the island.

No more than a half-dozen men knew of that island before the war, and probably nobody had learned of it since unless taken there by one of those who knew. Hidden from sight in a wilderness of moss-hung cypress, the approaches seemingly clogged by hyacinth or lily pads, the island was a quarter of a mile long, and at its widest no more than a hundred yards. The highest point was about six feet above the water, but without a guide who knew the area the island simply could not be found. From a dozen yards away it was invisible in the jungle of trees, moss and vines. The Caddo Indians had known of it, and a few of the mixed-blood Caddo-Negroes who lived in the swamp knew of it.

There were several of these islands, although the others were smaller and, but for one other, more exposed. Yet it was likely that none of them were known to these fellows who mostly had ridden down from Boston, Texas.

A heron flew up and spread wide wings ... poling on along the bayou, my head throbbing, muscles aching, finding a way through the lilies that would close after me.

How far had I come? A mile? Two miles? Moving as though in a trance, thinking only of putting distance between myself and the searchers who must now be looking for me. If they caught up with me before I reached the island I would be caught with nothing but the derringer to protect me, and it was useless at a distance. Moreover, I needed rest and a chance to gather my strength after the brutal beating I'd taken. My only chance was on that island where I was almighty sure Bob Lee, Longley and maybe Bickerstaff would be.

The sun was hot, and the water dead and still. Occasionally there were wide pools to cross, but mostly it was a matter of finding a way through the fields of lilies and hyacinth that choked many wide areas. If Ol' Joe had been around he certainly wasn't making himself known to me.

Every move of the pole was an effort now. Sometimes I could touch no bottom for some distance, nor could I always pole off the hyacinth although in most places there was enough thick growth to give a man some purchase. When I reached those places where I touched no bottom I just had to float, or paddle a bit with my hands to keep moving.

The sun was terribly hot and I needed water. The swamp water could be drunk if a man needed it bad enough, but folks got fever from it, I'd heard, and I was in trouble enough.

And I was still poling along, half-delirious when the log run aground. Several times I tried to force it on, and then looked up through a haze of pain and saw the bank of the island rising before me. But it was not a part of it that I remembered. Clumsily, I scrambled up the bank and fell flat, lying in the warm sunshine, letting the tired muscles relax. My brain was foggy and I seemed to have a hard time getting to my feet, but I knew that I must keep moving. The swamp has a way of destroying anything that becomes helpless, and to keep moving was my only salvation.

The earth was damp and in deep shadow once I left the shore, except where here and there the foliage overhead thinned out allowing enough sunlight to dapple the earth with light and shadow. Once, so weak that if it had been closer I could not have avoided it, I passed a huge diamond-back rattler coiled on a log.

Once, staggering, I fell to my knees and doubted whether I could get up—somehow I did. Vaguely then, my surroundings grew familiar. So on I went, although my strength seemed gone. Stumbling, falling, often entangled in brush, twice wading almost neck-deep in water, I kept going until struggling through the last forest of cattails I crawled up on a grassy shore near the camp. And there Bill Longley found me.

There were three days then of which I remember nothing. Then, slowly, the cuts and abrasions healed, and my head stopped its throbbing. The fierce anger faded, but left behind a sullen hatred. And there was desperation also, for it seemed a door was closing behind me, and that whatever I had come back for was slipping away, and would be lost.

Loafing about the island camp, I tried to think things out. This must not stop me. True it was that I had been set upon and beaten, yet if ever I was to be anything but what I was, I must make myself a man of substance, of property. And my only chance for that was to return to the land, to plant my crops, to buy my stallion and brood mares, and to win the fight on my own terms.

My immediate reaction was to get a gun and hunt them down, one by one, saving Chance for the last, and kill each man of them who had set upon me.

Yet there had been enough of killing, and, at the end, where would I be? An outlaw and a hunted man, without friends, without a place in the world. It would be too easy to be whipped, to sit back and admit that I'd been defeated. Down inside I knew they'd made me eat dirt, but it had been the dirt of my own field, and I could find it not unappetizing.

There were a dozen men on the island now. Bob Lee was there, so was Bill Longley and Bickerstaff, who was a good man and a hard one. All of these men were only a generation removed from those who fought at the Alamo and San Jacinto.

Listening to their desultory conversation I kept to my own thoughts with half my mind. There was that land Pa owned down on Big Cypress Bayou, the place called Fairlea. It was situated in an out-of-the-way place, surrounded on three sides by swamp and forest. On the west there was, as I recalled, a narrow grass-grown lane along the property line. It was fenced off, concealed, yet good land and a part of a place Pa had bought for a pittance. I strongly doubted whether anyone in either Boston or Jefferson dreamed it was owned by Pa. Fairlea was my best chance.

Bob Lee disagreed. "You've too many enemies. You'll not get a chance to get your crop in, to say nothing of harvesting."

"It's my feeling," I told them. "Nobody authorized my arrest. I've a thought it was Chance Thorne, acting on his own. There's still a chance they'll leave me alone."

"Maybe," Longley said dryly. "But there's some who will remember you and be afraid, and men try to destroy anybody they are scared of."

"There's something else we've got to talk about," Bickerstaff suggested, "and that's Barlow. We're getting blamed for every thieving, murdering thing he does while he hides out in the Thickets."

"He has friends tipping him off," Jack English declared. "He always knows where the Army isn't goin' to be."

While they talked of that my mind wandered back to that lonely field at Fairlea. With luck a man could get a crop into the ground there and nobody the wiser. Then with some feed to stash away I might even go wild-cow hunting down in the Thickets and come out with a herd we could drive to Sedalia or Montgomery.

Of this much I was almighty sure: they'd not take me again and treat me as they had just now. I'd see them all in hell first, and go with them if need be. And that brought back the problem of defense. Nothing could be done until I had a gun, until I had a carbine and a Dragoon Colt.

So I got to my feet and started toward my mule which Bill Longley had brought to the island for me. Jack English had gone with him to get it, and for that I owed them a debt that I must pay.

Lee watched me saddle up the mule. "You fixin' to go somewhere, Cull?"

"Figure I'll need my guns. I'm goin' after them."

Longley had been lying on the ground chewing a blade of grass. Now he sat up and regarded me curiously, but he let the others do the talking.

"You figure to do it alone?" Lee asked mildly.

"A man forks his own broncs in this country," I

told him, "but I've nothing against you riding along if you've a might to."

"Well, now," Longley got to his feet, "I sort of figure this might be somethin' to see."

Four of them rode along: Bob Lee, Jack English, Bickerstaff and Longley. I'd have wanted no better men, anywhere.

Jefferson lay lazy in the afternoon sun. A child rolled a hoop along the boardwalk, and a dog lay sprawled in the dust in the center of the street, flopping his tail as they rode by to indicate his satisfaction with things as they were and a willingness to let things be. Two men dozed against the wall of a store enjoying the shade and their chronic idleness.

The street was silent. A few men riding into the street meant nothing to anybody, not those days. There were loose men from everywhere, just drifting, hunting they knew not what, men who had lost what they had in the war and were hoping, away back inside their skulls, to find it somewhere else.

It wasn't likely any of them would know me on sight, although, come to think of it, Joel Reese had. But then I was on the place and where a body might expect me to be.

Stepping down from my mule, I glimpsed my reflection in the store window, a strapping big man in a cabin-spun shirt that was a size too small; my shoulders packed a lot of heavy muscle in them and it swelled that shirt considerable. First money I came by would have to go into clothes or I'd be seedplanting naked as a jaybird.

The black hair curled over the back of my shirt collar, and I guess I looked like an uncurried broomtail, one of those wild ponies folks find running in the swamps or the off-shore islands.

We had pulled up in front of the military head-quarters, and I walked right in, asking nobody yes or no. There was a soldier dozing on a chair near the door with a rifle across his knees. He gaped at me, then started to pick up that rifle but something in my eyes made him change his mind. Maybe it was because I was a-figuring to stretch him out if he made a move to swing that gun on me. And I was positioned to do it.

This soldier was the Reconstruction vintage, if you know what I mean. He was no veteran. Likely he never killed nothing more than a squirrel, or something he could aim at two hundred yards off ... It was a sight different to look up and see a full-grown man staring at him, just a-waiting for him. This boy had a uniform coat and cap, but only homespun pants—and he was asking for no trouble.

Colonel Amon Belser was there. He was tipped back in his chair looking at some papers and when he looked over them he saw me. I don't think he liked what he saw.

"Colonel," I said, "Chance Thorne came out to my place the other night and set on me. The men with him took my pistol and my Spencer, and gave me a sight of a whipping to boot. I came to get my guns back."

This Belser was surprised, but he was no fool. He sat very still, trying to think it out before he spoke. I had an idea Chance had operated on his own, but Chance was not a good man to cross and, unless I missed my guess, Chance was a man who would have influence.

"If you received a beating," Belser said stiffly, "no doubt you deserved it. I know nothing about your guns."

"This here country," I said, "a man needs a gun. Lots of mighty mean folks riding the roads these nights. I'd like my guns, Colonel."

Belser was angry. He was top man here and not used to being talked to like that. "Baker," he said to me, "you get out of here! And get out of town! I know nothing about your guns, but from what I've heard of you, you're better off without them."

Well, sir, right then I leaned over the desk and picked up the brand-new, spanking-new Dragoon Colt that lay there on the desk. Then I spun the cylinder and checked the action. It was in working shape and fully loaded.

"Then I'll just have to take this one," I told him, speaking mildly. "And it looks like a fine weapon."

"Put that down!" Belser could get authority in his voice when he was a might to. "That's my pistol!"

Well, now. Putting that pistol behind my waistband I shoved open the little gate in the fence that kept folks back from him, and walked over to the rifle rack. There were several guns there, but one of them was a Spencer carbine, a sight newer and much finer than the one I'd had taken off me. It was loaded too.

Belser got up suddenly and started for me and I just turned around. Holding the carbine belt-high thataway it was just almost naturally pointed at his belt buckle. Lead taken on a full stomach is mostly just indigestible, middle of the day, especially.

Belser stopped. He didn't want to stop, I could see that, but maybe he was having trouble with his digestion and didn't want anything to upset his stomach. Man like that, he has worries, and it doesn't pay to take anything on your stomach you can't rightly handle. He was mad with himself for stopping, but he stopped.

"Colonel," I told him, and I spoke quiet-like. "I came back to the Sulphur River country to mind my own affairs. When I came back here I wanted no trouble with any man, but I've been set on and beaten. Now I know the men who did it, and when I figure the time is right, I'll talk to each and every one of them. I'll read them from the Scriptures, Colonel, but in my own good time.

"Seems to me you'd want it quiet here. Seems folks back Washington way and down about Austin, seems like they might figure you weren't handling things right if a lot of trouble was stirred up down here. Now you leave me alone and you tell Chance Thorne to lay off me, and I'll make no trouble for you. You start something against me, Colonel, and I'll run you the hell out of the country."

That soldier, he sat right still, keeping his eyes on the floor, and wanting no trouble. So I just kept the guns I'd taken, and I walked right out of there into the street.

That tall, lean, long-headed Longley was leaning against an awning post right across the street, smoking a black cigar. Bob Lee was standing by the hitch rail on my own side of the street, looking mighty accidental-like. At the end of the street Jack English was squatting on his heels playing mumblety-peg with his bowie knife.

"Long as we're here," Longley said, "I figure we should have us a drink."

English, he stayed where he was, keeping an eye out for trouble, but the rest of us started for the saloon. Just about that time the saloon door opened and Joel Reese walked out.

He started to stretch and he caught himself right in the middle of it, and he stood there staring at me like his spine had come unsnapped, his face turning kind of sick gray.

"Bob," I said, "this gent is one of those who entertained me the other night. Fact is, he was one of those calling the numbers for the dance. I figure this man should be instructed in the Word of the Lord."

"Yes, sir," Bob Lee was mighty serious, "you take your text from Job, fourth chapter, eighth verse: 'They that plow iniquity and sow wickedness, they shall reap the same.' "

Joel Reese took a sort of half-step back, looking around for help. Longley had moved around to cut him off and he was standing there, lazy-like, his thumbs hooked in his belt, but boy though he was, there was nothing soft about Bill Longley.

Reese, he looked at me and he set up to say something but I wasn't figuring on much talk. So I slapped him across the mouth. Well, sir, I'm a big man and I have done a sight of work in my time, and I was remembering how they had closed in on me the other night, so that slap shook him up, somewhat.

He struck out at me, and I just shifted my feet to

make the blow miss and slapped him again. That time it started blood from his nose.

Colonel Belser came to the door and he had a rifle in his hands. "Here! Stop that!"

Now Bill Longley had him a Dragoon Colt in his hand and he was looking right at the colonel. "Mister Belser, sir," he said that, only he dragged it out a might, "you see a sinner being shown that the way of the transgressor is hard, and Colonel, sir, should you transgress any further with that weapon, you will transgress yourself right into a belly full of lead."

To bring his rifle to bear Colonel Belser must turn a quarter of the way around, and you could see with half an eye that he realized it. Bill Longley was standing there holding that pistol sort of casual-like, and down there at the end of the street, not too far off, was Jack English, just a-setting there. The good colonel must have had it brought home to him that there was no way he could turn without turning right into a chunk of lead. Right then I'd bet he was some unhappy with himself for not staying right inside and giving an imitation of a man gone deaf, dumb and blind.

While Belser stood there unwilling to chance a move, I remembered very clearly what had happened to me in my own yard, so I slapped Reese into a first-class beating. "Next time," I told the colonel, "it will be a shooting matter."

Now I didn't know this at the time, but in his office overlooking the street Judge Tom Blaine was watching all that took place, but the judge was no carpet-bagger. Judge Tom had fought in the Mexican War, and it had hurt him to see Jefferson folks afraid of these ragtag soldiers of the Reconstruction.

There were things we needed, so while the others mounted up and held my mule for me, I walked down the street to buy ammunition. It was just as I was finishing buying what I needed that Katy Thorne came into the store, and when she saw my face, I saw her own eyes go wide with surprise and hurt.

My face was still bruised and the cuts had only half-healed, and I suspect I was a sight to see. "Chance told me what they had done," she said, "but I didn't believe it was so bad."

"I'll have a talk with Chance."

She caught my sleeve. "Cullen, why don't you go away? They'll not leave you alone, you must know that! Even if the others will leave you alone, Chance never will. He hates you, Cullen."

"I'll not run ... and this land is mine. I would put seed in the ground here, and grow crops, and build the place as Pa would have built it. If I leave all this behind, his work was for nothing."

"His work was for you. It is you who are important, not the land."

"Are you so anxious to be rid of me?"

"No, but I want you alive."

Looking at her then I said something I had no right to say, no right even to think. "Where you are not—I would not feel alive."

Then I turned sharp around and walked into the sun-bright street, afraid of what I'd said, and not knowing why I'd said it, except that now it was said I knew it was the truest thing I had ever said.

Time was, any man who said such a thing and not

one of her own kind would have been horsewhipped or called out. Yet I had said it who had no right of any kind to say that to such a girl, least of all to her.

There was no girl of her kind likely to have an interest in Cullen Baker. What was I but a big, loose-footed wandering man with no money and nothing to his name? And who was nobody, nor likely to be anybody.

Remembering the reflection I'd seen of myself in the window, I knew there was nothing in that big, shock-headed and raw-boned young man in a faded red wool shirt that would be likely to interest a Thorne of Blackthorne, or anybody who married with them. I was a man carried a pistol. Folks had no good to say of me, and mostly they were right. I was not as bad as they painted in most ways, but worse in some others. No hand to lie, I never drank either, although often they said I did, but I'd killed men in pistol fights and rode a hard trail over a lot of rough country.

How could a man driven to the swamps like a wounded wolf mean anything to such a girl? A man who had nothing to his name but three shirts and one pair of pants, a man who had drifted and rode and fought with the ragtag and bobtail of the West?

My mother had been quality and my father of good yeoman stock, but there'd been nothing else to the family. Pa had worked hard all his life, but he'd been unlucky. Fire had wiped out one home, and grasshoppers had taken the crop two years succeeding, and there were things happened no man can fight off, things that saddled us with debt.

Bob Lee was a knowing man, and Bob Lee looked me over and said, "I don't blame you, Cullen."

"What did he do?" Jack English wanted to know. "What aren't you blamin' him for? Because he whupped that Joel Reese? I'd have done it myself, if excuse had been offered. There never was a good thing about that man."

"You would have reason, Cullen," Bob Lee said. "I think she would go wherever you wanted to ride."

"Don't speak slighting of her, Bob."

"No such thing. I never spoke slighting of any woman, Cullen. Only she's in love with you, that one is."

"Of itself that's a slighting thing. What woman of sense could look at a man like me? How much time have I got, Bob? How much time have any of us? We've our enemies, you and me, and all of us, too. You have the Peacocks, and I have Chance Thorne, and then there's the Reconstruction people who've no use for any of us.

"I tell you, Bob, even if she'd have me, and there's no thinking of that, I'll have no woman crying over my bloodstained shirt, as I've often seen them cry."

We rode silent then, and after a bit Bob Lee said, "There's little sense in loving, Cullen. Love has a sense of its own and I expect often as not it's the best sense. Folks love with their blood and their flesh, Cullen, not with their brains. The sense of love is as deep as the water in Black Bayou, rich as the color of hyacinth. It makes no sense but to the people who love, and that's enough."

"Not for her and me, Bob Lee. And she has no

such thought. It's only that we both liked her Uncle Will, I guess, and she may have sympathy for me."

"Have it your way," Bob Lee told me. "You've much to learn of women, Cullen."

Now no man likes to hear that. Each man believes he knows as much of women as the next, and in my time I'd known a few of them, and here and there women had been in love with me, or told it to me, but Katy Thorne was not likely to care for my kind of man, although she was a beautiful girl with a body that took a man's breath and embarrassed me to think on, not that I'm a man strange to women.

This day's work would bring trouble upon us all, but we had trouble already, and there was little they could do to us if we stayed to our swamps. Those carpetbagging soldiers weren't going to come into the swamp after us, not if they were in their right minds, but Colonel Amon Belser was a proud-walking man who would not like it said that he'd been made to look the fool, nor would he like to think that Bob Lee had been among the men, and Bob Lee with a price on his head.

What graveled us was the knowing that no Reconstruction was needed here. Texas had scarce been touched by the war, only men lost, and time taken from their work by it, but the carpetbaggers flocked to Texas because there was wealth to be had there and they wanted it.

As long as Throckmorton was governor he held them back, but when they'd thrown him out and put Davis in, we all knew we were in trouble. All state and local police had been disbanded and the Reconstruction were in power everywhere. Only we knew they wanted no newspaper talk, no publicity, just loot the state and get out, that was what they were thinking of.

Feeling had been intense up North when the war ended, but right-thinking folks were already making themselves heard and the old abolitionist group of haters were losing out to the sober-minded who wished to preserve the Union and bring business back to where it had been. The Reconstruction people had been told to use discretion because, if they stirred up a fuss, feeling might turn fast against them.

"This Belser," Jack English said, "I've had an eye on him, and he sets store by Katy Thorne, and that Petraine woman, too. He'd like to go after the both of them, but there's men would kill him if he said a word to Katy Thorne, and as for Lacy Petraine, she needs no man to care for her."

It was the first talk I'd heard of Lacy Petraine, but right then the talk began, and I listened as I rode. She was new to the Five Counties, a New Orleans woman, but who'd lived elsewhere before that, and she had cash money, which was a rare thing.

She was a beauty, they said, and a dark, flashing kind of woman who carried herself as a lady and let no man think of her otherwise. She had bought local property from folks who wanted to go West, but what she had in mind or why she wanted to stay here, there was nobody could say.

On the island that night there was talk of Sam Barlow again. Matt Kirby had come to the island with the news of how Barlow had burned out a farm near San Augustine. He had killed a man there and run off his stock.

"If he comes up this a-way," Jack English suggested, "I say we run him off. I say we run him clean out of the country, or hang him."

If a man would just sit quiet and listen he could hear all the news right there on the island, for the men who sheltered there had friends everywhere, and word came to them by several means: a man riding by on the trails might leave a message in a hollow stump, or he might arrange the branches in a certain way, or the stones beside a trail. We had our ways of knowing things, even in the swamp, but Sam Barlow was a dangerous man to us, for if people began to believe we were doing the things he did we'd have no more friends among the folks out there. It was Reconstruction law wanted us, and none of us had done any harm to the folks who lived hereabouts.

Next day I saddled up that buckskin mule and rode down the island. There was only one place where a man might walk a horse or mule to the mainland and it took sharp attention and the right knowledge of just where to turn. There was an underwater ridge a man could ride, but well out from shore a man had to make a turn. It was a Caddo who showed me the way, and the first of the others had learned it from me... if a man made to ride on he'd be off in mighty deep water or in places, in mud that was like quicksand.

It was to Fairlea I rode. The distance was short, and I wanted to look about and see what my chances were to make something of the place. Actually, it was a better place than our home place, and one which Pa had picked up while land was cheap—for that matter it was still worth nothing. There were men with thousands of acres and no money at all, nor chance to get any. Crops brought nothing but a mere living, and cattle were killed for their hides and tallow.

The point of land I'd been considering was separated even from Fairlea except by a narrow lane along the bayou. There was some three hundred acres in the piece, but it lay in a half-dozen small fields, each walled by trees and bayous, the land lying like a letter S with an extra turn to it, and the bayous bordering it until it was all but an island. The lane along the trees ended in a gate on another lane, rarely used now, and by going through the gate and crossing the land one was on Fairlea proper.

There had once been a fine mansion house on the place, but it had burned to the ground one night before we ever came to the place, and the owner lost his family there, and after that sold to my father and went off to New Orleans. I believe part of the selling price was money owed to Pa for work done, and that during the spell when the owner had thoughts of rebuilding and going on, but the memories were too strong, and he finally would have none of it. So Fairlea fell to us for labor done and a little money.

The soil was good, and it would not be difficult to get in here, plow a field and seed it without anyone being the wiser.

The sound of the oncoming riders had been in my ears for a minute or more before I realized what it meant. Somebody was coming along the unused lane at the end of the property...now in the old days it had been a rare thing for anyone to ride that way, and by the looks of the lane, all grown to grass, it was a rarer thing even now.

If riders came this way it would be a good thing to know who they were and if they came often, but I'd more than an idea they were themselves not eager to be seen, choosing such a route as this, out of the way as it was.

It was a fine spring morning, and the sun was warm and lazy. Off in the bayous behind me somewhere a loon called, a mighty far and lonesome sound, at any time. Walking right up to the fence I lay that Spencer across the top rail with my hand over the action in such a way I could cock and fire almost in the same motion. And it was well I did just that because the man on the first horse was Sam Barlow.

He was a wide, thick-set man with a sight of hair on his chest, revealed by an open shirt. Barlow had the name of being a mighty dangerous man to come up against. He had fought as a guerrilla in the war, and had been a renegade since. Under the cover of fighting Reconstruction he was raiding, looting and murdering up and down the state, and into Louisiana and Arkansas. Folks had laid much of what he'd done on Bickerstaff, Bob Lee and some of the others, but Sam Barlow was a man known for cunning as well as being mighty mean, and he seemed always to know right where the Army was so he never did come up against them. Behind him right now there were about a dozen unkempt, dirty and mangy rascals who looked fit bait for the hangman.

About fifty feet from where I stood, Sam Barlow saw me and at first he stared like he couldn't believe what he was seeing. Then he lifted a hand to halt the little column, but by that time he was closer.

Taking a stub of cigar from his yellow teeth, he said, "Howdy! You live around here?"

Imperceptibly the muzzle of the carbine shifted until it covered Sam Barlow's chest. That carbine was down on the rail and partly hidden by brush . . . I don't figure he saw it.

"I live all around here."

"I'm Sam Barlow."

Now if he figured I was going to start shaking he was a mistaken man. Names never did scare me much, and I'd come up against some men who had bigger, tougher names than this here Barlow.

"I know who you are. Mighty far north, aren't you?"

Barlow returned that stub of cigar to his teeth. "I'm comin' further north. I like it here."

About that time he saw the carbine, and his lips tightened down and when his eyes lifted to mine they were wary, careful eyes. "Who are you?" he demanded.

"This is my country, Barlow. Stay the hell out of it."

Barlow was mad, I could see that. Moreover he wasn't so smart as I'd heard because he was going to buck that .56 caliber. He was going to bet me his life I'd miss. It was in his eyes, when a man behind him spoke. "Sam, this here is Cullen Baker."

That stopped him. Maybe they had heard about that killing a long time back at Fort Belknap, or maybe something else but, when he heard the name, Sam Barlow changed his mind and saved his life— because if that horse had moved a foot I was going to kill him.

He knew it, too. It is one thing to jump a horse at

some scared farmer. It is another thing to buck a man who can and will use a gun.

Same time, he'd no wish to lose face in front of his outfit, for the only way you lead a crowd like that was by being tougher, smarter, and maybe more brutal.

"I could use a man like you, Baker. I've heard tell of you."

"Stay out of this country, Barlow. You stay south or west of the Big Thicket. You come north of it and I'll take it unkind of you. Fact is, you come north of the Big Thicket and I'll kill you."

Well, sir, the planes in his face seemed to all flatten out and he made to spur his horse and when he did I cocked that .56 caliber. In that still air you could hear that carbine click as it cocked and Sam Barlow pulled his horse to a stand.

"Get out, Barlow, and take your outfit with you. There's country south of the Big Thicket for you, and if you open your mouth even once I'll spread you all over your saddle."

Sam Barlow was mad—he was mad clean through—and I didn't figure to even let him open his mouth because if he did he'd say something to try to make himself big with his crowd. It had probably been a long time since anybody told him to shut up and get out, but it had been done now, and no mistake.

They would be back, I could bet on that. Sam Barlow could not afford to take water from any man, but he would think awhile before he came back, and he would do some planning, but if he stayed south of Lake Caddo then Katy Thorne would be safe.

"And that was what you were thinking about," I told myself. "You've heard of Barlow's ways with women."

Turning around then I saw four riders coming up the field toward me, and they were well spread out, but they were Matt Kirby, Bickerstaff and Bill Longley. On the far wing of the four was Bob Lee.

"Sam Barlow backed down," Kirby was saying. "He backed down cold."

"Means nothing," I said, "I had him dead to rights. And that .56 makes quite a hole."

"They'll come back." Bob Lee was a serious thinking man. He was looking past the moment, and he could see what it was we'd have to expect.

"Why, then," Bill Longley was grinning, "we shouldn't keep them waiting. We should go after them, Bob. We should go right down into the Thicket after them."

They were waiting for me, but when I reached a hand for the pommel of the mule's saddle I was thinking, "You've got to find a way to get a gun into action faster, Cullen Baker. Else they'll come up on you some time. You've got to learn how to get a Colt into action faster than any man would ever believe possible. You've got to think out how they might approach you and what you'll do in case.

"Otherwise they'll surely kill you."

CHAPTER 3

A PISTOL WAS carried in a holster or thrust into the waistband. The habit of carrying pistols on the hip had not developed to any extent, and hand guns were only becoming common now. The Dragoon and Walker Colts were too heavy for comfort. Usually, until now a pistol had been carried on the saddle, yet for a man who needed a weapon that could be brought swiftly into action, the pistol was the best.

Long ago at Fort Belknap I'd traded several surplus rifles for a pistol. The rifles were of the muzzle-loading variety then being sold to Indians, and which I'd won gambling.

That was the time a soldier taught me the Army method of loading the Dragoon Colt, when afoot or riding horseback, and he had drilled me until I'd become far more proficient than the average cavalryman ever became. Doing things with my hands had always been easy for me—I had the knack. Maybe that was because I'd worked with my hands since a boy, braiding rawhide ropes, splicing rope we used on the farm, doing what needs to be done. So more than most, I was handy with a pistol, and felt right at home with it.

No pistol would be any use to a man in trouble unless it was out and shooting, so the problem was getting the pistol into action, then firing accurately and with speed.

That last wasn't going to figure as troublesome. At Fort Belknap when I hung around there I'd done a sight of shooting with soldiers and proved then that what they could do I could do better. My shooting was better than any of them, and for some time I'd kept myself in money winning bets on shooting with both rifle and pistols.

Back on the island that night after the meeting with Sam Barlow I stretched out on a grassy bank just at the edge of the firelight and did some serious thinking. It was a problem I had to solve, and I'd never figured myself for too much of a thinker, but I do say I was persistent. I mean I could hold to an idea and plug away at it and size it up from all angles until it began to make sense.

After all, what's there to thinking? The way I figure it there was so much a body could do with a mind. You could take the various possibilities and line them all up, and then eliminate the ones that weren't practical. The main idea was to stay with an idea until all the possibilities were worked out.

Thinking was something I worked at like a prospector washing out gold. I'd take me a brain full of the coarse gravel of ideas and sift it down until the gold remained. Only sometimes I worked a long time and came up with no color showing at all.

That pistol would be in my waistband. That way I could lay a quick hand on it. What I needed was to get that pistol out and shooting, and I'd have to be prepared for a target from any direction. I wasn't to be able to shoot just where I wanted to.

This was easier said than done. Getting up I walked off down a path where I could be alone and unobserved. Standing in a little clearing I drew the gun and aimed at a mark—too slow.

Yet why should a man aim? When I point my finger at something I just point directly at the object, so why not the same thing with a pistol? And if a man could fire from wherever he had his gun, so much the better. It would have the advantage of the unexpected, and that was a primary concern. Of course, I'd have to be careful of that trigger squeeze. A man could pull his gun barrel out of line with the target if he gave it just a might too much. Still, I'd mostly be shooting from close up, and the target would be a man's body. I'd waste no time on head shots.

Whoever came against me would surely have help, and it was almost as sure that I'd be alone. Therefore if my gun was in action quicker then I might win with the first shot.

Nine out of ten fist fights are won with the first blow, so why not a gun battle with the first shot?

The problem was to get that gun out fast....

Right then I started to practice, drawing that pistol again and again, and sighting at whatever mark showed. The front sight had a way of snagging on my shirttail or beltband, so I would file that off. A thin white line on the muzzle would do most as good for close work, anyway.

The problem then was to draw swiftly, to fire at once, and above all to make the first shot count.

There was no use to waste ammunition firing until I'd developed some skill, and until I'd practiced turning and aiming at targets to the side or behind me.

The problem here was to focus on the target at once and let the gun muzzle go where the eyes went.

Right then I started, drawing fifty times by actual count, trying to break the draw down to its actual fundamentals. So I started trying to find the quickest and smoothest ways of grasping the gun—grasp counted for very much, and that first grip must be sure, clean and positive. If that was done half the problem was solved, for then the gun came up in line and didn't jump when the trigger was squeezed.

At daybreak the next morning I walked down to the far end of the island where nobody could see what I was doing and I practiced for three hours. After three hours I rested and thought about it for thirty minutes and then returned to work. My life depended on my success so I wasn't about to waste time. So I worked on steadily through the afternoon.

If the elbow was held loosely against the hip or the body above the hip my position seemed a little better, and the pistol could be pointed by the whole body.

The art of drawing a gun fast had never been developed by anyone. Until now there had been no particular reason for developing any such skill, for men fought duels on carefully paced-off ground, or they went looking for one another, gun in hand. Usually, disputes were settled by carefully arranged duels with gun, knife or sword. Moreover, the first successful repeating pistol made in any quantity was the Walker Colt, invented by Samuel Colt and designed for the Texas Rangers by order of Walker. But like the Dragoon Colt, it was heavy.

And the fast draw was of advantage only to a man

who might expect attack at any time, from any direction.

That first day I worked seven hours, until my hand was sore and I was some tired out. But I had a feeling that I'd hit on something new, and that what I was doing would work in practice, and that's the test of any idea.

Next day I rode to Fairlea and, with a team borrowed from a farmer who'd known Pa, I started breaking ground. After staying away for a few days so as to give nobody a chance for an ambush, I returned again. Each time that I came back to Fairlea I scouted all around before showing myself in the open. The chances were that Sam Barlow had no idea the field belonged to me, and most likely assumed I was merely passing through.

On the fourth day I finished my plowing, and later I dragged the field and planted my corn.

When I'd come back to Texas I'd had a little money, but most of it went to pay for the seed corn.

Time to time I'd find myself thinking of Katy Thorne, although I knew I'd no business thinking of her. But I'd keep bringing to mind the way her face looked in the candlelight, and how good it felt to be sitting in a home, with comfort around me and the sound of a woman moving about the house. But much as I wanted to, I stayed away from Blackthorne. I'd no desire to go to stirring up a lot of wishing that I'd no business with. I was a man with nothing, and with small prospects of living out the summer. Only I figured to have my say on that last point. I had most unfriendly ideas about dying, particularly from a gunshot by that riffraff that followed Reconstruction.

There had been no further forays by Sam Barlow into our neck of the woods. That country from Lake Caddo to the Oklahoma-Arkansas line he'd avoided. Bob Lee, however, and some of the others had ridden out and had themselves some gun talk with Reconstruction soldiers, in which they came off very well and the soldiers not so good.

The Reconstruction Act of 1867, followed by the removal of Governor Throckmorton from office, had been accepted by most Texans as another declaration of war. The carpetbaggers and Union Leaguers had come to Texas to get rich quick, and most of them were folks of low integrity and no morals to speak of. Here and there, however, to give them their just due, there would be one who amounted to something, and a few of these stayed on in Texas to become valued citizens. But they were mighty scarce.

Mostly those who came south were the wrong ones. They allied themselves with folks of the same kind in Texas, and they figured to force their will on us by shooting and burning which only stiffened resistance and drove many a good man into the swamps or the thickets, and most of us who took to the thickets had to learn to use our guns to live.

That section of East Texas was thickly forested with piney woods where even then folks had started a few small lumber operations, and here and there where the woods had been cleared out folks had started farming or grazing a few cows.

Unless you've seen an East Texas thicket you surely can't imagine what they're like—millions of acres covered by a dense, junglelike growth of pine, dogwood, chinquapin, elderberry, myrtle, blackjack and prickly pear. Above all, prickly pear. There was cat's-claw, of course, and even ferns as tall as trees and wild orchids, but all through it was a growth of tall, old prickly pear with spines that would rip a man's eyes out, and in places made a wall nothing could get through.

The Big Thicket to the south was over a hundred miles long and about fifty wide, but there were other thickets such as Mustang, Jernigan, and Blackjack Thicket, just to name a few. Here and there among the thickets there were streams or water holes, sometimes even good-sized ponds or small lakes, teeming with fish. There was a lot of wild game, and some of the most vicious wild cattle a man ever came across. There were wild cattle in there that would stalk a man like a cougar stalks a heifer, mean as all get out.

During the Shelbyville war between the Regulators and the Moderators these thickets and the swamps along the Sulphur had offered shelter for the fighting men and refugees as well as for outlaws from the Natchez or Trammel Traces. Growing up in those swamps and thickets, I probably knew as much about them as any one man...it would take a lifetime to know it all, believe me.

Few rivers on earth could twist and turn more than the Sulphur Fork of the Red. And few offered so great a variety of hiding places as did the curves, bends, islands and swamps of the Sulphur. When in the southern part of the area the boys hid out on the island in the Lake Caddo swamps, but farther north, not too far from Boston or the Arkansas line, there were hideouts at McFarland Island between the circle of Piney Lake, Spring Lake and the Sulphur itself. And there were two hide-outs in the Devil's Den region between the Sulphur River and Bell's Slough. Of course, there were others, some known to one group, some to another, but maybe I was the only one who knew them all, or so I figured. And most of them I'd learned from my friends, the Caddoes.

Bob Lee and the others left me alone. This was a time when nobody catered much to folks asking questions and a man's business was figured to be his own. Only sometimes the boys would get to riding me.

"Got himself a girl," Matt Kirby suggested.

"He's sparkin' that widow," Jack English said. "Most ever'body else is tryin'."

"Makes a man right uncomfortable, the way she looks at him sometimes," Bickerstaff told them. "She's all woman that one. Take a sight of man to keep her inside the fence."

It was Lacy Petraine of whom they talked. She was the subject of more talk than any woman I ever did see. Mostly they called her "that New Orleans woman," or "the widow" like that country wasn't full of widows, those times. But when a woman who looks like she does comes into a broke country carrying a sack full of hard cash, there's sure to be talk.

Chance Thorne was taking some rides, too. From time to time I heard talk of his being seen around the country, yet he rode quite a ways south, and what down there could be important to him? Could be he was sparking some woman himself, yet Chance was a man not likely to ride far out of his way for any woman, and who did few things without a mighty big reason. Who was south that was so important to him?

When the idea came it sort of shocked me into sitting straight up. Bob Lee turned sharp around, afraid I'd heard something that spelled trouble. "What is it, Cull?"

"Had a mite of an idea." I wrapped my arms around my knees. "Bill," I asked Longley, "would you do something for me?"

"You just give it a name."

"Try to find out where Chance goes on those rides."

Longley considered it. "You've got an idea where he goes?"

"I'm guessing, but I'd say the Big Thicket."

"Sam Barlow's country," Bickerstaff objected. "He wouldn't go there."

"Maybe."

Bob Lee took a stick from the fire to light his cigar. "You think he's the one who's been tipping off Sam Barlow about the Army?" He looked at me with one of those quick, sharp glances of his. "You don't like the man. You could be prejudiced."

"Might be," I admitted slowly. "It could be, of course, but I just don't believe I am, not to interfere with my judgment. Chance is a thinking man, a mighty thinking man when it comes to what is best for Chance. His side of the family were well-off, but never so much as the rest of the Thornes, and that never did set well with him. I believe he's out to make himself some money and I think he'd play all sides to do it."

Two days later when I was chopping weeds out of my cornfield there was a rider in the lane. The Spencer was leaning against a tree not too far off and I walked over to it, but when the rider showed up it was the horse that got me, not the rider.

"I am not flattered, Mr. Baker," she said.

When she spoke it was in a low, confidential voice, and I looked up into the eyes of the most beautiful woman I'd ever seen. I knew right off it was that New Orleans woman, Lacy Petraine.

"Beautiful horse," I told her.

Her expression did not change. "Yes, he is a fine animal. So are you, Mr. Baker."

That was direct talk and I looked at her, measuring what I saw, and what this woman had she wasn't pretending she didn't have. It was there, all right. Whatever else she was she was like they said, she was all woman.

"This was the sort of horse I was thinking about," I said thoughtfully.

"I came here to talk to you about a job, Mr. Baker."

"I'm not hiring anybody," I said. "I can't afford it." She ignored it. "I need a man—"

"Most women do," I told her innocently.

Her lips tightened. "Mr. Baker, apparently I am wasting my time. I heard of your trouble with the Reconstruction people and they are a group with whom I have some influence. If you accept the job I have for you, I can promise you that you will no longer be annoyed."

She was mad, but she wasn't backing off. Maybe I don't have any clothes to speak of, and I'm not much at dancing, but when I see that look in a woman's eyes I take it she's not thinking of playing whist.

"Mr. Baker, I am buying property. I sometimes carry a little money, and I need a man who can ride with me whom people respect and who can use a gun. With Sam Barlow and his kind I no longer feel safe."

"You'd be better off to talk to Colonel Belser. He would be glad to provide an escort, or do it himself."

"He offered, but I want no connection with him or what he represents. You see, Mr. Baker, I intend to make my home here, and I can imagine it will be difficult for those who were too friendly with the carpetbaggers when the carpetbaggers are gone."

"Somebody should tell that to Chance Thorne."

Putting a hand on the fence at a place where there was no brush, I vaulted it and walked over to her. She sat her horse watching me with a quirt in her hand and a pistol in a saddle scabbard, but I walked around the horse, sizing it up. I always had a good eye for horse flesh—but I was not missing the woman either.

When I was around on the other side I put my hand up as if to reach for her but just caressed the horse. She was looking at me, and I'll give her this, she wasn't scary. In such a position, lonely like it was, most women would have been. I figure she had an idea she could handle whatever showed up, any way she chose to handle it.

"If you are interested in fine horse," she said, "you should work for me. I have several of the very best."

"How'd you know to find me here?"

"You had been described to me, and I was riding by. I am interested in property, Mr. Baker, and have been looking for something I can buy."

"I am not for sale."

She got mad then, really mad. "You flatter yourself, Mr. Baker. I assure you, any interest I had in your working for me is ended."

She rode away, her back rigid with anger, but when

I walked back to my hoe the zest for work was gone. No question about it, I'd acted like a country bumpkin, which was what I was, only I needn't have acted it. And she was a sight of woman—most woman I'd seen in one package for a long time. The sort of woman who'd give a man all he'd ask for, and then some.

Hiding the hoe I mounted my mule and rode back into the swamp and dismounting in a quiet place I started working with the pistol. When the sweat was streaming from me and my hand was getting sore again, I let up. But it had seemed to be coming faster, with less lost motion and a surer grasp of the gun on that first grab. It had to be like that, for if danger came there would be no room for failure.

Seeing Lacy Petraine brought Katy Thorne to mind. Katy didn't have the flesh of that New Orleans woman, but her beauty was just as great. She had a way of carrying herself, cool, poised, and graceful . . . I must find some excuse for seeing Katy.

It was Matt Kirby who knew about Lacy Petraine. Or as much as anybody knew about her. She looked twenty-three or -four, but the way Matt figured it she just had to be at least six years older. Her Pa had owned a plantation near New Orleans, the way Matt had it, and Lacy was of French-Spanish-Irish ancestry, but by the time she was a girl her father had gambled away most of what they had, and she had moved into New Orleans with her father. The year she was sixteen he had died of yellow fever, and she married an Irish gambler named Terence O'Donnell.

He was, according to Matt, a gentleman. He was thirty-two when she married him, handsome, shrewd, and as skillful and successful at gambling as her Pa had been otherwise.

They left New Orleans for Atlanta, and later Matt heard tell of her in Charleston, Richmond and New York. Some said she had been in Havana, too. Then one night on a riverboat Terence dealt the wrong card to the wrong man, was challenged and killed. He left his young wife with a knowledge of cards and fourteen thousand dollars in money.

At eighteen she took off for Europe with two Negro girls for slaves and a big Negro man who was nearly sixty but mule-strong. Next two years she lived in Paris, London, Vienna, Rome, Venice and Madrid, and then she'd been in some sort of a mixup with a man, or so Matt had it from her maid. A love affair that turned out wrong, from what he said. She married André Petraine who was the bastard son of a prominent Frenchman. André tried to blackmail his father and was murdered, quick and simple. Same night they gave Lacy passage to New York and the suggestion she go there and stay.

On the way back some men taught her to play poker, and lost three thousand dollars doing it. Supplying money to an old friend of O'Donnell's, she opened a gambling house in Charleston. Before the war began she sold the gambling house and invested in cotton, sold it well in London and remained there during most of the war.

Matt Kirby had served during part of the war with the friend who had operated her Charleston place, and it was from him that he had pieced together much of the story. Without allegiance to anyone she had returned with sufficient cash to buy land, and it was East Texas she chose, feeling that with Reconstruction sure to go out in a few years she could be one of the wealthiest women in that area.

It was a good scheme, the way Kirby had it, and the way it seemed to figure out. We'd heard around that she was buying land, and that she wasn't a bit upset by the Barlow raids, or any other for that matter. The more folks were frightened the more apt they would be to sell out for a cheap price. According to all accounts she was a woman who knew what she wanted and how to get it.

One thing started me to wondering about how much she wanted me to work for her and how much she might have other ideas in mind. She owned the old Drummond place which adjoined Fairlea on the north, and she owned another farm south of my place.

No matter. I'd my own plans to think of, and with a crop in the ground I could start looking farther ahead. There were occasional drives of cattle to Shreveport or Sedalia, and in the Thickets there were thousands of head, unbranded, and whose ownership would be impossible to trace. Deep in the swamp, under the dark-leaved cypress and the hanging moss, I thought it out, figured just how it could be done, and how it had to be done. And no day went by when I did not practice with a gun.

———

ONE NIGHT, WE were sitting around the fire when suddenly out in the swamp, a fish jumped. We all knew the sound yet the suddenness of it caught us by surprise and in an instant there was nobody about the fire, nothing but the fire burning alone, the empty beds and saddles. In the thick shade of a cypress I looked down at the pistol in my hand and could not remember drawing it.

So that was the way it was then. I was learning, all right, I was faster, much faster.

Nobody moved. Here and there a rifle barrel gleamed in the brush around the clearing while we listened, and then we heard another noise, not of the swamp. A rider was coming who knew the way to come. We waited in the shadows, almost counting the steps. When the rider came into the circle of light it was Matt Kirby.

He was a broad, solid man with a wide face and jaw, a quiet man who drank too much, yet always managed to be where the soldiers were not. He dismounted and went to the fire, pouring black coffee into a smoke-blackened tin cup.

"Raid south of here," he said as we started to come in, "and a woman killed. They say Cullen done it."

"There it is, Cull," Longley said. "They'll mean it now."

"Three posses out," Kirby said. "That's why I hightailed it back here. The orders are to shoot to kill, and if you're taken alive, to hang you."

"That would be Barlow," I said. "I told him to stay away from here."

Bickerstaff got up. "Cullen, you've got to run. Even this place isn't safe."

"I'll stay."

"We can go to Devil's Den," Lee suggested. "It's farther north and no way they could find us there."

Devil's Den was one of the best places, difficult to

get at, and easy to defend. No posse in their right minds would attempt to even come near the place.

"You go ahead," I told them. "I'm going into the Big Thicket."

They all sat around looking at me, trying to see what it was in my mind. All I knew was Sam Barlow was there and the time had come for a killing, for an old-fashioned gut-shooting. I was going to see Sam Barlow. I was going to read him from the Scriptures.

"Heard something else," Kirby said. "There's a dozen riders camped on Blackthorne. They pulled in there while I was coming across country."

If these were Barlow's men on Blackthorne, and I had no idea who else they might be, Katy was in trouble. Getting up I walked to my mule and began to saddle up. It might be too late, even now.

Longley came over to me where I was cinching up. "What's bitin' you, Cull? You takin' off like a sca'ed pa'tridge?"

"Katy Thorne and her aunt live alone on Blackthorne."

"You set store by that gal?"

"I do."

"Then you just hold up while I get my saddle."

Bob Lee came up to his horse packing his saddle under his arm. "I take it mighty hard, you fixing to ride off into trouble alone, Cull. A man would think you had no friends."

"I'm obliged."

Watching them saddle up gave me a strange, warm, odd sort of feeling. There had not been many friends for me during the years I'd ridden the country, or wherever I lived, and there are fewer friends when trouble raises its hand.

Not that I deserved friends. I'd lived too much alone and with a chip on my shoulder, always wanting friendship but wary of folks, fearful of what might come of trying friendship. Thing is, if a man wants friends he's got to be friendly. Takes a man a sight of time to learn the simplest things, it seems.

Matt Kirby switched his saddle to Bickerstaff's spare horse, and when we rode out of there I felt better than any king with an army at his back, for these were good men who rode beside me, and like myself they were men driven to the wall with only ourselves to fight for, and the things in which we believed. If it was Sam Barlow on Blackthorne he'd better make himself scarce before we got there or he'd be planted in that swampy ground.

No moon lit the sky when we rode down the dark lanes, the sound of our horses' hoofs hard upon the roads, or whispering through the grassy fields, but we needed no moon for we were men to whom darkness was a friend. We rode dark horses and our clothes were dark, with no white shirts and no ornaments on our saddles or anything to make a target for a seeing man.

"They'll take time to settle in camp," Kirby said, reassuring me. "They'll be under the big trees between the house and the river."

The house they spoke of was the big house, Blackthorne itself, and some three hundred yards from Will's old place where Katy was...and Blackthorne closed these many months now, closed and still. No doubt they figured to loot the big house, and it would be a rich place to take, bank on that.

I cared just nothing for what they took from Blackthorne, but if Katy was touched, or even if they talked rough to her or threatened her, I'd bury Sam Barlow deep. For I was a man with one thought nor anything to lose but my life, which might be called a wasted thing, even now.

There was no moon when we started, but by the time we turned into the grass lane that led to a broken-down fence the moon was chinning itself on the horizon trees, and the vague light in the sky was lowering itself through the trees, but little enough of it was showing when we rode into the orchard and up through the aisle between the trees. With luck we would arrive unseen and unheard.

It was very still, with only the frogs croaking, but when we were but halfway through the big orchard we heard drunken voices near Will's house and then a pounding on the door. Looked like we'd arrived right on time.

"Open up! Open up in there or we'll bust the door!"

Inside me something started to swell and grow, and I knew what it was because I'd felt it before, the black angry rage, the choking fury that rose inside me until it filled me with a roaring anger, and then a strange and frightening coldness. I knew myself, and was frightened at these rages of mine, and fought them down, but not now.

From inside the house we heard Katy speak, heard faintly as we walked our horses on the grass of the long untouched orchard. "Go away! Go, or I'll shoot!"

"Now you see here," one of the men called persuasively, "you can't shoot us all and we sure enough aim to come in. Now you be a good girl and open that door. You can't shoot us all."

Now the night was still, like I said, and by that time we were right up to the house, and so when the sound of his voice died I spoke quiet but clear enough. "She can't shoot you all," I said. "But *we* can."

You might say there was a change you could feel. You might say these were startled men, and if you said it, you'd be right. Nobody much bothered Barlow men, they'd had their own way about things, but now they were called upon by a voice from the night.

These men standing there before that house where I'd been received in friendship were killers and rapers of women, they were horse thieves, deserters and rascals, and bad as I might be, I'd never touched the level of such scum as these.

"Stay out of this, whoever you are, and you won't get hurt."

Why, I was mad. I was mad and ugly and I laughed, and I am afraid it was not a good laugh. "Are you Barlow men?" I asked.

"We are, and what of it?"

"I told Barlow to stay the hell out of this country. You want to leave now or be buried here?"

The moon was behind the trees, but the light filtered through the cypresses and fell across the door of the house where Katy lived, and the Barlow men stood in the vague light of the coming moon, but we were scattered out on the edge of the orchard, its blackness behind us, and they could see nothing, but could hear a voice only.

There was muttering among them, uneasiness, too. They did not like it, but there might be only one man, and I saw a rifle move.

My Spencer was low across the saddle and on the body of a man standing nearest the door, with a streak of light from a shutter falling across him. I could see a vest pocket and the gray of a lighter shirt, and when that rifle moved I shot him in the stomach.

Along the front of the orchard to the right of me there was a rippling spatter of sound, of hard sound, and I saw men falling and then I was riding in. Going in I held on a man's skull knowing it was a chancy shot, but liking the target, and saw the man go down as the Spencer fired not three feet from his skull as I rode up to him.

The night was roaring with gunfire, and the Barlow men scattered and fell, and rose to rush on and staggered, then fell again. It was sudden, and it was complete and we saw one wounded man rolling on the ground trying to put out the fire the bullet had started on his shirt front. That black powder had a way of throwing grains—I'd seen men tattooed with it.

Their camp was beyond the big house and we rode through the trees on a dead run, weaving among them, shouting rebel yells and shooting at everything that moved in the flickering light among the tree trunks and the shrubs and the moonlight.

Then we saw their fire and a man running from it, and Bill Longley fired and the man stumbled and sprawled forward, falling in flight like a partridge landing, and then he started to get up and three bullets nailed him to the dark earth where he dug in his fingers and died, red blood joining the black earth beneath him.

"Good shot," I said, "we'll go goose-hunting this fall."

We swung down and Bickerstaff turned Bill's dead man over and there were finger-nail scratches on his face. This could be the man who had raped and killed the woman of whom we'd heard, or some other woman.

There were two Dragoon Colts in the camp and a Henry rifle which was brand-spanking-new, two old muskets and a Ballard rifle. There was also coffee, sugar, rice and some baked bread. We took it all, being hunted men who found it hard to get food. One of the Colts I took myself and tossed the other to Longley. Lee took the Ballard rifle.

When we walked our horses back across the lawn there was a moment when I drew in my mule to look up at the big house. "A long time ago," I told Lee, "they used to dance here. On the nights when they'd have a ball sometimes I'd watch from out in the trees. Folks would come up in their fine carriages, and they'd get out and go up the steps, and there'd be music from inside the house."

"Never see the like again," Bob Lee said soberly. "It was another world."

It was true enough, but I who had been no part of it regretted it.

The door was open when we pulled up and Katy was kneeling beside the body of a man who was badly hurt. She stood up as we drew near. "Will you help me get this man into a bed?"

"He was goin' to bust in on you, ma'am," Bickerstaff said. "He's better off dead. That's a mean man you've got there."

"You should have killed him then. I'll let no man die at my door, not even a wolf."

We carried him in and bedded him down, and Katy put water on the fire. We'd come off well, not a scratch among us, for our attack had been too sudden and they'd had no time to do anything but get off quick, unaimed shots in hopes they'd land.

Under the trees we found three dead men to add to the one killed by the door, and another badly wounded. At least two more men were wounded and out in the grass, and the way I figured it there was another dead man out there, and we'd best go hunting him.

"Sam Barlow won't like it." Matt Kirby was lighting his pipe. "I tell you he won't."

"He'll come," Bickerstaff said. "He'll come soon, I'm thinking."

"Then he'd better make it soon," I told them, "because if he doesn't I'll go hunting him."

"Keep the shovel after we've buried these others," I said, "because I'm going to dig Barlow a grave at the Corners. I'll dig the grave and put up a marker and leave it open for him."

Longley chuckled. "Now there's a thought, and I'd give a year of my life to see his face when he heard of it. I'll throw dirt from that grave myself, Cullen, and be proud to hold the shovel."

The wounded man looked at Cullen Baker. "You'll

dig the grave for your own body, whoever you are. Barlow will kill you for this."

"Whoever I am? The name is Cullen Baker, and I'll have the hide of any man who raises a hand against Katy Thorne."

Startled, the wounded man turned his head sharply toward Katy. "You're a *Thorne*?" He was shocked. "Relative to Chance?"

"His sister-in-law."

"Good God!" The wounded man's fear was a frightening thing. "Barlow will have my hide for this!"

"Barlow is a friend of Chance, is that it?" I asked.

Katy glanced at me sharply, but the wounded man merely stared at the ceiling and would say nothing more.

We dug the grave by moonlight as one should dig the grave of such a man, and we finished as the moon was setting behind the trees, and over the open grave we posted a marker with the words burned deep with a branding iron.

HERE LIES SAM BARLOW

COWARD

THIEF

MURDERER

KILLED BY CULLEN BAKER

Before the sun was three hours old the marker at the Corners had been seen by a dozen men and, the love of a good story being what it is, before sundown they were telling it in Lufkin to the south and Boston to the north. And in the swamps along the Sulphur where hard men relished a hard joke, the men in the hide-outs were chuckling and awaiting the fireworks.

And in the Big Thicket the story came to Sam Barlow, and they tell me his fury was a thing to see. They tell me that he raged and ranted and swore, but in the end he settled down into something cold and dangerous, and the men who heard such things and carried the news warned me: "Be careful man, he must kill you now or leave the country. He'll be coming north when you least expect."

And in the clearing back of my cornfield at Fairlea I practiced with the Colt, and it came to my hand with smoothness now, and it came with ease, and the muzzle found the target like a living thing. They could come when they wished, for I was ready now.

CHAPTER 4

MY CORN WAS growing tall when I rode again to the house of Katy Thorne. It had become a place I could not leave alone, nor my quiet talks with her, nor the good coffee in the candlelight. There was a softness in me that I'd nigh forgotten, and I'd sit tipped back in my chair watching her move about the room, listening to the rustle of her skirts, and at times talking to Aunt Flo.

It was a strange thing for me, a hard man grown accustomed to hard ways, to talk with this maiden lady and to Katy, but the house had a warmth for me that I liked. I knew I was not the only visitor, for Katy Thorne had a way with people, and even Chance came at times, although unwelcome I knew. And there was another, a man I'd not met, named Thomas Warren, and a teacher in a school not far away.

He was a stiff young man who rode uncomfortably in the saddle and who had a high-nosed way about him that drew some joking from the boys in the swamps who had seen him about. Yet he had much talk of books that Katy hungered for, and it was something I could not give her. I read whatever came to hand, but it was little enough, and mainly old newspapers and sometimes a magazine.

It was growing faintly yellow around the trees when I came again to the house of Katy Thorne. It was early, but there was smoke from the chimney, and knowing Aunt Flo was a late riser I surmised it must be Katy herself who was up and about.

She saw me coming and opened the door. "Put your horse away. I have breakfast ready."

It was a welcome thing, for I had worked until after dark the night before, and was too tired to prepare food for myself, so I'd dumped water over me from the well and sponged off and gone at once to bed.

These days I was staying at times in the old family house, but not often, and usually in the swamps, but I was a man wary of surprise, and not wanting to travel the same trail too often, so I shifted about and kept myself out of the way and out of sight.

There had been no trouble yet with the Reconstruction people, although there was talk of my arrest for taking the guns from Colonel Belser, in Jefferson. There'd been a note I sent him in which I protested any claim he had to the weapons, for his men taking mine from me.

There was a small shed in the orchard where I stabled my horse these days, and kept oats or corn for it, and some hay. There were two doors at opposite ends and the place was hidden in vines and behind a row of trees, and not many knew it was there. A great wisteria vine had grown over it, and the place had not been used in so many years that even those who knew the place had almost forgotten it.

Katy was at the door when I came, and there was worry in her eyes. "They may come for you, Cullen. It is a worrisome thing. Thomas was saying the other night that people want you arrested."

"People?"

"Some of those he speaks to, the farmers north of here, and the Reconstruction people."

"I've no doubt of it. There will always be some who will not like me. It is the old story of the dog with the bad name. There are some who blame me for anything Barlow does, or anything done by drifting renegades. I am sorry, Katy, but I warned you of what people would say."

She smiled at me. "Since when has the countryside told a Thorne who is acceptable and who is not? You will come when you like, Cullen, and stay as long as you like."

"Well, then. You've no worry right now about them coming upon me. There's a man on the highroad and another in the lane. We'll have warning enough."

Aunt Flo was in the bedroom with the wounded man. His recovery had been slow, and for a time it was doubtful that he would recover at all. Now, slowly, he was coming around.

Katy noticed the guns at my belt. "Must you always wear those?"

"Would you have me ride without them, Katy? They're as necessary to me as hairpins to you, or the ring on your finger, more so, because they are my life itself. I live by them, and perhaps shall die by them, but while I live they must never be far from my hand.

"There's a fine, strong feeling in the butt of a gun, Katy, for it's a man's weapon, but a gun is meant for death, and is not to be treated lightly or as a toy. A gun is like a woman or a horse, and not to be handled by a man who doesn't understand it."

"You understand women, then?"

"Only that like a fine pistol they must be handled

gently or they're apt to explode." I grinned at her. "You know the swamps are no place to learn of women."

"How about those Western lands? I've heard stories of you out there, and in the Mormon country. Did you have three wives out there?"

"Not one, Katy. Not even a small, quiet one. I'd a horse and a gun and little else."

She was pouring coffee then and she put down the pot and said, "Cullen, why don't you leave here? Why don't you go some place you won't be needing a gun? Are you always to live like this?"

"Can I give up all this, Katy, and make Pa's life a useless thing? And if I run this time, who is to say when I shall have to run again? And when shall I stop running? My father played to ill luck all his life, yet at the end he had this land, and little as land in Texas is worth, it was all he had, and it was left to me. And here I shall stay."

"There is hatred for you here, Cullen. Even the good people fear you. No matter what is to come, I am afraid they would never trust you or want you here."

The gloom was on me then for I knew the truth of what she said, and felt deep within me a sense of being fated for ill things.

"They are right to want to kill me," I said at last, "for there is a difference in me, and deep within every animal there is a need to kill what is different. There is always the feeling that what is different may expose them all to danger.

"When I came here as a stranger they attacked me because I was a stranger and seemed vulnerable. They believed me weak because I was alone, and I was not weak for the very reason that I was alone."

"You must leave. It is the only way."

"Maybe they are right to kill me," I repeated, captured by the trend of my thinking. "Wild animals often kill animals that are different, a white wolf among gray wolves must be a terrible fighter to survive, for their instinct is to kill, perhaps because a white wolf can be seen farther and may bring danger to the pack."

"Will Sam Barlow come looking for you?"

"He will. He must come. Stay clear of me, Katy. I'm a man who attracts trouble. And I must stay away from you, for I'll surely bring grief to you, and danger."

"You have saved me from danger."

"Yes...and if I am killed I want you to have Fairlea, and the crop I planted there."

She looked at me in sudden surprise. "You've planted a crop? How could you?"

"It was the first thing I did. When I came back here it was to make a new life, and I have not wished for trouble. They brought it to me, Chance first, and then Barlow, and those others with the loose tongues who talk of me as an outlaw and a bad one.

"The love of the land is in me, Katy, and it is all I have. Without it all I have is a horse and a gun and a will to fight. I'm as free as one of those soldiers of fortune of the free companies who sold their services to kings in the old days. Yet if there is anything will save me from what I am, it is the land. I am a man of blood and fury, Katy, perhaps it's the Black Irish in me, and if there is peace for me it will be on the land."

"If you harvest your crop, what then?"

"I'll store it for feed, and then with some of the others we'll round up wild cattle from the thickets and drive them off for sale in the north. With what cash I get I shall buy a stallion and a couple of good mares and start breeding horses. It is a thing I have been wanting to do." Pausing, I stared at the candle flame. "And I'll do it, too, if I am not killed."

"That isn't like you, Cullen, to speak of dying."

"It is though. I live with it. I am not one of those fools who believe it is always the other man who is killed by accident or a gun. I know it can happen to me, it can happen to anyone, at any time. Anyone who takes an unnecessary risk is a fool, and I don't want to die when I haven't lived."

"Go away, Cullen," she pleaded, "go West, or anywhere. You would not be running away, and if you live you will have defeated them. And what does it matter what they believe, anyway?"

At the door, when it was almost noon, I told her, "You shouldn't waste time on me. I'm no good."

"If you think that," she replied sharply, "others will think it. Respect begins with self-respect."

"You know you're right?" I told her. "You're damned right."

At the shed I led out the horse I was riding today, giving my mule a chance to rest. The mule was tough and seemed willing to go for hours on little food and less sleep, but nothing can stand up to that, and I must be in shape for a fast and long run, so the mule took turns now with a spare horse of Bickerstaff's.

When I reached Jack English who waited in the lane, we rode to the highway to join Bill Longley. We had agreed on a meeting with some of the others, and had gone but a short distance when Bob Lee came up to us with Matt Kirby.

There was news. Barlow had been riding again, and in the north. A farmhouse near Linden had been looted and burned and the stock driven off, but then there was an exchange of shots with some farmers who banded together and Barlow retreated, unwilling to fight when there was loot to be had without fighting. And the troops when called out had found nothing.

Three men had ridden up to Lacy Petraine's house and had ridden around drunk and yelling, but when they tried to force a way in, a man suddenly appeared around the corner of the house and spoke to them. Turning to look, two of them died in a blast of gunfire, and the third was carried away, seriously wounded.

"And you know who it was? John Tower is working for the widow."

Three men downed in the dark, and two of them killed outright. It was good shooting. And by John Tower.

He was a man to remember.

While they talked that over I walked away from them. Back in the field out of sight I waited until a frog croaked and then drew. The heavy Colt snaked out in a swift, fluid motion and was there in my hand, hammer eared back and ready to shoot. Lowering the hammer I tried it again. Yes, I was fast. Was I fast enough?

Gloomily, I strolled back to where they sat under the trees within a step or two of the road. What were we doing here, hiding in the brush like animals?

Weary, unwashed and beat, rarely a chance to sleep in a bed, rarely a well-cooked meal like today. They were always telling the foolish romantic stories of outlaws and men on the run...the writers of such stories should try it some time; they should try living in swamps, living with sweat, dirt and death.

"I believe," I told them, "that Chance Thorne is getting information to Barlow."

"Who would believe you?" Bob Lee asked. "They were saying today that you were raiding fifty miles south of here."

"Then we'll go into town and show them we're here, and raiding nowhere. We'll make liars of them."

Colonel Amon Belser was the first man we saw. "They say I am out raiding," I told him. "You see me here, and an unlathered horse."

Belser was stiff with anger, for he knew the townspeople were watching, secretly amused. They did not like me, but I was one of their own, and they liked him even less.

"I shall live to see you hang, Cullen Baker!" Belser said. My being here in town made him furious. It was a challenge to the authority he was proud of. "I shall be the first to put a hand on the rope!"

He might be, at that. These days in my dark moods I'd have bet no man that I'd not stretch rope before it was over, only the ones who took me for the hanging would leave some dead behind.

"Colonel." I put both hands on the pommel of my saddle. There were a dozen townsfolk within the sound of my voice, and I wanted them to hear. "Colonel," I said, "if you are in this county or any county that borders it one week from today you'll get what you deserve. It's time we ran all you carpetbaggin' rascals out of here."

"Now see here!" Belser protested. "I—"

"You heard me, Colonel. One week."

He stood there, his face white, and he was a mighty worried man. "You'll come to nothing, Cullen Baker," he said. "The very people who think you a hero now will be hunting you down as soon as we are gone."

And when we rode out of town I knew what he had said was true. Folks had never liked me here, and they did not like me now, although because they thought of me as resisting the carpetbaggers they were making me a talked-of man, but once it was over . . . well, they'd be the same then, and they'd start remembering that I'd been a tough lad to deal with.

With the word I'd given Belser I could expect an all-out hunt for me, and no matter what I did I was going to need money. Living in the swamps I'd needed little. A man could hunt himself a living out there, and the boys who had many friends were always coming back with supplies, but the money I'd brought home with me was about gone. Now, if ever, was the time to go after those wild cattle.

It would serve another purpose, too. They would be searching the swamps for me and I'd be down in the Thickets. But I must tell nobody my plans until the last minute.

IT WAS HOT and still in the Thickets. In a week of desperately hard work we had rounded up but three hundred head of wild cattle. They were big and mean, most of them, and we'd had our troubles. A man doesn't know how he can sweat until he starts working cattle in the brush. Sometimes for days there wouldn't be a breath of wind, and they grow horse-flies down there half as big as sparrows. We worked like dogs, nothing less, and now we had three hundred head together and we were talking it over.

"Barlow's holding about two hundred head of stolen cattle," Longley suggested. "We could go take them from him."

That Longley. He was already ready for trouble. And he was a salty youngster, too.

"We'll take them, Bill," I told him, "but that money won't be ours. Some of the folks that lost those cattle will be wanting the money."

"I wasn't thinking about the money or the cattle," Longley said. "I was thinking about taking them away from Barlow."

"Matt," I asked Kirby, "do you know Lost River?"

"Ought to, I fished along it as a youngster."

"Awhile back," I said, "a fellow was making talk one night and he said there were a lot of wild cattle down there, and that almost nobody lives down there now."

Kirby thought that over. "Well, there's a lot of big meadows down there, always ran to rich grass, and that's mesquite country. I'd say it was top country for cows. But I ain't been there since I was a boy."

We had word from the north. Belser and Chance Thorne were working the swamps along the Sulphur like they had never worked them before. Joel Reese was guiding them, but so far they'd found nothing but a couple of abandoned camps, unused for months.

And not ours, either. But what bothered me was word they had been watching the home of Katy Thorne.

One other thing we learned. Two men had come with a horse for the wounded man and had taken him away. She was not molested.

We went back to work on the cattle around Lost River. It was rough country, but a mighty handsome land, too. We had better luck there.

The first white men to come into Texas before the colonies' fight for independence had found wild cattle in the thickets and along the river, most of them descended from cattle left behind by Spanish travelers in the area. Later, cattle had escaped from ranches and fled to the brush, and during the War between the States thousands of cattle had gone unbranded and had run wild to join the herds already there.

Within the thickets there was grass, water and leaves for additional feed. The cattle had worn their own trails through the brush and had become wild animals, and some of them were as fierce as anything that walked, and incredibly huge. Why, down in those thickets I've seen many an old mossyhorn that stood seventeen hands and had a spread of horns better than six feet. Some have been found that I've heard tell of that were ten or eleven feet across.

Kirby knew many of these trails, and I'd scouted around the thickets some on my own. Working that Lost River country we rounded up three hundred head of cattle the first week, and with six hundred head we started north. We had us a big corral spotted.

This corral was in the brush itself, and had been made long since by some Mexicans who had interwoven the surrounding brush into a solid fence strong enough to hold an elephant. We drove our herd north and into that corral. There was water there, and grass enough for a while.

We were on the edge of the Big Thicket now, and we knew exactly where we were going. We entered the Thicket again at a place where a big old cypress leaned above a stream, and we took a dim path, used by game and wild cattle. We rode single file with brush snagging at us on both sides, and we rode armed and ready. This here was going to be war, and believe me, we were ready for it.

The air was stifling. A rabbit started almost from under the feet of the horse I was riding and several times we heard wild hogs grunting in the brush, but we didn't see any. Right then I wasn't wanting to meet a cross old boar right in that narrow trail—a wild boar can be a mean customer at close quarters.

We made a fireless camp that night in a small glade, and we didn't talk above a whisper. There was a hint of approaching thunderstorm in the air, and we spent the night cleaning guns and getting set. Sam Barlow had asked for trouble when he came north and now we were taking it to him.

My Spencer and two Colts were my weapons, aside from a twelve-inch bowie knife I always carried. For the time and the job it wasn't much to carry. Some of the Barlow men carried five and six pistols, for a cap-and-ball pistol can be a problem to reload, and a man needed fire power.

When I was with the Quantrill crowd that time for a few days I saw many men who carried several pistols stuck into their waistbands, in holsters and on their horses. That young horse thief called Dingus who was with Weaver when I rode away from them had carried four or five pistols. He had red-rimmed eyes and nervous affliction that kept him batting his eyes like an owl in a hailstorm. Nowadays they are talking of him as an outlaw. His rightful name is Jesse James.

It was past noon when we mounted up. The men we were hunting would have eaten and it was siesta time. When we got close to their camp I drew rein.

"We ride in shooting," I said.

Somewhere in the brush ahead of us a woman screamed and a man laughed loudly. Somebody else swore at them to be quiet.

We could see a corral filled with horses and there were a couple of cookfires going, and men lazing about in the shade. Mostly they were watching one man in the center of the group who had a young girl by the arm and a whip in his other hand. "Try gittin' away from me, will you? I'll give you a whuppin' to remember me by. Nothin' like a well-whupped woman, I always says."

There were nearer thirty men present than the fourteen our scout had led us to expect, but several of the horses were damp from hard riding so a party must have just arrived.

"Quite a passel of them, Cullen," Longley commented casually, "but we wanted 'em, didn't we?"

"One shot each," I said, "and then we go in. Make the first one pay." It was at least fifty yards from where we peered through the leaves to the opening into the clearing. "Looks like this will be all the Barlow men we get this time, so don't waste any."

Touching my heel to the horse I started him

walking. It was very still except for the laughter from the clearing and the bullying talk of the man with the whip. From each hoof-fall a tiny puff of dust lifted.

It was very hot. Sweat trickled down my cheek and I dried a palm on my jeans. Somewhere off over the thicket a crow called, cawing into the still afternoon. Saddles creaked, and we swung into line opposite the opening, and we were a mere handful to the men inside, but we had wanted a fight, and there was such a thing as surprise. As we swung into line we were within view of at least a third of the men in the clearing, but they were intent upon the struggle between the man and the girl.

Raising my pistol I dropped it dead center on the chest of the man with the whip just as he drew it back for a blow. "All right," I said conversationally, and shot him.

The sharp *bang* of sound was lost in the crashing volley that followed.

The man with the whip dropped the girl's arm and fell on his face in the dust. A man quicker of apprehension than the others rose up sharply from under the trees and dropped in his tracks in the volley that cut him down and several others, and then we went into the clearing at a dead run and swung into two ranks of four each and circled the clearing, shooting.

Men broke and ran in every direction. One who grabbed a shotgun took a bullet in the teeth and fell. Longley leaned from his saddle and grabbed a burning branch which he hurled into the roof of the nearest brush shelter and it went up in a puff of roaring flame.

We scattered out, firing at every target we could

see, but the clearing had emptied as though spilled over the edge.

Bob Lee caught up the girl who had been about to be whipped and swung her to his saddle and went out of the camp. Matt Kirby tore open the gate of the corral and stampeded the horses. A shot came from the edge of the clearing and three bullets smashed back a reply, and a man walked from the brush and fell on his face to roll over and stare up at the sun.

And then we were gone, and running. Behind us the Barlow camp was a shambles. The place was a mass of roaring flame, and what cattle and horses they had we drove ahead of us down the trail. Surprisingly, another woman ran from the brush and called out for help. Held prisoner, she had seen her chance, and Bickerstaff held one of the horses for her and she swung aboard with a manner that showed she was not new at riding bareback.

By nightfall we were out of the thicket and headed toward the Louisiana state line. The girl pointed out three cows and a horse that had belonged to her father and we cut them out and gave them to her. Once started we swung up a creek and then went up a road and headed for Fort Worth and the corral enroute where we had left the rest of our cattle.

The girl with her horse and three cows had started home, but she turned back. She had straight, proud eyes and a good, honest way of looking at a man. "Who shall I thank the Good Lord for?" she asked.

"This here is Bob Lee," I said, "and I'm Cullen Baker." Then I named off the others, and she looked at each of them in turn.

"Folks say Cullen Baker is worse than Sam Barlow."

"Don't you believe it," Bill Longley said. "Cullen's honest, but he's driven. The carpetbaggers give us no rest," he added, "and it was Cullen who brought us down here to teach Barlow to stay south of Caddo Lake."

"Thank you," she said, "it's most fittin', what you done. I shall tell folks that it was you saved me."

"You get along home," I said, "or make a new one if yours is gone. This trouble will pass," I added.

We rode to Fort Worth and some of our stock we sold along the way. But most of it we sold in Fort Worth itself.

Several days it had taken us, but we rode careful and stayed shy of the traveled roads, but we traveled less fast than the news of what we had done. In Fort Worth there was already talk of it, and folks were telling that Cullen Baker with fifty men had wiped out a camp of Barlow men. And most folks were pleased.

Actually, there were but eight of us charged the Barlows, and nary a man drew a scratch. We'd been less than three minutes inside that clearing and the surprise had been complete. It was the first time anybody had attacked a Barlow camp—or even found one.

Nor did we wipe them out. Near as we could figure no more than seven were sure enough killed, but we must have wounded that many more. They lost a lot of supplies, clothing, blankets and weapons as well as what stock we drove off.

"Must be a thousand people in Fort Worth," Buck

Tinney claimed. He was astonished, a body could see that. Buck, he had never seen a big town before.

"There's bigger towns," his brother Joe said. "New Orleans now, she's bigger. So's Natchez, I reckon."

"Don't seem possible," Buck replied.

We hired us rooms, and bought baths, shaves and haircuts. Comin' into town we looked a likely bunch of curly wolves, but when we got ourselves fixed up we all shaped up like a bunch of dudes.

The fort on the bluff was inside a picket fence, but the building had been abandoned. The log structure that had been the commissary had been taken over by civilians, and the buildings around it had been surrounded by more than a hundred small camps, tents and wagons. There was a blacksmith shop, supply store, saloon, a livery stable and various other businesses. Several dozen wagons loaded with bales of cotton were drawn up in the courthouse square.

We stopped on the corner by Haven's hardware store and looked around. The Tinney boys watched the crowd with excited eyes, while Bill Longley went over to the window of Bateman's grocery, nearby.

"Come sundown we meet at the hotel," I suggested. "If things look good we'll stay over, otherwise we light a shuck."

There was something vaguely familiar about a man across the square and it worried me. We wanted to see nobody we knew, although with herds of cattle coming in or passing through, any of us might be seen. There were more around who knew Bob Lee and the others than knew me, but they'd be apt to make a connection if they recognized any one of us.

So when we scattered out Bob Lee went across the

street with me for a drink. "I could use a decent meal and some clothes," I said to Bob Lee.

My clothes looked miserable and I'd been thinking of that. The cattle paid off in good money and I was feeling it. Also, good clothes would be a sort of disguise, for nobody had ever seen me in any, leastways not around here.

"Ever think of going West?" I asked it suddenly, so it surprised even me.

"My family are here," Bob Lee said, after a minute, "and we've a difficulty with the Peacock family. No telling when it will end. Yes, I've thought of it, or maybe Mexico."

"I was thinking about it."

"You've nobody here."

"Nothing but a tough reputation."

"Is that why you wanted this drive? To get money to go West?"

He never got an answer to that one because right then I lifted my glass and looked down the bar into the eyes of John Tower.

My left side was toward the bar and my left-hand gun was under the edge of the bar and out of easy grasp. It was my right hand held the drink.

Tower started along the bar toward us, and Lee caught my expression, knowing there was trouble. "Stand easy," I whispered, "it's the man rides for Lacy Petraine."

"Who used to ride for Belser."

Tower was carefully dressed in a black broadcloth suit, and was clean-shaven but for his mustache. "Having yourselves a blowout?" he asked.

"Looking around," I said. "We may open a ready-to-wear."

Bill Longley had come in. "Or a funeral parlor," he said. "Could be a lot of business in that line."

John Tower glanced at Longley. "I might contribute a little, myself. But don't start business my way. I'm not a trouble-hunting man."

"Neither are we," I said.

"There's a story around town that somebody named Cullen Baker cleaned up Barlow's guerrillas, and you would be surprised how much friendly talk it started about Cullen Baker. A few more operations like that and he could run for governor."

He put down his glass. "By the way, Mrs. Petraine is in town, and she'd like to talk to you."

"Later," I said.

Matt Kirby came up the street with the Tinney boys. "Dud Butler's in town," he whispered, "and four or five with him."

Butler I remembered. It had been him I'd seen across the street. He had been one of the boys with Chance the first time they set on me, but lately he'd been reported riding with Sam Barlow. A big, dirty, oafish boy he had grown into a man of the same sort.

"It's my fight," I said.

"He knows me," Bob Lee said. "He rides with that Peacock outfit."

In a tailor shop we got ourselves fitted into black broadcloth suits, and Tower came in. "You would do well to talk to Mrs. Petraine," he said. "She particularly requested you come to see her."

"Watch yourself," Longley advised. "It might be a trap."

"I don't need a trap," Tower replied. "I skin my own cats."

Lacy Petraine was in a small place on a street off the square where an elderly widow and her maiden lady sister served meals to the better class of traveler.

She was seated alone and for an instant she did not recognize me in the new suit. "You are quite the gentleman, Mr. Baker. You should wear such clothes all the time."

"You wanted to see me?"

"I wanted to buy your land—all of it."

So I sat down and put my hat on the chair beside me. All my memories of anything were here in Texas, and my folks had left their mark upon the house and upon the land. Pa was always a-tinkering at things, and he built every inch of fence on the place with my help, and some of it we had cleared together of brush and trees.

"It isn't for sale," I said.

"Cullen," she leaned across the table toward me, and she was wearing some fancy perfume like nothing I'd ever smelled before, "I know how you feel, but there's nothing here for you anymore. I know how you feel because we are much alike in many ways, but your only hope is to leave."

There was truth in that, more truth than I cared to admit, even though I was more than half-convinced already. The carpetbaggers would go, but Chance Thorne would stay, and he would have a glib story to tell, and with his family background, he'd be apt to make it stick. Meanwhile, who was to speak for me?

Would Bob Lee be left? Or Bickerstaff, or any of the others?

"Believe me, Cullen, you are facing a fight you cannot win. I tried to win it once, and then tried again and again, but my reputation followed me. But you could ride away into the West where you used to be, and nobody would be the wiser."

"Maybe, maybe you're right."

"You've frightened them, Cullen, and they're out to get you now, and believe me, they don't dare let you live."

Finishing my coffee I put money on the table and got up. Suddenly I felt cramped for space. "Not now," I said, "but thanks for the offer."

"Don't wait too long," she warned.

Turning away from the table I glanced out the window at the street. With Dud Butler out there Bob Lee was in danger, too. He should not be away from the others.

"Cullen," Lacy spoke very low, "if you're thinking of Katy Thorne it won't do. She's to be married."

My back was to her and I was glad. Katy to be married? That was impossible. She would have said something, she would have ... but why should she?

"I had not heard."

"It has been developing a long time, Cullen, even before you returned, and I am surprised you had not heard of it."

"Who is he?"

"Tom Warren, the schoolteacher. He began courting her over a year ago, and I believe his family have some distant connection with Katy's Aunt Florence."

She came up behind me where I stood looking into the street. "Don't sell me the land, Cullen, but go, please go."

"Why are you so concerned?"

The question stopped her, and I could see she didn't even know herself, and looking at her I knew I'd never seen a woman so beautiful, and somehow I had a sudden feeling if I was to reach out and take her in my arms that she wouldn't resist, not even a mite. And we were all alone in here, at this hour.

"I must go," I said, feeling a fool to have such ideas. What could she want with me?

Lacy put her hand on my arm. "Come and see me, Cullen. Please do."

"Why, sure. Sure, Lacy, I'll come."

My gun was thrust behind my belt under the edge of the coat I was wearing, and when I stepped out I looked one way and the other, but saw nobody.

The square was filled with wagons and as it was growing late in the afternoon folks were moving slower and the square was quieter. Yet suddenly the urge was on me to get out of town, to ride, to get away. I needed a campfire and time to think. There was no reason why I should be so wrought up about Katy marrying. What could she mean to me?

My eyes were busy and I figured I was seeing everything, that I'd scanned every wagon, every doorway, every spot a man could hide, yet suddenly the voice came from behind me and it was Dud Butler.

"I'm a-gonna kill you, Cullen!"

All movement stopped and I knew without turning that his gun was ready to kill me as I turned. Only I was already turning.

There was no thinking, no thought and response, just that challenge and the months of training I'd given myself and before he was through talking I was shooting.

The report of that Dragoon Colt cut a hard line across the silence of the square.

Dud lifted on his tiptoes, took one teetering step forward and fell flat, and he was dead before he touched the ground.

Dud had never known anything but a flash of flame and a stunning blow over the heart.

From nowhere they closed around me, guns drawn, facing outward. Lee, Longley and the Tinney boys, with Kirby coming up, leading all our horses. And by a cotton wagon was Jack English and he was holding a Spencer, and beyond him Bickerstaff facing the other way with a Henry .44.

A tall man with a gray mustache stepped over and stared down at Dud Butler's body, then he looked around at me. "I say it was a fair shootin'," he said positively, "but I never did see a man shuck a gun so quick."

The crowd was gathering, and one man stared hard at me and said, "He called a name, sounded like Cullen."

"He's no Cullen," Longley grinned at the man, "this here's our boss, he's a cattleman from the Gulf shore."

Matt Kirby reined his horse over to look down at Butler's body. "Why, this man looks like one of the Barlow crowd! I'd swear that's Dud Butler!"

We mounted up. After Kirby's comment it was not likely anybody would come forward and admit to being a friend of Butler, and therefore likely to be taken for one of the Barlow outlaws.

Riding swiftly out of town we took the trail west until we hit a cattle trail that would partly cover our tracks, and then we swung south and east, keeping to low ground so's not to be seen more than we could help. We expected no pursuit but operated on the idea that a man can't be too careful.

We camped by a small stream that flowed into the Trinity after riding several miles in the water to leave no more trail than we had to. It was past midnight when we bedded down, and when Longley was pulling off his boots he said, "That old feller back there was right. I never did see a man get a gun out so fast."

On the bluff across the river a lone coyote yapped a shrill challenge at the moon, and a faint breeze rustled the cottonwood leaves.

Taking my pipe out of my pocket I lighted up, feeling mighty solemn. Bob Lee was rolling a cigarette, a trick he had learned from Mexicans. "Could be you're right, Cullen," he said. "Maybe we should all go West."

CHAPTER 5

WHEN I CRAWLED out from under my blankets in the cold dawn I had an urge to cut and run. Prodding the gray coals with a stick I found a little fire and threw on some leaves and then some branches.

Why was I going back, anyway? I was away from there with a good start on the road west and I was a complete fool to go back and make a target of myself.

A stranger had camped with us, a man who came in late and wanted to bed down, and although none of us knew him there was no way we could shut him out. He was as full of news as a dry farm widow, and told us there was a regiment of soldiers moved to Marshall, and rumor had it that a company was to be located in Jefferson, and another in Clarksville. Nor were these raw, unseasoned troops we'd had around that neck of the woods, but tough veterans of the recent war, and real fighting men. Chance Thorne, this stranger said, had been searching the swamps with a bunch of Union Leaguers hunting for that there Cullen Baker.

When I had water on the fire for coffee I made up my mind. I was riding to Blackthorne.

Kirby caught me shaving and had to speak up. "A feller shaves he mostly goes courtin'."

"Business," I told them, "although I'm stopping at Blackthorne."

"They'll be ready for you, Cull." Kirby paused. "Want me to show some place? We're about of a size and build and color of hair. I've heard it said we favor, from behind, anyway. I could draw them off."

"No use getting shot for me. I'll manage."

"We'll be at the Elbow," Bob Lee suggested. "Come there."

It was a wearing thing, being geared for trouble at any minute when all I wanted was a little peace. Stuffing my gear in my saddlebags I considered that, realizing I was a hunted man drawing nearer to the hunters.

It was late when I rode up through the orchard to Blackthorne. I'd switched to the mule and I tied him in the old stable under the wisteria vine, but there was a horse tied outside the house and I felt irritation. I'd hoped to find Katy alone.

A glance through the window showed a young man, well-dressed, and a stranger to me. From the description I knew it must be Thomas Warren, that schoolteacher Lacy told me was to marry Katy. Right then I was a jealous man, and no reason for it; I'd no claim on her.

Aunt Flo had a quick warmth in her welcome that pleased me, not knowing how anybody would feel about me here, and Katy's smile was quick and excited. "Cullen! You were the last person we expected! We heard the Army was searching for you."

Katy turned quickly. "Cullen, this is Thomas Warren, he teaches school near here."

"A pleasure," I said, and held out my hand.

Warren wore a gun, probably a Patterson Colt, but carried it in his pocket. He ignored my hand.

"I cannot say the same. If you have friendship for Miss Thorne you will leave at once."

"Why, Tom!" Katy was surprised. "Cullen is a friend of mine, and a very good friend."

"That surprises me," Warren replied stiffly. "I cannot understand how a lady of quality can endure the presence of this . . . this. . . ."

Ignoring him, I said to her, "It's good to see you, Katy. Very good to see you."

It was a fine sort of thing to see her pleasure in my new clothes. In the dark suit I knew I looked well, but anything would have looked better than the clothes I'd been wearing.

"You look every inch the Southern gentleman," Katy said. "Have you eaten?"

"Camp fare by a man who is no cook."

Aunt Flo, to whom a hungry man was a delight, and reason for much bustling in the kitchen, was busy right off. Warren stood there at one side looking furious. Anybody else but him and anywhere else but this I'd have read to him from the Book for talking like he had, but this was Katy's house and I was her guest . . . and he, this Warren, was to marry her.

"Have you thought," Warren interrupted, "what would happen if the soldiers should come?"

Katy turned on him. "Cullen Baker was welcome in this house when Uncle Will lived here, and will always be welcome. I am sorry, Tom, that you disapprove, but if you do not mind being in the same house with Cullen Baker, we would like to have you stay."

His face paled, and for an instant I figured he would leave, then he sat down abruptly.

Katy asked about Fort Worth, so she had heard about Dud Butler. "I wasn't surprised," she said quietly. "He was always a cruel, trouble-making boy."

Warren glanced at her, shocked.

"Mr. Warren," Katy explained, "comes from New England. I believe he finds us somewhat barbaric."

"Not you!" Warren replied hastily. "Not you at all!"

"This is still a frontier," I said, "and there was a time when they carried guns to church even in New England."

"It was not the same. There were Indians."

"There are many kinds of savages."

"I scarcely believe there is basis for comparison." Warren was brusque. "Fighting off red Indians is very different from killing white men in the street."

"One time Will Thorne told me about the Puritans wanting to go down to Baltimore and burn out some folks just because they liked music, parties and dancing. That seems mighty savage to me."

Warren stood up. "I believe I must go," he said. "I did not realize you expected company."

When Warren was gone we sat silent, and I did not know what to say, or how to begin. If she was to marry this man it was her affair, but it was wrong; he was no man for her. And it was not only that he had not liked me, but there seemed something wrong about him, the feeling one has sometimes about a bad horse, yet what could be wrong about a school-teacher? Maybe it was that he was too sure he was right, he was almost, it appeared to me, a fanatic, and fanatics are dangerous men.

Yet why should I mind? She had been kind to me when there had been no one else. Turning my head to watch the candlelight reflected on her face I thought suddenly something I had not thought before—I loved her.

How does a man like me know what love is? There was nothing much in my life to tell me, but there was a feeling I felt for her that I had never felt before, for anyone.

"Your corn is tall," Katy said suddenly. "It is ready to harvest."

"I'm leaving Texas," I said.

"You're actually going?"

"Yes."

"When, Cullen? When?"

"Soon—in the next few days."

"Cullen, I— You've no idea how I've hoped for this!"

"You want to be rid of me?"

She put her hand on mine. "You know it isn't that. You simply haven't a chance here, and somewhere else you can make a fresh start, and you'll have a chance to live a decent life."

"Everything I have is here." I said it sullenly. "If I leave here there is nothing for me."

"There is everything for you, Cullen. You are young, strong, and you have intelligence. You can do anything you wish to do, if you wish it enough."

Looking at her I thought that there was one thing I could never have, no matter how much I wanted it. Anger stirred me and I got up, anger at myself and at the place life had given me. But she was right, and there was nothing here for me and the sooner I left the better.

"I must go."

"Wait." Katy blew out the candle and we opened the door and stepped out into the darkness. There was a faint breeze from over the swamp bringing a breath of ancient earth and rotting wood and dead leaves, the heavy scent of blossoms, too, and the coolness of still waters, those shaded waters where soon I would go no more.

Suddenly the anger welled up in me again and I knew that no matter who she was to marry I must say what there was in me to say. "Katy," I said, "would you—"

They stepped out of the darkness so quietly that I had no time to think or to act. There were a dozen of them with rifles leveled, and in the faint moonlight they were clearly visible. And my only thought was that if I made a move now Katy might be injured.

"Do not move, Cullen. This time we have you." The voice was the voice of Chance Thorne.

He stepped through the line of armed men and stood there in the moonlight, tall, straight and handsome. "And now, Cullen Baker, you'll hang."

A man came from behind me and took my two Colts. Katy remained beside me and, looking up at me, she whispered, "What was it, Cullen? What did you start to ask me?"

"A foolish thing," I said, "and nothing at all, really. Nothing at all."

How could a man who was to be hung ask such a question? And Chance Thorne would not let me escape again, and if I was not to be surprised, they would hang me before we ever reached Jefferson.

"Go inside, Katy," Chance said. "If anything is to happen I do not want you to see it."

"I'll stay." From behind the house Bert appeared. He was a former slave who had returned a few days before when he could find no work. "Bert, get my horse, will you?"

"I'll not permit that." Chance spoke angrily. "There might be shooting."

Katy smiled at him. "That is why I shall go along, so there will be no shooting. I want to be sure this prisoner really gets to prison."

Chance hesitated, not knowing how to stop her. I knew he intended to hang me, and realized that only Katy stood between the hangman's rope and me.

Yet I could wait and listen, and maybe there would be a spot of luck between now and the moment of death. At the same time the slightest wrong move would have me ballasted down with lead.

"It's all right," I told Katy. "Nothing will happen."

Joel Reese laughed sardonically. "Don't be too sure of that. I've already got the rope."

There were men here who feared me, and fearing me they hated me because of their fear, and Katy herself might be in danger if they became too drunk or too reckless to care. Yet any mob is composed of cowards, and each hopes to commit brutality and cruelty within the safety of the mob. He does not wish to be singled out.

So I chuckled, and never did I feel less like it, but I knew whatever must be done must be done now, while they were still sober-headed enough to listen and to know fear. "You have the rope, Joel, but have you eyes that see in the dark? Eyes that can see an aimed rifle before it hits home?"

Oh, I had their attention now, and I meant to push home the point. If I reached Jefferson or Boston or wherever they meant to take me, I would be a surprised man. Yet much as they wished to hang me they wanted to live even more.

"Did you believe I was alone here? The boys are out there now, just beyond the edge of darkness, and they're watching. If anything happens to me not one of you will live."

"You're lyin'!" Reese yelled at me. "You're lyin', damn you!" But there was a note in his voice that sounded from the fear in his belly.

We rode out, and I was tied to my mule which Reese had found, and my feet tied to the stirrups. There was a man on either side of me, three before and three behind, and others scattered about, and each man rode with a gun ready in his hands.

The words I had spoken as a warning had touched them to the quick. Once, when out in the forest a twig snapped, they jumped in their saddles, lifting their rifles.

"No use to fight," I told them. "When they want you they'll take you. Right now you are alive because they have seen that I am unhurt. If anything happens to me not one man jack of you will live to see town."

"Shut up!" Reese said angrily. "When we get you into town it will be a different story."

The stocky man on his right leaned toward him. "I want a hand on the rope that hangs you, Baker! That there rope will sell for a pretty penny. Feller could cut it into three- or four-inch lengths and sell them as the rope that hung Cullen Baker! I could stay drunk for a month on what I'd make from that!"

Out in the dark forest an owl hooted, only suddenly I knew all my talk had not been empty talk, for that owl hoot was Bill Longley! From the road ahead I heard it again, only that time it wasn't Longley who hooted, but one of the others.

A moment later and the sound was repeated from behind and on both sides.

Reese swore savagely, but the fright in his voice was plain to hear. The riders behind began to bunch up as if afraid of being caught alone.

"You'd be better off turning me loose," I said. "If I should fall off my horse there'd be a lot of dead men around."

There was no chance of rescue for my own crowd were outnumbered three to one, and I'd probably be killed in the fight. So bunched tightly we rode on into town, and the jail was opened for me.

Chance came to the cell door. "So now we'll see the end of you, Cullen, and we'll get the rest of them, too."

"Not a chance."

"We've drawn them close now, so we'll just bring in the soldiers from the other towns and draw a tight line around outside of them. Then we'll just move in toward town and bring them all right on in."

When I said nothing to that, Chance added, "We've informers. Bob Lee won't last any longer than his next visit home, and Longley will go with him."

"You had a bit of luck catching me," I told him, "you won't be so lucky with them."

He laughed. "We had word you were there, although not from a regular informer."

From the window I could overlook about an acre of grass-covered lot and could look diagonally up the street. Judge Tom Blaine's office was in view: he was an old friend of Katy's.

It was warm and still. Nothing moved outside in the night. From a few windows along the street, light fell into the black avenue, and overhead wind rustled in the leaves of the elms along the walk. Occasionally someone walked up the street and their heels echoed on the boards of the walk. Off across the town a dog barked.

Reaching up I took hold of the window bars and tried them with my hands. No man I'd ever met but one German in the mines of Colorado had been able to lift as much as I, or pull as much. Taking hold of the bars I tested them with my strength, for although set in stone such bars are often loose.

They held firm, and I tried a little harder, and nothing happened. Well, that was a remote chance, anyway. Prowling the square cell, which was about ten by ten, I tried to find some weakness, some way in which I could get out. The door into the space beyond the bars seemed the best chance, but I dared not try that with a guard in the outer office. It looked like the barred door might be set only in the wooden frame, and if that was true I'd have it out of there, door and all.

Somebody had informed. Who? Katy? That was impossible. What about that schoolteacher, Warren? But he had talked so much about Katy getting hurt if the soldiers came, and it was unlikely. He had no real reason.

Some time after that I fell asleep, and I opened my eyes with a rooster crowing next door, and I sat up.

One thing I had . . . the derringer.

When they had taken my Colts and rifle they had looked only so far as the bowie knife, and no farther. But in this country derringers were relatively unknown, and they were considered a woman's gun. There was nothing very feminine about those two .44 slugs.

The man who brought me food was a stranger wearing a blue uniform coat. He was tall, stooped and gawky. His big Adam's apple bobbed as he looked at me. "You that there Cullen Baker?"

"I'm Baker."

"They fixin' to hang you."

"When?"

"Maybe tomorry. I dunno." The guard eyed me thoughtfully. "You married?"

"I'm not so lucky," I said. "Only two things I'll leave behind are a mule and a corn crop."

He looked at me and blinked his eyes. "A corn crop? They said you was an outlaw."

"First crop I ever raised all to myself. I used to help my pa, but he died while I was out West. It's a good crop, only I couldn't do all I wanted, hiding in the swamps and all."

"What about the mule?"

"He's a buckskin riding mule with an ingrown disposition. Ornery most of the time, but once started he'll take you from here to yonder with less water and less food in more heat than any horse you ever saw."

"I got me a team of mules in Pike County."

From the front of the jail a voice raised. "Hey, Wesley!"

The food he brought me was not bad. Side meat, eggs and hominy grits, so I ate it, thinking of the night. The coffee was strong enough to float a bullet.

I'd not see that corn crop again. It was like my other dreams and would come to nothing, but one thing I did know, some way, somehow, I was not going to hang. The more I looked at that door the more I liked it, and the warmer I felt toward the slipshod carpenter who'd put it up. It did not look like it was bolted to the stones and if it was just fitted I could take it out of there like you'd take a picture out of a frame.

Wesley brought in a newspaper. It was a week old but it had things to say of me. They were calling me "the swamp fox of the Sulphur" and they were calling it a "new rebellion" and writing wild stories of all I was supposed to have done.

Standing at the window I saw Seth Rames out there. Seth was a hard man, and a close friend to Bob Lee. He had been through some fighting in that country, but he was not a known man in Jefferson. They knew him over west of here, and in Louisiana, but not right about here. He was standing on the street lighting his pipe.

Nobody needed to tell me why he was there. Seth Rames was a tough man and he was no Reconstruction man, but dead set against them with at least one soldier killing held against him. If Seth was here it was because he was a friend to my friends, and was a man not known in Jefferson. So they were thinking about me, and they were planning. But I almost wished them away from there. I wanted no man in trouble because of me.

While I was still figuring what Seth Rames might be doing out there, there was a footstep outside the cell door and I turned around to see John Tower standing there.

He glanced back toward the cubbyhole of an office that was in front of the jail. Then he said quietly, "Lacy was afraid of this."

"She warned me."

"She also," he spoke very low, "wants you out. And she'll still buy your land."

"Is that what she wants to get me out?"

John Tower's lips tightened and there was not much that was pleasant in the way he looked at me. "She's not that kind," he said, and his voice was mighty cold. "She wants you out, that's all."

"We won't have any argument there."

"Have you any ideas?"

Considering that, I decided I had none. All I knew was that somehow I was going to get out of here, but the walls were stone and they were thick and there was a guard around most of the time. The door frame was of two-by-sixes and they were fitted into the stone door in a mighty snug fashion, with the barred door hung on this frame. A man might take that frame out of there if he had time and there was no one around to hear. It would be a big job, but I was figured to be a mighty powerful man and might do it. But I didn't want my life to rest on that, but as a last resort I'd sure enough have a try at it.

At noon Katy Thorne came to see me. Her face was

pale and her eyes looked larger than I'd ever seen them. She was frightened, I could see that.

"Now see here," I said, "what's worrying you?"

"You ask that? Oh, Cullen! I've been afraid of this, so afraid!"

Well, I looked down at my hands on those bars and then at her. Maybe I should have kept my mouth shut, her going to marry him and all, but I'm no kind of a hero and a bad lot generally, and the way I figured it there was only one answer.

"Chance told me somebody tipped them off. And it was right after Warren left your place."

"Cullen!" she exclaimed. "You can't believe that! Oh, but that's absurd!"

"Who else then?"

That stopped her, and she stared back at me, as if thinking something out, then she said, "Maybe Judge Tom could stop this."

"The hanging you mean?" At her surprised expression, I added, "I know all about it."

We were quiet for a few minutes and then in a low voice I whispered to her to get hold of the boys, at all costs, and to warn them to stay away from Jefferson and me, that I was being used as bait for the lot of them. They were going to hang me, they'd said that, but one thing worried me. How were they going to do it? Now all they had to do was hang me, all right, but without a trial and all folks might start asking why, and some of those Reconstruction people might ask questions themselves. Some of them were honest, I'd heard.

Right about then I had an idea that I didn't like even a little: Suppose there was a jail delivery by Sam

Barlow? No sooner did I have the idea than I was sure that was just how Chance would want it, and no blame could fall on anybody but a fight between outlaws. It was just the sort of thing Barlow would want to do and that Chance would think of.

"Katy, you'd better get out of town. Go back to Blackthorne and stay there. There'll be trouble before this is over, but if you can stop the boys from trying anything I'll be forever grateful."

We talked then as folks will, about much of nothing, but making talk because I didn't want to see her leave, and from the way she acted she wasn't overeager to go.

Whatever happened now must happen here in town, and I could see trouble building around like the thunderheads piling up before a storm.

"Cullen, I'm frightened."

She was, too. Guess it was the first time since I was a youngster that anybody worried about me. Well, right now I was worried about me, too. I'd no idea of hanging to any tree for the pleasure of Chance Thorne and those others. But I didn't see much of a way out.

Sure, I had the derringer. In one way it was less than good to have. It had two bullets. It would be fine if nobody called my bluff, but if I had to shoot with that gun and only two bullets . . . well, it would be an invitation from them to mow me down, and they'd do it.

"You'd best go home, Katy. I'm afraid there'll be trouble here, and if there's careless shooting you might get hurt."

"I'm afraid for you."

Well, I grinned at her, although I wasn't feeling too much like grinning. "Forget it," I said. "There's no use both of us being scared."

When she turned to go she started to say something, but then she stopped and hurried out, and I stood there looking after her and I knew that no matter how she felt, that I was in love with her and had been for some time. Maybe I'd been afraid to admit it to myself, because I'm usually a man who speaks up for what he wants, and I back up for no man in trying to get what I want, but with her it seemed so hopeless that I guess I'd shied off from even admitting to myself that I was in love with her.

When she was gone something inside me exploded. Maybe it was anger: I don't know about that, for a man has many emotions and they are not as easily catalogued as folks would have you believe. Anyway, something happened and I just busted wide open inside, and I was suddenly frantic to get out of there. Not that I was wild or anything. I'm not the sort to go off my head. Inside I was wild but outwardly I was cold as ice, and I really began thinking. Get a man or an animal in a trap and they really do some thinking. There had to be a way out of here, and I meant to go out, but I didn't want to die in the process. There was no difference to me between being hung or shot. I just had a healthy urge to go on living, for no matter how bad it was there was always a chance it could get better, and that I could make it better. Now, with the whole West opening out for me, I wanted out of here.

So I paced the floor. Again I tried the bars on that window—nothing doing. So I went to the door and took hold of the bars of the door and I braced my feet. With all my strength I began to pull, not wanting to be free at the moment, but to test the strength of that door. Nothing stirred, yet somehow I had a feeling there was weakness there.

The floor was solid stone and well fitted together. Circling the walls I could find no weakness there. The door was a slim chance and it meant going out through the front, and if I made too much noise that guard would be in on me, but tonight I was going to try it. Believe me, I was.

So I went back to my cot and laid down. It was almost two in the afternoon, and it was hot.

Wesley came to the door with a fresh bucket of water. He put it down and handed me a gourd with a handle long enough to reach the bucket through the bars. "He'p yo'self," he said. "A man gits mighty dry."

Maybe I napped for a spell, but it couldn't have been long for the first thing I know Chance Thorne is there at the bars looking in at me. "Sleeping your life away?" he said. "If I had only a few hours to live, I'd be awake and enjoying it."

Well, I got up off that crummy cot and stretched myself, and took my time, looking bored all the while. Not that I was feeling that way. I was wishing I could get through those bars and have a try at him with my hands. "Don't let it bother you. I'll live to spit on your grave."

He didn't like it. Chance wanted me to beg, he wanted me humble, but surprisingly enough, suddenly I felt very good. Maybe it was because no man really believes he's going to die at a time like that. Right up to the last minute he's hoping something will happen to save his bacon. Whatever was going to save mine had better happen pretty sudden.

"Don't think you'll get out," Chance told me, "Bob Lee can't help you. Nobody can. Lee is too busy hunting a hole himself. This town is ringed with soldiers, and others are searching the swamps like they've never been searched. Peacock had men watching for Lee at his home, and you know how any Peacock hates a Lee, and Bob in particular. If he isn't dead within a few hours, he'll die within the next week or two."

Right now I was thinking of tonight and I wanted to feel him out. Turned out it didn't take any careful words to get at the truth, he was too sure of himself, and of me.

"You can't get away with hanging me without a trial," I said. "Folks will be down here investigating right off."

He chuckled, and couldn't resist a good brag. "Not if you're hung by somebody who isn't authorized," he said. "Supposing the soldiers should all hear about Bob Lee being some place and take off after him. No telling what might happen here in town, you've made a lot of enemies, Cullen, enemies like Sam Barlow."

Showed I could guess how he was thinking, anyway. The worst of it was, it could happen just that way.

What happened next I never heard of until later. It was Katy herself told me of it, and Jane Watson told me some more that she'd overheard. Jane was the name of that girl I'd helped take out of Sam Barlow's camp, the one who was about to get whipped.

If anybody was thinking of Jane Watson right then

it wasn't me, and I didn't even know her name, to tell the truth. She was one person I'd forgotten all about, and never expected to see again, but the way it turned out she hadn't forgotten me. I like folks, but never expect too much of them. We're all human, and most folks are apt to forget favors you've done them, fact is, they remember the favors they do for you far better. Right then I didn't know it, but Jane had come up to Jefferson with blood in her eye, wanting to do something for me, and later she came to see me at the jail, but first she heard a conversation that was repeated to me.

Seems Thomas Warren, that schoolteacher, met Katy in a store. Jane Watson, who knew neither of them at the time, overheard what followed.

Katy was looking at some yard goods when Warren came up to her. "Have you heard the news?"

"News?"

"They've arrested Cullen Baker. They plan to hang him."

"He will be tried first, I think." According to Jane it didn't seem that Katy wanted to discuss it.

"There are rumors that he will be taken out of jail and hung immediately."

"You don't like him, do you?"

"He's a common outlaw, a murderer. How could I like him?"

"You know that I do?"

Warren had shrugged at that remark. "You feel you should like him because he's from here and because your Uncle Will liked him. He will bring you nothing but trouble, and it will ruin your reputation."

"My reputation is my own concern."

"It may," Warren said stiffly, "some day be your husband's concern. That is why I feel concerned."

From what Jane said, Katy looked startled, and she said merely, "You have no reason to feel concerned, Tom. I like you, but the idea of you as my husband, if that is what you mean, why that's impossible."

"Why? Why should it be?"

Katy drew away from him at this point and perfectly composed she said, "Mr. Warren, I am afraid you are assuming an interest on my part that has never existed. As for Cullen, no matter what is said of him, I know him to be a good man."

Warren was excited then, or so Jane told me. He was so excited that it didn't appear just right somehow, or maybe that he was a little off balance. Anyway, he told Katy, "He won't look so nice at the end of a rope! He is an evil man! That's why I—"

"Why you—*what*?"

Abruptly he walked away from her, but at the door he had looked back. "You will feel different when you're rid of him," he said, "and then I'll be back."

Right then, as Warren went out, Lacy Petraine came in, and she walked right up to Katy. "Miss Thorne, we need your help."

And that was when Jane Watson went up to them both and told them why she had come to Jefferson. She knew how they both felt, and she said right out what she had come for.

There was one other thing Chance had said that stuck in my mind, and with good cause. Just as he was leaving he had said that he and Joel Reese and some others would be back before I was hung. They wanted, Chance said, a private session with me in the cell. They would, he promised, make it easy for me to die. They would make me want to die.

And that was enough to give a man something to think about.

CHAPTER 6

KATY HAD TOLD me a good bit about Warren, and some of it I could sort of piece together, seeing how he shaped up to me. He'd been born, she said, into a house that was run by two maiden aunts, and what happened to his folks, I never did hear. Only those two aunts must have made much of him as a youngster and, from what he told Katy, they had taught him to study hard, to stay away from rough boys and rough play, and to avoid all the vices named and unnamed in this most wicked of worlds.

A man brought up like that is likely to grow up but not out, and I expect the world he lived in at twenty-seven wasn't much different than it had been at seventeen. To me he seemed like a man mighty positive of his own rightness, and usually those sort are all torn up inside by a lot of petty worries and petty ideas. But with those aunts always telling him he would be somebody.

Maybe like some others he figured when the war was over that Texas was the place to come. A lot of young men had been killed, and there should be a lot of girls around with money. I heard talk of that sort, myself, and I wouldn't be surprised if something like that had been in his mind when he met Katy Thorne.

Right now he was probably mad clear through, but less at Katy than at me.

Standing by the window I saw Katy come out of the store with Lacy Petraine and Jane Watson. Now there was something to think about, and I was hoping that I was the only one doing that kind of thinking. Only I wasn't. Thomas Warren was standing across the street under a tree staring at them.

Why? Well, it sort of didn't fit, if you know what I mean. Three women might get together and talk, that's true, but Lacy wasn't considered a quite nice person and Katy Thorne was as much aristocracy as we had in that corner of Texas right then, and she would have been aristocracy anywhere else too.

Jane Watson? Well, she came of a poor family on a small place south of here. There was no likely reason for her to be in town, and less reason for her to even know Katy or Lacy. Maybe Warren was thinking what I was that the only common tie those three had was me, Cullen Baker.

It was hot in that cell with the sun beating against the outer wall. Sometimes I'd hear a rig go by in the street with a jingle of harness or the crack of a whip, or I'd hear people talking, or hear the *clank* of horseshoes from a vacant lot up the street where somebody was always playing.

From the outer office I heard simply nothing at all, so the guard must be sitting outside against the front wall.

There was nobody else in the jail but me, although there were three empty cells. If I could get that door out of the way I would have to go through that little office, overpower one or two guards and then would come out on a street where most of the crowd would be enemies and most of the remaining folks would want to stay out of it. Therefore that derringer was useless unless I could get out when nobody was around.

Once outside there would be the problem of slipping past the patrols and getting into the swamps. Chances were an easy thousand to one I'd never make it.

Unless I was altogether wrong, all hell was building up outside. Knowing the boys like I did, I knew no matter what I wanted they would try to get me out of there, just as I would try to help them. This was a fact known to Colonel Belser, too, and to Chance Thorne. It was a good guess they'd leave a hole for them to come through, then trap them inside, maybe right here at the jail.

And if my figuring was right, and from what Chance had said it was right, somewhere to the south Sam Barlow would be riding up to lynch me.

And right here in town three women were in a way to get themselves into a lot of trouble trying to help me. Whatever else happened this here had shown me how many friends I had, and for a man with a bad reputation, I was doing all right.

Only I didn't dare let them help me.

Somehow, some way, I had to get out and away before any of them could do a thing to help, before they could get their tails in a crack trying to help.

To have friends a man has to be friendly, and to get others to think of you, you have to think of others. I wanted no man dying for me, and the mere fact that Seth Rames was in Jefferson showed something was up, and whatever Lacy Petraine was in, John Tower was in, too.

It was closing in toward sundown. If all went as I figured, it would be some time after midnight before Barlow arrived, and right about midnight when I could expect the visit from Chance Thorne and his men.

That meant that some time before midnight I was going to have to be out of here, and the sooner the better. If I was going to help those friends who wanted to help me, I'd have to get out before they could get far enough in to be in real trouble.

Right then was when Jane Watson showed up. Wesley brought her in, blushing up to his freckled ears, and I could see he was mighty taken with her.

When he left she moved right up to the bars. "It will be at ten," she spoke quickly and quietly. "John Tower will hold up the guards and we will be outside in the buckboard. He will have two horses, and when the two of you start to leave, we will drive across the street ahead of anybody who might try to chase you."

It was silly, and I told her so. Same time I knew it was silly enough and simple enough to work. It meant making an outlaw out of John Tower, and I didn't see why he should do that for me. I said as much to Jane.

"It isn't for you, although he likes you. He is in love with Lacy Petraine."

She told me about that, and it added up to something none of us had known. Of course, I had my own bit of knowing about John Tower, but that's neither here nor there. According to what Jane said, John Tower had walked up to Mrs. Petraine and he had told her right out, "Mrs. Petraine, I am the man who shot Terence O'Donnell. I shot your husband, Mrs. Petraine."

Lacy being what she was, I could understand what followed. That was a sight of woman, believe you me.

"Terry," she said, "always believed himself a better man with a gun than he was."

"I am sorry."

"Yes, as he would have been sorry had he killed you. Mr. Tower, let me assure you of this. Terence would have killed you if he could. He was not a man to make foolish gestures with a gun."

"Is that all? I mean now that you know this you will probably want me to leave your employ?"

"That was long ago, Mr. Tower, and in another world than this. We have both changed since then. I believe I was very much in love with Terence, but now it is like a dream, and like all dreams, it has ended."

But from what Jane said it was there between them, and they knew they loved each other, and they both knew that in time something would come of it. So now he was to help me because of her.

Well, now. Maybe down inside I'd figured she would help me because it was me she liked, or because she thought me a fine figure of a man, like she had practically said, one time. Showed how wrong a man could be, and I felt kind of let down and cooled off, if you know what I mean.

Well, I was a wandering sort of man when it came to that, and once out of this fix, I'd wander again.

Come to think of it, there was nothing I'd rather be doing about then than just wandering, almost anywhere.

Surprising how proximity to a noose in the end of a rope can make man appreciate things. Living, just being alive, had never seemed quite so desirable as right now. When I started thinking of some of the fool chances I'd taken before I was dry behind the ears, it scared me...and did me no good at all. I was right here in these stone walls and time was closing in on me. Time was a noose.

"All right," I told Jane. "That there is a fool idea but it might work. My advice to you is to have an ace-in-the-hole, however, and get me a horse and saddle him up with a pistol on him and leave him in the trees back by Webster's stable."

She went out of there and Wesley put more water in my bucket. Wesley bothered me. That long tall boy had never done anyone any harm and I didn't want him out there when the shooting started.

Only two things I wanted. To get shut of this place and to put Sam Barlow in that grave at the Corners. And if I could pile Chance Thorne in there with him, I'd be more than pleased.

Belser? We don't worry about the Belsers of this world. Once I was free he would scare himself to death thinking what I might do to him.

Standing by that window and looking out on the street I could see the red sun going down behind the old Tilden barn, and I could hear the squeaky complaints of a rusty pump as somebody pumped water for coffee or maybe for washing hands before supper.

I could smell food cooking, cabbage, it smelled like, and sometimes hear a door slam as somebody came or went. Standing there I heard the first sounds of somebody milking a cow into a tin pail. It was suppertime in Jefferson on the night before they were to hang Cullen Baker.

That was me. I was Cullen Baker, and I knew they planned to have that hanging tonight, and if they were right and I was wrong, this was the last sun I would ever see, the last of these sounds I'd hear.

Like a jackass braying, or an owl hooting...an owl? It was early for an owl.

More than one kind of owl hoot.

It was something to figure on, that hooting owl. Soon he hooted again. Time was shaping up, it soon would be hanging time and unless I wanted to be the key man at that hanging I would have to get out.

The streets were growing empty as folks went for supper. All right then, this was what I wanted. No use waiting until ten o'clock and maybe getting folks killed. Right now while everybody was busy with supper and when it wasn't quite dark, right now and without waiting any further. I didn't want Wesley to get hurt but I wasn't wanting to be hung, either. So I walked over to that door and took a good hold of those iron bars. Like I said, I'm a man of strength, and so I took hold of those bars and gave them a yank.

Nothing.

Just simply nothing at all. I took hold of those bars and braced myself and gave it everything I had... nothing.

That carpenter I'd said was slipshod, the one I figured hadn't bolted those two-by-sixes into the stone, he hadn't needed to. They were set so close and solid you could pull that wall down before they'd be noticed.

Right then I was scared. All the time I'd had it in mind that I could rip that doorframe out of there, I'd been sure of that—and nothing happened.

Sweat broke out on my forehead. That rope was suddenly mighty close. Sweat began to come out on me and it was cold sweat and my throat felt dry like nothing in this world. You could have bought my chances right then for a plugged two-bit piece and been ahead of the game. I felt like a limp deuce in an ace-high deck.

So I tried it again. Sometimes a man can be right stubborn, times like that. I spread my feet and braced them against the stone floor and gave a yank that would have taken a tree out by the roots...nothing.

Then I looked up at the ceiling. I don't know why. I was just exasperated and I raised a hand to swear and looked up—and I kept on looking up.

The ceiling of that cell was of spiked plank, nailed to four-by-fours which served as beams, and it was high, just beyond the reach of my fingers when I jumped to touch it.

Spiked to those beams. With how many spikes? And what was above that? A shake roof? Well, now! A man thinks of many things, and I thought of them all, but mostly I thought of getting out. Suddenly I looked out and the sun was gone, only a few lonely red and yellow streaks in a graying sky.

Time was short.

The window...it had to be deep because the walls were thick.

Reaching up I grasped those bars and pulled myself up. Getting a knee on the sill, I hoisted a foot, then balancing myself against a fall back into the room, I straightened up.

Standing on the floor that sill had been just an inch below eye-level for me, now, standing on the sill, I had to bend my knees to stand and bow my back against those planks in the ceiling. To hold the position I had to keep pressure on the planks, and if I relaxed I'd fall forward and would have to land on my feet on the floor to keep from being hurt.

But my back was against those planks, and my knees were bent. The chances were mighty good that the carpenter who fixed that door had done a job on these planks in the ceiling, but I would see. Using my hands to grip the top edge of the window behind me, I started to straighten out my legs. It was no go. I couldn't get enough pressure on it to make anything budge. Turning around and squatting on the ledge of the stone window I gripped a bar in one hand and started testing the ceiling planks with the other. And the second one I tried seemed the best chance. Turning and gripping a bar with one hand I put a shoulder against the plank and started to straighten my legs. Almost at once a nail screeched, but not too loudly. Waiting a moment and listening, I tried it again, and the plank gave still more. A third time and the spikes pulled free. There had been but two. With one hand I moved the board aside and then listened for an instant before I caught the edge of the adjoining board and pulled myself up and through the space.

It was completely black in the space under the roof, but I could feel the underside of the shakes. Swiftly I worked my way along, testing each one to the very rear of the building. And there I found one that was not tight. Tugging, I pulled the shake around and then got hold of another. There was an ear-splitting crack, and I caught my breath, and waited. Down below I heard footsteps that came to the rear of the jail, paused an instant, and then returned the way they had come.

At any minute someone might decide to check my cell, so there was nothing for it but to make the attempt now. Crawling through the hole, although it was a tight squeeze, I worked out onto the roof, slid down and then dropped from the eaves to the ground. Only an instant I hesitated, and then started to walk swiftly away toward Webster's stable.

There was about an acre of ground that must be crossed, and the lower end of the street. Trying not to look excited or do anything that would attract attention I walked from behind the building and crossed the street diagonally. Behind me a man came from the door of a house and I knew he was looking my way, but I simply continued to walk, but the hair on the back of my neck was crawling, and I wouldn't have given two cents for my chances right then.

Turning the corner I went into Webster's farmyard and crossed the yard toward the stable. Webster was a Union Leaguer, and very close to both Thorne and Belser, so I could expect no help from him if he came from the house and saw me. I could expect nothing but trouble, and lots of it.

The worst of it was, I had acted before I was expected and there might be no horse for me.

Quickly I trotted down the little slope into the

trees and walked along the path where I expected the horse to be.

It was not there.

Turning I walked swiftly back along another way, searching the trees, but the area covered by trees was scarcely larger than a good-sized farmyard, and the horse had to be within sight if he was there, but he wasn't.

And then I saw him.

The horse was not tied; he was walking toward me, ears pricked, reins dragging. At almost the same instant I heard a yell from the street, then a shout and loud voices arguing, swearing. They had discovered my escape.

There was no time left. I started for the horse and in almost the same breath the brush cracked and suddenly a torch flared up and then another.

The first person I saw was Chance Thorne, and he was grinning. The second was Joel Reese, but there were at least six, and they had rifles.

Caught!

Reese lowered his rifle and from around his waist he unwrapped a short length of log chain.

Another man shucked a heavy belt with a large brass buckle, and several others had clubs. They stacked their guns and started for me.

"I've got the rope," Reese told me, "and when we get through you'll be glad to get it. Hanging will be a pleasure after this!"

They were all around me and they could see I was unarmed. Only I wasn't. Taking my time I tucked my thumbs behind my belt and stood looking around at them. "You've got it all your way, haven't you?" I asked. "But the first man who comes at me, I'll kill."

In the flickering light of the torch, and with them all unsuspecting, they didn't see the slight movement when my thumb at the base of the derringer pushed it up into my palm.

Two bullets, and then they'd have me. I wanted Chance Thorne and I wanted Joel Reese.

"Lucky we caught that girl bringin' you the horse," Reese said. "A girl with a horse going down here at that time of night, well, it shaped up as suspicious. We followed a hunch."

The flickering torchlight danced on the cottonwood leaves, and under cover of the talk they had been edging in on me. I had the derringer in my hand and I was ready as a man can be.

There were guns on the horse, which was just outside the circle. There was a rifle, and at least one pistol, and there were full saddlebags and a blanket roll behind the saddle. I could kill two men and make a try for it, but there wasn't a chance that I'd make it. They had stacked their rifles, but each man I could see wore a belt gun—three of them, anyway.

That was three too many.

"All right," Chance said, "let's get him!"

Reese drew back his chain and they started for me and I fired. For the second time I missed Reese, but I hit the man holding the belt with the brass buckle. He screamed and the sound, coming with the gun blast, stopped them in their tracks.

"*Look out!*" It was Reese yelling. "He's got a *gun!*"

One man grabbed for a pistol and I fired again and hit him right in the belly and at the same instant there was a wild Texas yell from somewhere behind me and a voice that yelled, "Hold up, in there! Hold it!"

The yell was followed by a shot that knocked another man to the ground with a smashed hip. I knew that yell. It had to be Seth Rames.

From behind them another voice spoke. It was cool, easy, confident. It was John Tower. "That's right, boys. Just stand fast."

Turning abruptly I walked to the horse and stepped into the saddle, and when I had my hand on a pistol I turned on them. "If you've hurt that girl, I'll see every man of you buried in the swamps."

Somebody spoke up. "She's locked up at Reese's place."

"She isn't now," Tower replied. "She's gone, and I let her go, and if she's ever bothered again, I'll add my weight to Baker's."

They stood very still. Two voices had spoke but there might be more men. They were sure there were more, and I had no idea how many there were, only that I had a chance and suddenly the future was wide and bright again... if we could just ride out of here.

So I walked the horse to where Seth Rames was, and saw his big, raw-boned frame sitting a horse in the shadows.

"Stand fast!" he repeated, and then he swung his horse. On the soft earth it made almost no noise, but he rode along with me until we reached the highroad, and then he turned. He was a big man, as big as me in weight, but taller. "We'd better ride, Cullen. Tower's already gone."

We took out.

Riding at a good pace, I checked the rifle, and it

seemed loaded. The pistol was okay, too. So we rode into the night.

Near the Corners, Seth drew up. "Got to reach the boys," he said, "and I've a soldier who'll let me through alone. You can make the swamps."

The roads were empty and still, and I knew them well. Luckily, I saw no one. Once I passed a house where a late light was shining, and near another a dog barked, but I rode on into the night with the cool damp air on my face, and the smell of the swamps. It was after midnight when I crossed the Louisiana state line heading for a place I knew on James Bayou.

Maybe they had expected me to keep going, to ride clear out of the country, but I wasn't about to go until I knew all my friends were safe. The place to which I was riding now was one nobody would connect me with, nobody knew I'd ever gone here, or had any friends here.

Avoiding Caddo Station I rode past the Salt Pits, and when daylight was gray in the sky I drew up near the dark bulk of a small cabin on the edge of the swamps. A dog barked, and a man came from the house and stood watching in my direction.

"It's Cullen, Mike, and I'm in trouble."

"Come on in."

Caddo Mike was a short, square man of powerful build, no longer young. This was solid ground, a little higher than most of it around here. Suddenly I realized this was one of the strange mounds that had been built here long before the oldest Indian could remember, and ages before the white man first came to the country.

Mike took my horse and dipped suddenly from

sight. Following him I found him tying the horse in an underground stable concealed among the trees, and dug into the side of the mound. The stable walls were of ancient stone, built ages ago. There were four other horses, all fine animals. It was cool there, and quite pleasant. Caddo Mike had opened a skylight on a slope of the hill which he had covered with canvas. It allowed a little light.

"White men dig for gold," Mike explained, "long time ago, in the time of my grandfather. No gold. The Old People had no gold. Just bones here."

Caddo Mike's face was seamed and brown. I felt as if I had known him forever. When I was a boy, the first month we had been here from Tennessee we had found Caddo Mike staggering and delirious with fever on the edge of the swamp. We had taken him home, and dosed with quinine, he had survived to become our good friend.

One night he was in bed, and in the morning he was gone, but a few days later we found a haunch of venison hung from the porch, and on another morning, two fine wild turkeys. It had been Mike who taught me most of what I knew about the swamps where he had lived all his life. He was now, I guess, at least sixty. But he was strong and able to travel for miles on foot or horseback.

Mike made black coffee that was more than half chicory and laced it with rum. Then he brought out some corn pone, brown beans and venison.

In this remote corner Mike cultivated a field of corn, and a good-sized vegetable garden. He rarely went into any of the towns, and almost never to the same one twice in succession. White men as a rule he did not trust, and he avoided their questions or any contact with them other than involved in his few business transactions.

Over the food I explained to Mike all that had happened, and ended by telling him, "Mike, I need to know what happened back there. And I must get a message to Katy Thorne."

When Mike had ridden away I stretched out on the bed with a pistol at my side, and trusting to the dogs who were wary of strangers, I slept.

In the late afternoon I awakened suddenly, and for a moment, as always when I awaken, I lay still, listening. There was no sound, so swinging my feet to the floor I padded across to the window and peered out into a sun-bright world.

Going out back I dipped a bucket in the tank and sloshed water over myself. The water was cold and it felt good. Four more buckets and I began to feel human and alive, so I dried off in the sun and then went back in and dressed.

First off I checked my guns. There had been a pistol on the horse and Mike had offered me another which I accepted. The rifle was my own Spencer, although how Jane Watson came by it I don't know and can't guess unless John Tower got it somehow.

It was a hot, still afternoon. There were a few scattered clouds.

Locating the feed bin I fed Mike's chickens, and then the horses. Somewhere out on the bayou a loon called, a lonesome sound. Returning to the cabin I sliced a chunk from a ham and fried up some ham and eggs, and made coffee.

The sun was low by the time I finished eating and I

was growing restless. Mike was not about to be back so soon, so I rummaged around for something to read. Right now I might as well admit I'm not much of a reader. I make out to read most things, given time, but I've got to have time and quiet.

Caddo Mike, whom I never figured to read at all, had a sight of old magazines and books around, most of them mighty old. There was a magazine there, a copy of *Atlantic Monthly* for August, 1866, and I started reading a piece in it called "A Year in Montana."

Reading that article, I'd nearly finished when I dozed off and awakened to find myself scared...I'd no business sleeping so sound or so much. And me with the light burning. Putting out the light I stood in the door until my eyes were right and then stepped out. One of the dogs came up and stood near me, and I spoke to him, mighty soft. His tail thumped my leg, and I walked down off the stoop.

The night was too quiet to suit me, edgy the way I was, and I walked out away from the cabin and turned to look back. A man could have stood where I was, within sixty feet of the house, day or night, and never known it was there.

Near Caddo Mike's the bayou described one of those loops so common among bayous, and even in the main stream of the Sulphur, which was well north of here. The bayou took a loop and then doubled back until it almost met itself, and at this point it was shallow and almost choked with hyacinth and old logs. The road at this point followed the outside of the loop, going up one side around the end and down the other side. Nervous as a bobcat about to have kittens, I crossed one arm of the bayou and started across toward the trail on the other side. Yet I'd gone not thirty feet when I heard riders.

Stopping dead still, I heard a voice grumbling, then another ordering silence. That grumbling voice was the Barlow man whom Katy had nursed, and this must be the Barlow crowd!

Listening, straining my ears to hear, I then heard someone ask a question of someone called Sam . . . and it figured to be Barlow himself.

They had drawn up, stopping on the road that cut me off from a return to Caddo Mike's. Did they know of him and his place? Had they caught Mike, and were they now searching for me?

No! Mike would die before he would talk, and there was no connection between us that anyone could figure out.

Nevertheless, I started on, moving across the narrow neck toward the other side. When I was on the inside bank of the bayou and hunting a place to cross its fifteen yards of water, at this point a fairly deep pool and clear of growth, I heard another party of riders.

Squatting on my heels, I waited.

This party was walking their horses and from the jingle of accoutrements could only be a party of soldiers.

The neck of land I had crossed was barely a hundred yards from bayou to bayou, but it was all of a half mile around the loop by following the road. The idea came to me suddenly.

Calling out in a low but clear voice, just loud enough for them to hear me, I said, "You fellers huntin' Cullen Bakuh, you better cut an' run! He's a-comin' raht down the road toward you all, an' he's sure set for trouble!"

"Who's there?" The voice had a sharp, military ring that I hoped couldn't be heard on the Barlow side. "Come out and show yourself!"

By that time I was moving back toward the other side. I wanted to get to Caddo Mike's and a horse just as fast as I could make it. If all went the way I hoped, all hell was going to break loose any time within the next fifteen minutes or less.

Barlow's boys had moved on when I reached the far side, but I was only in the middle of a log, crossing the bayou, when I heard a voice ring out, "Hey, there! Who's that?" And a moment later a ringing command, *"Fire!"*

There had been at least a dozen men in the Army command, and probably twice that many.

The blast of gunfire smashed into the night's stillness like a breaking of a gigantic tree limb, and like it was followed by a deafening silence.

The silence lasted a moment only, then there was a rattle of gunfire, a quick exchange of shots, shots, yells and then more silence.

On the edge of the bayou I started to cross the road, then heard a rush of horses' hoofs and a man riding. He pulled up, listening for sounds of pursuit. And then I heard someone running. He fell, scrambled up and came on, his breath coming in great gasps.

The man on the horse started, then stopped and walked his horse slowly back up the road.

"Bravo?" By the gasping breath it was the running man.

"Sam, anybody else make it?"

"Ed, I think Ed did. He dove into the swamp."

"The rest all gone?"

"Every man-jack of them."

Carefully, I eased myself across the road, then waited a bit. Sam Barlow was a man could stand some talking to, but shooting right now would bring the Army down on us, and I'd no wish to be captured again . . . I'd come too close to stretching my neck as it was.

"Somebody set us up like pigeons," Barlow was saying.

"Thorne, he figures he don't need us no longer."

"No, not Thorne," Barlow replied, but he didn't sound very convinced

"Let's get out of here," Bravo suggested. "Come daylight they'll shake this patch down like they was huntin' coons. We better be far off come daylight."

There was no sign of Mike at the cabin. Packing up some grub, I slipped away from the cabin and hid in the brush near the hidden stable. From where I lay I could observe the cabin and the road approaching it. The way I saw it I needed to talk to Mike before I moved, I needed to know whatever he'd found out about the others. There was no possibility of going home now, and somehow I wasn't sorry. Both Lacy and Katy had been right all along, for they'd give me no chance here. Out West, well I could find a place for myself and make my own way, maybe in the mines or the cattle business. Maybe I could, with

Katy's help, even learn to read and write better and make something of myself.

With Katy's help? I blushed there in the darkness. Who was I to think a girl like that would go on the dodge with me? The more I thought of it the more I figured she did indeed like me. But maybe I was wrong, and I'd no right to ask her, anyway.

To go West I had to go through the country I'd just come out of, or skirt around it, which was mighty near as bad, so whatever Mike could tell me would help. But most of all, I had to know those who helped me got clear; it just wasn't in me to go scot-free and leave a friend in the lurch.

Suddenly two riders came down the trail and drew up nearby, close enough to hear them talking. "Why waste our time? No matter what the sergeant says, they're gone. That wasn't Cullen Baker, anyway, that was the Barlow crowd. You think I don't know that bunch? I used to run in the Thickets my ownself."

There was a mutter of voices I could hear, and then the first man spoke out again. "Six Barlow men dead and nine wounded or captured. It was a good haul."

"Who d'you suppose that was who yelled at us?"

The first soldier chuckled. "Who d'you suppose?"

When daylight came again I went to the stable to saddle up, but before I could get the saddle on the horse, I heard the dogs barking and knew from the sound they were welcoming someone they knew.

It was Caddo Mike. And he was alone.

CHAPTER 7

RIFLE CRADLED IN the hollow of my arm, I stepped from among the trees.

"You got to git from here."

"Did you see Miss Katy?"

"You know Willow Bluff? West of the old ferry in Bowie County? She gonna meet you there."

Few people lived in that remote pine-covered area across the Sulphur, and there was a chance to reach the place unobserved. And it was on the way out of the country where I was known.

"She shouldn't be riding there alone."

"I don't figure she gonna be alone." Caddo Mike did not enlarge upon the statement, but went on, "They huntin' you. The sodgers huntin' you, the sodgers huntin' Sam Barlow, Sam Barlow huntin' you."

"What about Bob Lee?"

"He had a runnin' fight with sodgers. Joe Tinney, he dead. Buck ride back to pick him up, he dead."

It would be like Buck to ride back for his brother. It was the end for them all. The feeling was on me that I would never reach Willow Bluff, nor see Katy again. Their luck had played out.

The urge was on me to ride into Jefferson and kill Chance Thorne. Deeply, bitterly, I felt he was the cause of all that had happened, and that until he died there could be no peace for me, no matter where I

went or what I did. Had it not been for his hatred of
me Bob Lee and Bickerstaff might now be at peace
with the Union Leaguers.

No, that was untrue. They were men who would
fight and alone if need be, for whatever they believed.
They were men who got their backs up at tyranny.

"You ride careful, ride skeery," Mike advised.
"They bad people."

Mike insisted I take his dapple-gray mare, and she
was a good horse, a better horse than Jane Watson
had found for me. Still, I was wishing I had that
ornery buckskin mule of mine. He could eat a handful of grass, drink a cupful of water, and he was already to go again.

Stepping into the saddle I looked down at Mike,
reluctant to leave. "S'long, Mike," I said, and walked
the horse away, not looking back.

From this point every step was a danger, every mile
an added risk. Right then I was sure I was going to be
killed, it was a feeling I had not had before, and one
that I could not shake. I should never have returned
after the war, but to abandon the land would take all
the meaning from the years of labor Pa and Ma had
put in. Come to think of it, Pa himself had moved
on a couple of times, and in such a case, he would
move, too.

The mare was a good one with an urge to travel.
She stepped out with her ears pricked forward like
she knew she was going into new country, like she
wanted to see what was beyond the hill and around
the bend. This was a traveling mare.

So north we rode, away from Jefferson, away from
Caddo Lake. I was in Louisiana with the Arkansas

line somewhere to the north and the Texas line just to the west, only a few miles away. When I crossed into Texas I would be in Cass County, which was my home county, but I had just to hope that I'd see no-body who knew me. After crossing Baker Creek, I turned west.

Avoiding roads I kept to old trails the Caddoes used and that Cherokee hunting parties had used when they came down from the Nation. When I forded the river and rode up to Mush Island I took it almighty cautious to see before I was seen.

A broken branch with green leaves lay across the path ahead of me, so I walked the mare along until I saw the three stones beside the trail. The triangle they formed pointed into the woods.

They were signs our outfit used, but they might also be a trap, so I reined the mare over and hooted like an owl, waited, then hooted again.

After a minute or so a frog sounded back in the woods, and only Matt Kirby could do it so natural-like.

So I sat my horse and kept my eyes open for trouble, and waited for him to come up to me, but when he came he had a stranger with him. "It's all right," Kirby said. "This here's a cousin to Buck and Joe. I know him."

The stranger was as large as either Kirby or me, and he was almost in rags.

Mike had said Katy was bringing some clothes to their meeting at Willow Bluff so I dug into my saddle-bags. "You could use a shirt," I said, and hauled out my old checkered shirt and a pair of homespun jeans made by a Mormon woman near Cove Fort. They were none too good but better than what the fellow had on. "You take these," I said, "I've had my wear out of them."

"Thanks." The big fellow was mighty embarrassed. "I'm beholden. We uns are fresh out of cash money up on the Red. Man gits mahty little for his crops nowadays."

"What are you down this way for?"

He looked up, honest surprise on his face. "Why, they kilt my cousins. Somebody kills our'n, we kill them. That's the way it is up on the Red."

"You go home," I told him, "you just go back up there. You'll catch nothing but trouble down here."

"I got it to do," he said soberly. "Pa says so an' I got a feelin' he's raht. Them Tinney boys. I growed up with Buck an' Joe. Can't hear of them bein' laid away without the men who kilt 'em laid away, too."

"You go home," I insisted.

Bob Lee came up through the woods, Longley a length behind, and both of them grinned when they saw me. "Figured you for swamp bait," Bob said, "figured they'd tacked up your hide."

"Take some doing," I said.

"Bickerstaff went to Johnson County."

We squatted on our heels and talked commonplaces while Kirby and his new partner rustled wood and started some coffee. Bob Lee looked tired and even Longley, the youngest of the lot except for this new man, looked beat. Bob Lee, he looked around us. "I never liked this place; makes a man spooky."

"You going to Mexico?"

"Uh-huh. I figure to ranch down there." Bob Lee took the broken stub of a cigar from his pocket.

"Down in Chihuahua I have friends. I'll send for the wife later."

"I'm riding West."

It was on us now, the feeling that we were leaving was riding us, and a man could feel the uneasiness among us. All of us had been riding elbow to elbow with death for months, and yet now that we had a chance to get out we were more scared than ever.

I never figured it was a cowardly thing to be scared. It's to be scared and still to face up to what scares you that matters. A man in our way of life faces guns many times, and he knows a gun can kill, but now we had our chance to get out and away and we were ready. No sense in prolonging it. Taking the coffee Matt offered me I drank a mouthful. "I'm pulling out," I said. "I'm getting shut of this place."

Lee glanced up at me as I straightened up. Longley got up, too. Matt poked at the fire, and the youngster sat there and looked at us like he couldn't understand. All of us knew that we weren't about to see each other again, and we had shared troubles.

"Wait a spell," Lee told me, "and I'll ride as far as Fannin County with you."

My clothes itched me and I felt cold and lonely. A little wind came through the trees and I shivered. The feeling was on me that there was death in this place and it was my death that was coming. "Bob, I wouldn't go to Fannin County if I were you."

"I've got to see the wife."

"Don't go! Write to her. You light out for Mexico and don't stop until you've got Laredo behind you. I'm telling you, Bob, we should all get shut of Texas. You ride out, Bob, and you keep going. You're a good man, one of the best I ever knew, and there's no sense you spilling blood of yours for a cause that wasted itself away. You keep riding."

"Never saw you jumpy before."

Turning around I looked at that long, tall, handsome Bill Longley. "You hang up your guns, Bill. They'll get you killed, believe me."

"A man has to die," he said.

Holding out my hand to Bob, I said, "So long, Bob. Easy riding."

"Adios, compadre."

Longley got up. He looked awkward and embarrassed. "See you out West sometime. You watch for me."

"I'll do that."

Throwing the rest of my coffee into the dead leaves I looked into the empty cup, then I turned and dropped the cup and stepped into the saddle. For a long moment I sat my saddle unmoving, my back turned to them, for we all knew it was the last time, and the sickness of leaving was on me. Then I rode away.

"He should have waited to eat," Longley said.

Kirby glanced up. "A doom's on him, can't you see it? My old grandma told me when the doom's on a man and he knows he's going to die, he's like that."

"That's fool talk." Bob Lee dropped his cup. "I'm not waiting. I'm riding to Fannin County. Coming Bill?"

When they were gone the tall young man rubbed his eyes and looked sheepishly at Kirby. "You sleepy? I'm raht tard."

Only a a few yards away I'd stopped again, almost

afraid to go on, yet feeling like Bob Lee that there was something about this place that gave me a bad feeling. I'd sat there, listening to them talk, hearing the retreating sounds of the horses of Lee and Longley, and then I heard Kirby say, "Sleep, I'll wake you to take watch when I'm sleepy."

So I rode away under the trees, sitting easy in the saddle and shaped up for a long ride West.

At daybreak I was still riding, but the mare was dead tired and we both needed rest. There was plenty of time to get to Willow Bluff—but that was the trouble. A man always thought there was plenty of time, and there never was.

When I awakened and pulled on my boots I checked my guns and then scouted around. By the sun I judged I'd slept a couple of hours, and after a scout around I put together a small fire in a hollow place near a tree where the rising smoke could lose itself in the branches, and made coffee. Broiling a chunk of beef, I took a couple of swallows of coffee and then with the beef in my left hand, taking occasional bites, I strolled over to where the trail went through the trees.

There was no evidence that the trail had been used by anyone else, although I saw where an inquisitive deer had been checking my tracks. This was an old Caddo trail, and kept to high ground under the trees, dipping only occasionally to lonely springs or to the river. The days of Caddo wandering were almost a thing of the past, so the trail was unused. It was the same trail I'd taken out of the country once before. My camp was south of the Sulphur near Whiteoak Creek.

Both Barlow and the soldiers would be hunting me now. I'd escaped from prison now, and for that alone they'd be after me. But I was out of Cass County, and pretty much beyond Barlow's zone of action.

There was a mockingbird doing tricks in a treetop some distance away, but no other sound. At the fire I finished eating, finished my coffee and put out the fire with great care. I'd seen too much damage done by carelessly put out fires, or those left burning by some damn' fool.

It was a lazy, sunlit morning, and I was about three miles from Willow Bluff. In the silent woods a sound can be heard from quite a distance, so when I heard a sound I straightened up and listened.

It could have been a branch breaking, but animals do not break branches, and if broken deliberately it must be for a cooking fire. If otherwise, then somebody was sneaking around and I wasn't ready for that.

Moving easy-like, I saddled up and put my stuff together. Mounting up I walked the horse off under the trees, keeping away from my lonely little trail until some distance from the night camp. The main trail, such as it was, was several miles away, but there was another used occasionally that would touch at Willow Bluff. There was not a chance in a million anyone would guess my trail was here. Fact is, it would take a sharp man, just stumbling on it, to judge it a trail at all.

At no time had I failed to practice the technique of drawing a gun fast. Each day except when in jail I'd spent some time working at it, and I knew I'd become a sight faster than when I killed Dud Butler in Fort Worth. Accuracy had never been a problem. From boyhood I'd been skillful with all sorts of weapons.

At intervals I drew up to judge the silence of the woods, to sort out the sounds, and the closer I was to final escape the more jumpy I became. The very fact that I was getting out made every move more careful because I wanted nothing to go wrong at the last minute.

About noontime I rode down to the bank of the Sulphur. It was a dangerous river, many ways. Under the surface there was an entangling mass of roots, old snags, and masses of dead and long-submerged water lilies, sudden shallows or depths. The old ferry was several miles downstream, and the place where I now sat my saddle was an old Caddo crossing almost two miles upstream from Willow Bluff.

Approaching the bluff from the north seemed a likely idea, and I'd circled around, cutting for sign, and checking the country. Right about then I'd an uneasy feeling the woods weren't at all empty. Could be I was jumpy, but the feeling was on me.

Katy might come at any time, and she might not be alone, so I'd want to check whoever was with her before I showed up in plain sight. Also, there was always the chance she'd been followed. A man on the dodge can't rule out anything as unlikely. Walking the dapple into the water I waded him and swam him across the Sulphur.

The old trail divided here and a branch went northwest toward a couple of shacks called White Cotton. The other branch went northeast to intersect with a very poor trail running north to Dalby Springs and southeast toward the ferry. Turning off the trail before it reached the road, I worked a cautious way through the forest toward Willow Bluff.

Willow Bluff was one of several bluffs that were actually little more than high banks covered with willows as was much of this bottom in 1869. On the edge of a thicket near some pines I got down from the saddle. There was no reason I could think of for feeling like I did but there was panic in me. The silence of the forest was suddenly oppressive and I had to fight back an urge to climb into the saddle and light out of there and run like I never had in my life until I was far from here, far from Texas, and far from anything I ever knew.

Easing the girth on the dapple I squatted on my heels and lighted my pipe, and then I stayed right there, listening, making myself easy. The earth smelled of decayed leaves and rotting timber. Along a fallen log walked a big red ant, and a bumblebee bumbled lazily among the wild flowers—no other sound came through the trees.

Below me and to the right was Willow Bluff. There was a tumbled-down log cabin lurched half over like a sorry old drunk. There was a well, the remains of a pole corral and some unfinished fence, and not far off was the north bank of the Sulphur. I could hear the water running through the branches of a huge old tree that had fallen off the bank into the stream.

There was some open meadow down there, and from where I squatted on the slope I could see it all without being seen. A fly buzzed in the sunshine, my horse cropped grass, down on the river a fish jumped. Easing my pistols in my belt I knocked out the pipe on the palm of my hand.

Nothing moved anywhere, yet my stomach felt empty and I felt touchy as a boar with a sore snout. There was no sense to feeling this way: Katy would be here soon.

When they came it wasn't like I expected. Katy was there, but with her was Lacy Petraine and John Tower, and they were leading a pack horse. Tower got down from the horse and helped the two girls down, but I sat right still and didn't move.

Impatient as I was, I sat right still, just waiting and listening. If they had been followed, I wanted to know it. When ten minutes had passed I could wait no longer, so cinching up the gray, I walked down the slope.

"Cullen!" Katy ran toward me. "We heard you were dead! Warren said he'd killed you!"

It made no kind of sense. Not at first. Seems when they were well on their way they had spotted a rider coming toward them, and when he pulled up it was Warren and he was wild, and he was yelling, *"I killed him! I killed him!"*

"Killed who?" Tower had demanded.

"I killed that outlaw!" Warren was excited and his eyes had a glassy shine. *"I killed Cullen Baker!"*

"You killed Cullen Baker?" Tower had asked. "A sneaking little pipsqueak like you?"

"Don't you dare talk to me like that!" Warren's voice was shrill. "Don't you dare! *I* killed Cullen Baker!"

"I don't believe you," Tower had said. "You're out of your mind."

Warren had laughed, and Katy said she was shocked by his manner. He acted as if he were intoxicated. There was a queerness about him, an almost sadistic excitement that revolted them.

"Oh, I killed him all right! He thought he was so much! He was there in the brush with another fellow. I shot them both. Cullen was lying there in the checkered shirt he always wore and he never knew what happened. That other man, the one called Kirby, he started to get up, and—"

"You shot him when he was *asleep*?" Tower's face was white with fury, Katy said. "Why you little—"

"He didn't kill him, Mr. Tower," Katy said. "I just know he didn't."

Warren had turned on her, almost white with anger. "You fool! Can't you see now? He's dead! He's dead now, and nothing but a clod of empty flesh! And *I* killed him! *I!* There's no sense you mooning around over him. It will be me they talk about now. I'll be *the man who killed Cullen Baker*!"

"I think," Tower had said, "I think I'll kill him."

"No," Katy stopped him, "he doesn't understand. Down here," she said, looking at Warren, "a man is admired for daring to face another armed man with a pistol and for settling his quarrels bravely. It isn't a killing that is admired, it is the courage to fight for what you believe. You won't be admired as the man who killed Cullen Baker, you will be despised as someone who murdered a sleeping man."

They had turned then and ridden away as he stared after them. And the last thing they heard was a contemptuous laugh, but it was a hollow sound.

"I won't believe it," Katy had said, "I'm going on to Willow Bluff."

And in the end they had all come on along.

———

So THERE WE stood in the warm sunshine of the meadow, with the grass around our feet and a blue sky overhead with a few white puffballs of fleecy cloud drifting. We heard the gurgle of the water around that fallen tree, and I looked at Katy and she looked at me and I knew my home was going to be wherever she was, that I didn't need the land Pa had owned, that I didn't need anything, anywhere as long as I had her.

Tower, he turned to Lacy, and he said, "Something I've got to say. Lacy, I love you. I'm in Texas because I came hunting you, because I had to find you. I think I've loved you ever since you were Terry's wife, but Lacy, I didn't want to kill him, I didn't want to at all."

Right then Katy was in my arms and I wasn't thinking about anything else but I heard Lacy say, "John, I think we should go West, too."

And Katy was saying to me that she'd brought Sandoval for me, and then I looked up and threw Katy away from me.

Chance Thorne and Sam Barlow were there at the edge of the woods, just beyond the old well. And there were two others with them.

Four men standing in a scattered line, and they had us covered.

Fifteen feet away from me John Tower was facing them also.

"John," I said quietly, "it looks like we're going to do some shooting."

We both knew what could happen to the girls if we were killed without killing them.

"I'll take Barlow and Thorne, John," I told him, speaking low. "You get those others."

"All right, but you're getting all the best of it."

Sam Barlow was grinning. "Wish we were closer to that grave you dug for me. I figured you to fill it."

"John"—they were walking nearer—"I've been working on something. Getting my gun out fast, shooting from where it is, it worked against Butler in Fort Worth."

"I saw it."

"Takes them a moment to think, you know."

"All right."

They had come up within thirty feet of us now, and Chance was looking at Katy, and there was nothing nice in the way he looked. "You always despised me," Chance said, "and whatever happens here, nobody knows. Nobody will ever know."

"I'd like to take time to set fire to you, Cullen," Barlow was saying, "but we don't want to keep them girls awaitin'. They'll be impatient for some real men, seems like, so we're goin' to kill you."

"Sam." I was cold inside. I felt like ice. I could feel the sun and hear a mockingbird in the trees and I could see the wasps hovering about the well. "Sam," I said, "there's one thing I've got to tell you."

"Yeah? What's th—"

The brief lightning of my shot coming against men who believed themselves securely in command stabbed across the afternoon.

The months of hard practice, speeded now by the knowledge of waiting death. With complete coolness I fired a second shot into Barlow, then swung the gun muzzle and as a bullet blasted past me, a shot touched off by panic, I shot Chance Thorne through the body. My fourth bullet went through Chance's neck under his ear and drenched the falling man with his own blood.

I stepped around the well toward Barlow. Tower had to do what he must, these two were mine.

Barlow was trying to get up. He knew he had bought it. He knew what a bullet through the stomach could do and he had two of them right where he lived. He was dying and he wanted only one thing, to hurt me and to take me with him.

"They got Bob Lee," he gasped at me. "He was ridin' from his home to Mexico when the Peacocks ambushed him." He gasped hoarsely, sweat standing out on his forehead. "They got Bickerstaff over in Alvarado. Now I'm gettin' you."

He turned the gun muzzle on me and I kicked it from his hand, then I glanced over at Chance.

Thorne was twisting on the bloody grass, dying in the sunlight of a warm afternoon in Texas. "I wish . . . I wish . . ." Whatever he wished none of us knew, for he died there on the grass looking up at the empty sky through the leaves of the oak that stood by the well.

"It worked, Cullen," Tower said. "I'd never have believed it."

Lacy was ripping his shirt sleeve where a bullet had cut through the deltoid muscle of his shoulder.

"Warren said he had killed you," Katy said, "and if you don't appear again, it will be believed, so let

Cullen Baker die. Take another name, in another place."

We switched saddles so I could ride Sandoval and Katy the dappled mare. This much of the dream remained, that we had a stallion and a mare, and it was a beginning for any man, and most of all, I'd come up out of it with Katy Thorne.

So we mounted up and rode away in the sunlight, four of the living who left four of the dead behind.

And that was the way of it, although down along the Sulphur and the bayous around Lake Caddo some will say that Cullen Baker was an unreconstructed rebel who carried on a lone fight, and those who read a book written by Thomas Warren will tell you that Cullen was a drunken murderer and a thief. Only that was not the end....

A man can breed horses and cattle and still find time to read, even to study law of an evening when he has a wife to help and encourage him, and for a man with an education the world is a wide place and the opportunities are many, but the old habits and ways are not forgotten and on my desk today there lies a Dragoon Colt, polished, cleaned and loaded to remind me of the days along the bayous when I invented the first fast draw.

Tonight John Tower will drive out from town and we will walk down to the corrals together to watch the horses, two tall old men who long ago stood side by side in a green sunlit meadow on the banks of the Sulphur River, but that was long, long ago, and in another world than this, another time.

About Louis L'Amour

*"I think of myself in the oral tradition—
as a troubadour, a village taleteller, the man
in the shadows of the campfire. That's the way
I'd like to be remembered—as a storyteller.
A good storyteller."*

I T IS DOUBTFUL that any author could be as at home in the world re-created in his novels as Louis Dearborn L'Amour. Not only could he physically fill the boots of the rugged characters he wrote about, but he literally "walked the land my characters walk." His personal experiences as well as his lifelong devotion to historical research combined to give Mr. L'Amour the unique knowledge and understanding of people, events, and the challenge of the American frontier that became the hallmarks of his popularity.

Of French-Irish descent, Mr. L'Amour could trace his own family in North America back to the early 1600s and follow their steady progression westward, "always on the frontier." As a boy growing up in Jamestown, North Dakota, he absorbed all he could about his family's frontier heritage, including the story of his great-grandfather who was scalped by Sioux warriors.

Spurred by an eager curiosity and desire to broaden

his horizons, Mr. L'Amour left home at the age of fifteen and enjoyed a wide variety of jobs, including seaman, lumberjack, elephant handler, skinner of dead cattle, miner, and an officer in the transportation corps during World War II. During his "yondering" days he also circled the world on a freighter, sailed a dhow on the Red Sea, was shipwrecked in the West Indies and stranded in the Mojave Desert. He won fifty-one of fifty-nine fights as a professional boxer and worked as a journalist and lecturer. He was a voracious reader and collector of rare books. His personal library contained 17,000 volumes.

Mr. L'Amour "wanted to write almost from the time I could talk." After developing a widespread following for his many frontier and adventure stories written for fiction magazines, Mr. L'Amour published his first full-length novel, *Hondo,* in the United States in 1953. Every one of his more than 120 books is in print; there are 300 million copies of his books in print worldwide, making him one of the bestselling authors in modern literary history. His books have been translated into twenty languages, and more than forty-five of his novels and stories have been made into feature films and television movies.

His hardcover bestsellers include *The Lonesome Gods, The Walking Drum* (his twelfth-century historical novel), *Jubal Sackett, Last of the Breed,* and *The Haunted Mesa.* His memoir, *Education of a Wandering Man,* was a leading bestseller in 1989. Audio dramatizations and adaptations of many L'Amour stories are available on cassette tapes from Random House Audio publishing.

The recipient of many great honors and awards, in

1983 Mr. L'Amour became the first novelist ever to be awarded the Congressional Gold Medal by the United States Congress in honor of his life's work. In 1984 he was also awarded the Medal of Freedom by President Reagan.

Louis L'Amour died on June 10, 1988. His wife, Kathy, and their two children, Beau and Angelique, carry the L'Amour publishing tradition forward with new books written by the author during his lifetime to be published by Bantam.